BLOOD AND STONE

PAIGE N. REGAN

Book Illustration by Jessica Sherburn (Ouijacine).
Dinkus Illustration by Frederick Kroner of Stardust Book Services.
Author Photograph by Kaela Speicher Photography.

A Brief Word

*To the victims learning to heal
and all the thorny paths it takes
to get there.*

ONE

Frost bit through Eve Carter's gray knitted gloves. Her fingers were numb with cold, her freckled face far from feeling. She trudged through the snow anyway, each boot print left behind another reminder of how far she'd traveled.

It was fortunate that there was snow at all; if it were any other season, Eve was certain she would lose herself in these woods.

Not to say that she wasn't lost already. She pulled the thick black cloak tighter around her shoulders, all but shivering in the woolen dress she'd borrowed.

She didn't have a device to tell the time, but if she had to guess, six or seven hours had passed since Eve snuck out of the Bone Court manor. There was still sunlight to see by, but it wouldn't stay that way for long. Already the clouds were darkening as sunset made its way across the horizon. She would have another hour at most before she needed to turn back.

Eve pushed forward. She *would* find a way out of this place, one way or another.

Pain shot up her right leg. Eve dropped to her knees, muttering a curse under her breath as she grasped her calf. When she pulled her hand away, blood stained the glove.

A flicker of glistening wings caught her attention, followed by a faint giggle. Eve gritted her teeth and checked the wound. Five tiny scratches—the swipe of a tiny hand—tore through her tights down to her pale skin. The wound wasn't deep, but it stung. Eve flipped off the empty forest. "Stupid snow sprites."

Eve was learning about the creatures that inhabited the forest the hard way. Between the random yanking on her blonde hair, missing items from her bag, and the occasional clawing of her limbs, Eve was becoming a favorite plaything to the Unseelie Faeries.

"Be glad it's only tricks for now," Liam had said with a chuckle when she returned defeated to the manor yesterday with her hair full of brambles. *"The Unseelie are bloodthirsty. Once they're bored with the pranks, they'll resort to other entertainment."*

Eve had hoped to be out of Faerie by then. That wasn't likely.

Cursing under her breath, Eve fought against the pain in her leg and hobbled forward. One step at a time. If she could find the headstones of the church's graveyard, she could return home.

A strange lump in the snow ahead caught her attention. Eve approached it with caution.

"Christ," she gasped, covering her mouth.

The deer's—if she could even call the creature that—carcass was twisted and wrong, even for a corpse. The being's lips were spread wide in horror, rows of pointed teeth bloodied and beaten in. Its milky white eyes stared lifelessly into the trees. Two arrows stuck out from its broken legs, but it was the clean carve of its abdomen and the neat removal of its pelt that made Eve gag.

She had *seen* things in the woods—skirmishes between clashing Faeries and the messy, bloody bits of it all—but this was too neat. Too calculated.

Too intentional, a part of her whispered.

Eve's throat tightened as chills ran down her spine. She fled the scene, kicking up puffs of snow in her wake.

She *had* to get out of Faerie.

It was several minutes before she spotted a familiar set of footprints in the snow circling back where she had come from.

Eve followed the old steps, anger and dismay coiling in her stomach. They led straight back to the stone archway she'd first passed through on her journey this morning. The archway that was supposed to take her back to her world but stubbornly refused.

She had spent the day wandering in a circle.

Eve cursed and kicked a nearby tree. Small piles of snow fell at her sides from the shaken branches. This was her third attempt in four days to escape Faerie. Each time she'd tried to walk back to her small town in Vermont, Eve had been redirected back to the path from which she'd came.

That was her curse. Ever since she and Hailey had foolishly tasted the Faerie liquor at her birthday party, the girls had been trapped within the confines of this absurd plane. There was a time when Eve might have been grateful for the escape, but that was before she had the responsibility of caring for her grandmother on her shoulders. Before she had trapped her enemies in this realm.

Before she tried to kill the son of her captor.

It was too late to keep searching the woods. A part of Eve knew the effort would be fruitless if she tried. She trudged back to the manor with a bitter sense of shame, mentally retracing her path through the woods. It was as if the forest had a mind of its own: a living, breathing beast that enjoyed Eve's mortal anguish as it twisted and turned her around its branches. It was a miracle that she had been able to find her way out.

The Bone Court manor rose into view as a monstrous creature in its own right. It had taken Eve a few days to figure it out, but she could see that its structure was built entirely within the ancient ribcage of a dead beast. The bones curved into the ground, their age shown in the curling ivy and patches of moss that overtook their foundation. Eve had yet to come across a creature as daunting as whatever these bones belonged to—and she hoped the day would never come.

"Back so soon?"

Evren regarded her from the den, taking in the wound on her leg and the melting snow she dragged in from outside. Amusement sparked in his gold eyes as he sipped from his cup of wine. Every inch of him bespoke the Lord of the Bone Court, from his confident posture to the family crest signet on his finger. His long red hair hung in a loose braid over his shoulder, held back by clips of teeth. Bones were stitched into his clothes as embellishments, carrying an aura of death wherever he went.

Anger boiled in Eve's frozen veins, but she kept her mouth shut and stomped onward to the stairs. This was nothing but a game to him. He'd said as much on the first day of her imprisonment: *"Come the dawn after Yule, whoever proves themselves to be worthy of the position before nightfall on Ostara will inherit the Bone Court."* It was a game with simple rules—impress Evren and rule the court or die trying.

Evren had said that whoever inherited the court could choose how to dispose of the losers and their mortal "tools." She didn't know Preece enough to understand his morals, and Sage had made her opinion on Eve abundantly clear after she had failed to kill Liam. If she could not escape Faerie before Yule, Eve wasn't sure she would make it to next spring.

Liam lingered on the stairwell with a pointed smirk, his slender arms dangling over the curved ebony railing. Small crimson scales glittered on his cheeks, matching the vibrancy of his fluffy red hair. He took delight in the puddles Eve left in her wake and the defeat written on her face. "You gave up earlier than usual."

Eve passed him without comment. He was his father's son, alright. They couldn't resist a jab when Eve already wanted to sink into the bottom of the lake.

"You know, the spell should have worn off by now," Liam continued. She could hear him change direction and follow her, his footsteps soft against the moss carpet. "That is, the usual ones. I wonder what he used in the recipe this time? It's not *that* hard to trap mortals here, of course, but—"

"Have you found a way to break it or not?" Eve snapped. If he didn't shut up soon, she was going to shove him down the stairs.

Liam scoffed. "I've done you enough favors. If I recall, your idea of repayment involved a blade in my back."

"Keeping me hostage isn't a smart idea, Liam," Eve warned. Liam narrowed his golden gaze.

"We have a deal of protection," he reminded her. "You couldn't hurt me if you tried."

Eve was more than aware of that deal. Liam had given her his True Name in exchange for his life, and their first act of a limited truce had been to command each other's protection. No matter how many times he taunted her situation, Eve was stuck listening to him while her brain screamed at her to put up a fight.

See where that got me? she thought bitterly. Physical altercations with Liam had done nothing but screw her over. She needed another approach.

"Sure, I can't throw you off the roof, but I'm not the only enemy you have around here," Eve said. "Do you really want to make an enemy of the only person that's contractually obligated to protect you?"

"You certainly have a way with words."

Eve glared at him from the corner of her eye. Liam held his hands up in defense.

"I'll look into it," he said. "I can't promise anything more."

"That's all I need." That wasn't true—she needed to get the hell out of here—but Liam did not respond positively to pressure. Annoyed, Liam walked back downstairs, finally leaving Eve with a moment to herself.

She hobbled to what had become her bedroom, her leg still stinging with pain from the sprite's scratch. The room itself did not give any indication that it belonged to Eve aside from a few strewn pieces of clothes on the floor. Considering the other option was to sleep outside in the snow, she made do.

Eve cleaned the wound the best that she could with a poultice one of the servants had left behind for yesterday's injuries. It stung, but so did her pride. She collapsed back onto the bed, kicking her shoes and winter layers off onto the floor with a huff.

The sun sank low between the trees outside of her window, and Eve's heart sunk with it. Thoughts of her grandmother plagued her, a constant worry ebbing at the corners of her mind. Nan had dementia and couldn't be trusted on her own for long. Eve had been sent to live with her grandmother not only as a reprieve for her frustrated parents, but to watch over the ailing woman as a caretaker. Eve believed she was doing a shit job at it.

Had their neighbor, Mr. Stone, noticed Nan's abandonment and taken care of her in Eve's absence? Eve hoped so. She couldn't bear to think of the alternative.

It was never her intention to leave her grandmother vulnerable and alone. It was never her intention to *leave* in the first place.

Eve grabbed the nearest item from her end table and threw it across the room in a bout of anger. A decorative piece composed of small bones struck the wall and splintered into pieces.

Her bedroom door opened. Preece hesitated in the doorway, his light green brow raised at the destroyed figure on the floor.

"I take it that you aren't accepting visitors?" he said with a hint of amusement. In the few days that Eve had spent here, Preece had proved to be quite comfortable switching between his humanlike form and that of a frog—and more commonly, a horrifying myriad of forms in between. He was never *quite* human enough in appearance, with his sticky webbed fingers and horizontal pupils. Blinking required use of both his upper and lower eyelids. She had yet to see him steal any bugs from midair, but Eve suspected that had more to do with the seasonal change than Preece's habits.

"What do you want?" Eve grumbled. Preece picked up a few of the broken bone shards with the tips of his fingers and examined them with interest.

"My father requested everyone's attendance in the dining hall," Preece said. He flicked the bone shards back onto the floor. "Apparently, he has found another suitable player for his little game."

"Tell him I'm not interested."

Preece clicked his tongue. "I share the sentiment. Alas, we have been summoned."

Eve narrowed her gaze. "What if I don't show up?"

"Hm." Preece made an exaggeration of thinking about the possibility as he tapped his finger against his chin. "Then I suspect my father would send the servants to drag you down. He's unusually patient for an Unseelie Lord, but do not mistake his tolerance for kindness." He must have seen her consider disobedience anyway because he added, "Would it sway your opinion to know we'll be having honey cake this evening?"

The offer of food was enough. After trudging through the woods for six hours, the few provisions she'd snuck from their kitchen cupboards had been hardly enough to sustain her. And if the honey cake was similar to that delicious cake she had for her birthday...

Eve reluctantly climbed out of bed, half tempted to throw herself back on top of it when she saw the smug grin on Preece's face. She followed him downstairs into the dining hall, where the others had already gathered. Eve took the open seat beside Liam, refusing to even consider the empty chair between Preece and Evren. The meal had already been laid out before them—a large spread of roasted venison, root vegetables, and fruit compotes—but the plates remained empty.

The servants stood toward the back walls, their black cloaks blending in with the dark interior. Most of them were human—or had been. Skeletal faces hid behind the dark cloth, some with flesh and some without.

"His collection," Liam had explained upon Eve's horrific discovery a few days prior. *"My father thinks humans are fascinating. He keeps a glamour on them to cover the rot."*

"Are the skeletons alive?" Eve had asked.

"Not anymore."

Eve hated the sight of them. Liam would have subjected her abusers to the same fate if she hadn't unknowingly intervened. Eve wasn't sure if she regretted it or not; the idea of forced servitude while their minds and bodies decayed left her uneasy. She wanted revenge, but this was especially cruel.

She turned her attention across the table to Hailey, who was more restless than usual. She drummed her fingers on her lap, and her leg bounced while she stared at her empty plate. Upon noticing Eve's attention on her, Hailey tried to give her a reassuring smile, but the expression didn't reach her eyes.

Evren clapped his hands.

"I have some excellent news for you all this evening," he said, proudly extending his arms to make sure he had their full attention. "I promised you all the competition would begin the dawn after Yule, and make no mistake; I am a man of my word. We are but a day away, and it is only fair that each of you are given the tools you need to succeed."

"You mean to entertain you," Liam muttered.

"Without further delay, let us welcome the final piece to our festivities." The servants shuffled against the wall, practically dragging forward a skinny young man with untidy blond curls. Eve struggled to see him behind the shifting cloaks. They pushed him forward until he took the empty seat beside Preece.

Eve's breath caught in her throat as Logan Richards stared back at her.

Two

Eve grabbed her dinner knife and dove across the table. Porcelain and silver crashed together as she knocked them out of the way. Gasps and cries pierced the air. A single voice of laughter cut through it all as some idiot grabbed Eve and pulled her away from the cowering man on the floor.

"Let me *go*," Eve growled, thrashing her body in her captor's arms. Logan's petrified eyes were blue, but all she could see was red. Her head pounded. The knife tightened in her grip, demanding justice. "Let me *go!*"

"Your energy is delightful," Evren said between his laughter. His grip on her was iron. "But it has taken me quite some time to find a suitable partner for Preece. I will not delay the competition. Do you understand me?"

When Eve did not relent, Evren's grip tightened, his elongated fingers gripping her arms tight enough to bruise.

"Do you *understand* me?" he emphasized. Eve stopped struggling and Evren let her go. "Good."

Logan slowly rose up from the floor. She wasn't sure if she'd pushed him there or if he fell. His cheeks were splotched pink. He flitted his attention from one face to another, avoiding Eve's gaze directly.

Coward. Anger simmered deep within her, a pent-up rage that burned hotter than the depths of hell. The pounding inside of her skull beat harder the longer she stared him down.

"Eve." Liam reached for her, but Eve slapped his hand away. Evren was watching her, his warning ringing in the back of her head. When she did not make another move to kill her competition, Evren gestured toward the seats.

"Let us eat before the food gets cold," he said. No one moved. "*Sit.*"

Everyone else reached for their seats. Liam's gaze urged her to follow suit. Logan kept his attention focused on his empty plate.

Eve threw her knife at him.

It missed and clattered onto the ground.

Eve turned and stormed from the room before she could face another lecture. The pounding in her head wouldn't stop. Her skull was going to *burst*. She squeezed her eyes shut as she fled the mansion, desperate to put as much distance between herself and Logan as she could. The adrenaline faded as the freezing temperatures hit her, working against the heated flush on her cheeks.

What the hell was she going to do? She couldn't go back in there. Eve raked her fingers through her hair as she paced back and forth across the narrow dirt road. The mansion was far enough away now that she could breathe but still provided a beacon of light before the forest swallowed her whole.

"I hope you don't plan to sleep out here," Liam said as he approached from the manor. He was closer than she'd expected, his cloak forgotten in his haste. He tightened his arms over his chest, clutching his arms through the thin material of his black peasant shirt. "Unless humans are more resilient than I thought. My balls are freezing."

"I'm not staying in there with *him*." The air briefly left her lungs. Her hands shook, but she shoved them into her pockets where Liam couldn't see.

Liam gauged her stubbornness. "Shall I get you a tent?"

"Keep him away from me." The words tumbled out before she could catch them. "*Liam Thistle Fogtree,* you will keep his ass out of the mansion or so help me God—"

The use of his True Name made Liam rigid. He scowled at her before turning around and marching back to the estate, forced to do her bidding. A pang of guilt etched itself into her heart. They had been avoiding the use of each other's True Names since their pact to protect each other, but her panic had overtaken her sense. She hoped Liam wouldn't use this opportunity to abuse his power over her as well. This needed to be done, though. She couldn't sleep in the same building as Logan. The mere thought made her queasy.

Hailey left the mansion a few minutes later, her thin arms crossed against the chill. Concern and reproach appeared on her face when she spotted Eve several yards away.

"You okay?" Hailey asked once she was close. She towered over Eve, long and gangly, as if someone had taken her limbs and stretched them out in all directions.

"Yeah, great." Eve's voice was scathing. She kept picturing Logan across the dinner table, his eyes wide with horror. "I'm having the time of my fucking life."

"You and me both." Eve was surprised to hear the bitterness in her voice. Hailey twisted the end of her ponytail until it resembled a dark strip of leather, then let it go. "Who's the guy?"

There wasn't any point in playing stupid; Eve had given herself away as soon as the knife was in her hand. "We went to school together. He graduated before me."

Hailey's brows shot up in surprise. Eve never talked about her past, much less the parts involving Logan. "I take it you guys didn't get along?"

"We do not."

Hailey waited for Eve to elaborate, but she did not. Hailey exhaled, her breath vaporizing in the air. Eve could see that her friend was cold, both from the way she kept glancing back at the mansion and from the sudden flush to her cheeks, but Hailey placed a gentle hand onto Eve's arm instead and asked, "What happened?"

Eve pulled back. She couldn't stand the sensation of someone touching her. Not now. "I don't want to talk about it."

"You might feel better if you did," Hailey said.

"There's nothing to talk about." Eve's voice became cold, callous. Her mind was too preoccupied with images of her knife pressing through Logan's flesh, carving her hatred into him until he, too, experienced the pain that never left her.

She could have ended it there if they hadn't held her back. Now what? Would she still be able to act on her threat the next time she saw him? Or would she freeze up the moment he walked in the room as she had with Nick? Her stomach lurched. She couldn't risk that, not when it came to Logan—and definitely not when it would come to Colton.

Hailey's concern for Eve battled with the exhaustion pulling at the dark circles under her eyes. Had she gotten thinner since they arrived?

Worry for her friend broke the spell on Eve's internal schemes. Something was clearly bothering Hailey, but all Eve could think about was her own miserable situation. After everything Hailey had done to pull Eve out of her shell, she deserved better than that.

"Are you okay?" Eve asked, internally cringing at the simplicity of her question.

"Yeah, I'm fine," Hailey answered too quickly, her reassurance lacking. "I haven't taken my ADHD meds in a few days. It can be hard when I'm not on them consistently, but Sage has been helping me through it."

Eve wondered about that. She knew that Sage cared for Hailey more than anyone, but Eve had seen firsthand how fragile Sage's friendship was.

It had only been a few days since Eve made the deal to kill Liam—and failed. Even though Eve had Liam's True Name, their promise to protect each other prevented Eve from ever fulfilling her end of the bargain.

Still, there were worse things than death. Sage knew that Eve possessed Liam's True Name—did she intend to use that against him? If Eve failed to make it up to her somehow, she suspected Sage would find cause to end her life as well.

"Has Sage talked to you about the competition at all?" Eve struggled to keep her voice casual. There was even more incentive for Sage to act against her now that the court was up for grabs.

Hailey bit down on her lip and, after glancing toward the estate, dropped her voice to a whisper. "Sort of. I had no idea she wanted to inherit the court this badly. I've been trying to talk her out of some of her plans, but she's making me nervous. I don't know if she's listening to me."

Alarming, but unsurprising. Sage was putty in Hailey's hands—whether Hailey was aware of that or not—but there was something Sage wanted more that even her true love could not dissuade her from: power.

"Has she said anything specific that's worried you?" Eve pushed.

Hailey shook her head. "It's not always what she says, but the way she says it. I don't think she cares what happens as long as she wins."

"Was she always this way?" Eve asked. She didn't know much about Sage's past, but if there was a chance she could quell the pixie's ire, she had to take it.

Hailey considered for a long moment. There was a faraway haze in her eye as she thought, her presence growing dimmer by the second. "I'm not sure."

"It's fine," Eve said quickly. Guilt pooled in her stomach as Hailey stared off into the forest. Of course Hailey wouldn't know—her memory had been tampered with by Liam several months ago. Whatever she had wanted to forget was locked away along with her other memories of that summer. "Don't worry about it."

"Right." The empty gaze that overtook Hailey whenever she tried to recall a missing memory lingered. When she blinked, it was gone again.

I have to tell her, Eve thought. It would be one thing if Hailey was willingly keeping her memories locked away, but according to Liam, she couldn't even remember that her memories were gone.

"She wanted her memories erased; everything involving her recent romantic pursuits," Liam had said on the balcony. In exchange, he'd taken away her ability to experience romantic acclimation at all.

Hailey could remember that she made a deal—that was how she'd convinced Eve to seek Liam's help in the first place—but how much of it did she remember? Could Eve try to pry those memories from her?

Before she had a chance to try, Liam strode out of the estate and slammed the front door behind him. They watched him approach from down the dirt road, his glare reserved solely for Eve.

"He's out of the house," Liam said. His tone insinuated that it had not been an easy task to accomplish. "You can come back inside."

"Where is he?" Even if he was out of the mansion, Eve didn't trust Evren—or Liam—not to screw her over. As far as she knew, Logan would be lingering outside, waiting for her to go in before he rejoined them at the table. Eve wasn't sure she could stop herself from strangling him if she saw him again that soon.

"He'll be staying in the servant's quarters," Liam explained, gesturing further away from the estate. "They have their own facilities near the forest—and before you ask, I've placed an enchantment on his feet to prevent him from entering the mansion. Is that satisfactory?"

Eve ignored the bitterness in Liam's voice as he grit his teeth through each word. Her own concerns clung to Logan's relocation; the mansion's grounds were still too close, but at least she wouldn't need to worry about him creeping down the hall. It also allowed her to keep track of him on some level. When the time came for her to strike, she would be ready.

"It'll work," she decided.

"Does that mean we can go back inside?" Hailey asked. She rubbed her arms for emphasis, her breath coming out in small puffs of frost.

"No one's keeping you out here," Liam said.

She rushed ahead of them, practically sprinting back to the warmth of the estate. Eve and Liam followed behind in silence. Neither anticipated Evren and his miserable festivities.

"So," Liam said once Hailey was out of earshot. "What was that about?"

This was the last conversation Eve wanted to have. "I don't know what you're talking about."

Liam rolled his eyes. "He's one of the men you had me capture. I'm no fool. You've never spoken of the reason for your hatred, though."

Eve shrugged. "It's not part of our deal."

"No, but it leaves me to speculate. Obviously, this man has wronged you in some way. Or you find stabbing men with pointy objects to be a new hobby of yours. If that is the case, you've proven yourself horrible at it and should seek a new activity immediately. Might I suggest knitting?"

"Are you done?"

"Are you going to tell me what happened?" Curiosity practically radiated off him. It only served to piss her off more. He wasn't concerned in the slightest; Liam lived for entertainment, and this was fresh gossip to stave off his hungry soul.

"It's none of your business," she snapped. "Leave me alone."

"Very well. Instead, why don't you tell me why you tried to kill me?" Eve's breath caught in her throat. "You owe me that much."

I didn't mean to. That wasn't true. Going into the ball, Eve had fully intended to murder Liam in exchange for Sage murdering her rapists.

Something had changed, though. She didn't want to kill him. Eve couldn't bring herself to do it.

And Sage had made sure Eve couldn't tell anyone what had happened.

Eve choked on her confession. The truth squeezed her neck, rendering her silent. With her words held hostage, Eve managed to get out, "It doesn't matter now."

"You know, Evie, we're supposed to be working together. Don't you think that calls for an ounce of trust? If you won't tell me what I did to warrant murder, the least you could do is tell me why you tried to kill—"

"No." Eve whirled on him and stomped her foot in the snow, not caring that the cold flakes had soaked through her spider silk slippers. Her temper flared, both at herself for her foolishness and at Liam for putting her in this predicament. "I didn't leave you alive to bug the shit out of me. When I say *leave me alone*, I mean it. Do not ask me about that man again. Ever. I will not repeat myself."

Liam was stricken. As usual, his pestering had gone too far—but Eve had nothing left to defend herself. She left him standing in the snow, too angry to look back.

THREE

By the time Eve returned to the dining room, guilt had wormed its way beneath the layer of fury seizing her heart. She shouldn't have snapped at Liam, but it was too late to take it back now. Her inability to control her temper further proved how rotten she was on the inside, a tooth grown brittle from decay.

The others were already eating. Sage caught Eve's eye as she entered, her pale brow raised with interest. She wore a human glamour, the sharp angles of her face no different from any mortal aside from her golden eyes. It must have been for Hailey's benefit; if Eve squinted enough, she could see the barest outline of Sage's pixie wings and long lilac hair peeking through.

Sage caught Eve's elbow as she passed, tugging her down to whisper in her ear. "Be sure to spare some of that anger for my brother next time."

Eve yanked her elbow away and returned to her seat. Sage didn't press her, but she saw the pixie's impish smirk out of the corner of her eye. Eve stared at her plate, her appetite lost. Sage still hadn't come to her with a plan for Liam's demise. Eve wondered if Sage had lost interest since learning of Eve and Liam's pact to protect each other—she wondered if that made her a potential victim, too.

If Sage was willing to do anything to win, Eve didn't have much confidence in her own safety. Logan might not be the biggest threat in the mansion after Yule.

Eve's mind turned once again to the possibility of escape. There was a shoddy map in her room that she'd drawn up and tucked under her bed, marking off areas of the forest she'd searched for an exit. Nothing about it was accurate—Eve was no cartographer—but it was better than wandering blindly in the forest.

I hope Nan's alright. Her chest ached as she thought of her grandmother, alone and confused, without anyone to watch over her. Eve had no idea how to contact Nan to let her know she was missing, let alone check up on her.

Liam returned to the table, as uninterested in holding a conversation as Eve was in starting one. They sat in silence as the others jabbered on, their chatter overlapping into static noise. Eve ran through the outline of the map in her head again. She had it memorized by now: the winding dirt road to the wisteria arch, the lake inhabiting sharp-toothed asrai, and the ever-expanding forest that *should* have reached the cemetery—but never did.

There was a reason for that, according to Liam: the cemetery did not exist in this veil.

"What are you talking about?" Eve had confronted him about it two nights ago when she had failed—yet again—to return home. Liam had been lounging on the chaise in the den, tossing chestnuts into the open fireplace and watching them pop.

"What did you think was happening when you stepped down the stairs?" he'd said. *"You crossed through the veil to Faerie. Our world here is not the same as yours, although we are close enough to brush against each other."*

"You're telling me that I'm in an alternate dimension?" Normally, Eve would have laughed at something this absurd. She did not laugh then.

"Not quite, but call it what you wish," Liam had said. *"Regardless, you aren't going to cross back easily."*

Eve did not want to think about what other veils or dimensions could be out there. It was bad enough she landed in this one.

Upon probing him further, Liam had told her of a few other known weak spots to access the other side of the veil from the Bone Court. A cracked well tucked between a ring of brown mushrooms. A half-finished bridge over a mountain pass. A rope ladder that dangled from the highest pine tree.

None of them had worked.

After poking at her meal, Eve took a slice of honey cake and holed herself back up in her room. She spread her map out over her desk and marked off the spots she'd visited today with angry red X's. It was time to think of another route. She had to, or else...

She had to.

FOUR

Eve did not sleep. She tossed and turned in her bed, twisting against the heavy velvet blankets until they were suffocating. She couldn't shake the sensation of eyes watching her from the shadows. The dark interior of the room did nothing to help her nerves—everything was unfamiliar, from the paneled wood walls to the earthy scent that rose from the moss carpet. She feared the bedroom was going to swallow her whole.

With a huff, Eve kicked off her blankets and strode to the window, pulling on a thick charcoal cape over her chemise. The mansion was freezing, even with the dwindling fire striving for life in the fireplace across the room. The staff usually came to tend to the fires in the middle of the night, but Eve had refused them, keeping her door locked tight. She didn't care what kind of spell Evren had over them—Eve would not be caught unawares by a stranger in her sleep.

She shuffled to the window and glared down at the snow-covered lawn. Frost crept up the glass panes, blurring her vision, but she knew. She knew. Somewhere, tucked between the trees, was the servants' quarters—was Logan.

Clutching her cloak tighter, Eve pulled on her borrowed slippers and wandered out into the hall. Darkness curled at every corner, shadows dancing against what little moonlight leaked in. Silence enveloped the hall. The mansion resembled the sleeping beast it was made from.

Eve wandered the manor without purpose. With her breath as the only sound, she was no more than a ghost trapped within these walls. Is that what she would become? Escape became less viable with each passing hour. Yule was tomorrow. She had one last chance to get out before the competition doomed her.

Do I even want to leave yet? The question haunted her. She'd been eager to take her revenge—and now Logan's demise had been handed to her on a silver platter. What better opportunity to kill him than in a competition where she was encouraged to do it? *Isn't this what you wanted?*

What about Nan? Another part of her fought. After she killed Logan, it wasn't as if she was allowed to go home. Someone had to win, and Eve knew Sage wouldn't mind taking her out to do it. If she didn't find a way out now, who was to say she would ever see her grandmother again?

"Damn it." She wasn't any closer to deciding, and time was running out.

She took refuge in the kitchen without meaning to. She was still hungry from dinner. Whether she left or not, Eve needed to eat.

None of the food was labeled, but Eve was able to pick out fruits and vegetables she was familiar with from the pantry. Most food in Faerie came with a cost to mortals. Some brought an insatiable hunger, another trapped them in this realm—but it was distinguishable by the strange, almost pearlescent sheen that coated the food native to Faerie.

It was easy to miss at first. Liam had to point it out to her days ago when she'd almost eaten a particularly shiny apple, but she was learning to distinguish between mortal fare and the Fae's. The Fair Folk were lucky; their food was far more appetizing, with lush ripeness and a plum shimmer that somehow made their meals even more delectable.

It was fortunate that whatever meals made with the Fair Folk's native ingredients carried that sheen over to their finished product. So long as she avoided the never-ending temptation that came with admiring the Fae's spread, she would be fine.

Probably.

Her thoughts pulled toward the weird concoction Evren had tricked her into drinking at her birthday party. She hadn't noticed a sheen in it then, but she also hadn't been searching for it. Eve did not want to add more time to her sentence in Faerie, but who was to say that the drink wouldn't keep her there until Ostara anyway? What if it kept her there forever? Evren certainly wasn't telling her, and no one else in the mansion knew, either.

Her stomach growled and Eve dug through the cabinet, setting jars and raw produce on the counter as she deliberated what was safe.

"The nuts appear to be edible."

Eve gasped, nearly tossing said jar at her intruder until she saw that it was Preece. She took a deep breath and set the jar down on the counter. That was the second time today she'd almost attacked him.

"You *have* to stop doing that," she hissed and popped the lid off. Dull, ordinary pecans sat inside, nowhere near as succulent as the Faerie food. Yes, these had to be safe. She plucked one from the jar and tossed it into her mouth.

Preece watched her, bemused. He took a seat on one of the wooden chairs at the kitchen table and gestured for her to join.

"You certainly livened up our meal tonight," he said. "My father thought your little stunt was hilarious."

Eve swallowed a cheek full of pecans. "It wasn't supposed to be funny."

"I know." Preece's gaze flickered to her throwing hand. "If you're intent on killing my partner, you'll need to learn to wield a weapon first. Your aim is terrible."

"Thanks," Eve said icily. She didn't come down here for a lecture. She wondered why she even came down here at all.

"How is it that you two know each other?" Preece asked, cocking his head to the side. Eve scowled.

"I'll tell you the same thing I told Liam: it's none of your business."

"Oh, but I wish to *make* it my business." Preece leaned forward, his slit, frog-like eyes bulging with interest. "I am a collector of stories, you see."

Eve regarded him suspiciously. "You're a librarian?"

"Oh, no, nothing of the sort." Preece waved the idea away with a webbed hand. "The librarians and archivists are such *strict* professions, mind you. I'd hate to be in their department." He shuddered. "No, I am as I said: a collector." He must have seen the confusion on her face, because Preece quickly asked, "How much do you know about the other courts?"

"Not much," she admitted. Sage had told her bits and pieces about them a few weeks ago—something about Faerie splitting into the Seelie and Unseelie Courts and overseeing several smaller courts in between. There were independent courts, too, but all Eve could remember of it was that the Bone Court was a part of the Unseelie Court.

Preece nodded with understanding. "I work in the Court of Knowledge, under the Seelie Court. We keep a record of every myth, story, and history that passes through our ears. It's grueling work, I must say, but at least I don't need to archive it; I'm merely the messenger."

"Messenger?"

"A collector of information," Preece said, splaying his webbed fingers out eagerly. "I can't resist a good story, and many love to tell them."

"How do you know if something is true or not?"

"We don't, but when you get enough accounts of a story, you tend to find a thread of truth there," Preece said with a grin. His smile was unnatural, white teeth against his amphibian face. It unsettled Eve, but she did not sense danger. She chewed another pecan in thought.

"You work in a court of gossip," Eve finally decided. Preece laughed.

"You'll find that much of Faerie is gossip." He leaned forward, his eyes dilated with interest. "I'm much more interested in stories from beyond the veil. There are a variety of fascinating perspectives. Won't you share yours?"

Eve grimaced. "I'll pass."

Preece shrugged and rose from his chair. The placid smile on his face told her that he was accustomed to rejection. "No matter. The truth tends to come out eventually."

A lump formed in Eve's throat. Preece left before she could find it in herself to make another remark. She put the pecans away and returned to her room even more anxious than before.

FIVE

It was past dawn when Eve found sleep. She awoke in the late afternoon, her hopes for a last-minute escape dashed when she saw the lowering sun.

She was too late.

Eve managed to drag herself out of bed and unlock the door before a handful of waiting servants rushed in. Their cloaks swept across the floor in swaths of shadows as they carried in several large boxes. Eve did not want to think of how long they'd been waiting out there for her to wake up, silent as the grave and eternally patient.

From the boxes, they unloaded an assortment of clothes in fabrics she'd never seen before: dresses carved from tree bark, corsets made from beetle carapace, and several pieces adorned with clattering bones.

"What is all this?" she asked but knew they wouldn't answer. The servants never spoke.

Eve stood awkwardly to the side until they finished. After they left, she browsed through the new additions to her wardrobe, unnerved to find that—unlike the borrowed attire she'd been wearing—these were made to her measurements.

Dunla, she guessed, recalling the dwarfish seamstress that had made her birthday dress. Eve cringed to think of what Dunla would say if she saw the poor state of the gown now.

She picked out a black dress made of wool and some thick stockings to wear underneath. The dress came up to her chin and teeth were sewn around the lace cuffs as an adornment. Eve considered ripping them off, but that meant she would have loose teeth lying around her bedroom, which was somehow worse.

"There you are!" Evren greeted her on the stairs with a wide smile and open arms. Eve expertly dodged him. "The others are waiting in the den. I will be ready in a moment."

He didn't give her a chance to ask what he needed to be ready for—Evren was gone, their brief interaction sapping her limited energy.

Exhausted, Eve trudged to the den.

The room—as with the rest of the manor, Eve noticed—had been decorated for the occasion. Cranberries hung in twine garlands near the ceilings, and fresh pine had been wrapped around banisters and pillars. Lit candles had been placed in every window, while large wreaths of dried orange slices, pinecones, and cinnamon decorated the walls.

Christmas, but not quite. The likeness startled her. Eve found she preferred these natural decorations over the plastic and glass that accompanied her childhood holidays.

Everyone appeared to have been gifted a new shipment of clothes. Sage and Hailey lounged by the fire with new thick velvet dresses of ebony and gold, their hair pinned up by combs made of bone. Preece read a book across from them, his vest and trousers a unique black leather that resembled oil.

There wasn't any room on the chaise for her, but even if there were, Eve wasn't interested in Sage whispering plans of murder in her ear.

Her attention snagged on a sleeping figure hunched over a nearby table. Liam slept with his head in his arms beside a Yule log—a real one, with candles and pine and oranges covered in anise—unaware or uninterested in the people around him.

She settled into a chair beside him, angling it to keep some distance. It was only then she wondered how long Evren would make them wait and if she should have brought something to occupy herself with.

Eve glanced around the room for something; all the books were on the other side, held hostage by a potential conversation with Sage. That option was out.

Great. She sighed. Maybe Liam had the right idea by taking a nap.

He wasn't exempt from the new attire either. Bones made up a vest—or was it a corset?—stitched up together to wrap around his puffy black tunic in an external ribcage. Eve was almost jealous, until she remembered that they likely *were* someone's ribcage.

You're not doing any better, Eve thought, running her thumb across one of the teeth at her wrist. Its carnivorous curve was inhuman, but Eve had met plenty of inhuman creatures in Faerie.

Liam's high collar did much to hide the disease creeping up the back of his neck. Patches of gray stone that had protected him from her dagger only a few nights before. But he did not bother to hide his true appearance behind a human glamour. He hadn't done so since her birthday. Red scales resembling ruby freckles dotted his cheeks, and the black tips of his ears were as sharp as his teeth.

"I cannot possibly sleep if you keep staring at me," Liam said. He turned his head up in annoyance. "I'm aware of my unbelievable beauty, but you will need to control yourself."

You wish. Eve scowled, her cheeks heating up in embarrassment at being caught. She kicked his leg under the table. Liam grabbed his shin and let out a noise of pain.

"How's that for no sleep?" she muttered. Eve scooted her chair even further away, ignoring Liam's glare. Evren strode into the den and clapped his hands, demanding their attention. He was the most ridiculous of them all in a cape made entirely of bones. They rattled and clacked whenever he moved.

"Merry Yule!" he said. "Let us begin the festivities. Everyone, into the carriages now."

Unease crept into Eve's stomach. "Where are we going?"

"You'll see," Liam whispered when Evren ignored her. Eve pressed her lips into a tight line, but there was no use fighting back. Evren would not allow it.

She followed the others to the carriages and hoped that Evren was not taking them to their deaths.

They arrived at an enormous clearing in the forest, far outside of the boundaries of the Bone Court. A giant pine tree decorated with candles, berries, and other elements of nature sat proudly in the center of the grounds. Large arrangements of food were spread out evenly, so no one would have to walk far to partake. Candles were strung up around the surrounding trees, providing plenty of light, while a small orchestra played hauntingly beautiful ballads near the center of the clearing.

Eve climbed out of the carriage with Liam and Evren, relieved that she was not forced to ride alongside Logan. Eve was certain she would have killed him before they left the mansion grounds.

I guess Liam has his benefits, she thought. Being Evren's favorite child was certainly at the top of that list.

Their second carriage arrived, and Eve made a point to keep her distance, refusing to even turn in its direction in case she saw familiar tufts of blond hair. She heard Hailey and Sage leave the wagon first, their gowns rustling as they stuck close together.

"Is any of the food here safe?" Eve overheard Hailey whisper to Sage.

"Probably not. The other courts aren't nearly as fond of mortals as we are." Sage noticed Hailey's frown and squeezed her shoulder. "I'll make sure we get you something to eat when we return."

Eve tucked this nugget of information away, already regretting skipping dinner last night—and sleeping through breakfast. It would be hours before she ate a meal again.

Stupid, she thought to herself and pulled her cloak tighter. Her new dress was warm, but not warm enough to keep out the bitter chill. Clouds shifted overhead, dark and ominous. She had no idea how she was going to last the night out here without freezing to death.

"There's a bonfire later," Liam said from beside her. Unlike his father, Liam wasn't eager to rush off to greet the other nobles. "The fire kicks off the festivities."

"And they couldn't have it ready when we got here?" Eve muttered. Liam made a noise of agreement under his breath. "This space is huge. One fire isn't going to be enough."

"It will," Liam said. "We needed a space big enough to host the guest of honor."

"Guest of honor?"

Liam smirked but did not elaborate. She followed him into the festivities as more guests arrived, their thick cloaks collecting a dusting of snow as they mingled. Eve recognized many of them from her birthday party; it was hard to forget hoofed feet and translucent wings. She watched them gather in groups, mentally noting that their attire coordinated with the party they had arrived with. Some wore red as rich as blood, while another group bore a variety of dried flowers and herbs stitched into their garments. Every member of Evren's court bore some kind of bone in their attire, her cuffs included.

I knew I should have ripped them off, she thought bitterly. The freezing temperature made that impossible to accomplish now. Why didn't she think to put on a pair of gloves?

Eve's attention landed back on the tree centered in the field. It echoed a Christmas tree pulled from nature. Hefty branches were decorated in pine cones, orange slices, bundled herbs and cinnamon sticks, and pillar candles attached with solidified wax. Dried berries made up a garland that draped over the pine needles in an elegant splash of red.

It was more beautiful than any tree her family had decorated growing up. It did not share the same nostalgia as her family's collection of glass blown ornaments and twinkly lights but made up for it in its wild embrace of nature.

The holidays with Eve's family had been strained in recent years, but there were aspects she had enjoyed. Decorating the Christmas tree had always been one of them, along with her family's tradition of competing to see who could make the best salt dough ornament. Eve usually won.

Would they do that without her this year? Bitter realization squeezed Eve's chest. It was a small thing, an inconsequential event, yet it bothered her in a newly unfamiliar way. She'd known things would be different for the holidays since moving to Nan's, but was this how it was to grow up? Would this ache continue to last as she lost more pieces that made up her past?

Liam nudged her. A crowd had gathered around the tree, their focus reserved for a smaller group of Fae. There were five of them, each one more dignified than the last. The tallest of them, a bipedal one that was more owl than man, stood with their chin raised and a macabre crown of twisted branches dipped in silver atop their head. They observed the crowd with a keen eye. The other Fair Folk behind them—family, Eve assumed, or close to it—showed less interest, their support no more than a formality. In each of their hands was a large candle, each lit with an unnaturally black flame.

Eve gasped as Liam suddenly yanked her into a kneeling position beside him. The other courts followed suit. "What—"

"Shh," Liam shushed her. His hand was still on her shoulder, as if she might run off. "The king is here."

Eve glanced back at the owl-like man. He was regal, with dark jewels glittering over his cape and vest. The woman beside him—an elven creature with high cheekbones and black thorns across her skin—wore a silver crown as well. Sage had mentioned something about a royal family overseeing the Unseelie Court. This must be them.

A well-dressed creature with the beak of a vulture and legs of a goat introduced the family. "Welcoming His Highness, High King Àrdghal Ironsiege."

The crowd clapped and cheered, but did not rise to their feet.

"Merry Yule," the sovereign owl said. Eve struggled to comprehend how he spoke through his beak. "And many blessings to you all. May your darkest days be alight with your desires."

The High King and his family turned and tossed their strange candles into the tree. The black flames took to the branches at once. The Yule tree burst into flames, an enormous roaring blaze that instantly warmed Eve to her core.

"Let the festivities begin!" High King Àrdghal shouted with a laugh. "Bring in the guest of honor!"

The king's attendant gestured toward the trees. "Welcoming, the Yule Cat."

"The what?" Eve turned to Liam for an answer, but he nodded to the line of forest instead.

The clouds shifted again. Eve realized they weren't clouds at all but great gray tufts of fur that had blended in with the overcast sky. A great beast lumbered forward, carefully stepping around pine trees that came up no higher than the cat's shoulders. The moon blinked. Then a second appeared beside it: eyes, it dawned on her, so dilated with excitement that the vibrant yellow underneath had been mistaken for the moon itself. It slinked to the edge of the clearing, its tail high and curled with delight.

Eve's breath caught as fear overrode her senses. She couldn't even scream. Every inch of her body froze with terror, waiting for the beast to descend and swallow her whole.

Cheers erupted around the clearing as the crowd jumped to their feet. Eve did not join them. She was too busy trying not to have a heart attack.

"What the hell is that?" she demanded.

"The Yule Cat," Liam explained as he removed his cloak. One of his servants took it without question. Eve held up her palm, intent on keeping hers close. "It rules over Yule itself."

"What does that mean?"

"The Yule Cat works outside of the courts, although it tends to favor the Unseelie. If you aren't given new clothes for Yule, then..." Liam motioned with a finger across his neck.

Eve blanched. She touched the cuff of her new dress and toyed with the teeth. "How would the cat know if you got clothes or not?"

Liam pointed to the beast as it made its rounds through the party. The Yule Cat's head bent low as it sniffed through the attendees, its muzzle occasionally scrunching in disappointment before they moved on.

"Over here, kitty!"

Eve saw a handful of creatures wave the Yule Cat over. One of the larger men with horns at his brow yanked on a rope. A human man on the other end stumbled forward.

The cat's pupils widened. It crouched low, wiggling its butt before pouncing atop its first victim. The mortal man shrieked, begging others for help as the Yule Cat dug its claws into his flesh. Creatures surrounding the scene laughed and cheered.

Eve made herself turn away as nausea roiled in her stomach. "You find that kind of thing *fun?*"

"Not particularly," Liam said, grimacing at the gory scene. "I thought you might, though, considering you have a fetish for killing men. Or at least trying to."

"That's different," Eve hissed. "That man was innocent."

"And I'm not?"

Eve paled. "I..."

The words caught in her throat. Even if she wanted to tell him the truth, she couldn't; Sage had made sure of that. Eve glared at her shoes instead, her hands balled into fists at her sides.

"I didn't imagine you had justice to your method," Liam continued after a long beat of silence. "I'm afraid you won't find any justice here. The Unseelie Court enjoys its freedoms."

The Yule Cat moved on, its muzzle splotched in red as it happily explored the party. There was nothing left of the eaten man except a patch of snow steeped in blood.

"This party is full of monsters," she muttered to herself.

"On that, I can agree," Liam said, surprising her. "Let's make sure you and I avoid the worst of them. You've already seen the High King and his family—undoubtedly worth avoiding. Do you see that man in the red cloak?"

"There are a lot of red cloaks."

Liam's lips pressed into an annoyed line. "The one with the antlers."

Eve scanned the crowd. She came across a tall, slender man with a pair of black antlers and a cloak so deeply scarlet that she almost mistook it for blood. He moved with an ethereal grace only given to the Fae, his smile as sharp as his cheekbones. Eve watched the way his long black hair moved as the sea, rippling in waves that crested the shore.

Hair as liquid as ink. Eve suddenly remembered part of the riddle that Liam had given her weeks ago. The quest that would cure the stone-spreading disease on his body. It was the last item she needed.

"That's Lord Foxglove's son, Killian, of the Blood Court," Liam explained in a low voice. "I would stay far away from him if I were you. His court is not the kindest to mortals."

Eve scoffed. "And you are?"

"I am kinder than most you will find here." He pointed toward the other side of the clearing. "That group with the ugly pine vests over there are poisoners; neutral for the most part, but I would avoid touching them. Don't consume anything they offer you, but that goes without saying."

"Why are you telling me this?" Eve asked. Suspicion twisted in her gut; nothing in Faerie came for free, information included. "Why are you helping me?"

"It would be a waste of time if you were to die on me before you fulfilled your end of the bargain," Liam said with a sigh. "We are bound to protect each other. If you are determined to remain oblivious and risk your life, though, you have every opportunity to do so."

Liam flippantly gestured to the festivities around them. Eve had not fully been paying attention before, but now she couldn't resist. Between the carefree dancers twirling to a chaotic beat and the Faeries gorging themselves on wine and delicacies, many of the courts had found deadlier forms of entertainment.

Mortals danced until their feet bled, tears clouding their sight as their bodies jerked unceremoniously to the heavy thrum of stringed instruments. Horse-like creatures with riders infused into their backs and elongated mouths jeered and trotted around a cluster of human hostages whose bodies decayed when the creatures' mouths got too close.

Even weaker Faeries were not immune; Eve watched in horror as larger beasts plucked the wings from screaming sprites, gnomes with bloody red caps gutted unsuspecting attendants, and a slew of Faeries dined and played with discarded human entrails. Crude laughter intermingled with screams as the savage celebration carried on.

Eve watched the party spiral into madness. Her hands trembled, and she tucked them against her sides, hiding them within the folds of her cloak. This was not the place to show weakness.

"Do you see what I mean?" Liam asked. Eve gave a stiff nod. "Not all courts celebrate this way. Preece says the Seelie are more civilized in their holidays. I have never attended myself."

Why not? But Eve let the thought fade as she grew accustomed to the cruelty. Terror weaned off into grim acceptance—this was simply how things were done in the Unseelie Court.

There must be something wrong with her. Perhaps it was the shock. The longer she watched the bloody scene, the less it affected her; there was disgust, yes, but her mind kept wandering back to Nick's death and her role in it. She did not share the perverse pleasure of the Unseelie Court, yet she had participated in brutal violence just the same. How much blood on her hands did it take before she would be no different from the monsters painting the snow crimson at their feet?

"I need a moment." Eve pulled away and made for one of the buffet tables in the back. There was nothing she could eat, but she needed something to do with her fidgeting. She grabbed a leg of meat and settled against the forest's edge, as far away from the festivities as she could get. Creatures became no more than black shapes dancing against the light of the fire, their hooves and heels and toes creating a winding maze of crunched paths in the snow.

She took a deep breath. Then another. The hammering of her heart caught up to her, squeezing her chest tight enough that Eve thought she might rupture. She crouched down and squeezed her eyes shut to cut off the rest of the world. She prayed none of the Faeries noticed her. She was supposed to be the frightening one, the thing that her abusers would fear chasing them in the dark.

Why was it that she felt so weak right now?

Eve lifted her gaze—and immediately wished she hadn't. The Yule Cat sat in front of her, its gray tufts of fur dappled in scarlet as it peered down with interest. Its enormous fluffy tail flicked back and forth, but Eve couldn't tell if it was irritated or wanted to play.

What do I do? Standing up might encourage it to pounce on her. Running away would ensure it would. The reminder of the Yule Cat swallowing the mortal whole lingered in the back of her mind. Was this how she was going to go out?

The cat's eyes followed Eve's hands—the leg of meat. Of course.

Slowly, Eve lifted the food up as an offering. The cat leaned forward and sniffed the meal.

Gently, the Yule Cat took the leg of meat from Eve's hand. Its purr rumbled the ground she sat on, vibrating through Eve's bones as it happily trotted off with its new snack. Eve stared, amazed, as the Yule Cat curled up in front of the fire and consumed the meat with the flick of its tongue.

It's a big house cat, she thought. Eve took a shaky breath of relief and staggered to her feet. It was a miracle she could stand at all.

Eve searched for Liam or Hailey from the edge of the clearing, but neither stood out from the crowd. It was hard to make out anyone amid the array of bodies, but Eve caught sight of Logan and Preece by one of the tables of food and quietly seethed. Out of all the gore and chaos of Yule, how was it that Logan managed to escape unscathed? If anyone deserved to be eaten alive by the Yule Cat, it was him.

She turned her head away and kept searching. It wasn't safe to linger by herself. She needed to stick close to the Bone Court before someone else mistook her as another toy to play with.

Huddled in her cloak, Eve stuck to the outskirts of the clearing, avoiding direct eye contact with any of the Faeries that glanced her way. She spotted Liam snaking through the crowd when Logan turned his attention toward her. Eve tensed, hoping that something else would catch his eye. He leaned in toward Preece to say something, then made a beeline for Eve.

Shit. Eve reached for the dagger strapped to her thigh—but it was gone. In her mind's eye, Eve saw it sitting on her desk where she'd left it. She'd been too tired when she woke up to remember to bring it. *Shit.*

Eve pulled her hood low and pushed through the crowd in the opposite direction.

"Eve!" Her name on his tongue grated against her eardrums. Eve ducked her head, sparing only a glance over her shoulder to see how far he was. Logan, against his better judgment, pursued her, but it didn't last long. He hesitated near each group of Fae he came across, rightfully afraid to draw their attention. When Eve turned, she lost him.

Eve sagged with a sigh of relief. She didn't know what he wanted, and it didn't matter; Eve had no intention of facing him without a weapon. She turned to leave—and smacked right into one of the Fair Folk.

"Sor—" Eve's apology caught in her throat when she met the gaze of Killian Foxglove of the Blood Court.

Six

Killian was more ethereally beautiful up close, even as his nose wrinkled in disgust at Eve's accidental touch. He was younger than Eve realized—certainly not much older than Liam—with sharp cheekbones and dark, mesmerizing eyes. His black antlers glinted against the firelight as he raised his chin haughtily.

"It was an accident," Eve blurted out before he could name a punishment for her. She took a significant step backward and nervously curtsied. "It won't happen again."

"I should think not," he sneered. Even his cruel words came from a voice smooth as silk. He brushed the area of cloak that she'd touched, as if infected, and inspected her. Other red-cloaked members of the Blood Court paused, regarding her with the same hostility. "The Bone Court. I should have presumed as much."

Eve knew she should leave—Liam had warned her about Killian—but his response pulled at her curiosity. "What do you mean by that?"

Killian's gaze flickered over her, but he gave no indication of answering her question. Instead, he said, "You're the mortal they hosted that revel for."

"You mean my birthday party?"

He watched her, and Eve realized that his pupils extended across the entirety of his eyes. Black and fathomless, they were glistening tar pits that glued her to her spot.

"The Bone Court is fond of wasting resources," Killian mused. "Especially in regard to their pets, however unremarkable they may be. If not for their wine, it would be a wonder that the king allows their presence in court at all."

Heat crept up Eve's neck, but she reined her temper in with a tight smile. "A wonder, indeed."

Screams captured their attention. The twist of a smile on Killian's lips forced her to turn toward the sound.

Eve's heart plummeted as a group of skiers was dragged into the revelry. Four humans bundled in thick winter gear stumbled forward, one clutching their broken skis as they were pushed to their knees. One, to Eve's horror, was a child no older than ten.

The skiers were tossed into the center and the Yule Cat padded toward its sacrifice. Eve searched the faces of the Fair Folk, silently pleading for someone to step in. They did not—they delighted in the violence, their faces twisted with mad glee. Preece and Logan watched in disgust from afar, while Liam averted his gaze. Sage stared straight ahead, but even her ruthless facade cracked as Hailey trembled in horror at her side.

"Their bloodline breeds weakness," Killian said, following her stare. His dark eyes flashed in delight as the Yule Cat's mouth opened wide. "If you'll excuse me."

It was not a request. Killian left with the others in his court to join the rowdy Fair Folk in their display of carnage. Screams pierced Eve's skull as the first man was devoured. The skiers huddled around the child to shield her eyes, but there was no hiding the cat's blood-stained teeth.

Eve tore off her cloak and rushed to the mortals.

She heard someone call her name as she broke through the crowd, but Eve ignored it. If she thought too hard, her nerves would catch up to her. Adrenaline pumped through her veins as she dropped beside the skiers.

"Put this on," she ordered, thrusting the cloak toward the group. They did not budge, whether out of terror or suspicion, Eve wasn't sure. The Yule Cat was almost finished with its meal. She shook the heavy fabric in front of them with an edge of desperation to her voice. "*Someone* put the fucking cloak on. I'm trying to help."

A small hand shot out from the huddle. One of the skiers—the mother, Eve presumed—pulled away enough to let the child grasp the cloak. Eve kept a wary eye on the Yule Cat as she kicked off her shoes, ignoring the freezing bite of snow through her stockings as she passed them on. The other skier—another woman—took Eve's shoes and swapped them for her own.

There was nothing left to give. Eve searched her outfit for something, anything—

"Eve!"

Hailey's hair comb flew toward her. Eve caught it, stumbling back into the snow. Sage stood at Hailey's side, worry creasing her brows with every inch Hailey moved forward. But her friend smiled, and Eve's anxiety eased.

There was no time to ask for permission—she tore the skier's hat off and tucked the bone-made comb into her hair. Eve hoped the woman wouldn't ask what it was made of. Perhaps she could already guess.

A solid crunch signified the end of the Yule Cat's meal. The furry beast padded toward them with eager, dilated eyes. Eve held her breath as the Yule Cat sniffed. All eyes of the revelry were upon them, waiting for judgment.

She had managed to save herself with a leg of meat once, but Eve wasn't certain this would work. How new did the clothes have to be? Would it matter if she and Hailey had already worn some of them during the night? Questions ricocheted through her mind as the feline took its time sniffing them out.

Finally, the Yule Cat made its decision. It turned away.

Eve practically collapsed onto her knees, but held herself steady. She grasped the skiers' shoulders and pulled them close.

"You need to run out of here as fast as you can. Do you understand me?" she said with grave severity. "Do not stop, do not believe what anyone says, *run*. Whatever way you came. Can you do that?"

The women glanced at each other, then nodded, one lifting the child onto her back. They did not question what had happened—perhaps they did not want to think any more of it. Eve watched them run from the revelry and hoped the skiers would make it out safely. Eve had done all she could.

"What an excellent idea." Eve recognized the High King's voice from earlier and spotted him standing before the angering crowd before they could pounce on her. "We all enjoy a good hunt. The first to bring back the mortals' heads shall receive a boon."

"No—" Eve started, but members of various courts were already fleeing into the woods with weapons drawn. Her stomach clenched. *Please make it out alive.*

Servants of the Bone Court descended upon the man's remains like vultures, sweeping up any remaining bones into their cloaks. Eve grimaced and stepped away. Evren caught her eye from beyond his servants. His dark gaze pinned her in place; he was not pleased with her behavior.

The feeling was mutual.

Seven

The gore-splattered snow haunted Eve's mind on the way back to the Bone Court. She thought of the child and her family as she stared out of her window into the gloomy forest and wondered if they'd escaped safely. Eve could still hear the crunch of bone paired with the little girl's screams.

Liam sat beside her, his expression neutral, but she could sense him watching her alongside his father. Where Liam was uncharacteristically quiet, Evren more than made up for the silence.

"Of course, His Highness chose the *Blood* Court to host, of all people," Evren muttered. He held out an empty wineglass to the cloaked servant beside him, who obediently filled it to the brim with a peach-colored liquid. "The food was hardly edible—dare I mention the wine? One would think they were serving vats of blood. Far too thick and metallic."

"The Unseelie King favors the Blood Court," Liam said.

"Not for long." Evren tapped his long nails against the glass with a steady, rhythmic clink. "We have been the official vintner for centuries. His Highness wouldn't dare insult our good name by forcing a replacement. With a new heir behind the title, he will be forced to renew our contract before the summer."

Liam sighed and threw his head back against the top of the seat. "That is not guaranteed. Do the rumors mean nothing to you?"

"I am aware of what the Unseelie have to say," Evren snapped. "Idiots, the lot of them, but you would do well to dispel their gossip." Eve pretended not to notice that his attention had shifted to her. "As for your spectacle, it is a small miracle that His Highness did not order our heads in exchange for your insolence. You do us no favors by playing hero, girl."

"You were going to let a child die," Eve said incredulously.

"The more the merrier." Evren took a large gulp from his glass, then held it out for a refill. "It is a celebration, is it not? You are lucky His Highness has a fondness for hunts. The Fair Folk would have eaten you alive."

Eve didn't doubt that. If Evren said it, it must be true. The Fair Folk couldn't lie.

She swallowed hard and stared out the window. The carriage had become claustrophobic, the air stifling with disapproval and tension. Eve squinted into the blackness of the forest until her eyes burned. As they passed the stone archway that signified her way back to the mortal world, her breath hitched with longing. She could picture the spiral stairs on the other side, leading her back home. For now, it was hollow, an empty reminder that she was trapped.

A rumble shook the ground. Eve gripped the carriage door handle as fear spiked through her core. The carriage teetered but did not stray off course.

A giant beast prowled through the trees. The Yule Cat. It tromped through the forest, shoving trees and debris out of the way as it crossed the road—and trampled right down on the archway.

Eve let out a strangled cry, throwing the carriage door open. Liam pulled her back inside, but not before she saw the damage. The ancient stone crumbled and turned to rubble in the snow. Wisteria wilted between the cracks, flattened by the giant paw that had crushed it. The Yule Cat carried on through the forest, chasing some unseen prey. Unaware that it had ruined Eve's hope of escape.

"Are you insane?" Liam hissed after Eve settled back against the cushion in defeat.

"It crushed the arch." The words rang hollow. Eve gripped the seat numbly. Although she'd searched for alternative routes, her plan had always come back to somehow making the arch work again. Now, she was truly at a loss.

"All the more power to it," Evren said absently, taking another sip of his wine. "That ghastly thing was an eyesore."

That eyesore was my way home, she thought. Eve dug her nails into the cushion as the manor pulled into view. There would be other ways to get back, she told herself. For her own sanity, there had to be.

She left the carriage before it fully stopped. The smell of blood clung to her dress, her stockings. Her feet were still cold and wet from the mixture of snow and carnage. Eve longed for a hot bath and the comfort of her pajamas.

"Eve." Logan's voice sent a chill up her spine. He simultaneously appeared both afraid to approach her and urgent to catch up with her as he hurried out of the second carriage. Eve picked up her pace. "Eve!"

"Get away from me," she snarled over her shoulder. She was all but sprinting to the front door. Of all nights, why did she have to leave her dagger in her room *now?*

"Please. It'll only take a minute. I need to talk to you," Logan pleaded. Eve grasped the door handle, but her hands were too slick with sweat to turn it. She banged on the wood instead, startling when Logan spoke up behind her, "Eve, I—"

"*Don't,*" she hissed, whirling on him at once. "If you take another step near me, I'll slit your throat. I mean it."

Logan hesitated a few feet away, his raised hand slowly lowering to his side. There was a pathetic quality to him that Eve had not seen before. Her fingers flexed as she imagined the easiest way to pin him down and choke the life out of him.

He opened his mouth to speak, but the door swung open and Eve dove inside. She could hear the others enter as they returned home, but it wasn't until Eve was almost to her room that she realized Liam was close on her heels.

"What were you thinking, trying to save those people?" Liam demanded. Eve clenched her fists at her sides. She wasn't ready for this conversation.

"Leave me alone."

"You could've gotten yourself killed."

"I didn't," she said, and Liam shook his head. She reached for the knob to her room, but Liam blocked her path. "Let me through."

"Talk first," he said, pointing to another open door down the hall: the study. Eve glared up at him.

"You don't tell me what to do." Liam did not relent, his finger stubbornly pointing at the doorway. Eve considered barreling him over, but her will to fight this evening was diminishing by the second. With a huff, Eve stomped into the little study, scowling at the books on the shelves as though they were the reason for her fury.

"I don't see why you care," she snapped once Liam had shut the door. "I thought you were still angry about me trying to kill you."

"I am," Liam reassured her hotly. "Don't think that I've forgotten. But we've made a deal to protect each other; if you put yourself in danger, I'm forced into it, too."

Eve opened her mouth to argue but found herself at a loss. She hadn't thought about that. All she could think about was saving that child. "I didn't mean to put you in danger, but they would have died if I didn't do something. I won't apologize for that."

Liam was silent, his twisting expression betraying his conflicted emotions. He collapsed into an armchair with a sigh. "You are abhorrently reckless. I'm going to die before the new year at this rate."

"Without my help, you might die sooner," Eve pointed out. Liam frowned, his fingers brushing across the rough stone embedded in the back of his neck. Seriously, she asked, "How is it?"

His gaze narrowed. "Don't burden yourself with false sympathy."

Guilt twisted in Eve's stomach, but she didn't deny him. She couldn't. Eve buried her remorse instead, silently accepting that whatever tentative friendship she'd built with Liam was ruined.

She just hadn't expected to *miss* it.

Eve cleared her throat and crossed the room, balling up her ruined stockings and tossing them onto the floor. Liam's brows shot up as Eve settled on top of the desk and stretched her toes, pleased to be free of the wet garment. Her feet were *freezing*. Perhaps giving her shoes away had been a mistake.

"Do you know how to fight?" she asked.

Liam's gaze flickered to her face, uncertain. "Yes. Why?"

"I want you to teach me." It was the best solution she could think of. Eve knew her own weaknesses, and strength was one of them. She barely survived Nick's attack; if she was going to kill Logan and Colton, she needed training.

"Why? So you'll have an easier time stabbing me in the back?" Liam laughed without mirth. "I think not."

"You still need me alive to finish your quest, don't you?" Eve pushed. "We both know I can't survive in the Unseelie Court without any way to defend myself."

Liam inspected his nails. "I wouldn't say that; you've done a decent job thus far."

"How long before that luck runs out? Our pact to protect each other is lopsided right now, don't you think?"

He pressed his lips into another thin line. Eve suspected that she might have won.

"This wouldn't have anything to do with Logan, would it?" Eve glared in response. "I thought so."

Eve jumped to her feet, ignoring the pain that shot up her injured leg. "If you aren't willing to teach me, then—"

"Then, what? You'll command me to do it?" Liam's tone was mocking, but she could see the anger—the hurt—in his gaze. He had not forgotten her outburst last night.

"I'll ask someone else. I don't need your help," Eve insisted, but the ire had left her. Guilt had a funny way of doing that.

Liam twisted in his chair to sit sideways, his long legs dangling over the edge as he rolled his eyes. "Have you considered the consequences of what you're asking? If you learn how to kill someone effectively, are you going to be able to live with yourself afterward?"

"Of course," Eve said. "I killed Nick, didn't I?"

She was already in the hall when she heard him mutter under his breath, "Sometimes I wonder about that."

Eight

Eve missed showers the most. A bath didn't do the same job, especially when she had to rush cleaning herself before the water cooled. There was also a matter of boiling the water—something usually done by the Bone Court's staff, but Eve wasn't comfortable relying on them given their circumstances.

I wish I knew how to free them. Eve had tried a few things—pinning the brooch of protection Hailey had gifted her to their uniforms, gifting them berries and flowers and anything else she thought might break their trance—but none of it had worked.

"I used to free them myself," Liam had told her one evening after she'd sat one of the servants down and begged them to wake up, to no avail. *"Glamour them out of their glamour in a way. It worked, but my father would always replace them."*

"Why did you stop?" Eve had asked. She never imagined he would do something so... empathetic. Liam frowned at the servant in the chair, not much older than either of them but skinnier than any human had a right to be.

"I hated to find their bodies after."

Eve gathered her things and made for the bathroom, determined to quickly scrub herself with whatever frigid water she found and be done with it.

Her fist barely brushed the door before it swung open. Hot, welcoming steam poured out into the hallway as Hailey stood on the other side, her damp hair pulled back into a loose braid. Surprise crossed her face, and she opened the door wider.

"Sorry, were you waiting on me?" she apologized, stepping to the side.

"No, you're fine," Eve reassured her. Hailey smiled, but the tension in her shoulders didn't ease.

They hadn't had a chance to see each other at all during the Yule festivities, aside from their meddling with the skiers. Eve could see the toll the night had taken on her friend. Hailey's soft brown eyes were rimmed in red, and she gripped the peachy linen of her nightdress until her knuckles were pale. Neither of them had been prepared for the party, if one could even call it that. The revelries they'd attended at the Bone Court were tame in comparison.

"How are you holding up?" Eve asked in a quiet voice. Hailey's smile was instinctual and unconvincing.

"I'm fine," she said, and straightened up, as if the additional height could ward off the horrors they'd witnessed. "It—it was a lot to take in. Sage tried to convince me to stay behind, but I didn't listen."

"That's not your fault." Eve's heart cracked at the daunting horror in her friend's eyes. Had she witnessed the same things Eve did? Or something worse? "Someone should have told us what was going to happen."

Hailey glanced away, but the color had drained from her face. Eve noticed a tremble in her hands. "I saw a girl, and the cat... She couldn't be older than twelve, Eve. Who laughs at something like that?"

Eve swallowed hard, glad to have missed that particular scene—and wishing Hailey had too. "They're not human. They don't value human life."

Hailey shook her head, but it wasn't in disagreement. Eve wondered if she was trying to erase the memory before it permanently ingrained itself into her nightmares. "Sage didn't even react. I asked her to do something, and she told me that this is how things are."

A bitter taste rose in Eve's mouth. For as much as Sage praised her love for Hailey, it was as though she knew nothing about her.

"She probably didn't want to get involved with the other Fair Folk," Eve muttered. "You saw how dangerous they are."

Hailey's arms crossed over her chest, gooseflesh rising as she hugged herself. "You didn't hear her, Eve. She wasn't *afraid;* she *praised* them."

"What?"

"I mean, not outright—" Hailey stumbled over her words. Her ironclad defense of Sage was crumbling. "She wasn't saying what they did was great or anything, but..."

"But she wasn't condemning it, either."

"Exactly."

Uncomfortable silence permeated the hallway. Hailey's fingers flexed around the fabric of her nightdress. She tried to smooth out the wrinkles, to no avail.

Questions burned on the tip of Eve's tongue. *How much do you know about Sage? How much do you remember?*

I need to tell her.

But not now. Not after witnessing... that. Eve knew that Hailey had enough existential crises for one night.

Hailey reached for her hand and gave it a squeeze. In a small, hopeful voice, she asked, "Have you had any luck finding a way back home yet?"

If I did, I wouldn't be here, Eve thought. The shame of her bitter failures burned in her chest. It wasn't only Eve that was relying on an escape; Hailey was trapped, too. Unlike Eve, her family must be worried sick. *Do my parents even know I'm missing?*

"Not yet," Eve confessed. If she wasn't exhausted, she would try again now. Eve knew her body couldn't handle another sleepless night. She had a better chance of freezing to death in the woods than finding a miracle route home.

Disappointment flickered across Hailey's face. She gave Eve's hand another squeeze. "We'll figure something out. I'll poke around the mansion and see if I can find anything helpful in the meantime."

Eve forced a tight-lipped smile. "Thanks. I appreciate it."

Hailey gathered her things and, finally, relinquished the bathroom. Eve dragged herself through the motions, using the leftover bath water to scrub what dirt she could until her freckled skin burned raw against the brush's bristles. Once she was dressed in her own nightgown—some ivory thing that reminded Eve of Gothic heroines—Eve brushed her teeth and returned to her bedroom.

She collapsed onto the bed when she heard a steady knock at the door. Eve rolled onto her side, glaring toward the unknown intruder.

What if it was Logan? The thought sent a shiver down her spine. Even though Liam had reassured her that Logan was magically banned from the premises, Eve had little hope that restriction would hold permanently. She recalled how he'd chased her through the crowd tonight.

Another knock.

Eve climbed out of bed and remembered to grab her dagger off the desk this time when she answered the door. If it *was* Logan, there was no one to stop her from slicing his throat this time.

To her relief—and confusion—Preece smiled at her from the other side. He wore a pair of silky blue pajamas and a nightcap that hung to the side of his face, reminding her of a storybook character. Eve kept the door open a crack.

"Oh, good, you're still awake," Preece said happily, his gaze drifting to the dagger in her hand. If he was concerned, he didn't show it. "I have a message to deliver to you."

"From who?" Suspicion twisted in Eve's gut. Preece held out his closed fist, and Eve opened her palms to accept whatever he held.

Her heart dropped.

The silver cross necklace winked up at her under the candlelight, her initials marked clearly in the center. Dirt and dried blood tarnished the snapped chain.

"Where did you get this?" she whispered. Eve hadn't seen the necklace since it had gone missing at Liam's party. Since Nick had been dragged into the lake.

"Logan requested that I deliver this to you as a sign of peace."

Eve scoffed. *Peace.* The only peace she would get was when she sliced his head clean off. If he thought returning her necklace would make up for the torture she'd endured, he was dead wrong.

There was a gleeful twinkle in Preece's eyes, and Eve suspected there was more to say.

"What else?"

"He also has a message," Preece said. His smile was too eager: that of a man who reveled in what scraps of information passed through his sticky fingertips. She could see him trying to put the puzzle pieces together. "*Colton knows.* Rather cryptic, wouldn't you say? Do you know what he refers to?"

Eve gripped the necklace tight enough to leave indents on her palm. "Yes."

Preece waited for an explanation that she had no intention of giving. *Colton knows.* Eve didn't have to ask what it meant; the necklace was proof enough. Nick was dead, and Eve had been responsible.

When Eve did not elaborate, Preece changed tactics. "Shall I deliver a message in return?"

Oh, she had a message in return. It came in the form of her dagger in his skull. Eve's last attempts at bargaining for death with the Fogtree siblings, however, had been less than satisfactory. Instead, she shook her head, too angry to speak.

"If you are certain," Preece said. His shoulders slumped in slight disappointment. "Sleep well."

"Goodnight." Eve shut the door before he had fully turned. She dumped the broken necklace onto her desk as if burned.

A sign of peace. The exchange turned over in Eve's mind with sickening realization. *Colton knows.*

Eve had lost the element of surprise against them. Logan might have wanted peace—Eve had her doubts about how genuine his request was—but Colton would not forgive her for killing Nick. He valued his friends, and no matter how horrible they were, Colton protected them. She had seen the extent of his protection—his wealth, his connections—firsthand years ago.

A horrific thumping startled Eve awake. It came from the window, an unsteady *thump, thump, thump* followed by a deafening whine.

The Yule Cat sniffed outside, its snout larger than the frame. It nudged its head against the wall, pressing its enormous nose against the glass.

What the hell was it doing *here?*

Eve lay in her bed, petrified, and silently pleaded with the beast to go away. Had it realized she had given her clothes to the skiers and wanted revenge? Was that why it lurked now, searching for its next meal?

If she stayed completely still, maybe it would leave. Eve held her breath, praying for it to be true.

The Yule Cat did not leave. It pushed and pawed at her window, not hard enough to break the glass but enough to gain her attention. An elongated meow rattled her bones. Then another, as if it was begging for something.

Is it hungry? she thought. Eve had heard the same cry from her baby cousins when they needed to be fed. She recalled the leg of meat she'd given the creature at the festivities—and how it had trampled the stone arch before arriving home.

Did it follow *me here?*

Eve stared at the cat in contemplation,

Slowly, she crept out into the hall. From the tossing and turning she heard through passing rooms, the Yule Cat must've woken up the entire household. Eve tiptoed down to the kitchen and grabbed whatever meat she could find. Maybe if she fed the beast, it would leave her alone.

The Yule Cat wailed impatiently upon her returned. Eve's arms shook when she opened the window.

"Don't eat me," she ordered, carefully setting the meat down on her windowsill and taking a large step back. "I can't feed you if you eat me."

To its credit, the Yule Cat waited until all the food laid on the windowsill before driving its enormous tongue down the line. Eve stumbled back, afraid the pink muscle would scoop her up as well.

Its two large yellow eyes glanced around the room, searching for more.

"That's all I have." Eve swallowed hard. If it wanted to, the Yule Cat could swipe its giant paw and drag her directly into its maw. "There's no more."

The Yule Cat glanced around the room a final time before reluctantly taking off—presumably to beg at the next Fair Folk's house. Eve sunk to the ground, her entire body trembling.

She quietly hoped that it would not come again.

NINE

"You're late."

Liam tapped his foot impatiently against the ballroom floor, the noise bouncing off the high walls. Strapped to his hip was a black-hilted sword.

"What are you doing here?" Eve hesitated in the hallway outside. She'd woken up early with a plan to practice using her dagger in Sage's meadow before anyone else was up. The blade weighed heavily in the pocket of her cloak, along with a few apples she had intended to use for target practice.

"You requested an instructor, didn't you?" Liam raised his brow.

"I thought you weren't going to help me."

"I won't if you keep standing there." Liam sighed and played with the hilt of his sword. "Do you want to learn how to fight or not?"

Drawing her dagger, Eve met Liam in the middle of the room. "What do I do?"

"That depends," Liam said. "What sort of experience do you have?"

Not much. Eve had been relatively well-liked growing up. There had only been two fights in her class, and she hadn't been involved with either of them. No, her violent streak had been more recent. She could easily imagine the damage she wanted to do, but when it came to her fists, they wouldn't cooperate.

"I fought you," she said after a long moment.

"And?"

"And what? That's it."

"That's *it?*" Liam was aghast. He stared at her, scrawny and miserable as she was, and Eve knew that he was also wondering how she'd managed to best him at her party. "Show me what you can do."

He stood to the side of the room and gestured for her to move. Eve hesitated. Athleticism had never come easily to her, especially with an audience. That much became apparent to her as she clumsily darted throughout the ballroom, wielding her dagger with the same skill as a crab waving a spoon. Liam watched from the sidelines, mouth covered but face pink with laughter.

"What?" she snapped. "I'm *trying!*"

"Is that what you call it?" Liam asked between peals of laughter. Eve wanted to throw her dagger at his stupid face. "No—No, go on. Pretend I'm not even here."

Eve scowled, refusing to budge another inch until his hysterics ceased. Liam wiped a tear from his eye.

"Are you done?" she demanded.

"Hardly. That *terrific* display will live in my head for years to come." Shaking his head, Liam detached his scabbard with a loud *clunk* on the floor. "As for your training, I suppose we'll have to cover the basics."

"Hey!" Liam plucked the dagger from her hands and tossed it with his sword into a discarded pile.

"You won't need it," he said. "Let's start with the metals."

Liam pointed to the dagger and sword on the floor. "The metals in Faerie are similar to the ones in your realm, but not quite. Ours are stronger, and the Unseelie Court is renowned for our blacksmiths. You will not find finer weapons than the ones here, with the exception of iron."

"Iron weapons?" Eve asked.

"Weapons, jewelry, wires—anything," Liam explained. "We have a variation of iron here in Faerie, but it's more of a mixture of metals with such low iron content that it barely counts. Pure iron from your realm, however... nothing here compares. If you wish to fight the Fair Folk, your best bet is to find iron."

"Okay. Can I go out and buy it, or...?"

Liam laughed. "Hardly. It rarely passes through here anymore.

You would be hard pressed to find someone willing to part with pure iron."

"Do *you* have pure iron?"

Liam annoyingly tapped her nose. "That, Evie, is a secret I will carry to my grave. Now, let's give you a proper lesson."

Eve tensed as he pressed one hand to her waist and the other on her back, straightening her spine.

"I'm going to grab you roughly," he said. "Manage to get me off you."

The moment his hands fell upon her shoulders from behind, Eve spun to escape his grasp. Liam grabbed her forearms instead and yanked her toward him. She pulled against his grip, but no amount of squirming would loosen his hold.

"By now, you would be dead," Liam said. His voice was hard and unsympathetic. He touched her neck, the gesture sending a tremor down her spine. "I could have sliced your throat open, or broken your neck, or—"

Eve jerked her head and bit his hand. Liam yelped in surprise. He pulled back at once. In his moment of shock, Eve careened her knee into his groin.

Liam released a sharp gasp of pain and bent over. Eve raised her knee again—this time for his nose—but Liam snatched her leg and tugged hard. Eve fell onto her back with a painful thud.

"At least you know how to take someone by surprise," Liam wheezed. He released her leg and stepped back, indicating surrender.

"Sorry," Eve apologized instinctively.

"I do not accept your apology." Eve winced, but Liam collected himself and offered her a hand. Confused, she took it, and Liam steadied her on her feet. "The Unseelie folk do not fight fairly. You responded aptly."

"So, fight dirty," Eve concluded. Liam's lips twitched with amusement.

"If that is what you wish to call it," he said. "Your balance needs work, though, as does your strength. Surprise can't carry you through every fight. Formal training will benefit you."

Eve thought back to her fight with Nick, and again to her botched murder of Liam. He was right. While she'd had an upper hand during her moments of surprise, her lack of experience and her weakened body couldn't keep up.

If she ever wanted to kill her abusers—to escape Faerie—she needed to be stronger.

"Teach me," Eve said, instilled with a new purpose.

"Only if you promise not to use what I teach you to kill me."

"I promise."

Liam scrutinized her for a lie, but there was none. Eve had no intention of trying to murder him again, for her sake or otherwise. Still doubtful, Liam gestured for her to return to their starting position.

For the next hour, Liam guided her through a series of exercises focused on balance, strength training, and self-defense. Eve did not lack coordination as much as she had previously lacked motivation. Her best fighting had come out in clumsy spurts of desperation amid a high of adrenaline. Now that she had the motivation, Eve could see every clumsy fault she had made before and grew increasingly frustrated as she repeated those same mistakes in practice.

Liam scoffed as she found herself once again struck down, only hard enough to bruise her ego.

"It would have dishonored me to die by your hand," he mocked with the shake of his head. "I'm embarrassed it even came to that."

Eve gritted her teeth and hopped back to her feet. They ran through defenses again. And again. They'd both removed their shoes somewhere along the way, stockings, socks, and vests bundled into a sweaty pile on the floor as Eve fumbled through each step. She did not bite him again, but his bossy, patronizing attitude made her want to.

"When can we move onto the weapons?" she demanded after another miserable defeat.

"Not any time soon," Liam said. "You can barely wrangle me off you without falling over."

Anger boiled within Eve's veins. Maybe it was the fact Liam had bested her all afternoon, or maybe it was the sinking realization of how screwed she was without his help. "I need to learn how to wield a weapon."

"You'll learn eventually, but not now," Liam said. He was already back in what they had decided as their starting position, ready to throw her onto the ground again. Eve wondered how much joy he received from tossing her across the ballroom. "There will be times when you have none. You should know how to survive without it."

"What *time?*" Eve threw her hands up in the air, refusing to participate. "Your father's stupid competition is underway, Colton knows I killed Nick, Logan is *in the backyard,* and if I don't get home and check on my nan, my parents are going to *kill me*—if something here doesn't do it first!" She snatched the dagger from the floor. "Tell me how to use this thing before I kill both of us."

Liam rubbed the tension between his brows. She could see that he was weighing whether it would be worth it to continue arguing with her. "Pick something else."

"What?"

"Give me that." Liam snatched the dagger from her hand and held it in front of her face. "This is for close combat. If you aren't willing to learn the right way, then pick something that'll at least give you a fighting chance.

Something with distance. Bows, throwing knives, a whip, it won't matter to me."

"Those are too noticeable," Eve argued. "I need something I can hide. The dagger is perfect."

"You can hide plenty of things with enough creativity," Liam argued, but Eve shook her head.

"You don't understand," she snapped. "Everyone underestimates me—I can use that to my advantage. Who thinks a skinny brat like me is going to stab a guy in the stomach? No one. It'll be over and done with before they know it."

Liam twisted the dagger in his hands—the same one Eve had tried to murder him with—and muttered, "Anyone would be a fool to underestimate you."

Shame struck her fast and hard. To Liam, Eve had pulled off that exact scheme. She stared at the blade and tried to fight back the guilt that had haunted her since.

I'm sorry, she wanted to say. *I'm sorry I betrayed your trust.* But she couldn't explain why. It was another sin she would have to live with.

"Can I use the dagger?" Eve pushed, gentler. He did not meet her gaze, focusing instead on the blade that had nearly plunged into his throat days before.

"I cannot stop you from using it," Liam resigned. "I'll think you're terribly foolish for doing so, but that hasn't stopped you before."

He moved to offer it to her, but Liam paused, pulling the blade back for further inspection.

"Where did you say you got this?" he asked, turning it over in his hands. The hilt's and scabbard's designs were unique, with smooth jewels encrusted in silver. One cracked stone winked up at her under the light, a reminder of her failure on the balcony.

"I didn't say." Eve watched him examine it, a part of her hoping—willing—for him to recognize the blade. To see who was behind his assassination.

"It's Faerie made," Liam explained, more of a commentary to himself than her.

It's Sage's. Sage gave me the dagger, Eve wanted to say, but the words caught in her throat when she tried. The admission was too close to confessing Sage's involvement with the planned murder. She managed to get out, "It was a gift."

That was true, at least. Sage had given her the dagger both as a birthday present and a weapon, a perfect excuse should anyone ask how Eve acquired a Faerie blade. She was surprised it took Liam this long to notice it.

Eve waited for him to ask more, but whatever interest Liam took in the blade waned. With reluctance, Liam returned the dagger to Eve's hands. She could see how uneasy it made him for her to have it. The crack in their tentative friendship had become a chasm, and Eve had no one to blame but herself.

"I'm better educated with swords," Liam said, moving on. "In truth, Sage would be better equipped to teach you how to wield a dagger, but I can assist with the basics. To start, you're holding it wrong."

Liam stepped forward and twisted the dagger's pommel to face the blade the other way.

"What's the difference?" she asked.

"The side closer to you is called the spine; it's not as sharp as the edge. See?" Liam took her hand and pressed one finger lightly to the spine of the blade, then to the other, sharper side. "This isn't a toy. You'll hurt yourself if you handle it incorrectly."

"I know how to hold a knife, Liam," Eve said, rolling her eyes, but did not push him away when he readjusted her grip on the pommel. Despite her discomfort with physical touch, Eve was surprised by how willing she was to accept each of his brief adjustments to get her body into a fighting stance. Perhaps it was because of the dagger in her hand and the threat it posed to him. Or maybe it was because she was certain he had no interest in her beyond another set of hands to complete his quest.

They practiced in the ballroom for some time. Eve lost track of the minutes—maybe hours—that ticked by as she tried to mimic Liam's movements. A slash here, a parry there. No matter how simple his instructions, Eve failed to match Liam's agility and speed. The way he made her twist the dagger in her palm was instinctively unnatural. She kept dropping it onto the floor by mistake.

Liam grimaced. "Perhaps you are better off poisoning those boys."

"Don't make me use this," Eve muttered, but meant none of it. She picked up the dagger again.

"You're not gripping it tight enough when you switch positions," Liam said.

"I'm gripping it fine."

"Clearly," Liam drawled. "You're holding it out too far from yourself. It's not a sword. You need to be prepared to keep it close and seek out your opponent's vulnerabilities."

Eve clenched her jaw and tried to mimic a parry that Liam had shown her earlier. The blade twisted in her hand, and she slashed backwards in defense.

Eve hissed through her teeth. A thin stripe of red blood colored her bone-white blouse. Another mistake; she'd pointed the edge of the blade toward her instead of the spine.

"This is why I said you need a different weapon," Liam chided. "Roll up your sleeve. How bad is it?"

"I can take care of it." Eve clutched the sleeve down, the fabric wet with her own blood. The cut had been close to the straight-lined scar on her wrist. It would not be the first time Liam noticed that scar, but the last thing she wanted to do was discuss it.

Liam raised his brow as though he might argue but decided against it. "Bandages are in the kitchen. I recommend bringing some tomorrow when we practice."

Eve nodded, too embarrassed to put up a fight. With a last lingering glance, Liam picked up his clothes and sword and left. It was only once he was out of the room that Eve rolled her sleeve back and surveyed the damage.

It stung worse than it actually was. Already the cut had stopped bleeding. She would need to change clothes, but that was going to happen anyway; sweat clung to her body and shirt in a sticky second skin. She grimaced, peeling the cloth away as she bent to pick up her discarded things.

When Eve stood, her gaze trailed to the window—and stopped. Logan lingered outside, his blond hair poking out of a knitted hat as he waved to get her attention from the grassy hill below.

Eve's stomach churned in disgust. How long had he been standing there? Was he watching her this whole time? From the lack of fallen snow clinging to his clothes, she had to guess it hadn't been long—but she wasn't sure.

Kill him, a small part of her whispered. The balcony door was right there, and the dagger was in her hand. She imagined herself stepping out, feigning a listening ear to whatever cursed thing he had to say before she drove the blade into his back. It would be a merciful death compared to what he put her through.

The sting on her arm reminded her how impractical that plan was. *Surprise can't carry you through every fight.*

Furious, Eve turned on her heel and stormed out of the ballroom.

TEN

There had been many awkward family dinners in Eve Carter's life. On the dinner of her seventh birthday, her Aunt Sam had gotten into an argument with Ben, Eve's father, and was excommunicated from the family. When she was fourteen, Ben was laid off and drank himself stupid while Eve's friends from church were over for dinner. And then, of course, there was the dinner after *the incident*.

In short, these miserable evenings prepared Eve for the discomfort of the Fogtree family dinners and all the familiar misery that accompanied them.

Cloaked servants ushered in savory meals on bronze platters, a mixture of cinnamon and nutmeg wafting through the air. The staff doled out side dishes of glazed berries, roasted nuts, hearty vegetables, and a large meat pie took up the center of the table. The pastry dough was intricate, depicting a murder of crows devouring the innards of a frightened deer. Eve paled as she remembered the not-quite-a-deer's corpse in the forest.

Despite the gruesome depiction, the Fair Folk's delicacies were far more appetizing than the safe meals Eve and Hailey were provided. Venison in a cherry jam and an array of cooked vegetables sat on their plates; safe for mortal consumption, but dreadfully boring in appearance. Eve pushed the green beans across her plate with a grimace. She couldn't fathom their appeal from one realm to the next.

"The Yule Cat is still lingering in the Bone Court," Evren said irritably. "Yesterday, it squashed two of my brownies in the courtyard."

"Odd," Preece mused, tapping his chin with the end of his spoon. "It should have returned home by now."

"One would think," Evren grumbled. "You've heard nothing that would change its circumstances?"

"Not a word."

Evren hummed in annoyance, and Eve carefully took a bite of her venison to avoid his gaze. *She* knew why the Yule Cat was still around—and she had no idea how to get rid of it. Nearly every night, the beast had showed up at her window, pawing for food.

It had ceased its whining at least. Only her sleep was disrupted by the Yule Cat's needs. Eve gave it what she could, but the staff would complain in the morning about the missing meat and send someone off to fetch more.

Better than it eating me, she thought. It was a small price to pay for her survival.

"I've had some correspondences with Lady Acacia recently," Sage interrupted, addressing her father in a businesslike tone. When he didn't look up from his meal, she added, "From the Seelie Court?"

"I know who she is," Evren said with disinterest.

"She is interested in trying some of the mulberry wine you made," Sage continued, striving to grasp her father's attention. "She requested a delivery to test at her Imbolc celebration."

Evren's fork scraped across his plate, and he finally met his daughter's gaze. "You told her no, I assume."

"I told her to expect a delivery within a fortnight." Sage's brows pinched in confusion as Evren glared at her. "It's a reasonable time frame."

"Perhaps you ought to have considered speaking to me before making such promises," Evren said with a thin smile. "The High King has requested exclusivity with certain wines."

"I know that," Sage huffed. "Mulberry wasn't on the list."

"It is now." Evren set his glass down on the table with an aggressive clink. "No matter. I shall have to visit Lady Acacia myself and suggest an alternative."

"I can do it," Sage said. "We've already spoken—"

"You have done enough," Evren snapped, then redirected his attention to Preece. Sage moodily sunk in her chair, dismissed. "You, at least, are kept up to date on things. Tell me, what news have you acquired recently?"

Eve tuned out their conversation as Preece delved into the gossip of the Unseelie Court. His stories of gory recollections and mundane cruelty did nothing to help her appetite. She chewed her vegetables instead and stared longingly at the decadent arrangement on Liam's plate. Maybe the risk of starving herself after a taste of Faerie food was worth it...

No, it wasn't. Eve tried to ignore the tempting scents from the dishes in front of her. Evren didn't care one way or the other if Eve and Hailey gorged themselves on Faerie meals and found themselves unable to stop. If it wasn't for Liam and Sage's interventions with the cooks to make sure certain ingredients weren't used among their mortal guests, they already would have. Eve had to wonder if Liam's intervention had to do with their protection pact, or if he'd suddenly grown a conscience.

"—concerns regarding the unusual amount of Fair Folk slain in the woods." Eve's interest was piqued by this familiar piece of gossip. She thought of the not-deer's corpse and the clean carve of its removed flesh.

"It's not unusual for the Unseelie Court to get rowdy now and again," Evren said, clearly bored by this piece of information.

"It is when none of the denizens will own up to it."

Evren paused. "Now, that *is* strange."

"There haven't been any similarities between the victims," Preece continued— too enthusiastically, Eve thought. "Nothing to indicate a rivalry of some sort, but their wounds have been consistent enough to assume it's the same murderer each time."

"And how did you come across that piece of information?" Evren mused. "Were you caught digging up corpses again?"

Preece smiled wanly. "It is said that the dead cannot speak, but I tend to disagree." He took a bite from his plate, chewing thoughtfully. "Mutilations aside, the number of bodies is supposedly higher than the High King is letting on. There are whispers that he's offering a reward for the head of this serial murderer."

"A reward?" Eve spoke up without thinking, earning the men's rapt attention.

"Yes, a boon," Preece said with a devilish grin. "Any wish within his power, the High King will grant."

"A rare gift indeed," Evren mused. "Well, power is bestowed upon the strongest contender. I am sure he will have plenty of ruffians vying for the challenge. Things truly must be dire for the Unseelie Court if the High King is involving himself in petty deaths."

"Not as petty as one may presume. Killian Foxglove's father was among the dead."

Evren choked on his wine. "Lord Foxglove was murdered?"

"It would appear so."

Evren's expression became grave. "Yes, dire times indeed."

Their conversation fell silent, but Eve's mind was racing. A boon. Any boon she wished. The way home had suddenly opened to her; a chance for her to escape this miserable place before the Fair Folk decided to turn on her. Or worse.

Plates were cleared shortly after and were replaced by smaller bronze dishes with individual slices of pie. Dark berry juice oozed out of the sides, mixing in with the brown sugared sauce on top. Eve dug into her slice absently, too preoccupied with thoughts of how to track down this serial killer to savor her dessert.

Her vision blurred. Eve blinked slowly, her movements sluggish and disorienting. She coughed once. Twice. Each one came more violently than the next, rattling her body as her throat seized.

"Eve?" Hailey said, pushing a glass of water her way.

"I'm fine," Eve choked. Panic clawed at her chest, but she pressed her cloth napkin to her lips to hide her fear. "Excuse me."

Eve stood, fighting past the dizziness, and staggered out into the hall. Her legs were lead, trudging forward with each shallow breath. Cold sweat erupted on her feverish skin.

A horrible sense of wrongness enveloped her—but she couldn't catch her breath to vocalize it. Her stomach churned. Eve got as far as the first floor's landing before she collapsed.

Eve slammed onto her knees and retched. Her body gave out under her, a horrible chill sinking through her veins as she struggled to breathe. Somewhere, she heard footsteps. Shouting. Shadows moved around her while Eve's head spun.

Her heartbeat hammered at a violent speed in her chest. Eve was shutting down, her body convulsing against whatever had entered her system. It tried to fight back in a way Eve couldn't.

It wasn't enough.

ELEVEN

Eve was alive. Somehow.

She woke up in the den, her body stiff and heavy as she shifted against the chaise lounge. A throw blanket rested over her lap. Feverish heat flushed her cheeks as she tried to sit up. A hand appeared from her side and pushed her back down.

"Stay," Liam ordered, and Eve was too exhausted to argue. She sunk back against the cushions, grateful that her vision returned to normal.

"This is the second time I thought I died and woke up to you barking orders at me," Eve mumbled. Liam stared at her, momentarily caught off guard.

"Don't make a habit of it," he said. The hint of a smile teased the corner of his lips. "How are you feeling?"

"Terrible." Eve sighed, rubbing her cold hands underneath the blanket. The dizziness was still faintly present, but she could breathe again. "I'm not dead, though."

"You were close to it." The concern in his voice surprised her. "Your pie was filled with belladonna berries. If we hadn't heard you fall, you would've been dead."

"Belladonna?" Eve racked her brain for some kind of connection. It sounded familiar, but she couldn't place it.

"Deadly nightshade. You have it in your realm, too," Liam said. Eve understood then, recalling the name. "It's more potent on our side. It doesn't take much to kill."

"Did anyone else eat the pie?" Eve thought of the slices across the table. She thought others had consumed it, but was she the first? Did anyone else know?

"Yours was the only one made with belladonna," Liam said quietly. "Everyone else had blackberry."

The news sank in with deafening silence. "Someone tried to poison me?"

"And nearly succeeded." He kept his voice unusually low, leaning on the edge of his seat at Eve's side. "Who did you piss off this time, Evie?"

She didn't know. Eve had some ideas—Logan, Colton—but she couldn't imagine Colton going for poison, and Logan was banned from the manor.

He was glamoured with the staff once. I guess he could have snuck it in somehow? Had one of the other servants plant it for him? But even that was doubtful. Logan was a despicable human being, but clever wasn't a word Eve would use to describe him.

Pushing her suspicions aside, Eve found herself at another loss. "How am I alive?"

"Sage had an antidote," Liam said. "She keeps a collection of poisons in her room, you may recall."

Eve tried to ignore the sting in Liam's voice. Of course she remembered—the dagger she'd nearly killed him with had been coated in some sort of poison. Eve never asked what it had been; she didn't want to know. She didn't want to think of what additional suffering Liam might have gone through if she'd finished the job.

Wait, he knows?

Eve grabbed his sleeve, halting whatever he had to say next. "You know about Sage?"

Liam regarded her for a moment, his expression softening. "Poisons are not necessarily common in the Unseelie Court, Eve. Not the *method* of poisoning, anyway. The victims are seen as weak, and the perpetrators weaker still for their cowardice. The Seelie Court, however, is well-versed in a subtle death. There is only one person I know that keeps her poisons stocked in the Unseelie Court."

Eve swallowed hard. "The only people here from the Seelie Court are Preece and Sage."

"Preece is uninterested in poisons. I've never seen him show much interest in any weapon. Sage's daggers are hard to miss, though. She's always had a flair for the dramatic."

Eve stared at him as if truly seeing him for the first time. "You knew, but—why? You..."

"I do not need to know why Sage took a roundabout route to take my life," Liam said with a humorless smile. "She is my sister. I understand her intention to inherit the court. You, however... I still do not understand why you agreed to it."

Eve tried to tell him, but the words mangled in her throat, resulting in gibberish. She tried again. Again.

Nothing. Not a word would escape.

"I can't tell you," Eve murmured, casting her shameful gaze onto her lap.

"I see." He sighed, his lips drawing into a tight, troubled line. He stood, flexing his fingers. "Regardless, without evidence, we only have speculation. We can't say for certain she was behind your poisoning."

"But the chances are high."

"I would say so."

Eve gripped the blanket on her lap. Murdered. She'd nearly been *murdered*. Nausea pooled in her stomach, sloshing in her gut in lapping waves. It had all happened so quickly. She would be dead, if it weren't for...

"Liam?" Eve said before he could leave. "Why did you stay with me? Why did you help me?"

"We have a pact of protection," Liam reminded her, but there was something off about his tone to suggest otherwise.

"And that's all?" she pushed. If he had managed to save her, that would have been enough—but he'd stayed until she woke up. He made sure she was alright. Had that been a part of the pact, too?

Liam paused for a long time, and Eve suspected that even he didn't know why he did it. Then, "Not all of us relish in seeing others die, Evie."

Guilt coiled in her chest, and Eve's fingers dug into the blanket until her knuckles turned white. Even knowing the truth—that she had not acted alone—Eve still shouldered the blame.

She could still picture her borrowed dagger against his neck, the blade coated in a thin layer of poison. Eve had threatened to cut his tongue out, threatened to *kill* him. Yet, when she had nearly died, Liam watched over her with the affinity of a guardian angel.

I'm sorry for trying to kill you. I'm sorry for ruining everything I touch. The apology burned on her lips, but the words did not come. Her heart ached, desperate and longing to confess everything. To try to repair the tentative friendship she'd burned to ash.

Liam turned instead to leave. "Rest well tonight. If you are in no position for training tomorrow, you are welcome to take the day off."

"I'll be fine," Eve said hastily, then winced as she sat up too quickly. Liam raised a doubtful brow, but shrugged, and left her to recover.

Eve groaned as she shakily rose to her feet. The recovery from the belladonna berries left her weakened and sapped of strength. Eve moved slowly through the estate and toward her room, careful to mind her steps as she went.

It was not lost on her that Sage had been the one with an antidote—and a collection of poisons in her room. Eve had missed them among all the strange figurines Sage decorated her desk with. Considering the state of the dagger on her birthday, Eve was confident that Sage had better access to the deadly tinctures.

Why kill Eve, though? She'd already bargained for her life in exchange for her silence on Sage's part of Liam's attempted assassination. The agreement was that Sage would not kill her for her transgressions that night. So, what had she done now to earn Sage's ire?

Does it matter? Sage wanted to be heir to the Bone Court more than anyone. This sort of retaliation was exactly what Eve had feared.

She dragged herself up the stairs and to her room, collapsing onto the soft cushion of her bed.

If someone came to finish the job, she would be too tired to notice.

TWELVE

Eve was rearing for a fight. The fear of her near-death experience had gradually faded throughout the night, leaving her with nothing short of pure, unbridled rage in its place. Her early training session should have been the perfect time to release those pent-up emotions that rocked her to her core.

Instead, her anger found another direction.

Liam parried her strike with his mock sword, as he had done for the entirety of their session thus far. He hadn't tried to hit her once—Eve knew she'd left plenty of opportunities—and Eve suspected that he was taking it easy on her.

Eve's faux dagger clashed again with his sword. It was nowhere close to his neck, where she'd been aiming, but Eve knew Liam wouldn't have let it reach. She'd been instructed to practice with fake weapons today, and Eve wondered if it was out of a sense of self-preservation when Liam had seen her temper flare this morning.

She backed away, her chest purposefully exposed and open for retaliation. Liam did not take the bait.

"Are you going to take me seriously or not?" Eve snapped.

"Your body is still recovering," Liam said. His calmness irked her. "I will not push you too hard."

Eve gritted her teeth. Liam might not be willing to take the opportunity, but her enemies gladly would. Vulnerabilities were not a risk she could take.

"I didn't ask you to go easy on me. I asked you to train me."

Liam raised a stark red brow. "I'd say that making sure you don't prematurely kill yourself is fine training."

Eve struck again, this time aiming for his chest. Liam blocked her with his sword, then dodged her next attack. She goaded him on, one reckless attack after another, until she was panting and out of breath. Eve could sense his growing irritation, which only fueled her own temper when he refused to hit back.

"I'm not weak," Eve gasped. Her body ached as she pushed herself, but Eve didn't care if she hit him or not so long as he gave her some kind of response. "Give me a fair fight!"

"Is that what you want?"

"*Yes!*"

Pain shot up Eve's leg as Liam's wooden sword came down against her calf. She inhaled sharply through barred teeth. Another blow came to her back, and Eve crumpled onto the ground, barely catching herself on splayed hands. Her faux dagger clattered onto the polished floor, skidding away.

The wooden sword's blade nudged her back. "Do you give up?" Eve glowered up at him. Liam met her stare, unfazed. "You wanted a fair fight."

"Again," she said.

Eve switched out the false dagger for her real one, and they practiced. She kept a closer eye on his blade, nearly tripping over herself to avoid some of his strikes. Eve loathed to admit it, but her body hadn't fully recovered from the poison's effects. Weakness toiled in her stiff limbs, and the energy she'd had in the morning dwindled with each misstep. If she could get even one hit on him today, Eve would consider herself lucky.

Liam stumbled back, one hand pressed to his chest. He grunted in pain, and Eve teetered to the side in her confusion. She didn't believe she'd hit him—and she was right. In the thin gap of his airy shirt, Eve saw the gray stone creep across his skin, solidifying before her eyes.

"If you continue to ogle me, Evie, I may blush," Liam said, but pulled his shirt to conceal the spot. Picking up his wooden sword, Liam crossed his arms over his chest, his movements stiff. "That's enough practice for today."

He shuffled out of the room, his expression wrought with pain, but Eve couldn't think of any way to ease his suffering. What did you do for a man that was turning to stone?

Sighing, Eve picked up her dagger and swung it in a lazy arc through the air. She wanted to keep practicing, but she wasn't about to call Liam back. Eve sheathed her dagger. It was already lunchtime; if she couldn't fight, she ought to eat. She hoped that whatever she found wouldn't be poisoned.

As Eve neared the kitchen, she heard a commotion from inside. Two cloaked figures held the head chef, Gotwin, between their arms. He was a little thing—a brownie, Preece called him—that came up to the middle of her calf. His curly brown hair was tucked underneath a drooping chestnut-colored cap, and he wore a white linen dress shirt that came down to his knobby green knees. Eve had only seen the chef once and had promptly been yelled at for her rudeness when she watched him work.

He was not the sole brownie in attendance. The other brownies that worked under him remained invisible, but Eve could hear their nervous shuffling as they watched their boss thrash in the air.

"Yer crossin' a line ye shouldn't be nearin', Lady Fogtree," Gotwin snarled, his stumpy legs kicking out violently. "We knows the rules! I been workin' under yer papa for years!"

"Then how do you explain this?" Sage lifted a small burlap bag and dumped its contents onto the kitchen island. Belladonna berries rolled out across the surface and bounced at their feet. "It was found with your belongings in the servant's quarters."

If Gotwin recognized the berries, he didn't show it. "Tis not mine. Gets my produce fresh from the market every morn."

"But this *is* your bag?" Sage pressed. She turned the burlap sack over in her hands to give him a full view.

"'Tis my bag, Lady Fogtree, but the contents ain't."

Sage clicked her tongue and walked around the island. A pie sat in the center with a single piece cut out. Beside it was another pie, with several more removed. "Are you suggesting that you had nothing to do with this, then?"

"I used blackberry—I swear by it!" Gotwin shouted. He struggled in the servants' grips, but their hold on the little brownie tightened.

Sage's gaze narrowed. She cut a slice of the darker pie—the belladonna pie—and set it onto a clean plate. "Then perhaps I'm mistaken."

She slid the plate across the island and waited. The brownie visibly paled.

"Ye don't mean for *me* to eat it?"

Sage cocked her head. "I thought you said the pies weren't poisoned?"

Gotwin glared at her, then at the slice on the table. "When yer papa hears 'bout this—"

"My father agreed to let me handle the investigation," Sage said coolly. "He already knows."

Eve heard someone coming up behind her. She swung an arm out, blocking Hailey from entering the kitchen. Confusion flickered across the girl's face and only increased tenfold when she peered in and saw what was inside.

"What's going on?" she whispered to Eve.

"I'm not sure," Eve admitted. "I think Sage might have caught who poisoned me?"

Hailey bit her lip, and there was doubt on her face that Eve had never seen before. "*Gotwin* poisoned you?"

"I don't know," Eve admitted. "Did Sage say something to you?"

"No," Hailey whispered. She hesitated, and there was disappointment in her voice. "She didn't have to."

When they redirected their attention to the kitchen, the slice of pie remained untouched on the table. Baring his sharp teeth, the chef spat on it. "You'll rue this day, little Fogtree. *I curse you, and I curse your home. May your good prosperity fall and with it, the eldest daughter.*"

Sage sneered. "And may you and your family remain exiled from the Bone Court for as long." To the servants, "See to it that he and his kin are removed from our borders."

Gotwin thrashed in full now, writhing against the servants' grasps as he shouted obscenities and curses at Sage until he was fully removed. Eve and Hailey watched as the brownies became visible again, glowering at Sage with disdain. She raised a challenging brow at them.

"Do not scowl at me so. You can thank your dear Gotwin for your fate," she said, then airily waved toward the door. "Consider it a mercy that he was not executed on the spot."

There was grumbling, but the brownies fled through the back door, kicking over pots, pans, and ingredients in their wake. Eve and Hailey reluctantly stepped into the kitchen once they'd cleared out. The room was in disarray, but the servants swept through and cleaned at once.

"Did you enjoy the scene?" Sage asked, her sharp attitude easing into annoyance as she tossed both pies into the trash.

"He said he didn't do it," Eve said. "I thought the Fair Folk couldn't lie."

"Not directly," Sage clarified. Her long nails clicked against the pie dishes before she dumped them into the sink. "What he *didn't* say was confession enough."

Eve's stomach grumbled. "I take it the Bone Court is too far to order delivery?"

"There will be a new kitchen staff by tonight," Sage said. "There are always Fair Folk seeking employment."

Eve said nothing, lingering awkwardly near the entrance of the room. She watched the servants sweep up the plump blackberries before dumping them into the trash. They were nauseating to see. The weakness in her limbs did nothing to help as the sickening memory of last night resurfaced.

"Why did you fire him?" Hailey asked.

"I didn't—he and his family are exiled," Sage replied calmly. "It is a better offer than most. That pie could have gone to anyone. It could have gone to *you*—"

"But it was supposed to go to Liam, wasn't it?" Hailey's question took Sage by surprise. "Liam was the target."

"I couldn't say."

"Can't you?"

"Where did this come from?" Sage's voice had gone quiet, but there was a defensiveness to her. She squared her shoulders, her fingernails tapping against the countertop in displeasure.

Hailey hesitated. Eve could sense her contemplation, an inner debate that would only wrought tension between them. Still, she said, "You've been scheming ways to get rid of Liam ever since Evren brought up this stupid game."

She's been doing it for a lot longer than that, Eve thought. It was a relief that Hailey believed Sage to be behind the poison, too. Eve hadn't been sure how wary Hailey was of Sage, but this was a clear sign of where she stood.

"You're saying I tried to kill my brother," Sage said, dumbfounded. "Do you hear yourself?"

It wouldn't be the first time. Eve found her act frustrating. Sage wasn't fooling anyone, least of all Eve.

"I don't know," Hailey said, her voice carrying doubt amid her frustration. "You haven't been like yourself since we got stuck here. You've made it pretty clear you want to be the heir. If Eve hadn't eaten it, the pie would've gone to Liam, right? Then there would be no one in your way."

Sage stared at Hailey as though she were a stranger. "Is that what you think?"

"I don't know what to think!" Hailey threw her hands up in the air, frustrated. "Can you honestly tell me that you didn't try to kill him?"

Sage opened her mouth to speak, but nothing came out—because, Eve realized, she *had* tried to kill her brother. On the balcony and again with the pie.

Something cracked in Hailey's expression. Whatever trust she'd built with Sage dimmed in her eyes.

Sage glanced toward Eve, and there was no mistaking the hostility found there. "Can't we discuss this in private?"

"I don't think there's anything to discuss." Hailey left, and Sage went after her. One hand outstretched, but always out of reach.

Thirteen

Tension ran in an undercurrent through the Fogtree household. As Eve washed up for the night, she could hear the dribble of a ball outside, followed by a slam and Hailey's grunts of frustration.

Isn't it too cold for this? Eve glanced at the frost clinging to the single window. Nighttime had fallen, bathing the room in moonlight.

Eve finished her bath and loped downstairs, tossing on a borrowed cloak from Preece before stepping out into the cold. Liam had promised to replace the one she gave away—along with the boots—but Dunla had yet to deliver. Preece's cloak hung too long on her body, its heavy navy fabric catching under her feet as she walked.

At least it keeps me warm.

Hailey paced across the courtyard outside, her attire as tight as the ponytail on her head. She glared at the ball in her hands—not quite as large as a basketball, but bouncier—as she slammed it against the ground.

"I didn't know you could play basketball in the snow," Eve remarked, settling down on one of the cold stone steps that descended from the patio.

"You can if you want it badly enough," Hailey replied. She tossed the ball into the makeshift net attached to the patio's ledge. The threads were too thin to be rope; Eve wondered if it was crafted from the same spider silk that made up her slippers. "Want to join?"

"I'll pass. Not a sports person."

Besides, Eve thought to herself. *I think Hailey needs this more than I do.*

Hailey groaned as she missed her next basket. Her brown leather boots slapped harder against the snow-dusted stepping stones as she made another attempt.

Eve never had a chance to see any of Hailey's practices or games in school—not with Nan needing her there as a caretaker—but her skill was evident. She moved with the practiced grace of an athlete, leaping and shuffling over the stones as if it were no different from the court.

How could her parents push her into nursing school over this? Eve wondered. *Have they even seen her play?*

But Eve knew why. It was the same reason her own parents would condemn her for studying art; such a career was unreliable, and school was too expensive. Eve could accept this—she didn't need a degree to paint, after all—but Hailey's situation was far more fraught.

Eve hugged herself, toying with the hem of her cuffs. It was unnerving to see her friends plan for the future. Graduation. College. The workforce. It overwhelmed her, forming tight knots in her stomach that begged an answer for a question she was afraid to ask.

What am I going to do?

Eve pushed the thought away and tried to focus on Hailey's practice instead. The tension in Hailey's muscles betrayed her anger, and Eve didn't have to guess what—or who—caused it.

"Are you okay?" Eve asked.

Hailey dribbled her ball hard on the ground before trying to score another basket. The ball bounced from the stone with a resounding *thump.*

"I'd be a lot better if we could go home."

Me too, Eve thought. The irritation in Hailey's eyes was off-putting on a girl so bubbly. For the duration of their time trapped within the Bone Court, Hailey had become increasingly irritated at petty things. Tripping on a stair. Smacking her toe against the furniture. Untangling knots in her hair.

The ball flew too high and bounced off the patio's upper railing. Hailey grunted in frustration before trying again.

It can't be easy without her medication. Time slipped through Hailey's fingers the longer her ADHD went untreated, leaving her restless, disorganized, and moody. Even now, Eve wondered if her friend knew she'd been practicing in the dark for almost two hours.

"I haven't found anything in the mansion yet," Hailey continued, softer now. Thoughtful. "I'm still looking, but it's kind of hard when I don't really know what I'm looking *for*."

Eve understood that. She'd had her own trouble skimming through the estate, peering at labeled bottles and magical herbs without the slightest hint of their intended use. Many of them weren't even in a language she understood.

Nausea from last night crept up again. Eve covered her mouth to subdue it. She'd hardly eaten, sticking instead to fresh water and light foods she'd seen others in the house consume first.

Her stomach ached for more substance, but she couldn't bring herself to give in. The idea of experiencing that level of poison again, of nearly dying... Eve had to be cautious.

"What did Sage say to you after the kitchen fiasco?" Eve asked, swallowing back the creeping bile in her throat. They hadn't spoken to each other at dinner, and Eve couldn't help wondering if Sage confessed.

"She said she didn't do it."

"Of course she didn't," Eve muttered. She toyed with the lace on her cuffs, then paused. "Was that exactly what she said?"

"What?"

"That she didn't do it?"

"More or less."

A dissatisfying answer, but likely all Eve was going to get. She wasn't sure if it mattered anyway. Logan wasn't allowed in the manor, and Eve couldn't imagine another culprit responsible. The Fair Folk had proven their ability to twist the truth into something unrecognizable. Sage was no exception.

"Do you believe her?" Eve asked reluctantly.

Hailey hesitated. "I was worked up when I accused her. Sage hasn't been herself lately, but none of us have. I don't think she would kill her *brother*."

Or maybe you don't want to see it.

Hailey picked up her ball and turned to face Eve. "What do you mean?"

Crap. She hadn't meant to say that aloud.

Eve chewed on her lip. "I think that you and Sage have a soft spot for each other, that's all."

"Sure, but..."

"But you forget that she isn't human." Hailey blanched, despite the cold. "We can't expect her to think the same way we do."

Hailey gripped the ball, but did not move to continue her practice. She turned the ball in her hands with uncertainty. "You don't think Sage is human?"

"Liam isn't the only one that can make glamours," Eve said.

Silence followed. Hailey dribbled her ball again, but lacked enthusiasm. She moved automatically, the routine drilled into her from years of repetition.

"What do you think Evren wants?" Hailey asked, promptly changing the subject.

"I'm not sure." Truth be told, Eve hadn't put much thought into it. There had been plenty of other things preoccupying her mind. "He said he wanted to be impressed, right?"

"Sure, but he hasn't been impressed by anything yet." Suspicion crept into Hailey's voice, something that Eve wasn't used to hearing from her. Hailey was usually trusting, but some of that had been lost in Faerie. "Sage has been working her butt off to expand business, and Preece is always giving him new gossip and stuff, but Evren doesn't care."

"Well, Liam's not putting in any effort," Eve said. A part of her wondered if he even had to. Despite Evren's competition, he still clearly favored his youngest son. She couldn't guarantee that would be enough to win, though.

"I don't think Evren wants an easy way to win," Hailey said softly.

"No, probably not." Eve sighed. The thought troubled her. She planned to bring the serial murderer's head to the High King in exchange for a favor, but what if someone else got to them first? She would need a backup plan, and that involved Liam winning, lest Sage take over and decide Eve would be better stuffed and mounted to the wall. "What do you think he wants, then?"

Hailey gripped the ball in her hands. "You saw how he was at Yule."

Memories of gore and bloodshed pooled in the front of Eve's mind. Yes, she had seen what kind of pleasure Evren and the other courts relished in.

It hadn't occurred to her that Evren might want something more sinister in his future heir. If Sage found out what he truly desired, poison would be the least of Eve's concerns.

FOURTEEN

The rumbling woke her first. A deep tremble in the ground shifted Eve in her bed, clattering the sparse items from her desk onto the floor. She rolled over, yanking the velvety blankets over her head in a bleary attempt at sleep.

A horrible, pained screech echoed through the forest. Eve sat upright. Another yowl resounded outside, followed by an unnatural, wretched gust of wind. Or what Eve thought to be wind.

Something was wrong. Eve was not sure what possessed her to go investigate. Before she knew it, her shoes and cloak were on, and she was stepping out into the cold, peering over the frozen courtyard out back. If anyone else had heard the noise, they did not join her.

Eve squinted, her eyes slowly adjusting to the dark. Fresh snow glittered under the pale moonlight. Pine trees and their barren friends twinkled under the snow, peaceful and undisturbed. The night was calm; Eve wondered if she'd imagined the disturbance.

The Yule Cat came barreling through the forest. Its enormous paws trampled through the courtyard, trees bending like stalks of wheat as the Yule Cat pushed them out of the way. Clouds of dusty snow puffed down from their branches, collapsing in slumped heaps on the ground.

The cat's thundering steps rattled the earth. Eve grasped the patio's railing, her feet slipping on ice. Something protruded from the cat's face—small sticks of some kind, but she was too far away to see clearly.

It's hurt, Eve realized.

The cat let out another pained cry and dove through another copse of trees, its fur rustling in the wind.

Before sense could catch up with her, Eve ran out into the courtyard and through the forest, following the Yule Cat's destructive path.

The cat was much larger—and faster—than Eve. She struggled to keep up, following the enormous paw prints left behind. Despite her cloak, the long nightgown she wore did little to protect her from the cold. As did the lack of gloves. She huffed warm air into her hands, her breath coming out in soft wisps of frost. Her face and hands stung, but the cat's pained cry echoed in her mind, and Eve knew she had to help.

She found the Yule Cat curled up inside of a cave that was too small to house it. Its large gray tail flicked irritably outside of the opening as it tried to remove the sticks on its face with the swipe of its paw.

Not sticks. Arrows.

Was the Fae murderer behind this? Eve glanced at the forest, but all she saw was darkness.

Damn it. She hadn't had any luck tracking the murderer in the woods on her own. For someone leaving numbers of mutilated corpses in their wake, the killer was surprisingly elusive.

Eve swallowed hard, lingering at the cave's mouth. The Yule Cat had not noticed her. Yet. Would it be angry when it did? Hungry, even? She had nothing to feed it—nothing to protect herself from being eaten.

This was a stupid idea. The idiocy of her plan dawned on her later than it should have. It was one thing to rescue a regular animal in pain. It was another to help a cat two hundred times her size with a penchant for eating people.

Eve took a step back to return to the mansion. The Yule Cat's head snapped up.

Her breath caught. The cat's pupils narrowed, and it hissed, the same harsh sound Eve had mistaken for the wind earlier. Her whole body trembled under its gaze, but she couldn't bring herself to move. Now that it had seen her, Eve knew running away would only ignite its predatory instincts.

She needed to earn its trust instead. How the hell was she going to do that? Eve racked her brain for anything she knew about cats. She never had a pet growing up, much less experience with wild animals.

Think, damn it. Her sleep-addled mind did nothing to help the situation. Eve's eyelids droop in slow, steady blinks as she tried to stay awake and think of her next step. The Yule Cat watched her, the tip of its tail lazily flicking toward the sky.

Then it blinked. Slowly, its large eyes slid down, then back up. Tension eased from the creature's posture. Eve waited for a pounce, but nothing came. The beast was calm.

Eve took a reluctant step forward. The beast's posture did not change. She continued until she reached the paw of its back leg. Its individual pads were huge—easily the size of Eve's head—but she drew her gaze to the arrow stuck in one. It had gone deeper when the cat fled, the arrowhead embedded within the pink flesh.

She grasped the wooden stick. The Yule Cat let out a low growl and pulled its leg away. Eve stumbled with it.

"I'm trying to help you," Eve pleaded with the beast, and hoped that it could understand her. There was a layer of skepticism on the creature's face. Eve feared doing more should the creature turn its agitation on her.

Taking a deep breath, Eve grasped the stick again and yanked it out. The Yule Cat hissed. Eve held up the arrow, its iron tip dripping with blood.

A sudden kick sent Eve flying against the cave's entrance. She gasped, her body crashing against the sharp rocky walls. Pain shot through her limbs as Eve slumped into the snow, breathing hard.

The enormous creature bent to lick its paw, tending to its wound. Pity swelled in her chest. The arrow must have hurt more than she'd realized.

Eve gripped the bloody weapon in her palm. The beast flicked its gaze back to her, ready to strike again. Eve wasn't sure she would survive another one.

Despite the bruises forming on her back, Eve met the cat's gaze and snapped the arrow in two. She tossed it to the side, out of sight. The Yule Cat watched, glancing between her and where the arrow had gone.

"I need to take out the rest," Eve said. Her body cried out in pain as she stood. Nothing had broken, thankfully, but Eve knew those bruises would ache for some time. She blinked slowly again, noting that the creature calmed and respond similarly when she did so. "I can't say it won't hurt, but I'll try to make it easy, if you'll let me."

The creature's tail swished to the left. The idea of going anywhere near its face—and those sharp, dangerous teeth—nearly sent her running. Unfortunately, that was where most of the arrows were.

I'll work my way up to it, she told herself. Maybe the Yule Cat would accept her help once it realized what she was doing.

Eve worked slowly along its body, taking care to remove any stray arrows she found stuck between its fur and paws. Eventually, the cat stopped hissing, and Eve continued to break each arrow in its sight before tossing it away.

She was hesitant to climb the creature but had no choice. As she scrambled up its side, grasping tufts of gray fur to get close to its face, her confidence wavered. The Yule Cat's bright yellow eyes watched her, and Eve couldn't help staring at its maw, fully aware of the sharp teeth hidden underneath.

Limbs shaking, Eve gathered her courage and gently removed the arrows across the Yule Cat's face. It was not pleased with her touch. Its eyes narrowed in irritation, and it let out rumbling noises of dissatisfaction.

"I know, I'm sorry," Eve said, gently rubbing her hand across the beast's muzzle as she worked. That eased some of its agitation. "Just a couple more left."

Once the last arrow had fallen, Eve groped around her cloak until she pulled out a clear jar: her healing salve. After countless injuries during her training, Eve found it handy to keep it close.

Opening the lid, she rubbed some of the sticky yellow poultice onto the Yule Cat's nose, then moved to coat its other wounds.

A loud rumbling erupted from the beast. Eve gasped, grasping onto its fur as she nearly toppled onto the ground. It took her a moment to register that the Yule Cat was *purring*.

Pleased with herself, she climbed down and administered the last of the tincture.

The Yule Cat shifted and gave her a gentle butt with its head. Surprised, Eve grinned and pet its nose, careful to avoid the wounds.

"Do you have a name?" she wondered, more to herself than the cat. It continued to purr, lowering itself flat onto the ground so she could more easily rub its face. "I know you're the Yule Cat, but that's more of a title than a name. What do you think about... Cinder?"

The beast—Cinder, she would call it—purred, although Eve was uncertain if it was because it enjoyed the name or if it was simply relishing in her attention.

Suddenly, Cinder lifted its head, its ears perked toward the cave's entrance. Eve listened, waiting in silence.

"What is it?" she asked, giving the Yule Cat another pet. It took off instead, forgetting Eve entirely as it bound through the forest. She watched it go, stunned.

Without Cinder's fur to provide warmth, the cold settled back into her limbs. Grasping her cloak, Eve braced herself against the snow and trudged back to the manor.

Fifteen

Eve found it difficult to keep track of how much time had passed. Each day came with a new worry—particularly for Nan, confused and alone in that little house.

If she couldn't check on her herself, she would need to find someone that could.

Eve paced in the den, trying her best to figure out how to ask for this favor. *Who* to ask. Sage was out of the question, as was Evren.

Liam might do it. Eve suspected she wouldn't even have to use his True Name to get it done. Seeing how rigid Liam had become during their trainings, though, she was hesitant to ask for more. Even if she did, Liam might ask why she tried to kill him in return, and Eve simply couldn't answer.

That left only one option.

"Leaving already?" Eve caught Preece in the foyer as he laced his shoes. She wasn't sure how he spent most of his time, but he rarely stayed in the estate during the day and always returned with fresh gossip to share over dinner.

Preece—in his typical half-frog state—nodded, wrapping a charcoal gray scarf around his neck. "An accurate observation."

"Do you think you could do me a favor?" Eve asked. Preece's attention caught on the word *favor*.

"That depends," Preece said with feigned disinterest. "Are you inclined to indulge my curiosity?"

"What do you want to know?"

"The question we're all asking, little one." Preece tapped Eve's nose with his webbed finger. She scrunched her nose in disgust as a thin string of mucus trailed off when he pulled away. "Why did you try to kill the Logan boy? What is your story?"

Eve had expected as much. She was prepared.

"I *could* tell you," Eve hedged. "Or I could offer you something more valuable."

Preece cocked his head at her, as though appraising the reliability of such a statement. "And what would that be?"

"I'll give you my church's tabernacle." She hadn't found much of a use for it anyway. Liam had stolen it for her in a bargain a few months ago to prove himself. Aside from making an interesting art project out of the bronze display, it was busy collecting dust back at Nan's.

Preece drummed his sticky fingers against his crossed arms, considering. "And that is...?"

"An expensive box. It's sitting in my closet at home," Eve explained. "It's shiny—when it's not coated in paint."

Preece sighed. "I have no interest in trinkets, little one. My services are exchanged for a more informative currency."

Eve feared that might be his response. The story he wanted, though, was too much. "You can have the box, and I'll tell you how I made Liam steal it for me."

He wavered, torn between this new story and the information he wanted. "I presume you made a bargain for it."

"You won't know unless we make a deal."

Preece thought about it for a long moment. "Does this box serve any purpose? Why is it valuable?"

"I can tell you, if you agree to my favor," Eve said.

"Clever girl," Preece mumbled, but she did not get the sense he was annoyed. Disappointed, maybe, but the potential of new information dangled before him. An unfamiliar story waited to unfold. "If you tell me of this box, how you acquired it, *and* transfer ownership of it to me, then I suppose I can do something for you in exchange."

"Thank you." Eve beamed. Even an update on her grandmother was more than she could ask for, but making sure Nan was cared for in Eve's absence was even better.

"Don't thank me yet," Preece warned. "What is it you want?"

"My nan is sick," Eve explained, somber. "She's been alone in our house since I left, as far as I know. I need you to check up on her. Make sure she's alive, eating, that someone can watch her."

"And that's all?" Preece was genuinely surprised. "I would have thought you wanted me to find you a way out of here."

"Can you?"

"No," Preece said, crushing her short-lived hopes. "I merely presumed that's what you would have wanted. Checking in on your... what is it, nan?"

"My grandmother," Eve explained.

"Ah. Yes, checking in on your grandmother's wellbeing is far more doable." Preece opened the door, and Eve shivered against the cold. The snow was falling hard and fast. White flakes blurred against the overcast sky, making it difficult to see. "I am eagerly awaiting this information, Eve. Be ready when I return."

"I will," Eve promised. Preece grinned and disappeared into the snowfall.

Eve moved to close the door, but another figure lingering outside caught her attention. Logan stared at her from behind a tree in front of the manor, shuffling his feet awkwardly for warmth beside one of the nearby windows. From the flush of his cheeks, he'd been standing there for some time.

He'd been *watching* her for some time.

Logan's eyes widened, realizing he'd been caught. He turned on his heel and ran—or tried to. Thick, white crust kicked up under his heels, and his sprint was more of a hurried series of high kicks through the snow.

Eve gave chase.

Old pain resurfaced again: violation, terror, shame. Prom night haunted her. Changed her. Logan's face stood out among the ghosts who coveted what they should not have. There had been a fleeting freedom when she thought him dead.

Eve intended to make that permanent.

She tackled him into the snow from behind, taking the monster by surprise. Logan gasped as he fell into the cold. He tried to inch away. Eve unsheathed her dagger and pressed the point against his back, hard enough to recognize through the thick wool of his cloak.

"Don't. Move."

He froze. Logan trembled underneath her, his face nearly pressed into the snow. She grabbed a fistful of his dirty blond curls and yanked his head up.

Logan had always been thin, but he felt *small* under her. Frail. His bones poked out underneath his cloak, and there was a new sallowness to his cheeks. His time in Faerie had not been kind to him.

"Why are you stalking me?" Eve moved the dagger's blade to his throat. "Don't lie to me. I'll cut out your tongue."

"Please," he begged. "Don't do this. I'm—I—"

"Eyes up here," she snapped. Logan twisted his neck awkwardly to do so, his pale gaze wide with fear. "Begging doesn't work, remember? Now, answer the question."

Logan shrank beneath her, his forehead slick with nervous sweat. It would be easy to shove his face into the snow and let him drown. Eve imagined him struggling under her as she once had under him. The terror in his eyes, the pain once he realized that nothing he did could save him. It...

It didn't satisfy her as it should have.

Eve tried to push away the gnawing sense of wrongness that tugged at her. The piece of mercy that still existed in her soul. Logan was pathetic. Weak. If she didn't kill him now, what would that make her?

Dagger at his throat, Eve sliced into the flesh.

"I'm sorry!"

The dagger faltered. Eve held it still, a trickle of blood dripping down the blade from the tiny wound in his throat.

"I'm sorry," he choked out between sobs. "I'm so sorry. I never—I never meant to—"

Her hands shook. Eve gripped his hair tighter, and Logan winced.

"You never meant to *what?*"

"Hurt... you." He couldn't meet her gaze, which only made her angrier. "W-We were drunk. Nick brought the alcohol, we drank too much, and—and I don't remember all of it but—I'm so sorry, Eve."

"You think"—Eve's voice cracked—"You think *sorry* is going to make up for what you did to me? You think any of that is an *excuse* for—for—"

"No! No." He broke off again, hiccuping through more sobs. "I don't—Please, I've been trying to find a way to tell you. I-I'm in therapy. I'm trying to be better. I went to rehab for a year."

"That's not what your socials say."

"I haven't used them in years," Logan explained. His voice was hoarse, mournful. "I-I hadn't spoken to the other guys since graduation. Not-not until we woke up here." His body sagged into the snow beneath her, trembling with his tears. "I wanted to reach out and apologize, b-but I didn't know how you'd—I didn't think you'd want to hear from me—"

"I *didn't!*" His apology sliced through her, gutting her to the core. Grief and anger sloshed inside, a poison mixing in her lungs. "But you kept coming back. Each fucking night, every time I close my eyes, you three"—Eve gritted her teeth until her jaw ached—"You *ruined* me! You ruined *everything! Look at what you did to me!*"

Eve pulled the dagger away from his throat and shoved her arm forward, pulling up her sleeve. Logan blanched at the scars on her wrists. At the pale, fading ones that crisscrossed up her arm. Shame clouded his face, and tears fell from his cheeks as he realized what he'd done.

She scrambled off him at once. His touch burned, his body made of angry coals and acidic grief. Her breath came out in quick huffs as panic seized her chest tight.

Eve fled to her room before he could see her cry.

Everything was wrong. Wrong wrong wrong wrong wrong *wrong wrong wrongwrongwrongwrongwrongwrong—*

The air couldn't reach her lungs fast enough. Her heart pummeled against her ribcage until she thought it would crack. Eve flailed in her room, the dagger still wet with Logan's blood gripped tightly in her white knuckles.

She couldn't do it. She couldn't kill him. She was too *weak*—weaker than that groveling piece of shit she left trembling in the snow. She wasn't better than him. She was *worse.*

If this wasn't death, it was close enough. Sorrow too painful to bear had seized her body and her mind. It was a familiar ache that left her breathless and broken, clutching the dagger like a lifeline. There was no God to forgive her and no punishment but her own to give. Pain seared up her arm.

"What are you doing?"

Liam's face twisted in concern as he barged into her room. Her breath still fraught, Eve could not speak. She watched him silently as he held up her arm and examined the blossoming cut on her flesh.

Funny, she did not remember doing that. The blade was heavy in her hand, redder than before.

"Leave me alone," she choked out, pulling her arm away. Liam gripped it gingerly, making sure not to press into the wound. "I said go away!"

"If you want me to leave, then order it," he said firmly. Eve glared at him through her tears. They both knew what would happen if Eve was left alone.

She did... not want to be alone.

Liam took the weapon from her, then disappeared. She stared at the wound, blood dripping in soft splats against the mossy carpet. He returned a moment later with a couple of cloudy bottles and a roll of bandages.

"Sit," he ordered. She obeyed, too numb to object, and settled on the edge of her duvet. Liam tended to the cut on her arm, his brows pinched with worry. "Why would you do this? I've told you; these weapons are stronger than anything you mortals have. You could've cut your whole arm off."

"Why are you helping me?" Eve whispered. Her ragged breaths calmed, and the shame of it all mortified her.

"You're hurt," Liam said, as if it were the most obvious answer in the world. "Why wouldn't I help you?"

"I tried to kill you."

"But you didn't."

Tears welled up in her eyes. Eve stared at the ceiling, her eyes burning in tandem with her throat. "You should hate me."

"I should," Liam agreed. He secured the bandages on her forearm, his thumb lightly brushing against the older scars. Her skin tingled at his touch. "It's strange, the things I am willing to forgive. Do you still want to kill me?" Eve shook her head, too emotional to speak. "Then why did you do it, Evie?"

She opened her mouth to speak, but the words caught when she tried. It was as though a block had been shoved down her throat. Everything was carefully filtered through, rendering her silent when she dared approach too close to the truth.

Eve turned away instead, but not before she caught the hurt in Liam's eyes. "I don't want to talk right now."

"Very well," he said. She waited for him to leave, allowing the suffocating thoughts to consume her once again.

Liam settled on the floor beside her instead and laid his head against the duvet. His vibrant red hair brushed against her leg, but Eve could not bring herself to make him move. Something shifted inside of her. It brushed against her heart and she shoved the sentiment as deep into her soul as she could.

They did not speak, nor did they meet each other's gaze. Liam stayed by her side, and Eve was grateful not to be alone.

Sixteen

Yesterday's breakdown lingered in the back of Eve's head as she dressed for training the next morning. She bore a throbbing headache from crying and the subsequent dehydration. Now that the emotional stagnation wore off, the cut in her arm hurt plenty and Eve was ambushed with the full force of the embarrassment that came with Liam finding her in that state.

She'd chosen to take her dinner in her room last night; they hadn't spoken since he left long after the incident. She kept brushing her fingers over the bandages and remembering the care he'd taken when putting them on. There was a soft touch of his hands when he'd examined the wound, as though handling something delicate and fragile. Liam had been kind. Caring, even.

Eve didn't know what to make of it.

Dangerous feelings stirred in her chest. Eve buried them deep inside of herself, abandoning them in the shallow pit of memory where the rest of her repressed emotions lived. They had no place here. Not with her.

Liam stepped out of his room at the same time she did. They paused, and the awkward silence that followed was enough that Eve wanted to crawl into a hole and let whatever Fae lived in the soil take her. She waited for him to mention last night and make her relive her shame all over again.

Mercifully, he did not.

"You'll want to wear something warmer," he said, glimpsing her airy blouse and slim trousers. His gaze lingered on her injured arm, the bandages visible through the fabric. "Make sure to wear comfortable shoes."

It took Eve a moment longer to register his instructions. "Are we practicing in the snow?"

"We're taking a break today," Liam explained, tying a scarf around his neck in a loose knot. "I have some errands to run."

Eve watched him, turning suspicious. "Why am I going?"

"I think you'll enjoy it."

His words took her by surprise. Liam pulled on a set of worn leather gloves. There was a hole in one of the thumbs.

Eve touched the bandages under her sleeve. There wasn't any reason to include Eve on his errands unless her pathetic display from last night had haunted him, too.

"You don't have to invite me anywhere because you pity me," Eve said. It was the last thing she wanted, especially from Liam.

"Did I say that I invited you out of pity?"

"You didn't have to."

Liam sighed, exasperated, and met her stubborn gaze. "I am not inviting you out of pity, Evie. I am experiencing some pain, and you are in no position to train today." Eve opened her mouth to argue, but Liam gave a pointed look that shut her up. "I think that a change of pace would be beneficial for both of us. Surely you're tired of the manor by now?"

Eve was hesitant to deny it. Staying cooped up inside of the mansion *was* grating on her. The Bone Court had its charms, but there were only so many hours Eve could spend training.

The rest of her time was filled with avoiding Sage, plotting revenge, unsuccessfully searching for the serial murderer, and reading books left in the den. She thought that one of them might clue her in on how to break the spell Evren cast over them.

Unfortunately, a considerable number of the books were written in languages she couldn't understand. The rest were a random collection of mortal novels that might have been scavenged from a flea market.

Her search was too narrow. There were other creatures out there—other courts—all armed to the teeth with knowledge Eve lacked. It was a reasonable enough guess that one of them might have a way to break the spell.

If not hers, then maybe Liam's.

It was becoming difficult to ignore the young man's grimaces as he walked, his movements stiff with pain. He managed it in front of his family, but even Preece had raised a brow at his brother's rigid gait after dinner.

The easier choice had been to avoid them altogether. Aside from their training and meals, Liam either sequestered himself in his room or skulked through the halls, playing small pranks that resulted in little payoff. Eve had not been pleased to find her shampoo switched with olive oil any more than Evren had been when he realized his wine had been replaced with dyed water.

But as Liam's disease grew worse, his pranks grew small and infrequent. His amusement dimmed with each passing day, leaving a despondent man in its wake.

Yes, leaving the manor would be good for both of them.

"I'll get changed," Eve promised. She returned later in a thick woolen gown the color of winter berries and a new charcoal cloak—provided by Dunla—that brushed her calves. Satisfied, Liam led her downstairs, where he called for the carriage.

Eve stared out the window as they jostled forward, watching the snow fall in tiny crystals from the sky. A snow sprite fluttered by, twirling amid the flakes. Despite their vicious nature, Eve regarded her with awe. The sprite's bare body was made entirely from ice, and her sharp wings swirled into a beautiful frosted pattern. Little bursts of snow puffed under her feet as she danced, keeping her afloat.

"You can thank them for this miserable weather," Liam said from beside her. She was surprised to find that he was watching the Faerie too. "Her and the rest of the bloody Winter Court."

"There's a Winter Court?" Eve asked.

"Of course. How else would we get seasons?" Liam scowled at the little creature as she spun a miniature figure of herself made of snow.

"Is that where we are?" Eve guessed, unfamiliar with her surroundings. She had explored plenty of the area around the estate, but she'd never been this far.

"No, we're closer to the Unseelie Court proper," Liam said. "Although the Winter and Autumn Courts are nearby; our courts share an alliance. I suppose you've never been this far from the manor."

Eve craned her neck to get a peek down the road. Dense forest stretched as far as the eye could see. She searched for some sign of life, but the woods were empty and still. Snow-covered branches hung over the winding path, their shadows clawing at the carriage. The further along the path they went, the dimmer it became as boughs twisted together, creating a canopy dark as nightfall.

The carriage slowed as a figure came into view: a statue made of stone and thrice as tall as Eve balanced atop a circular base. It depicted a slender man with long pointed ears and hair that fell to his ankles. His head turned down toward the sword in his stomach, his handsome features pressed in displeasure as he gripped the handle. A crown sat atop his head, cracked and worn with time.

Liam climbed out of the carriage first, gritting his teeth at the effort. Eve was reluctant to take his offered hand, but Liam gripped her palm in his and assisted her.

"Who's that?" Eve asked, nodding to the statue. She hadn't seen it in the carriage, but a large gray slab of stone rested in front of the statue's feet. It reminded her of a coffin.

Liam peered up at the statue with admiration. "High King Earnan. He was the first of the Fair Folk to split the courts and created the Unseelie Court as he saw fit. It is said that his statue faces the Seelie Court to ward off those who bring harm to his beloved and their home."

Eve stared at the statue, taking in every detail of the deceased High King. It was incredibly lifelike, with stone so thin across his enormous tucked wings that she thought they could be real. His name was etched into the base, along with text in an unfamiliar language.

"How did he die?" she asked.

"The sword didn't give you any clues?" Liam asked sarcastically. Then, "No one knows. Some say it was his bride who was a spy for the Seelie Court. Others think he was murdered by someone of his own court that envied the throne. His body was never found, but the statue says it all, I think."

"What do you believe happened?"

"Who knows?" Liam shrugged. "I've certainly never asked him."

Eve glanced at the statue one last time, quietly wishing she had the artistic ability to render anything half as beautiful. *Maybe someday.*

She heard the scrape of stone.

"What are you doing?" she demanded as Liam shoved the slab out of the way. A part of her couldn't contain her own curiosity as she glanced into the slit he'd created. What would an ancient corpse look like, anyway?

"I told you that I had errands to run." Liam finished pushing the stone aside with a huff, his face flushed. The hole dipped down into a set of stone stairs. Unlike the ones Eve had entered Faerie in, these descended into blackness, with only a few torches for light. "Are you coming?"

"You want me to go down *there?*" Eve tried and failed to keep her voice even. For all she knew, this was a direct descent into an early grave. Liam could push the slab shut after her, leaving Eve to suffocate with no one the wiser.

Yet, she knew he wouldn't. Her cheeks warmed at the memory of his gentle touch on her wound, and Eve couldn't resist glancing at his gloved hands.

"You'll enjoy it," Liam promised again, one foot already in the hole. Eve was less than enthusiastic to join him.

Still, what choice did she have? She wasn't particularly eager to freeze her ass off in the carriage while she waited for him to return.

Eyeing him with suspicion, Eve ignored his offered palm and took a few steps down. She pressed her hand against the wall for support as the light dimmed ahead. Liam shifted the slab back into place, sealing them inside.

Seventeen

Stone mixed with packed dirt the deeper they went. Eve used the walls as a guide, soil digging under her nails as she ventured lower into the earth. She wondered how far down this tunnel would go. The torches along the walls did little to provide enough light to see. She relied on the sound of Liam's breathing to know where to step, occasionally reaching out to brush his cloak in reassurance that he was still in front of her.

As they came to the bottom of the stairs, a mixture of torches and candle sconces lined the stone walls. A myriad of tunnels stretched before them. Eve brushed her hand against the wall, only for her palm to grasp something hard and rounded.

She shrieked, yanking her hand back from the skull that was set upon a shelf in the wall. Liam swiveled to her, his immediate concern shifting into barely suppressed laughter when he saw what happened.

"That's no way to greet the dead, Evie," Liam teased, his shoulders shaking in amusement.

"You brought me to a *crypt!*"

"Not *any* crypt," Liam chided with the wave of his finger. There was an excited gleam in his golden eyes that made Eve bite back her retort. "This is the entrance to the Unseelie Court proper. A part of it, anyway."

"And what are we doing in the Unseelie Court?" Eve wiped her hand on her dress and followed Liam down one of the labyrinthine tunnels. There was no point in threatening to leave—Eve was certain that one wrong turn down here would spell out her doom. "Why are they located in a *crypt?*"

"Has anyone told you that you ask too many questions?" Liam asked. Eve glowered up at him. "I cannot speak as to why High King Earnan built his court underground, but I can assure you that we are here for a purpose."

"And that is?"

"This." Liam led her around a corner, where a faint buzz of conversation down the tunnel turned into an acoustic cacophony of haggling and deals. What Eve had thought to be stone coffins or altars had been re-purposed into stalls with eager merchants ready to sell their wares. They filled the room, this one wider and well-lit compared to the rest. A few used canvas banners to advertise themselves, but the artisan goods spoke for themselves.

"This is the Unseelie Court's central market. The Bone Court's denizens are scattered compared to the other courts, but they all come here during the day for trade," Liam explained with fondness. "It may not seem as such, but my family *is* important. Our job is to oversee the denizens in our jurisdiction and work to make improvements to their livelihoods."

"I didn't realize you did all of that." Eve glanced over the array of peculiar faces, wondering which ones belonged to the Bone Court. She recognized a few of them from Yule and mentally noted to keep her distance.

"To be fair, my father usually handles the particulars," Liam said. "But I've sat in on several meetings. He prefers to handle his work with the court outside of home. Although, his advisers do most of the work."

"Why is that?"

"He prefers to reserve his attention for winemaking. I presume that's why he's suddenly interested in picking an heir."

"So that he can relieve his official duties onto you or your siblings?" Eve guessed with a hollow laugh. Liam met her gaze with a grim smile.

"Precisely."

Irritation simmered in her chest. "If he wants to be a merchant, then he should do it. I don't see the point in dragging us all into his game."

Liam was not inclined to argue, but his lips twisted in resignation. "He can't give up his position as Lord of the Bone Court."

"Why not?" she huffed. "It would save you all a lot of trouble."

"You don't simply leave your position in the Unseelie Court, Evie. No one does." The drop in his voice and the seriousness behind it gave Eve pause. He ran a hand through his vibrant red hair, the tension in his shoulders easing. "The position isn't as awful as my father makes it out to be. Most decisions are already decided by the High King; we merely need to carry them out."

Eve nodded uncertainly. She knew Liam and his family were important, but she didn't grasp the scope of it until now. Watching the crowd bustle through the market and knowing that the Fogtrees oversaw a portion of the people there and more, was hard for her to wrap her head around.

"Do you have any interest in being his heir?"

Liam blinked, caught off guard by the question. "Why do you ask?"

"It matters, doesn't it? What you want." Eve recalled how heartbroken Hailey had been filling out applications for nursing schools as her parents demanded of her. She herself wilted under the undulating pressure of her parents' commands. "Is ruling the Unseelie Court what you want to do?"

Liam fiddled with the belt on his trousers, snapping and unsnapping the leather pouch attached at his hip. "Not in the slightest."

"Why not?"

Liam's expression twisted as he struggled to conjure the right words to say. "It is perhaps the most isolating role one can take in the Unseelie Court, second to the High King himself. Allies are rare here, friendships even more so. The ones that form tend not to last."

"That sounds lonely."

"It is."

Eve waited for Liam to elaborate. He did not. "What do you want to do instead, then?"

Liam narrowed his golden eyes at her. "You'll laugh."

"I will not." But now she was curious.

He pursed his lips, then shook his head with a wry smile. "Another time, perhaps. Not here."

One glance around the market's crowd and Eve understood. These were not the kinds of creatures one wants their admissions overheard by.

"Does Evren know?"

"Of course he does." Liam scoffed, his mood taking a bitter edge. "It does not matter to him what I want. He has already decided that I am to be his heir one way or another."

"Why *you*, though?" Eve pushed. It didn't make sense to her, what Evren saw in his youngest son. Liam was... not what she'd expected, but a leader was still not on that list. "Why not one of your siblings?"

Liam hesitated. Eve wasn't sure she would get an answer until it came through clenched teeth. "Because I've already proven myself capable."

"Then why even bother with the game?"

"You're unusually inquisitive today." He sighed, staring out at the market. "He wants to be sure that it wasn't a... fluke. That I am still what he imagines me to be."

"Are you?" Eve peered up at him, noting the tension in his muscles and jaw. Whatever he'd done to prove himself to Evren, it had taken something from him, too.

He did not answer. Liam nudged her lightly and moved toward the crowd. "Stay close."

She didn't need to be told twice. Yule was still fresh in her mind, as were the corpses left behind. Eve trailed close to Liam's elbow, careful not to touch him amid the mass of bodies they maneuvered between.

The musty scent of the crypt tapered off as she passed booths that smelled of smoked meat and other edible delights. It was hard to see what each one offered, and harder still to remain close to Liam while she craned her neck for a better view.

"I'm told that this isn't as glamorous as the market in the Seelie Court," Liam said as they sidestepped a tall, hefty creature made of rock. "But ours has a certain charm, wouldn't you agree?"

Eve eyed a stall decorated with dried intestines hanging from the rafters.

"Charming is... a word for it."

The crowd dispersed some the further they went, and Eve got a better idea of the market's offerings: nightmares in bottles. Trinkets both cursed and enchanted. Crystals, weapons, and magic as far as the eye could see.

Her attention veered toward a section of homemade goods, and Eve was captivated by the array of the strange artisan tools and handcrafted items on display. One woman used a hook attached to a handle to carve a beetle from raw emerald. Another had set up a glassblowing station and performed demonstrations with unusual dyes that turned into images of hissing snakes in the glass once heated.

A pale man with sharp canine teeth gestured Eve toward his booth of ruby-red jewelry. Liam dragged her away, muttering that they had no need of anything that the Blood Court had to offer.

"Wait," she said before he could rush her past another stall. A booth of leathers caught her attention, each one meticulously crafted in varying shades of black. It was not the whips or the armor that she was drawn to, but a basket filled with gloves of all sizes. Eve picked up a pair and held them up to Liam's hand.

"These are too big for you," Liam said, but Eve shook her head.

"For you," she explained, poking at the hole in his current pair. Eve held the pair out to him for examination. "What do you think?"

Liam wordlessly took the gloves, turning them over in his hands before trying one on. As he removed his old pair, she caught a glimpse of gray upon his wrist.

It's still spreading, she thought with dread. Eve kept putting the task off, convincing herself that she had more time to acquire the final piece of Liam's quest to find a cure for his ailment. But the clock was ticking, and Eve was running out of time.

Hair as liquid as ink. She'd been close to it at Yule. Killian's hair was a perfect match—but Eve had no idea how she was going to get it. The marketplace might have been a good place to search, but nothing she'd seen had come close to the riddle.

Besides, something about Killian's hair resonated with her. It *had* to be the final piece.

Liam, oblivious to her inner turmoil, tested out the pair of gloves. The stone on his wrist disappeared under the leather, and he flexed his hand in the air.

"These are quite nice," he approved. Reaching into his pouch, Liam exchanged a few trinkets for the pair and shoved his old gloves aside to get rid of later. As they meandered to the next stall, he asked, "Has anything caught your attention?"

"Plenty of things," Eve confessed, thinking back to all the artistic displays she'd seen. "I don't think Evren would be happy if I brought back an entire glassblowing studio."

Liam laughed. "No, I think not. I would love to see his face if you did, though."

Eve grinned, imagining Evren's irritation upon finding his den completely replaced with whatever nonsense she brought back from the marketplace.

"I cannot promise an entire studio," Liam continued. "But if there is something that appeals to you, you should get it."

"I can't afford anything here," Eve said, gesturing toward the booths.

"Who said that you were paying?"

She regarded him skeptically. "You're paying for me?"

"Why not?"

"Because I tried to kill you," she reminded him flatly. Not to mention the care he'd taken with her last night. Eve shoved the memory back before it became a permanent fixation.

Liam waved off her concerns, rolling his eyes. "Don't flatter yourself, Evie. You'd hardly be the first to try."

Eve wondered at this, but before she could ask who else was responsible for his near-death experiences, Liam's step faltered. He hissed a sharp breath and righted himself quickly, but Eve could see the tension in his jaw as he moved forward.

"Does it hurt a lot?" she whispered.

"Unimaginably so," he replied, his voice equally quiet. Liam glanced across the marketplace to make sure no one overheard.

"When did it start?" Perhaps if she could pinpoint the timing, Eve could find some kind of connection to its origin. Some way to stop it before it could spread further.

"Years ago," Liam said. "It was a small piece then, but I suppose it's finished taking its time. I've sought out higher powers for a cure, but..."

"You need the items to pay them," Eve finished for him.

"There is a cure of sorts—something to reverse the effects before they take over—but it's hard to come by," Liam explained.

Guilt squeezed Eve's chest as he absently rubbed at his wrist.

"Who are the items for?" Eve asked. If she knew who they were completing the riddle for, maybe she could bargain for a different item instead. Something that was easier to get than stealing a lock of hair from the Lord of the Blood Court.

The pained expression Liam gave her was enough to squash such thoughts. His time was already limited; did she genuinely think she could waste it with more bargaining?

Liam pointed out a stall instead, moving their conversation onto lighter ground. "I think you'll appreciate this one; she creates all of her supplies from scratch."

Eve allowed the distraction, her eyes lighting up as she took in the wide variety of paints. Each color sat in its own little jar, the shades vibrant with an intensity she'd never seen in her mere mortal realm. One teal bottle sloshed with the waves of an ocean. An amber bottle dripped thicker than honey, and a golden one beside it managed to capture the exact shade of Liam's eyes. Eve stared at the collection in awe, her heart beating fast as creative inspiration struck her with each new shade.

The stall's owner threw her head back in a cackle, revealing several gaps in her teeth. Her long, bedraggled hair was made of tree roots, and there was something serpentine about her face. "Likin' what ya see, girl? Bet ya never seen this stuff in yer measly realm."

"I haven't," Eve admitted, too stunned to take offense. Not since her work on the tabernacle had Eve been this excited to paint. Her hands itched to open the jars and test each shade.

"Cause ye won't find 'em anywhere but here." The woman slapped a wrinkled hand onto the slab with force. "I make everything myself."

"How?" Eve picked up one of the bottles and turned it between her fingers, admiring the red sheen under the torchlight. The woman snorted.

"If I go tellin' everybody how to do it, I wouldn't have a business, would I?" she scoffed. The woman held out her palm toward Eve. "If ye aren't gettin' anything, then scram. I got other customers to handle."

Liam caught the woman's hand before she could snatch the bottle of paint from Eve's hand.

"This isn't any way to win over customers, Zinnia," he chided. Zinnia scoffed.

"Yer still here, aren't ye?"

Eve weighed the bottle in her hand before reluctantly putting it back. Liam regarded her curiously.

"I don't have any money," she explained quietly, averting her gaze from Zinnia. "Besides, I have no use for them. There's nothing at the mansion to paint."

Liam waved her off and plucked a few bottles from the shelves. "You sell supplies, do you not?"

Zinnia glared at Eve from the corner of her eye but nodded. With the creak of her bones, she rose from her threadbare chair and removed a few blank canvases from behind the stone slab.

"Brushes are in the basket. My supplies are quality. Don't expect to get 'em for cheap," Zinnia grumbled as she set up the canvases for display. Eve noticed a strange discoloration to the fabric stretched over the thin wooden frames.

"What kind of materials are those?" she asked.

"I've got mortal flesh, pig's hide, hemp—"

"We'll take the hemp," Liam said quickly. Zinnia muttered something under her breath but grabbed the few normal canvases among her display. Eve took them between pinched fingers, doing little to hide her discomfort.

They left the stall with Eve's new supplies and several trinkets short of what they'd arrived with. Eve observed the paint bottles in her new canvas sack with more caution, wondering what was inside those little jars to create such rich colors.

"What's the catch?" Eve asked, gesturing toward the supplies.

"There is none. I am doing this because I want to." She raised a skeptical brow. "I thought indulging in your hobbies might help you unwind."

Eve prepped a smart-ass comment, but his concern gave her pause.

Is he worried about me? The wound on her arm ached. She brushed her fingers over the sleeve, pushing back against the tightening in her chest. Liam had claimed to come here for errands, but all they'd purchased were painting supplies.

The shame of last night crashed into her with breathtaking ferocity. She wished to bury herself somewhere in the crypt and let the worms whittle her down to the bones that decorated Liam's sleeves. If it was pity he offered her, Eve would rather let Zinnia turn her into one of her fleshy canvases.

"I know how things work in Faerie," she said. "You can't get something for nothing."

"You're so stubborn," Liam groaned. He ran a hand through his hair. "Very well. You wish to make it up to me? Paint me something."

Eve nearly laughed in disbelief. "You don't want something I've painted."

"Why not? It is a fair enough payment."

"It won't be any good," she argued. It wasn't a threat, but the truth. "Not worth what you paid for all of this."

"That will be for me to decide," Liam said. Eve scowled at his silhouette as they meandered further into the market. Liam turned back to her with a wry grin. "If it's truly terrible, though, we'll put it in Sage's room."

Eighteen

Logan's visits were intermittent. Days of training went by without even a glimpse of him, while others were soured by his presence outside. The final straw was when she arrived in the morning and found him perched on the tree across from the ballroom's balcony. He sat up and waved for her attention, his voice silenced by distance and the intrusive winter wind.

Eve wanted to punt him out of the tree. Instead, she turned to Liam.

"He's outside."

"Again?" Liam peered over her shoulder. "He's awful set on freezing out there, isn't he? Maybe you won't need to kill him. The elements will do that soon enough."

"I want to practice somewhere else," Eve said. She wasn't comfortable with him watching their training sessions. Watching *her*. Even now, Logan tried to get her attention, waving at her to come to the balcony before breathing into his palms for warmth.

"Did you have somewhere in mind?" Liam brandished his mock weapon, twisting the wood between his hands.

"Anywhere but here." Eve glared back at Logan, who seemed less certain about his position in the tree. She hoped the branch would snap, and that he would break his neck on the way down. "There has to be somewhere outside of the mansion that we can go, right?"

"There are plenty, but do you honestly think he wouldn't follow?" Eve scowled. "At least he is forbidden from entering the estate. I can't promise the same for anywhere else."

"Damn it." She hated when Liam was right. "Fine. Any other ideas, then? I can't concentrate with him watching my every move."

"We could go out and talk to him, for starters," Liam said. His calmness irked her. "He looks as though he wants to talk to you, anyway. If you're lucky, he might leave you alone after."

Eve gritted her teeth. He would never leave her alone. Did Logan think they were on friendly terms after she'd spared his life?

"I have nothing to say to him that a dagger won't say for me," she grumbled. "Why don't you teach me how to throw it? I wouldn't mind shooting him out of a tree."

Liam's brow arched as he watched her pace across the floor. "Would killing him grant you that much pleasure?"

"Obviously."

Liam frowned. "Evie, what did these men do to you?"

Eve stumbled. She cursed, tripping over her own feet before resuming a more frantic pace. Damn him. Why did he have to ask that?

She considered telling him everything. Then her mouth dried up at the thought. Liam had already spared her abusers' lives through a loophole. He had been their friend once. Was he still?

Such thoughts sickened her. Had he taken part in the kind of cruelties her abusers had? Eve didn't want to believe it—but trust was not a resource she had much of.

"We've wasted enough time," she said, and unsheathed her dagger. "Are you going to train me or not?"

"I simply thought—"

"I didn't ask you to think." Rage simmered under her flesh. It took a life of its own, lashing her tongue at anyone who dared come too close. "I asked you to train me."

"Is that an order?" Despite the sour note in his voice, Liam stepped into his starting position opposite her.

"If I have to make it one."

Liam frowned but motioned her to begin. Eve dove forward, her mock dagger aimed at his heart.

Liam easily parried her. They moved across the ballroom floor, their weapons clashing and bouncing off one another in a twisted dance. Eve's mocking turned into concentration as she focused on each of Liam's attacks. Eve was improving little by little, but she still lacked the agility and training Liam had taken years to attain. She stayed on the defense, managing only a few offensive strikes to his chest that Liam had no trouble countering.

"I know you can do better than that, Evie," Liam taunted, smacking her dagger away easily with his wooden sword. Eve gritted her teeth and struck again, only for Liam to slap her calves with his stick. "Still too slow. Try to keep up, Evie, dear, or you'll find a blade in your back before you know it."

Eve gasped as his mock weapon struck her hard across the spine. She stumbled forward but caught herself and spun around as Liam had taught her—blade out to strike. Liam narrowly sidestepped her attack, but the small grin on his face bespoke approval. She was learning.

The wooden sword came down across her chest, and Eve fell back. She groaned as she hit the hard tile floor.

"I believe that's another win for me," Liam said, offering her a hand. Eve stubbornly refused and rose to her feet on her own.

"Again," she demanded. Liam's brow arched, but he fell into position without argument.

With each spar, Eve realized nearly murdering Liam on her birthday had been a fluke. She couldn't even get close to him now. How was she going to kill Colton and Logan, let alone defend herself in Faerie, if she couldn't win against *Liam?*

Sneaky, arrogant Liam. He had a way of riling her up during their spars. It was only when her head cleared after their fights that Eve realized that his taunts were often interlaced with instruction. She mentally parsed through the corrections hidden in his jabs, and Liam left plenty of opportunity for her to practice them in their next match.

Sweat dripped from her brow as they finished. Her limbs ached with bruises and shame. It had been four days, and she hadn't won a single match. Eve knew it would take time, but that was another luxury she didn't have.

Eve winced as she stood, struggling to catch her breath. Her lungs and limbs were on fire. Her body screamed for a break, but Eve forced herself into position again, gripping the dagger until her knuckles were white.

Liam rolled his shoulders but did not match her stance. "We'll stop here for today."

"I can keep going," Eve insisted. Her calves screamed with each step.

"I'm too tired to indulge in your masochism, Evie," Liam said. He rubbed his shoulders, his position stiff. "You won't achieve perfection overnight. Take breaks when you can, or you won't improve at all."

He was right. Again.

Eve hated it. Even as her muscles spasmed in her leg, she wanted to keep fighting. She wanted to win.

Liam ignored the glare piercing into his back as he bent over to pick up his things. Eve's frustration subsided as she saw him struggle to pick up his scabbard on the ground. She bent over and offered it to him.

"What's wrong?" she asked. His movements were stiff as grinding stone. He wasn't as lithe as he had been on their first day of training. At times, he barely countered her. Even now, he grimaced in pain.

"I'm tired," Liam said with a hint of annoyance. "If you insist upon continuing to practice today, you'll have to do it on your own. Or, better yet, you could make some *actual* progress and finish finding the things I asked you for."

Eve grimaced. Even if she knew where the Blood Court was, Eve doubted she could simply waltz in and ask for a lock of the lord's hair. Certainly not without payment.

"I'm working on it," Eve ground out. "What about getting me and Hailey out of Faerie? I don't see any progress there."

Liam's brow furrowed. "It's complicated. I don't know what my father used in the wine, and he refuses to say. Until I can figure out the ingredient, I can't say how long it'll affect you—or how to counter it."

"Of course," Eve muttered. Nothing ever came easily to her, after all.

"In my defense, there hasn't been any time," Liam continued. "Since *someone* has insisted that I train them."

"You wouldn't have to train me if I were home," Eve snapped. Her anger at Logan, at her own ineptitude, at *everything* poured out in a hissing stream before she could catch it. "Honestly, why don't you win this stupid thing with your family so I can leave? Win-win for everyone."

Liam gave her a hard stare. "I have bigger priorities than playing games, Evie."

Eve flushed, gripping the mock dagger in her palm. "Then why don't you get the last item yourself?"

"Rest assured, I have spent nearly every waking hour trying to figure out how to do just that," he quipped. "Especially since you've proven yourself to be inept in this regard."

Eve gaped. "Excuse me?"

"The last time you made an effort to finish this quest was the same night you tried to kill me," he pointed out. "I'm not sure you had any intention of finishing it in the first place."

Eve found herself speechless. Yes, she'd put off going to the Blood Court, but not for the reasons he accused her of.

Does he think I can't do this? She thought. Bitter guilt soured on her tongue. *That I won't even try?*

Liam brushed past her. Eve watched him go, wincing with each slight jerk of his movements.

The spreading stone's effect on Liam was impossible to ignore. She could see it in the tension of his shoulders. The lean of his body. She imagined the gray patch crawling across his skin, inching closer to his heart.

He's given up on me, she realized. *He doesn't think I can do it.*

Eve glowered in the direction he'd left, her heart thumping with renewed vigor. She clutched her dagger and looked to the window. Logan was long gone, disappeared somewhere during her training.

She imagined his face at the other end of her blade as she practiced alone in the ballroom.

Nineteen

The tabernacle was a hit. Eve watched, bemused, as Preece—in his tiny green frog form—settled on a thick cushion inside of the brass box, his eyes slitted with contentment. He'd already decorated the inside with dried flowers and a selection of scarves and hats tiny enough to befit his smallest form.

"I'm glad you're happy with it," Eve said, setting the tabernacle down on Preece's dresser as instructed. He hadn't bothered to bring it up himself—he was too excited and left it in the hallway as someone else's burden to carry.

There was nothing to distinguish Preece's rooms from the empty guest beds down the hall, except for the mounting books and unwound scrolls piled beside his armoire. Aside from the typical accommodations one would expect from a guest suite, the room was devoid of any personalization whatsoever. She knew Preece lived in the Court of Knowledge now, but Eve had to wonder if he'd ever lived in the Bone Court at all.

"What isn't there to be happy with?" Preece gushed. Hearing his voice come out of his frog form took some getting used to. It was better than him indignantly *ribbiting* at her all the time. "The stories behind this device are quite interesting. You say it's a place where man meets a god?"

"Sort of," Eve said, tracing her finger along one of the spires. She had painted over the tabernacle a few months ago, after Liam had stolen it for her. Each panel on the heavy piece displayed a forest through the changing seasons. "That's kind of what the name means. It's a place to store the Eucharist during mass."

"What is a Eucharist?"

"The body and blood of Jesus."

"Cannibalism," Preece mused. "I've been told that some mortals can be as savage as the Unseelie Court. Truly, I'm fascinated to know how you fit an entire body in here."

"It's not a real body," Eve explained. "They're papery wafers."

"You dry the body out first? Fascinating."

Eve shook her head and decided against explaining the symbolism of the Eucharist. It would only end in a thousand more questions, and Eve had more pressing matters on her mind.

"You visited my nan," she said, inching closer. "How is she? Tell me everything."

Eve tried to keep calm, but her heart pulsed erratically with anticipation. It had to have been at least a week since she left her realm. Days were hard to keep track of in Faerie. Who knew how long her grandmother had gone without help?

Guilt was a hard pill to swallow. Eve had never meant to leave Nan alone. Not while she...

While she sought her own revenge.

The selfishness of it all was not lost on her. If she were given another chance, would she do it again? Eve thought of Nick's body sinking into the lake. Her knife against Logan's throat.

She would, and Eve hated herself for it.

"Your nan appeared perfectly fine," Preece said. Eve nearly sank to her knees in relief. "She was resting peacefully."

Resting peacefully. Oh God. "She wasn't dead, right?"

"Quite alive," Preece reassured her. He placed his little hand on hers. "You need not worry so. Humans acquire wrinkles too easily."

Eve relaxed into Preece's desk chair. Her anxiety was only marginally subdued. "Was anyone there with her?"

"I did not see other mortals in her presence."

Eve chewed on her lip. That troubled her. Nan was well enough to rest on her own, at least. For all Eve knew, Mr. Stone from next door had been coming over to take care of her during the day.

Still, Eve couldn't shake the worry that ticked in her heart. Nan was nearly ninety years old with dementia. What if she wandered off somewhere and forgot her way home? What if she fell and couldn't remember the number for emergency services? One dreadful scenario played after the next. Whatever the outcome, Eve knew it would be her fault.

"How long has it been?" she asked. "Since we've been here. I don't... I lost count."

Preece thought for a moment. "Time works differently in Faerie. Sometimes it will be minutes. Other times, weeks. Months. Occasionally years. It is not consistent, not when compared to your realm."

"Do you have any idea, then? What were the decorations?" Eve asked, thinking of how thorough her grandmother's small town had been in churning out Christmas decor on every block.

Preece thought for a long moment. "I'm afraid I did not make an astute observation in my time there. The lights were still upon the houses, if that is of any help."

It wasn't. Some people left their Christmas lights up for months after. Eve took a staggering breath to ease her racing heart. Nan was okay right now. She had to take comfort in that.

"I have another question for you," she said before Preece could fall asleep where he sat. Eve envied how cozy and at ease Preece was in the tabernacle. If only she could feel half as secure. "How do I get to the Blood Court?"

Preece's beady eyes twinkled with amusement. "The Blood Court? Why do you want to go there?"

"They have something I need." Eve had been putting off the last of Liam's quest for too long. He missed practice this morning, and after everything he spent on her supplies at the market, Eve would be damned if she didn't repay her debt. "I don't expect to get something for nothing."

"Then you know I require information in return," Preece said. Eve didn't know if frogs could grin, but his green lips eerily quirked into something resembling a smile.

She took a deep breath. Preece desired knowledge as a trout required water, and his thirst for her past was no secret. Eve wasn't prepared to speak her truth—to him or anyone.

But she could offer a taste if it got her to the Blood Court.

"One question," she said firmly, holding up a finger. "I will answer one question of your choice."

"Tempting, but I imagine you want directions to the Blood Court immediately." Eve swallowed hard. Preece chuckled and settled further into his cushion. "I'm a rather patient amphibian; I'm willing to wait for knowledge to spill on its own."

Eve scowled. Her leverage of withholding information only worked as far as her desperation. If Preece knew how badly she wanted to go to the Blood Court, there was little stopping him from bargaining to get what he wanted.

"I'll find it on my own if you don't tell me, and then you'll have nothing in return," Eve countered. It wouldn't be the first time she had gone wandering in the forest. Evren had to have some kind of map around here, didn't he? Certainly one better than the chicken scratch map in her room.

Preece almost laughed. "And risk dying by some creature in the woods? Have you no self-preservation?"

"No," Eve said, more stubborn than truthful.

"Either you are blindingly arrogant or incredibly foolish. One question," Preece conceded. "And you must answer truthfully."

"Fine. Let me know when you think of one," Eve said, turning to leave.

"Oh, I already know what I wish to ask. Why do you hate the Logan boy?"

Her throat tightened, but Eve fought to keep her face impassive.

"He hurt me," she said simply. Preece rolled his eyes, something she did not expect a frog capable of doing.

"Yes, that much is obvious. I suspect there is more to it, though."

"I answered your question," Eve said stiffly.

"You answered it partially. Shall I only give you partial instructions as well?"

Eve bit her tongue against the angry string of words that threatened to come out. She was doing this to pay off her debt to Liam. She couldn't risk giving Preece a reason to ask for more.

"He did something unforgivable to me," Eve murmured, pretending to find interest in a crack along the wall. She fought against the memories that resurfaced. The touches that scraped her mind like nails on a chalkboard. Nausea wormed its way through her as it had that night, leaving her sick and numb. She focused on the crack and imagined crawling through it, sinking into the darkness where she'd never be found. "It ruined my life, and I want him dead. Is that enough to satisfy you?"

"It shall suffice." There was a moment of quiet, and when Eve finally met Preece's gaze, beneath the curiosity, she saw a glimmer of what she hated most: pity.

Preece climbed out of the tabernacle and hopped onto the ground, where he was suddenly humanoid again. Eve hadn't even seen the transformation happen, although her eyes had never left him.

He gathered some writing utensils from the desk and jotted down a set of directions—which he promptly had to throw away and start over once Eve pointed out that she couldn't read the language he was writing in.

"These should provide you a relatively safe path to the Blood Court," Preece said, crossing his arms when he finished. "Although you could simply ask the carriage to take you there, no directions needed."

Eve tucked the directions safely into her pocket. "I'd rather not; you're the only one who knows I'm going."

"Shall this be our little secret, then?" Preece asked, somehow thrilled by the idea. I must warn you that going to the Blood Court alone is a marvelously stupid idea. Even father wouldn't dare attempt it."

"If it wasn't for your *father*, I wouldn't be in this mess in the first place," Eve muttered. "Do you even know why I'm here? How the hell am I supposed to help Liam impress your dad?"

There was something odd in the way Preece regarded her. As though he wanted her to be something more but was disappointed with what he found. The differences in their realms—their species—became apparent as he pressed a hand against the wall, mucus clinging to his palm. Compared to the Fair Folk, Eve was small and inconsequential. Human in the worst sense of the word.

"Mortals are regarded poorly in Faerie," he said slowly. "But it is especially apparent in the Unseelie Court. My father is of no exception to this."

"Why would he want us here, then?"

"Who can say? I am not always privy to the inner workings of my father's mind." He cocked his head in thought. "I would be willing to share my theories, however."

"For a price," Eve deadpanned. Preece grinned.

"For a price."

"I'll pass." Eve rested her hand on the folded parchment in her pocket. Her fingers brushed against the ink scratched into the parchment, as if she could memorize the directions by touch alone.

She would repay Liam. She would kill Logan and Colton.

Then she would go home.

TWENTY

Preece's directions were shit. Eve cursed under her breath as she trekked through the snow, searching for the landmarks written down.

Keep left at the road where the redcaps raged war against the dryads. Walk forty paces until you see the remnants of Orkalea's burned tower. Follow the right path but avoid the síoga—Cú Sidhe wander these parts.

"What does any of this *mean?*" Eve hissed. She glanced between the directions and the forest, lost. She could have sworn she passed a tower somewhere, but was it the right one? What were síoga? Why couldn't Preece give her some *normal* directions?

Eve crumbled the paper into a ball and shoved it in her pocket. Useless. These directions were utterly *useless.*

I would've been better off taking the carriage, she thought. She hadn't wanted Liam to know where she was going. He would have stopped her, and then what? How else would she get the last item for his quest?

With a hefty sigh, Eve trudged forward. While foreign, Eve was growing accustomed to the landscape of the Unseelie Court. She recognized the snow-covered mounds as homes, the smoke billowing up from their stone chimneys blending in with the overcast sky. She noticed the hollowed-out trees versus the ones that were intact, their little doors no taller than her ankle.

The critters had two categories: sentient and non. There were stags and bears that roamed the forest as any animal would. Birds that sang in the morning, and rabbits that burrowed in the ground. For all she knew, they had been plucked and bred from her own realm for the Fair Folk's pleasure.

Then, there were the *others*—creatures that resembled deer, goats, or bears but were not. Some walked on their hind legs. Others spoke, their words guttural and not entirely meant for human ears. They did not bother her, nor did Eve seek them out. She kept her head down, hood up, and minded her own business.

Until she met the beast.

It could have been a dog if it were not for its size. The wolfish creature was as large as a small cow with fur so deep a green it was almost black, and eyes that burned with the flames of hell. The beast stood some ten yards away, blocking her path. It snarled. Lips pulled back to reveal sharp, bloody teeth.

Then it was gone.

Eve stared at the empty spot where it had been. The sensation of being watched did not fade, and Eve's muscles tensed as she glimpsed through the trees for its figure.

The stillness of the woods was alarming. Even the birds had vanished, holding their breath alongside her lest they give themselves away.

A low growl set her nerves on edge. It was close—too close—and still Eve saw nothing but fallen snow. Hot, invisible breath brushed her face.

Then she saw the paw prints.

Enormous, they pressed without a sound into the fresh snow, circling her. She watched as they appeared from thin air and grew indistinguishable with its steady pace. They crinkled in the path it made behind her.

Eve ran.

Snow kicked up in her wake as she fled, scrambling to keep herself from tripping on the forest debris. A skull-shattering bark pierced her ears. Eve pressed her hands over her eardrums, fighting against the distraction.

She didn't dare turn back, but she could hear the beast behind her, its jaws snapping at her neck.

The beast howled. A spike of fear drove through Eve's heart, chilling her to the bone. Adrenaline kept her upright, but it was a supernatural terror that pulled her senses into hyperdrive. The howl rattled through her mind, consuming her with dread.

Eve had no hope of outrunning this monster. Tears blurred her vision as she tried anyway.

The beast was upon her—she could smell its foul breath with every growl from its maw. Panic made her breaths short and thoughts reckless.

The next howl hurt worse than the first. Fear coincided with pain as the sound drilled into her head. Eve's limbs trembled, threatening to give out.

Keep running. She *had* to keep running.

Eve thought her chest would burst from fright. Never had she experienced such fear before. Phantom images played in her mind's eye of the creature's jaw clamping down on her neck. They invaded her thoughts, less of a threat and more of an agonizing promise.

Faster. She had to go faster. Escape. Escape. Esca—

Eve crashed chest-first to the ground. Air knocked out from her lungs with the impact. The beast ground to a halt over her, and Eve watched in terror as it dove for her throat.

Two great javelins plunged into the beast's neck.

The magically heightened fear vanished at once. Eve gasped, rolling onto her back as the creature fell with a heavy thud beside her. Blood matted the beast's fur and seeped into the snow underneath. Eve fumbled to her feet, avoiding the crimson splatters on the ground.

Sharp laughter caught her attention. Eve stepped out of the way as two large ogres in black leather uniforms approached the monster. They yanked the javelins from the creature's neck with ease, licking the blood from the tips.

"Cú Sidhe blood," one said, scratching his scraggly gray beard. "This'll be a rare treat."

Eve grimaced, peering at the beast again.

Oh. So *that* was a Cú Sidhe.

"And what of this one?" his friend asked. Eve froze under their scrutiny. "Another mortal? We can toss her in with the others."

"You aren't going to *toss* me anywhere," Eve snapped. "I am in the middle of something."

"Getting eaten?" The ogres snickered, nudging each other. Eve pressed her lips into a tight line.

"I'm trying to find the Blood Court," she said. "I need to speak with Killian."

"What right has a mortal to address the Lord of Blood by his name?" the first ogre sneered, his fist tightening around the javelin.

Eve straightened her shoulders and did her best to suggest her importance. She hadn't noticed the red insignia on their uniforms earlier, but the symbol of a vial of blood shrouded in roses was unmistakable. She'd found the Blood Court, if under undesirable circumstances.

"I'm here on behalf of the Bone Court," she explained, only half-lying. *Technically*, she was here on behalf of Liam, even if he didn't know it. "There is something important I need to discuss with Lord Foxglove. I need to see him immediately."

"The Bone Court? Why didn't ya say so?" Eve detested the mocking tone the second ogre used as he approached her.

"You'll make a lovely gift."

The bearded guard hoisted her up from underneath her shoulders with ease while his companion slung the dead Cú Sidhe over his shoulder. Eve screamed and kicked, swearing to every god under the sun and moon her hatred as they dragged her away.

TWENTY-ONE

Eve knew she was doomed when they carried her over the blood-red creek. They crossed over an ancient stone bridge that was frosted over, the rushing stream underneath loud in her ears. She did not know where the water got its scarlet color, nor did she want to find out.

This was the Blood Court.

Her captors dragged her into a twisted manor carved from the mountainside. She wouldn't have even noticed it if it were not for the stained-glass windows and red banners with the court's insignia. A small crimson waterfall poured out from the mountain, far enough from the side to not erode the estate. It was not close enough for Eve to tell if the water smelled as bloody as it looked.

The sharp scent of minerals hit her when they passed through the entrance doors. The air reeked of iron—not pure iron, but the sort only found beneath flesh and bone. It was overwhelming. Nauseating. The stink came from every crevice of the hall, and Eve did not think a thousand hours of scrubbing could remove it.

She squirmed in the ogres' grasps as they carried her through the grand hallway and into a dining room with vaulted ceilings high enough to reach the heavens. A long, deep oak table stretched to the back where Killian and a few members of his court dined. The bearded ogre dropped her in front of Killian with the grace of a falling boulder.

Eve grunted as her knees hit the floor. Her captor gripped her shoulders with his large hands, forcing her still, while his friend tossed the Cú Sidhe onto the table. Tableware rattled under its weight, but no one bothered to pause their meal, suggesting this was a common occurrence.

"We caught a fresh one in the woods, my lord," the bearded guard said, pinching Eve's shoulders. "Along with its prey."

"I was *not* its prey," she huffed. They ignored her, which only served to demean her more. She glared up at the smug ogres, her cheeks flushed with anger. "I said I—"

"Hush," Killian interrupted as he took a long sip from his goblet. "You're spoiling my appetite. Redgar, what is this human doing here? Put her with the others."

Redgar—the ogre holding Eve in place—shifted uneasily. "We thought you might be interested in her, my lord. She says she's here on behalf of the Bone Court."

"The *Bone Court?*" Killian barely suppressed a laugh. He spared Eve a cursory glance, then did a double take, lowering his goblet to the table. "You're that little wretch that stirred up trouble during the Yule festivities."

"I have a name," Eve said evenly. Killian smirked.

"May I have it, then?"

Eve opened her mouth, then promptly closed it as his true meaning settled in. "No."

He shrugged, as if such power meant nothing to him either way. "They've taught you well, little wretch. What is it you have come to deliver on behalf of the Bone Court?"

"It's not a delivery," Eve explained. "So much as a... request."

"Oh?"

Members of Killian's court took interest, peering down the enormous table to watch. To Eve, they all appeared to wear masks above their lips of various animals—both real and mythical—but she knew Faerie well enough to recognize how real it all was. They shared the ravenous hunger in their eyes—and the sharpness of their teeth.

This was not how Eve had wanted to do this. She had imagined asking to speak to Killian privately, where she could bargain on her own terms. To have the eyes of his court watching her, judging her, did nothing for her nerves. "Is there somewhere else we could—"

"You have already interrupted my meal," Killian said. "Speak now before my patience leaves us."

Eve swallowed hard. She tried to stand but was promptly pushed back onto her knees.

Fighting against the humiliation, Eve said, "I need a lock of your hair."

Tittering and laughter echoed across the table. Even Killian's lips quirked into a mocking grin.

"Whatever could you need a lock of my hair for?" Killian asked, twirling one of the graceful black strands around his slender finger. "You aren't intending to perform a love spell, are you?"

"*No,*" Eve said in repulsion. Killian's black eyes narrowed slightly in offense. "No, I need it for a... quest."

"Is that so?" Killian held his empty goblet out, and a maid with pointed ears and poppy-red eyes filled it from a questionable brown jug. "And to whom are you delivering such a valuable item?"

Eve suspected that telling him the truth—that it was for Liam—would not serve her well in this instance. The gazes of the court bore down on her, their amused smirks placing their sharp fangs on display.

"It's for a troll," Eve said, her gaze meeting Killian's. She did not dare look away should he detect her lie. "In the woods."

Killian appeared unconvinced, but there was still a glimmer in his eye that bespoke amusement. If he was entertained, Eve was safe. Relatively.

"Why must it be *my* hair?" he inquired. "Surely you've come across a substitute elsewhere."

Eve shook her head. "Yours is the only one that matches. *Hair as liquid as ink.*"

"I'm flattered that you should think so." Killian chuckled, running a hand through his long black locks. The members of his court whispered, casting deriding glances toward Eve. "I fear that I have little interest in parting with what is mine, though I am rather curious. What is it you would be willing to trade for a lock of my hair?"

Eve tried to reach into her sack, but Redgar's hold made it impossible. "Do you *mind?*"

Killian waved Redgar off, and the ogre grudgingly obliged. Eve stood and, after brushing herself off, dug into her sack.

"I have a few things that might interest you," she said, placing a handful of trinkets on the table. Members of the court crowded together to see what she had to offer.

A goblet inlaid with obsidian. Two silver rings. Hair pins that hadn't been touched in decades. A tooth with a golden filling. Discarded things not likely to be missed that Eve had plucked and dusted from the unused spaces of the Bone Court and made shiny again.

She hoped one of them would make a fair trade. Eve was tired of bargains that asked more of her than she could give.

The Blood Lord observed each trinket with a critical eye. Eve waited, trying not to let her impatience show.

"I have no use for these," he finally said, sitting back in his chair. Eve inhaled sharply.

"Are you sure?"

Killian sneered. "I am certain. What use would I have for a goblet with the Bone Court's insignia?"

He gestured at the cup, and, to Eve's dismay, the family crest of a skull and nightshade was proudly engraved between the gems. How she'd missed it, Eve wasn't sure, but she hurriedly tucked it back into her sack.

"What about the rest of it?" Eve pushed. "All of it? Wouldn't that be enough?"

"No." Killian flicked his hand, and the ogres grabbed Eve's shoulders. Her heart leaped into her throat. "She will make a fine hostage. Take her to—"

"Wait! There must be something else I can give you in exchange. Something..." Eve racked her brain for an offer. She scanned the empty walls, pleading with them, searching. The bottles of paint sitting on her desk raced to the forefront of her mind. "I can paint you something. Anything. You can hang it up in the dining hall."

He laughed in her face. "Why would I want anything crafted by a mortal?"

"I have already been asked to paint something for the Bone Court," Eve said, thinking quickly. "You would have it first before anyone. Before Liam."

Killian paused, his lips brushing the edge of his goblet as he considered her offer.

Killian mused, raising his chin in observation.

"Unlike anything you've seen." Eve was careful with her words. She shuddered to think of what he would do if she boasted to him and couldn't deliver. Licking her dry lips, Eve held out her hand. "Does that mean we have a deal?"

"Not on your terms." Killian snapped his fingers, and Eve gasped as the ogres snatched her up by the arms. She struggled in their grasp, but it was no use. "You have three days to paint something to my satisfaction. Should you succeed, I will grant you a lock of my hair."

"And if I don't?" Eve was not naive enough to think that he would allow her to fail without consequence.

Killian smirked, and a chill ran down her spine. "Then my court will decide your fate."

TWENTY-TWO

Mold grew through the cracks along the walls of the Blood Court's dungeon. Eve's cloak brushed against the spores as she ventured down the spiraling staircase where the number of prison cells grew as frequent as the screams that echoed from below.

They advanced through a heavy door at the bottom—but another hall of cells stretched out before them, and more stairs remained at the end.

Eve passed by a cell much larger than the rest. Figures huddled against the shadows, cowering away from Redgar and the other guards that stood watch outside.

Redgar leaned in close. "That's where you'll end up if his lordship wishes."

He met her gaze with a malicious grin. She squinted against the darkness and tried to work out the creatures' shapes.

Humans. Dozens of humans crowded inside of the cell in the same frightened huddle as cattle prepared for slaughter. Eve covered her face with her scarf against the thick stench of stale urine and decay that wafted from inside. Most of the captives were alive, but a few bodies hunched on the opposite wall against the floor, slack-jawed and unseeing.

A pair of guards came down the stairs after them. Eve watched as they entered the cell and grasped the nearest body—a woman with blond hair and a raggedy blue dress. Eve thought she couldn't be much older than herself.

"No," the woman gasped, breaking into hysterics. "No, no, nonononononono—!"

The guards lifted her up under her arms without effort. She kicked and screamed, her high-pitched voice echoing through the hall as she begged and sobbed for the guards to choose someone else instead.

"What is she being picked for?" Eve asked, uncertain if she wanted the answer.

Redgar glanced over his shoulder at the frantic woman as she is dragged up the stairs. "Probably dessert."

The guards pulled the woman out of sight. A heavy door above slammed shut, silencing her screams. Unsettling quiet hung in the woman's absence.

Redgar delivered Eve to a cell on a lower floor that was half the size of her room at Nan's. Eve squinted past the dim candlelight that flickered on the sconce outside. There was no bed. No privy aside from another bucket that had been overdue for a cleaning. Murky brown splatters stained the floor and walls, which Eve pointedly chose to ignore.

"Homey," she muttered. Frigid air brushed her cheeks and created a small fog with each breath. Eve was grateful for the thick layers she'd worn on the way here. If she *did* have to stay overnight, at least she wouldn't freeze to death. Probably.

She jumped as the cell door slammed shut behind her. Redgar vanished and returned with a plain canvas, a single paintbrush, and a bucket of crimson blood. Eve stared at the bucket, her nose crinkling in disgust.

"What am I supposed to do with this?"

The ogre grinned. "You said you're a painter, yah? Get to it."

Eve glared at Redgar as he locked the cell and meandered back upstairs, leaving her alone to her task.

The supplies were far from adequate. Eve turned the paintbrush over in her hand, disappointed with its thickness. Details would be difficult to accomplish. The canvas had the same discoloration she had seen at the marketplace as well, and Eve did not want to even think of the bucket as her paint.

Eve had promised a painting unlike anything the Lord of Blood had seen. She should have worded it as a painting unlike anything *she* had ever seen.

There was no certain way for Eve to know what kind of art Killian would enjoy. She had seen a few tapestries in the hall and typical family crests adorning banners, but Eve suspected the style belonged to the recently deceased Lord Foxglove.

What kind of painting did *Killian* want?

Eve thought back to their meeting at Yule. They had barely spoken to each other. The Blood Lord enjoyed the chaos and carnage, but so did most of the Unseelie Court.

Eve drummed up the image of Yule in her head—the blazing fire that consumed the enormous tree, the dark silhouettes that danced with glee around its destruction. Backgrounds were not the strongest among her talents, but Eve did her best, focusing on the stark contrast of shadows instead.

Blood was a difficult substance to work with. It was too thick for water-color but too thin for oil painting. Eve learned quickly that she needed to lay the canvas flat on the ground before the blood dribbled down over her painting.

Eve gritted her teeth and dabbed away another defiant drip that threatened to ruin her tree with the hem of her skirt. It was getting increasingly hard to concentrate, and not only because of her frustration with her tools.

She tried to tune out the torture happening down the hall. Screams and cries floated in her direction, a reminder of what was to come if she failed.

Eve couldn't afford any distractions. Still, her heart beat fast as guards meandered past her cell in search of their next victim.

Eve was adept at numbing herself to her surroundings. She had done this with her father countless times. The pain was real, but Eve could distance herself from it. From herself, even. Begging got her nowhere—but action did. If karma was a bitch, Eve was the worse one of all.

Her hands were stained red by the time she finished. Eve wiped the blood off on her skirt, analyzing her work.

It was a decent painting. At least, Eve thought so. Dark figures with fae-like features danced around the lit Yule tree, casting long, ominous shadows over the snow. Cinder watched with pleasure in the background, its face blending in with the pine trees and dark clouds. A momentous occasion for a court so depraved.

Redgar came back a while later and, without a word, took the canvas from the cell and carried it away. Eve's stomach clenched as he dragged her painting out of sight. She could picture mistakes on the canvas in her mind, ones often overlooked and disregarded for the sake of the project. She wished she could slip through the bars and snatch the portrait back before Killian ever laid eyes on it.

Too much of her future relied on the arbitrary opinion of a lord she knew little about. Eve tried to quell the racing of her heart as the screams down the hall echoed in her ears. They were harder to ignore now that her fate was in another's hands.

The ogre came back much sooner than Eve had expected with a blank canvas in his arms. He tossed it carelessly into her cell.

"What is this?" Confused, Eve picked up the canvas. "Did Killian see my painting? What did he think?"

"His lordship was unsatisfied," Redgar said with a tone of mockery. Eve's heart sank, but she tried not to show it.

"What didn't he like about it?" Eve asked evenly, holding back her annoyance. If she could figure out what Killian's tastes were, she could get through this trial before her first day was over.

Glancing around the cell, Eve realized she had no idea how much time had already passed. There were no windows or clocks to indicate the hour had moved at all, let alone the sun. She could only go off the increasing hunger in her stomach as any sign that the day was nearing its end.

Redgar offered no insight into Killian's tastes. Eve watched him go, wondering if it was even worth the effort to ask him for food. After seeing the woman dragged out of her cell for "dessert," Eve didn't trust anything they would try to feed her anyway.

Fighting against the increasing cold in her cell, Eve picked up her brush and brainstormed her next painting. A part of her wondered if anything she painted would be enough to satisfy the Lord of Blood, but Eve shoved those doubts aside. She didn't have time to worry about hypotheticals.

The first day of her trial had already vanished before her eyes. She couldn't let tomorrow be the same.

Eve painted late into the night. When her body was too tired to withstand another minute awake, she reluctantly placed her cloak on the floor and slept.

Sleep was a generous word. She tossed and turned on the hard stone floor, the cloak doing little to provide her with any semblance of comfort. Half the time she was awoken by screaming down the hall, and the other half was due to her own stiff posture.

When she couldn't stand it any longer, Eve fought against her aching limbs and moved onto the next painting.

Emotions passed over her in a haze. Her hunger came and went, returning each time stronger than before. Nausea at the constant reek of blood from her paint bucket ebbed and flowed, eventually diminishing to yet another part of the background as she worked. Eve's patience thinned with each new canvas she received, forced to start over with a fresh idea every time.

Nothing had satisfied Killian. As the hours passed, Eve experimented with different art styles and techniques, challenging herself repeatedly until she was a dried sponge squeezed of every creative thought she'd ever had.

When Redgar brought down yet another blank canvas, Eve nearly screamed.

In truth, she was terrified. It was becoming increasingly difficult to hide her panic with the lack of food and sleep. Eve put her heart and soul into her paintings, yet Killian dismissed them without a word. What if nothing she painted was good enough? How arrogant was she to claim to be able to paint something to please this otherworldly creature?

The cell of captive humans lingered in the back of her head as Eve struggled through her next piece. Her ability to concentrate was decreasing by the minute. Forget being able to save Liam with a lock of Killian's hair—she'd be lucky if she was able to save herself.

"Can't I have water?" she asked Redgar when he took her portrait for judgment. This time she'd drawn Killian's head inside of a toilet bowl to spite him.

Redgar nodded to the bucket of blood. "Ya got that."

"I'm not drinking *blood*," Eve snapped. "I need water. And *food*. I'm starving down here."

The ogre shrugged as if to say *that's not my problem*. Eve gritted her teeth, fighting against the ache of her empty stomach as it released a low growl. She picked up the blank canvas and debated tossing it at his head, but Redgar had already left, and Eve knew it wouldn't solve any of her problems anyway.

With grumbling reluctance, she moved on to the next painting.

Her thoughts drifted to Liam and Hailey as she attempted a serious portrait of Killian himself. Had they noticed she was missing? What would they think of her absence? Eve regretted not leaving a note behind. As much as she wanted this to be a surprise for Liam, leaving without confiding in them about her location had not been her smartest moment.

Eve's anger dulled throughout the night. Her arm moved on its own, her joints cramping as she forced another painting onto a blank canvas. Exhaustion numbed her senses. Eve hardly knew what she was painting anymore—just that she wanted to finish it and never see it again.

Off it went, and Eve wondered if this time Killian would set her free.

She was not surprised when Redgar came back with another blank canvas, but Eve was too tired to argue.

TWENTY-THREE

One day left. Eve didn't know how much time had passed when she woke up, but knew she had to start right away. She *would* earn Killian's satisfaction and leave with a lock of his hair. She had no choice.

All that determination did nothing to offset the growing weakness in her body. She hadn't slept soundly in two nights and hadn't eaten a proper meal for even longer. Eve's hands shook as she painted—not from fear, but from her tanking blood sugar. Dehydration pounded against her skull.

Would she die here, painting with blood until Killian and his court feasted on her corpse?

Footsteps echoed from the stairs. Eve frowned at her painting, acknowledging its flaws with remorse. It was nowhere near as beautiful as the first one she'd painted for him. Killian would never be satisfied with this. Hell, *she* wasn't satisfied with it.

Eve picked up the canvas, ready to turn it over, but nearly dropped it when she saw what was in Redgar's hands.

"Is that water?" she croaked, her voice squeaky from disuse. She licked her chapped lips, her entire mouth dry and cracking. Redgar set the heavy goblet down on the floor through the bars, ignoring how a third of its contents sloshed onto the ground with his reckless movements.

"Drink," he ordered.

She grabbed the goblet and forced herself to take small sips lest she make herself nauseous. It only occurred to her after the cup emptied that the water may have been poisoned. Eve didn't find it in herself to care—a death by poison would be better than whatever Killian had planned for her.

It wasn't enough water to hydrate her—not by a long shot—but it gave her the boost of energy she needed.

"You mortals are weak," Redgar sneered. He watched her lick the water from her lips in disgust. "Lord Killian wants you alive. It is his choice, not mine."

Eve didn't care whose choice it was if it meant she could drink more water.

Redgar took the canvas, scowling as he tucked it under his arm and retreated upstairs. She didn't bother trying to stop him. He would come back down with another blank one, and *this* time Eve was certain she could win their bargain.

When the ogre descended to her cell, his hands were empty.

Eve eyed him cautiously as he unlocked her cell and gestured for her to leave. Killian couldn't have been satisfied by her last painting, could he? Even Eve was disappointed by her handiwork, but at this point, she could hardly remember what she'd drawn. Her paintings from the past few days blurred together in a sea of red.

"Are you coming or not?" Redgar barked. Eve gathered her cloak and hurried out of the cell, wrapping it tightly around her shoulders as the ogre led her upstairs.

Maybe she *had* satisfied Killian somehow. It wasn't as though Eve was privy to Killian's artistic preferences. For all she knew, the guy had bad taste.

Redgar led her up into a large, open room filled with cushions of velvet and silk in rich, dark colors. Members of Killian's court lounged in a drunken stupor on the floor, drinking from goblets and smoking from long pipes as they conversed with each other. Eve was careful to step around them, ignoring the chill that ran down her spine when their predatory gazes landed on her.

Killian sat in the back of the room in a large chair with black cushions and red stones embedded into the frame. He twirled a red vial between his fingers, inspecting it under the light with amusement. A few ladies sat by him, flashing their fanged smiles with Eve's approach, but it was not his court that caught Eve's attention.

It was Liam.

He stood in front of Killian with his chin raised and a glare colder than the frozen landscape outside. Liam was ashen, worse for wear with his disheveled red hair and wrinkled clothes. Purple bruises under his eyes emphasized his exhaustion.

"See? All in one piece," Killian said, flippantly gesturing to Eve. "You are free to leave, unless you are inclined to stay for dinner."

"A generous offer, but we must decline." Liam did not hide the acidity in his voice. When he turned to Eve, his expression softened. "Let's go."

"Wait," Eve said, pulling away when Liam reached for her. Something flashed across his face, but it was too quick for her to catch it. "What's going on? I thought we had a deal."

"Pay it no heed," Killian said with ease. "I had never intended for you to leave in the first place, but it appears the Bone Court can offer something better than a measly mortal meal."

Eve stared at the vial of blood between his fingers. Then at Liam's pale, almost greenish hue. Her hands balled into fists at her sides, tight enough that her knuckles turned white.

"We made a deal," she repeated, her anger and hatred for this man and his court escaping in the venom of her voice. "I am not leaving here until I finish."

"Eve," Liam warned. He reached for her again, but thought better of it, awkwardly tucking his hand into the pocket of his trousers instead. "Whatever deal you made with him doesn't matter. We should go."

"No." She wouldn't budge on this, not after Liam had saved her. Again. She owed him this much.

"You should listen to the little Fogtree," Killian said with a smirk. "I am not often so generous."

Generous. Nothing about the past three days had been generous. Eve wanted to lock him in the cells and see how he liked it.

"Did you even see the paintings I made?"

"Of course not." Killian laughed. "I had them burned the moment they left the dungeon."

His confession was a punch to the gut. Eve braced herself but couldn't stop the shaking of pure, unbridled rage. If Colton, Logan, and Nick were demons, *this* was the devil himself.

"Let's settle this now," she said, the cool iciness of her voice a mask against the vitriol hatred she kept locked inside. "I will paint for you here and now. If you are satisfied, then you'll keep to the terms of our agreement."

Killian observed her, his dark hair brushing over his shoulder as he cocked his head. He set the vial of blood down in his lap. "Do you intend to keep to the original agreement should I find myself unsatisfied as well?"

"No, she—" Liam's eyes widened with panic, but Eve cut him off.

"Yes."

Killian grinned, and the absolute delight on his face was the most terrifying thing Eve had ever seen.

"Bring up her materials," he ordered Redgar. The ogre obliged without a word.

There was nowhere for them to speak privately, but Eve noticed Liam staring at her with mixed emotions, his lips drawn into a taut line. Whatever anger he felt was quelled only by the presence of their audience.

If she lived through this trial, Eve would never hear the end of it.

Redgar arrived with her familiar tools and set them on the floor. For the severe lack of artwork in the manor, Eve had to wonder where they had all these blank canvases stashed. Considering their unusual texture, she was better off not knowing.

Eve settled down on the floor and picked up her paintbrush. There was a renewed sense of determination as she drew her first lines. This painting needed to be perfect. She didn't care how long it took. Eve wouldn't leave this room until Killian was satisfied.

Her best chance at success would be to paint something familiar. Something she had seen a thousand times, that she could conjure the proportions of without a second thought. A piece that was as gruesome as it was mundane. An image that had been burned into her brain since birth.

Eve knew exactly what to paint.

Creatures of the Blood Court slowly crowded around Eve as she worked, craning their necks to get a better view of the drawing. At first it was merely light sketches, shapes and figures that didn't quite connect. Then a face formed. Downcast eyes in mourning. A man's body slumped against the cross. Nails dug into his feet and palms, holding him in place, while a crown of thorns drew trickles of blood down his face.

Eve may not have been Catholic anymore, but she knew the image of Christ's crucifixion as if it was her own. It was painful to draw. Memories of the miniature statue banging against the wall whispered to her, recalling that wretched night in the boys' dormitory.

For once, Eve did not shy away. She embraced that pain, pouring her agony into the stark shadows on the canvas. Into the blood that dripped from Jesus's body. She wanted this painting to be as wretched and disgusting as she felt. No one was safe in this world—not even the son of a god.

"What a gruesome display," one of the court's members mused with delight. Pleased murmurs picked up behind as she sharpened the thorns and placed emphasis on the wounds.

Liam was unusually silent. While Eve did not regard him, she could sense his gaze boring into her back with each stroke of her brush. She was glad for his attention; let him see that she did not need pity. Eve was stronger than anyone gave her credit for.

Her refinements done, Eve pulled back from the painting and gave it a final once-over. The canvas did not depict Jesus with the same reverence her church would have. There was no light, no halo, no sense of a noble sacrifice by a man who would rise to life again three days later. Eve's depiction was that of an unwilling martyr—someone forced into the role and hated for it all the same.

Eve lifted up the canvas and carefully displayed it in her arms.

No one said a word. Killian observed the piece without emotion, his black-eyed gaze slowly drifting from one corner of the canvas to the other. Eve held her breath when his attention flickered back to her.

"It is... satisfactory," the Blood Lord relented. He seemed irritated that he should enjoy such mortal art. Killian flicked his hand, and Redgar snatched the canvas from Eve. "You carry such a brutal imagination. Are you sure you do not wish to stay among the Blood Court, little wretch? I'm sure your cell would make a fitting art studio."

Liam bristled at her side, but Eve stood tall.

"I'd rather yank my teeth out with pliers," she spat.

Killian grinned.

"We can always have that arranged."

Eve crossed her arms and fought against the urge to slap him. She wasn't sure how she ever found Liam frustrating—Killian was a thousand times worse.

"Don't forget my end of the bargain," she said, holding out her open palm. Killian's smile dropped, his mood soured by the reminder.

"Indeed. Let us be done with it." He gestured toward his court, and a feminine creature with feathers for hair fetched him a pair of gold scissors. Killian glared at Eve as he carefully snipped a lock of his hair and tossed it at her feet. "Do not let it go to waste."

Eve picked up the lock from the floor and tied it together with a loose thread on her skirt. Her task was complete, and now... now she could repay Liam properly.

Liam grabbed her elbow and they finally, safely, left the Blood Court.

TWENTY-FOUR

The Bone Court's carriage door had barely shut before Liam rounded on her.

"What were you *thinking?*" he hissed, perched on the edge of his seat across from her. "Going to the Blood Court *alone,* making a deal with *Killian* of all Fair Folk—"

Eve tossed the lock of hair onto his lap.

"I finished the quest," she said. Her body relaxed with the admission. It was done. The final piece to Liam's quest was finished, and now he could trade everything in for a cure.

Pride swelled in her chest. She bested Killian on her own. She escaped the Blood Court on her own. She was as capable as any of the Fair Folk and, for the first time in her life, she felt that she *belonged.*

Eve waited for the relief to settle in for Liam. This was what he'd been waiting for. With her debts paid, Liam had everything in the world to be happy for.

He did not so much as crack a smile.

"You shouldn't have done that. I didn't *ask* for you to do that." He ran a hand through his hair in frustration, but the gesture was rigid. Stone ground together as he moved. "The only reason you're free is because I intervened."

Eve's jaw ticked with irritation. "I'm *free* because I fulfilled my end of the bargain."

Liam laughed in disbelief. "Killian was never going to let you go. You heard him yourself; he didn't even look at your paintings."

"I would have found another way," Eve argued. "Even if you hadn't shown up, I could've handled things myself."

"I sincerely doubt that."

She hated how easily he cut down her victory. Why couldn't Liam accept that she could manage things on her own?

"Why do you have to fight with me? I got you what you wanted," she gritted out, gesturing toward the lock of hair on his lap.

"I didn't want this."

"Bullshit. Why can't you be happy that I—"

"Because you could have died!"

Eve was taken aback. The fight promptly blew out from under her sails. Why would Liam care if she died? Wasn't this all a means to an end?

The pact, she remembered. He must have sensed the danger she was in. Of course it had been him to rescue her.

"Why don't we break off the pact of protection, then?" she suggested. It was impossible to hide the bite in her voice. "Then you won't have to worry about putting yourself in danger for me."

Liam stared at her incredulously. "You think this is about the *pact?*"

"Isn't it?" Eve challenged. "You knew I was in danger, right? You—"

"Yes, I could sense that, but it's not—" Liam struggled to find the right words. "This has nothing to do with the pact."

Then what is it? Her thoughts demanded. *It can't be because you care.* Couldn't it?

Sure, he'd helped her bandage her wound when she'd cut herself. And he *did* come to rescue her from the Blood Court. Maybe they enjoyed spending time together, and had their own secrets together, and *maybe* Eve found herself preferring his company at a rate that alarmed her. But none of that meant Liam cared about her. He pitied her—Eve had seen it on his face.

Or she thought she had.

If Liam didn't pity her, what did he feel?

And why did *she* care?

The carriage ride back to the Bone Court was wrought with uncomfortable tension. Eve pointedly stared out of the window, determined to look at anything but Liam.

Regardless of their affection—if such a word was even accurate—she was still angry that he'd dismissed her hard work. It had been reckless, but necessary. Eve saw firsthand how sick Liam had become. Time was running out, and Eve couldn't afford to wait.

They were almost home when Liam finally spoke.

"Thank you," he murmured, so quietly that Eve wasn't sure he wanted her to hear. "For getting the lock of hair. It... it means a lot to me."

He didn't need to say that last part, but Eve was grateful that he did.

"You're welcome," she said softly. Her earlier anger fought to hold on, but Eve pushed it away. There was plenty for her to be mad at; Liam, for once, wasn't one of them.

"You must promise me not to do something that reckless again," Liam voiced seriously. "Not on your own. You should have asked me for help before you even thought about going there."

"It wasn't your responsibility. It was my quest. I—"

"You don't have to do everything alone," he cut her off. "You want to do everything on your own, and I understand that. I'm not experienced with asking for help myself. But rely on me or at least try to.

There are people that care about you, Evie. How many of them do you think you would have hurt if you'd died at the Blood Court today?"

Shame coiled inside as she immediately thought of Hailey and Nan. Her grandmother might not remember her, but Eve knew somewhere in her core that she would have been missed. That she *was* missed. And Hailey...

"Hailey would be crushed," Eve mumbled, more to herself than to Liam. "Nan, she... I think she'd be sad."

Liam nodded, turning his gaze away. "They aren't the only ones."

Eve didn't know what to say to that. She stared out of the carriage window instead, telling herself that the blush on her cheeks was due to the cold.

Twenty-Five

Hailey threw her arms around Eve the moment she stepped out of the carriage. Eve reflexively stiffened under Hailey's touch. Then she softened and gently hugged her back.

"Hey," she whispered. Her voice cracked, and she hugged Hailey tighter. Everything that had happened at the Blood Court came down on her all at once. Exhaustion pulled at her weary bones, and there was nothing Eve longed for more than a deep sleep.

"Where *were* you?" Hailey demanded, her serious voice pitched high with worry. " I thought you left, or you found a way home, or something happened to you, or—"

"Hailey," Liam interrupted. He stood close enough to Eve that she could smell the dew and smoke on his cloak. It reminded her of autumn rain. "I think Eve could use some time to recover, don't you?"

Hailey held Eve at arm's length and scrutinized her.

"I'm fine," Eve said as Hailey's frown deepened. "I'm just hungry and dehydrated."

"I'll get you something to eat," Liam promised.

"You don't have to—" He was gone before Eve could finish her objection. She wasn't given much time to mull over her confusion, either; Hailey clung to her arm and ushered her inside.

"Let's get you into a bath. You're *freezing*."

She was too tired to argue about her self-sufficiency as Hailey dragged her upstairs and heated up a warm bath.

Once Hailey left, Eve sank into the tub, savoring the water's burn against her flesh. Grabbing a bar of soap that smelled of cranberries, she scrubbed the blood and dirt from her flesh until her skin was as raw and pink as poultry. Eve raked her fingers through her blonde waves and scraped the grime from her scalp. She washed her freckled face three times until she decided it was clean.

The water was abhorrent when she stepped out of the tub. Eve tried not to think of how she must've looked—how she must have *smelled*—in the carriage. It had to have been a nightmarish sight if Liam didn't even crack a joke about it.

Stomach grumbling, Eve pulled on the silky nightshift Hailey had laid out for her and followed the scent of beef stew to the dining room.

"You're back."

Sage met her at the top of the stairs, her lilac hair loose and wavy around her waist. She did not hide behind a glamour this time, allowing her alien features to appear on full display: the pointed ears and shimmering skin. Pale green translucent wings on her back fluttered as she moved. Sage's golden eyes flickered over Eve, her cool gaze marred by the pinch of her eyebrows.

Eve didn't have it in herself to be kind tonight. "Upset you couldn't kill me yourself?"

The pixie scoffed. Whatever flicker of concern she'd displayed vanished. "Death from my hand would have been a mercy compared to what the Blood Court had in store for you."

Eve didn't doubt it. "You're not wearing your glamour."

"I'm not." Sage picked at one of her long nails with feigned interest. "Hailey demanded to see what I am."

"And?"

"Now we're not speaking."

Oh. A lot more had happened in her absence than Eve realized. She held a twinge of pity for Sage, despite her mind screaming that this girl had tried to poison her. She knew firsthand the betrayal of opening herself up to someone only to face their rejection. Her own parents could barely stand to acknowledge her.

People didn't want the truth. Truth made people question the things they believed and the friends they knew, warping their reality into something frightening and unknown.

Lies were comforting. They were safe. Easy.

Until they weren't.

Sage left, and Eve proceeded downstairs to enjoy the first hot meal she'd had in days. Each bite was a mouthful of heaven. Eve forced herself to eat slowly, lest she get nauseous from the heavy meal. Once she was full and satisfied, Eve retired to her room with Hailey in tow.

"You don't need to watch over me. I'm not going to go anywhere," she said as she absentmindedly straightened her room. It was too early to sleep, but Eve was anxious to be away from Hailey's and Liam's worried glances. They'd watched her eat with rapt attention, and if it weren't for how painfully hungry she was, Eve would have insisted they leave her alone.

"I know," Hailey said unconvincingly. She plopped down on the edge of Eve's bed, interrupting her attempt to adjust the duvet. "I missed you. I haven't had anyone to talk to."

"Like Sage?" Eve hadn't meant it to be a jab. Her threshold for conversation was horrendously low today. Still, she winced upon seeing the flash of hurt on Hailey's face. "Sorry. I didn't mean..."

"It's fine." Hailey pulled her hair out of her signature ponytail and nervously braided the locks over her shoulder instead. "We're not talking right now."

"I heard." Hailey cocked her head, confused. "Sage told me. I ran into her in the hall."

"Oh." She resumed braiding her hair, got to the end, undid it, and repeated it again. Eve thought Hailey was quite pretty with her hair down, but such a style wasn't practical for a basketball player.

If Hailey still wanted to be one. If they ever got back. Eve sighed and dropped onto the bed, collapsing onto her back with a thump.

"You really didn't know Sage was one of them?" she asked. Eve found it hard to believe. Even she suspected something was off about Sage before she saw the truth for herself. Hailey was dense, but she wasn't stupid.

"I mean, I knew *something* had to be off with her," Hailey admitted. "You've seen her family. She can't be *totally* normal. But she didn't tell me anything! Why wouldn't she tell me? She's my best friend!" She caught herself. "No offense, Eve. I don't mean—You're my best friend, too, I—"

Eve held up a hand before Hailey dug herself into a hole. "It's fine. Continue."

Hailey sighed in relief. "I just don't get it. Why wouldn't she tell me? Doesn't she trust me?"

"Maybe she was afraid you wouldn't react well," Eve pointed out. "Kind of like you're doing now."

Hailey bit her lip, abashed. "I'm not angry that she's different. I'm angry that she kept it a secret."

But that wasn't the only secret Sage was keeping from her. Or Eve, for that matter. Eve thumbed at the Fogtree family crest embroidered on the breast of her chemise.

What would Hailey say if she knew about the deal Eve and Sage had made to kill Liam? What about Sage's unrelenting love for her, or Eve's own plot to kill her rapists? Hailey was forgiving, but Eve wasn't naive enough to think she could overlook the stockpile of secrets that kept adding up.

"Sage said you knew about it once," Eve murmured, recalling a conversation she'd had with Sage in the meadow some weeks ago. It felt that ages had passed since then.

Eve separated time into two categories: before Faerie and after, with the latter occurring after her disastrous birthday party. Everything before was as blurry as fogged glass during a storm. What she experienced was real, yet incomplete. Eve had lived life through a haze of mundanity, accepting the pain wrought each day with all the tenderness of a cancerous sore.

As much as she loathed to confess it, living in Faerie had awoken something in her. Revenge was not a sin but a way of life for the Fair Folk. Lies and trickery came as easily as breathing, and Eve could indulge in such behavior without the fear of any god hanging over her shoulder. In Faerie, she was not a terrible girl. She was herself, as selfish and flawed as any other Faerie here. Eve could be *Eve*.

Hailey leaned against the bedpost to Eve's canopy. She tucked her knees up to her chin, her troubled expression only partially obscured by her hair. "That can't be right. I don't remember that."

"You don't remember a lot of things, Hailey."

"Yeah, that's kind of what ADHD does—"

"It's not the ADHD." Eve sat up, meeting Hailey's gaze. "What do you remember about your deal with Liam?"

"Liam?" Hailey startled. "What does he have to do with—"

"Just humor me."

Hailey hesitated, but Eve could almost see the wheels turning in her head. "It was late August, I think. I was, like, really upset, and I couldn't find him. I came here..."

The hollowness in her eyes was coming back. Eve pushed, "Then what?"

"Then..." Hailey tried to fight it. Eve could see it on her face, the way her lower lip trembled and her forehead scrunched in concentration. "I don't know. I know that it worked—I can't tell you why, it's just a feeling I have."

"Hailey." Eve gently touched her shoulder. "You can't remember because Liam took your memories."

Hailey's lips parted without a sound. Eve could see the puzzle pieces clicking in her eyes, one mystery snapping into place after another. "Why would he do that?"

"Because you asked him to."

A million questions flashed in her eyes. As the words sunk in, Hailey curled further into herself. "I didn't do that."

"You did. You just don't remember it."

The heavy confusion that clouded her face shifted as grim understanding took place. She swallowed hard, glancing down at her feet.

"I... I thought it was my ADHD," she whispered. "I forget things all the time. Like, that's just how it is. That's how it's always been.

But there are these... these gaps in my memory, where everything is cloudy and I can't see straight. People tell me things happened, but every time I try to remember, it's like I'm trying to hold on to a wet rope, and it keeps slipping away from me."

Eve's heart ached. "It doesn't have to be this way. You can ask Liam for your memories back. He can—"

"Do I *want* to remember?" Hailey cut her off. "You said I asked for this; do I even want those memories back? Everything God does is for a reason, right? If they're gone, I should trust His intentions and let it be, right?"

"God didn't make you forget your memories, Hailey," Eve said.

"Okay, but if God wanted me to remember them, He'd make it happen, wouldn't He?" Hailey pleaded with Eve for an answer she couldn't give. Hailey was trying to convince herself that this was the right thing. Eve didn't think it was.

"I'm not sure," Eve said. "Maybe that's something you need to ask Liam about."

"Maybe," Hailey agreed solemnly, although Eve suspected that was where her friend's intentions ended.

Humans, after all, feared the unknown.

Twenty-Six

Moonlight streamed across the still lake of the asrai, creating a single beam in the water's abyss. Eve wasn't sure how she got there. She wasn't sure the lake was even the right one. Something about the landscape was off, a poor imitation that didn't quite capture the real thing.

Eve searched for the stars, for the moon, noticing their absence. Acknowledging the wrongness of it all.

A figure appeared in the center of the lake. Dread cemented her in place as the water lapped at his ankles. Nick Palenti glared at Eve from the center, his body impossibly still. Impossibly whole.

Blood poured from the wounds in his head, leaky as rusted faucets. He did not try to stop them. Eve knew the lake was deep, but Nick did not tread. He stood, as if the water were thick enough to hold him in place.

Then he dropped.

Nick bobbed in and out of the water, gasping for air he couldn't reach. Scaly asrai with their webbed toes and vicious teeth circled him as the vibrant blood took over every ounce of the lake. It shimmered scarlet against the untouched snow at her feet.

The asrai chittered and cheered at this development. Their black hair pooled around their shoulders, shifting in the water. Nick gurgled and gagged on his own blood as he sank into the crimson lake. The asrai mimicked him between laughter, clawing up at the night sky. Their yellow eyes glowed with delight.

All at once, they turned to Eve. Her heart went still as their sharp, pointed grins stretched impossibly far across their pale blue faces.

Eve fled through the woods. She gasped each breath as she wound through the trees. Eve had explored much of the forest by now, but this part was unrecognizable. Fear held her in a viselike grip as Eve understood that she was lost.

The sensation of being stalked as prey stuck with her as she searched for familiar ground. The mansion, the arch, anything would do if she could orient herself.

Up ahead, the statue of High King Earnan stood forebodingly in a small clearing. Eve raced to the statue, relieved to find some semblance of familiarity.

The stone slab to the crypt was already ajar. Eve shoved it the rest of the way and climbed down.

As she descended two steps at a time, Eve realized the stairs did not lead to the Unseelie Court. The walls morphed as she walked, contradicting her memory as they shifted into something else entirely. But she was moving too fast. Her legs wouldn't obey the fear begging them to hold back.

Her hopes shattered as Eve fell into the Blood Court's dungeon—directly into her cell. She skidded to a halt, but it was too late—the door slammed shut behind her with a final locking *click*.

Let me out! she screamed, but no sound would come from her lips. She tried again, desperately rattling the bars. *Let me out! Let me out! Please! Let me out!*

She reached out to a passing guard, grasping the fabric of his sleeve. *Please! Let me—*

Colton smiled at her from behind the guard's uniform. His angular features were twisted, his brunette locks sticking out in unnatural angles under his cap. He snatched her wrist, pulling her close against the bars.

"You've committed terrible sins, Eve," he sighed. Eve tried to pull away, but he wouldn't budge. His touch made her skin crawl.

He reached for her throat. Eve clawed at his hand, but Colton was bigger. Stronger. He squeezed, his brown eyes dead and devoid of emotion as the oxygen cut off from her lungs.

Eve bolted upright in her bed. Something pierced her ears and burned her throat, a horrific noise that it lifted the hairs on her arms. Eve choked on the sound, sluggishly realizing that it was coming from *her*.

Clamping her mouth shut, Eve silenced her scream and frantically scanned the room. It was pitch-black now—the sun had been setting when she'd fallen asleep—and it took a moment for her eyes to adjust.

The Bone Court. That's right; she was still in her room at the Bone Court. Eve loosened her death grip on the sheets. Sweat clung to her skin in a film, sticking her nightdress and the sheets to her skin. Breathing deeply, Eve peeled the fabric away. *Gross.*

The nightmare played over in her head, the frightening images still fresh. Tears pricked her eyes as she recalled Colton's hand on her throat. It had only been a dream, but the terror had been real.

A sob hiccuped in her throat. Eve squeezed her eyes shut and brought her knees up to her chest. She buried her face into the fabric until she couldn't tell what stain was sweat and what was her own tears.

A knock at the door splintered her nerves. Eve's head shot up. After a beat of silence, she wondered if she'd misheard.

Another knock. Louder this time. Eve fumbled for the dagger under her pillow.

Adrenaline pumped through her veins as she swung open the door.

Liam stumbled back in confusion, his fist still raised for another knock.

He glanced at the dagger in her hand. "Is now a good time?"

Sheepishly, Eve lowered her weapon. "What are you doing here?"

"You were screaming," he said, taking in her tear-stained face and sweat-drenched nightgown. "I thought something happened."

"It was only a nightmare." Eve took a deep, shaky breath. Everything was fine. She was fine.

Liam lingered in the hall. "May I come in?"

Eve shrugged. She didn't have the strength to turn him away—not while she still struggled to calm her racing heart. She had no intention of going back to sleep anytime soon.

"I didn't mean to wake you up," she said, placing the dagger back under her pillow. Liam sat at the foot of her bed.

"You didn't. I've been having trouble sleeping."

"Is it...?" She gestured toward his torso. Liam nodded.

"Lying down is rather uncomfortable when you have a body made of stone." He laughed bitterly, knocking his fist lightly against his chest. It rapped against the rock under his tunic, solid and unyielding.

"That sucks."

"I've had more pleasant experiences," Liam admitted, his expression turning serious. "How are *you* faring?"

"I'm fine. I told you—it was a nightmare."

His voice softened. "I'm not talking about the nightmare."

Eve struggled to meet his gaze, busying herself with flattening out the creases in her skirt instead. "It's no big deal. My body needs to adjust to eating again, that's all."

"They didn't feed you that entire time?"

"I had some water."

Liam shook his head. "No wonder you were so weak when they brought you up."

"I'm not weak," Eve snapped. Liam held up his hands in defense.

"No, you're not," he agreed. "You... we were worried about you. We'd been searching for days. Preece finally told us where you had gone. You could have been hurt, or dead, or worse." Liam turned his haunted gaze toward the window. "When I saw Killian's guards bring you back upstairs... I can't express to you my relief."

Eve searched his face for the lie. It didn't make sense. She was a means to an end. Once she completed his quest, Liam would have no use for her.

He did not care about her. He couldn't. He... Maybe...

"People die all the time," she said. Liam cocked his head, waiting for her to continue. "I don't know why mine would cause you grief."

Liam flinched as though he'd been struck. Eve could see that he was thinking up a response, but whatever came to mind wasn't satisfactory. It took him a while to find the right words—or any words at all—to say.

"Hailey would be sad if you died." It was an excuse, and both knew it.

Eve scrubbed her tear-stained eyes with the back of her hands. "I don't know why that matters to *you*."

"Must you always have a reason?" Liam huffed indignantly. Beneath the red scales that dotted his face, Eve saw a hint of pink rise to his cheeks and the blackened tips of his ears. "Some things simply are."

That long forbidden affection stirred inside of her chest again. Eve tried to push it away, but every glance in Liam's direction—at his flustered expression that he desperately tried to hide—pulled her in.

Eve thought it would be impossible to feel this way again. She'd quashed the emotion more than once. Any time a creeping hint of a crush lingered, she'd strangle the thought and bury it with the others, abandoned and left to rot. Eve was better off on her own. It was too dangerous to get attached. Too dangerous to care.

Yet, no matter how many times she pushed Liam away, he always came back.

He's not human, she reminded herself with a tinge of sadness. *He doesn't feel the same things mortals feel.*

It was comforting. It was agonizing. Even if she developed a crush on Liam, his interest surely would not last—if it existed at all. They were still repairing their friendship. She wasn't ready to let it fall apart again.

"I still owe you," Eve said, quick to change the subject. Liam's brows furrowed.

"For what?"

"Saving me at the Blood Court. I don't know what you traded to help get me out of there, but it couldn't have been cheap." Liam grimaced, confirming her suspicion. "What is it you want? Within reason."

"I desire nothing in return," he said with the wave of his hand, as though the mere suggestion was foul.

"No. We're not doing this." Eve shifted on the bed to face him fully, tucking her legs under her. She sat taller, her face stern. "You've saved my life *twice.* I'm not letting you rack favors up until I can't pay them."

He found interest in everything but her face. "I have no intention of doing that, Evie. Believe me."

"Then why rescue me at all?" she pressed. "You're the one that told me favors come at a price. What is it?"

"*Nothing.*" His whole face was red now. Eve wanted to strangle him. "Would you kindly stop asking?"

"Not until you tell me what you want."

Liam finally met her gaze. His golden eyes burned as they bore into hers, yet she had never seen him so nervous. Even when she had put a knife to his throat. "You're certain you want to repay me?"

"Yes," Eve insisted. She wouldn't be caught with another debt to Liam that she couldn't repay. She wouldn't be pitied, either.

Liam's gaze softened. Something stirred in Eve's chest as he leaned closer, slow but deliberate. A sudden realization that she was alone with a boy in her room settled in. Fear struck her core. She wanted to repay her debt, but there were some things she could not do.

His gaze dropped to her lips. "Then allow me to kiss you."

Eve's brain short-circuited. She tried to process his request—and what the hell kind of motivation he had. Eve searched for a nefarious reason, some trick behind his words.

She found none.

"Just a kiss?" she finally asked.

"Are you asking for more?" Liam's brows rose in genuine surprise.

"No!" she squeaked. "N-No. No, no more. Just... a kiss. I wasn't expecting that. Are you... You're sure that's what you want?"

"It is." His voice was steady with conviction. She had no idea where it came from. No idea why he would *want* this.

Why *she* wanted this.

At another time, Eve might have panicked at such a suggestion and tried to toss him out the window.

But this was Liam, the boy who'd saved her life not once, but twice. The one who learned her boundaries, and when he apologized, meant it. He was the boy who frustrated her as much as he made her laugh, and had seen her in one of her darkest moments and didn't bat an eye.

Liam was the one whose attention kept flickering to her lips with each unsteady breath.

"Okay," she whispered, the word barely passing through her lips.

Liam moved toward her gradually, his gaze meeting hers as if to ask for permission for each inch he closed between them. Eve did not move. Her heart thundered in her ears when his soft fingers traced a line along her jaw, leaving a tingling sensation in their wake. His thumb stroked her other cheek with a gentleness she was unaccustomed to. He treated her delicately, as if she were something precious.

She almost wanted to tell him. The words hung on her parted lips, ready to confess what had been done to her. How ruined she was in the eyes of every man she'd ever known. How brittle and frail she still was inside, no matter how many times she told herself that such things had no meaning.

Eve couldn't bring herself to do it. She didn't want to ruin this moment, this rare instance, where someone's touch was magic instead of acid. Eve leaned lightly into his cupped hand, craving the kindness she found there.

Liam's lips pressed against hers, featherlight and fleeting. Eve's breath caught, unsure if it even happened, until his lips found hers again with more intention.

Admittedly, she did not know how to kiss. Such experiences had been stolen from her, but Liam did not mind. He guided her, first with his lips, and then with the gentle prodding of his tongue. She let him take the lead, bunching her skirt in her fists to quell the eager flips in her stomach.

The panic settled in. It came with the subtlety of a freight train in the night. Horrible memories flooded her vision, Liam's touch twisting into the unwanted advances of her past. The contrast was stark. The touches she'd endured were nowhere as gentle, but now her heart raced fast, waiting for Liam to push further. To cross that line.

He never did. Liam ended the kiss slowly, his fingers tracing lightly down her arm. His bashful smile eased some of the anxieties that twisted her heart—but they did not disappear altogether.

"Now, we're even."

Liam pressed his forehead to hers, the gesture as kinetic as another kiss, and pulled away. Eve watched, stunned, as he got up to leave. The bed suddenly felt cold in his absence. A part of her wanted to pull him back but couldn't bring herself to do it.

"Sleep well, Evie," he said from the doorway. "May sultry dreams of my beautiful face give you a different reason to wake up screaming."

He ducked out of the room, laughing, before her pillow could hit his face.

Twenty-Seven

There was no fear greater than that which came with vulnerability. To trust, to love, to care—all of that was easy, if kept to oneself.

Eve had broken a cardinal rule: do not let others in. If she should, do not let them know. How miserably she'd failed. What a frightening thing she had allowed.

And still, she could taste the blackberry on his lips.

If it were possible to rewrite history, this would have been her first kiss. Fumbling and awkward and anxious, but safe. Impossibly safe.

She shouldn't have let him kiss her last night. Eve had unraveled something that was better left alone. Even in the gentlest of touches, the fear lingered; a foul rot that blighted every ounce of tenderness she received. Men were never satisfied with idle kisses for long. They always asked for more, devouring the object of their desire until there was nothing left to take.

It had taken her almost three years to be comfortable with a kiss. The thought of anything beyond that was incomprehensible.

Things could only go downhill from here.

"You're up early," Eve half-yawned as she strode down the stairs. Liam lingered by the front door in the foyer, his gloved fingers pinching the laces on his boots. He fumbled with the strings nervously, tying and then retying them again when they came loose. The circles under his eyes told her that he hadn't slept much.

Neither had she.

"I'm trading in the items," he said. Eve glimpsed her twilight scarf peeking out of the pouch holstered to his hip. "I'm afraid our practice will have to wait until later."

"That's fine. Let me get my cloak."

Liam reached a hand out to stop her. "That's unnecessary. You would be better off here."

Eve hesitated on the stairs, grateful that she'd turned away so he couldn't see the hurt on her face. He'd barely glanced at her this morning. Had she wildly misinterpreted what had happened last night? Was his interest lost already?

She gripped the handrail tight. Insecurities pulled at her heart with the masterful tug of puppet strings.

Pathetic. This was what Sage had warned her about. What she knew would happen if she got too close. *"How long do you think it'll take before he gets bored and decides you get to be his next toy?"*

"Have fun," Eve said rancorously. "Don't turn to stone on your way there."

Liam peered at her, incredulous. "You're angry?"

"I'm fine," she snapped, trudging back up the stairs. Liam sighed and ran a hand over his tired face.

"Wait a moment, will you?" Tempted as she was to leave him there, Eve paused at the landing with a scowl. Liam finished tying his boots and readjusted his scarf. "Before you add me to your little killing spree, I want to clarify that I don't believe you should accompany me because I don't want you to get *hurt*, you dolt."

"For the pact?"

"No, Evie, not for the pact."

She shifted, fighting against the relief that bubbled inside of her. The warmth of knowledge that he didn't want to put her in danger. That was... new. She was usually an afterthought, her emotions a helpless casualty to the whims of others.

Eve was unused to people caring about her. Not as Hailey did. *Definitely* not as Liam did.

"You don't think I can handle myself?" Eve crossed her arms over her chest. If she squeezed hard enough, maybe she could contain her conflicting emotions forever.

Liam, ignorant of her inner turmoil, rolled his eyes. "Not everything revolves around your ability to hold a dagger, Evie. No, you shouldn't come because it is dangerous." Eve opened her mouth to argue. "*More* dangerous than the Blood Court."

"It can't be worse than the Blood Court."

Liam leveled his gaze. "Yes, it can."

That gave her pause. The Blood Court had been plenty dangerous, and Eve had managed to avoid the worst of it through sheer luck alone. Still, she'd survived. She had managed to befriend (perhaps that was too strong a word) the Yule Cat, too. A rare surge of confidence lifted some of the dread in her chest.

I will make them fear me, she reminded herself. Colton, Logan, the Fair Folk—all of them. Let them see how dangerous a woman scorned could be.

"Where are you going?" she asked finally. It didn't actually matter where he went—Eve had every intention of going, if only to prove how resourceful she'd become.

Liam must have seen her decision by the scowl on his face. "To see the Hag of Three."

"The what?"

"She is an ancient being that roams the land of Faerie," Liam explained with a grimace. "It is said by some that she is Fate itself, although that remains to be seen. I would not openly discuss her age, regardless. I quite prefer my head attached where it is."

"If she roams the land, how will you know where to find her?"

"There are ways to summon her. Usually with an offering." Liam shifted in front of the door. Eve caught him wincing as he bent his knee and stone ground together.

It progressed that far? Even though she couldn't see it through his thick clothes, Eve's gaze lingered on his chest where she'd last seen the stone crawling toward his heart. If there was anyone that should be worried about dangerous situations, it should be the man that couldn't move without pain shooting through his body.

"Do you have an offering picked out already?" she asked, unable to take her eyes off his chest. Was it moving across his body now as they spoke? How much longer until he turned to stone completely?

"I do." Liam sighed. "It should be a relatively quick exchange. You would better serve yourself with some sparring practice while I'm gone."

As if she was going to focus on parrying the air while he met with what was potentially Fate itself. Even if she wasn't worried about his health, Eve was too curious to pass this opportunity by.

Maybe she'll have some insight to killing Colton. He was still there, lurking in the woods—although Eve wondered if the cold had already done him in. How long could a mortal survive a winter in Faerie on their own?

I can ask her about the murderer instead. Finding a way home was more important, Eve decided. The High King wanted the killer's head, and Eve was glad to give it to him—if she could figure out where they were... and how to effectively decapitate them. She didn't exactly have a guillotine on hand.

"I'm going," Eve said decidedly. She turned back up the stairs, ignoring Liam's poor attempt to shuffle forward and stop her.

"Evie, don't be stupid."

Eve stopped short. "*Stupid?*"

Liam grimaced. "I am simply saying that you are being foolish—"

"*Foolish?*" Her voice rose, and Liam winced. "You think that I'm *stupid* and *foolish?*"

"On occasion, but—" Eve reached the bottom of the stairs and smacked his arm hard. Liam was ready to dig himself into another hole, but something in Eve's expression mercifully stopped him. "You want me to stop talking, I gather."

Eve glared. "That would be wise."

He sucked in a sharp breath through his teeth. "See you in the carriage, then?"

"If you leave before I'm ready, you'll wish I'd stabbed you at that party." She jabbed her finger in his chest for good measure before retreating upstairs.

When she returned to the carriage, properly dressed, Liam didn't object—but she could see the disapproval plain on his face.

He thumped the roof of the carriage with his fist. The carriage lurched forward.

It had not occurred to Eve when she insisted on accompanying Liam how awkward it would be riding alone with him for an indeterminate amount of time. It didn't help that the compartment was small, with Liam pressed against her side as they rolled over the snow-trodden road.

Eve stared through the frosted window, pretending to find interest in the mischievous snow sprites along the road. The smell of morning dew and smoke drifted from Liam's cloak. It drew her in, bringing with it memories of his fingers on her cheek and the softness of his lips. She wanted to bury her face in the fabric and soak it into her lungs.

Jesus Christ. She prayed he wouldn't see how red her ears were. What a fool she was. One kiss, and Eve had come undone.

"Did you sleep soundly for the rest of the night?" Liam asked, breaking the silence. She could practically hear the smirk in his voice. "Any pleasant dreams?"

Damn it. He definitely noticed.

"No," she answered evenly. "I didn't dream at all."

"Hm," Liam hummed, but didn't press her. That was odd. Eve had half-expected him to tease her—perhaps mock her as he'd done upon their first meeting—but he didn't. He hadn't in quite some time.

Was she being too harsh on him? Eve clasped her hands tightly in her lap. If this was all a ruse to poke and prod at her insecurities, Liam had several opportunities. Instead, he'd been kind. Considerate, even, as much as Eve mentally rallied against it.

And that kiss... Maybe she hadn't misinterpreted what he meant after all.

"I knew you should have stayed back," Liam said, pressing a hand to her burning forehead. "Are you ill? You look terrible."

"What every girl wants to hear." Eve smacked his hand away with more force than intended.

Liam, to his credit, realized his mistake and grimaced. "I only meant that you haven't taken nearly enough time to recover—from the Blood Court *or* the belladonna. Mortals are fragile. I fear that you are pushing yourself beyond your limits."

He had a point, even if Eve was too stubborn to admit it. She *was* exhausted; every limb in her body ached, and the slight nausea in her stomach had not gone away since she was first poisoned. Eve tried to be diligent with her weapon training. She spent extra hours practicing in her room, but Eve found herself making careless mistakes, the effectiveness of her training tampered by her body's limitations.

What else was she supposed to do, though? She needed that favor from the High King. If she wanted to find a way home, failure was not an option.

"I'm not sick," Eve said. She blinked heavily—the snow outside was too bright to stare at for any length of time. "Tired, maybe. I'll be fine."

Liam shifted in his seat. "It may not be comfortable, but I tend to sleep against the window. Or, if you prefer—" He gestured at the space between them, offering his arm as a place of rest.

Hesitantly, Eve leaned against him, burying her face in his cloak. Liam stiffened, then relaxed, tentatively draping an arm around her side. Exhaustion from the past few days weighed her down.

I'll only close my eyes for a few minutes, she told herself. The scent of autumn rain filled her head, and the moving carriage gently rocked her to sleep.

Twenty-Eight

"We're here," Liam whispered, nudging her awake.

Eve grumbled as she sat up, squinting against the bright reflection pouring in from the snow. "How long was I out?"

"Not long," he reassured her with a grin. "Did you know that you snore?"

She reeled on him. "I do *not.*"

"You most certainly do. Unless you can name another beastly creature in this carriage."

"*Beastly?*"

"Not that *you're* beastly, per se." Liam raised his hands in defense. "I am only implying that it sounds incredibly similar to a mangled goat—"

Eve shoved away from him. How she had even *considered* having a crush on this jerk was beyond her. Eve climbed out of the carriage, her boots tromping through the snow gracelessly. Liam chuckled, following behind.

The forest was eerily still as they ventured through the woods. Twisted trees cast dark shadows over the ground, their branches a web of knots and bark dense enough to hide the sky. The snow remained untouched by footprints or debris, aside from the soft crunch of Eve's own feet. Not even the calls of birds broke through the silence.

Patches of briar poked up between the snow, creating a fence between the trees. The tangled thorns grew taller as they ventured forward, stretching high as fortress walls. Eve and Liam followed the path between them until they reached a small tunnel formed by the briars.

Liam crouched first, hunching low as he shuffled forward. Eve went in after, cursing under her breath as she was poked, prodded, and scraped by the mess of thorns. Some caught her hair, yanking hard on the curls.

They came out into a hut made of a briar patch. It was large—tall enough for Eve and Liam to comfortably stand—and warmer than she had expected. The briars were too dense to let in snow, and a thick layer of yellow straw kept the earthen floor dry.

Liam removed a spool of charcoal thread from a pocket in his cloak and buried it beneath the straw. Then they waited. Eve did not breathe a word as the air shifted around her. A magnetic electricity clicked into place, raising the hairs on her neck and arms.

"Little lordling, returned at last," a voice rasped from the shadows. *"As fate would have it before he passed."*

In the dark, Eve could not tell if this was one woman or three. The figure shifted in number, never settling on one—or two, or three—for long. She was twice as tall as Liam and hunched in the briar hut as if it could barely contain her. A black robe hid her body, but her skeletal face was ancient, with onyx pits where her eyes ought to have been.

Eve understood now why Liam was hesitant for her to come. If there were gods in this world, this creature was undoubtedly one of them.

The woman—for it appeared feminine, although Eve could not be certain—snatched the spool of thread from the ground and examined it up close. *"Uncertain, the choices he will make. Determined, his resolve will stay."*

"I brought what you requested," Liam said, removing the pouch from his waist. The hags' empty eye sockets—for there were three of them standing there now—widened with delight.

Liam emptied out the pouch onto the straw. Eve recognized a few of them—the butter turkey from Thanksgiving, Killian's lock of hair, her scarf the shade of twilight—but then he removed more. A molar with a silver filling. A vial of red-orange berries. Two identical coins of unknown currency.

Eve didn't recognize any of the extra stuff. Was there more to the riddle than what Liam had told her? Did he search for these by himself?

The hag was against the wall—and then she was not. Eve lurched back as the crone reappeared several feet closer, crouched low to the ground. She inspected each item before tucking them away individually into the void that was her robe. Eve wasn't entirely sure she wore fabric at all and not the night itself.

"A name as fleeting as the sun?" she asked, peering up at Liam. More voices chimed in—her own, but echoed. Eve fought against a shudder.

"Mary," Liam said, his tone less certain. "I give you Eve's... the name..."

"My confirmation name," Eve cut in. "It was part of my name for a year or so, but not anymore."

The hag observed Eve with the sharp cock of her head. Her empty eye sockets bore into Eve, their darkness as vast and all-seeing as space itself.

"A name as fleeting as the sun, accepted from the vindictive one," the hag decided. She was in front of Eve instantly, her wrinkled face inches from Eve's own. With one clawed hand, the hag reached into Eve's chest, carving through her flesh like pudding.

Eve gasped, but it was not her skin the hag was piercing. The invasion was deep in her soul, the hag's claws caressing her core. The hag plucked something from within her and tore it out, snapping it from Eve with the flick of her wrist. A small, white wisp of smoke rested between her fingers.

The hag inhaled it deeply through her nose. Eve pressed her hands flat against her chest, keenly aware of the hollow spot where her confirmation name had resided.

Liam watched her with grave concern. Neither of them had expected that. "Evie?"

"Unscathed she will be." The hag waved him off, pulling the scarf from her robe to wipe her nose. *"The little lording, not so."*

"What do you mean?" Liam hedged.

The hag tsked, twisting the colorful scarf between her brittle hands. *"Idle hands make idle cures. Time halts for none."* She pointed a bony finger at his chest. *"To the heart it will finish before I am done."*

Eve's stomach lurched. *I was too late.*

She dared a glance in his direction, noticing how still he'd become. Shame burned deep inside of her. If she hadn't wasted time getting the items, this could have been avoided. Liam could have been saved.

Eve wondered if he was thinking the same thing.

"What do I do?" Liam asked evenly.

The hags pursed their lips and repeated, *"To the heart it will finish before I am done."*

Liam slumped, crestfallen. Everything he'd been working toward for the past few months—maybe longer, considering how much he offered—crumbled at his feet.

And Eve had let it happen.

Eve spoke up. "There has to be something we can do to stop it. Anything."

"To the heart—"

"What about after?"

At this, the hags smiled with thin lips that peeled back against their skull. *"Blood from stone, bind with thine own. Ash to root, a seed awaiting her fruit—lay to rest, the newt."*

Eve and Liam exchanged a cautious glance. More riddles?

The hag—singular, now—turned to leave.

"Wait." Eve reached for the hag but quickly thought better of it, drawing her hand back. "I need your help. There's someone I'm searching for. I need to bring their head to the High King."

The hags' gazes narrowed. "*Huntress, we are not.*"

"I can do the dirty work myself," Eve said. "I just want to know who they are and how to kill them."

The hag stared past Eve with a vacant expression, as though she were seeing something beyond the briars that the others could not. "*That which you seek has hunted before.*"

"Hunted the Fair Folk?" Eve asked, confused.

"*You.*"

Eve's blood ran cold. She swallowed hard, understanding settling deep in her gut.

"Colton," she murmured. A question. The hags did not answer—their hard, scrutinizing gaze was confirmation enough.

He's murdering the Fair Folk, she realized. A new, sickening fear rattled her bones. The not-deer's mutilated body stained the back of her mind in a permanent fixture. If he was capable of doing *that,* what would he do when he found *her*—his best friend's killer?

The hags' arms suddenly drove into the straw. The one in the center pulled out a silver sewing needle and offered it to Eve. The others' hands stayed empty. "*Bind the threads with no eye, unravel the ones seen.*"

What the hell does that mean? she wondered but knew there was no point in asking.

"What do I owe you for this?" Eve asked, twisting the metal between her fingers. The thin needle pulsed against her skin, alive with a magic she could not name.

"*Free those which have been cast in stone, behold an empire grown. A new age is upon us.*" Their eye sockets widened as they chanted, "*A new age is upon us.*"

"I—"

"*A new age is upon us.*"

"*A new age is upon us.*"

"A new age is upon us."

The hags vanished.

Twenty-Nine

It was a solemn ride back to the Bone Court. Eve stared out of the window, squinting past the frost toward the barren trees. Their carriage bounced over compacted snow, shifting the company inside.

Eve shivered, drawing her cloak tighter. She twisted the sewing needle between her fingers, then shoved it in her pocket. What use would this be? It didn't even have a hole for thread.

More riddles and not a moment spared to solve them. She glanced at Liam, who had not spoken a word since they left the briar hut.

He's dying. She had been too late. The Hag of Three offered the solution with another riddle, but how was she meant to solve it before Liam transformed entirely?

Another glance in Liam's direction told her that this truth weighed on him as well. She wanted to reach across the gap between them and squeeze his hand. To tell him everything will be alright—that they would find a way to fix this.

But she didn't know that they could. To instill false hope was cruel, so she did nothing, letting the tension settle between them with the heaviness of a funeral procession.

Liam adjusted in his seat. When he did speak, it was not the conversation she'd expected.

"What did the hag mean? About Colton being the hunter?"

Eve played with the hem of her dress, picking at the thread until it was loose. She almost wished he'd focused on his inevitable death instead. "Probably because he's hunting Fair Folk."

"We both know that's not what she meant," Liam said. "She said he hunted you, specifically. Is this why you wanted to kill them all?"

Yes. She stared at her lap, unraveling the lace on her skirt. "I don't want to talk about it."

Liam was quiet for a moment. His eyes lingered on her, searching her face for clues. Eve worked to keep her expression neutral. He didn't need to worry about her. No one did. Eve was no damsel in need of rescue—she was a monster, a demon worthy of her parents' litany of insults and more. She'd killed a man and would do it again. *Wanted* to do it again.

Letting Logan go had been a mistake, a moment of weakness. It was not one she would be repeating.

"They did something to you." There was an edge to his voice that Eve took for pity. Her anger flared.

"I *don't* want to talk about it."

"Evie... Whatever happened, you can tell me. I want to understand."

His earnestness caught her off guard—but it was not enough to convince her. "You couldn't understand if you tried."

"Won't you *let* me try?" he urged. Eve ignored him, her stomach twisting in knots. There was too much conflict inside of her—to tell him or not to tell him? To hate the pity on his face or crave the moment of vulnerability he'd let her have? The walls she'd built were crumbling around her and solidifying again, unable to take solid shape. Unable to protect her.

Liam reached for her hand, but Eve pulled away. "What did they do to you?"

"Don't."

"Evie—"

"Shut up!" It was too much. She didn't know what she wanted or who she could trust. Eve pulled back sharply, her breath coming fast and short. Last night she almost told him, but today the truth clawed in her throat, grasping her bloody heart until it threatened to stop beating.

You're fine, she told herself. *You're fine. Everything is fine.* But Eve was unraveling like the loose threads of her dress. The thought of Liam knowing how she'd been violated terrified her. She knew the way his face would twist into grim understanding, the judgment and pity she'd faced a thousand times over, coming back to fruition. There wasn't a soul she'd told who hadn't found fault in her own actions. Her own appearance. Why would Liam be any different?

She'd rather he see her as strong. Frightening, even. Eve wanted Liam to think twice if he ever thought of touching her the wrong way. She wished to be as vicious as any other Faerie in the Unseelie Court.

If he knew what happened to her—

The carriage jolted. The wispy horses outside cried out and picked up speed. Eve grasped the door handle to keep balance as she fell forward against the opposite seat. The carriage rattled and bounced over the forest debris as it veered off course.

Liam tried to open the door to see what was happening. The horses took a sharp turn. Eve shrieked as the compartment teetered onto its side—and crashed into the nearest tree.

Their movement stopped. Eve sat up uncertainly, pulling her hand away from the broken glass and the cracked window underneath her. Liam rubbed his head. Eve guessed he had knocked it in the fall.

"You okay?" she asked, hoping that nothing had broken.

"Only a bump," Liam reassured her.

"What was that?"

"I'm going to find out." He shifted onto his knees and tried to unlatch the door now above them. It took effort, both because of Liam's current state and the crushed roof that had pinched the door out of shape. Liam eventually managed to toss it open, letting in a cold burst of air.

Liam took one glance over the side before shutting himself back in.

"The driver's dead," Liam said. He settled onto the floor of the carriage with a grunt, propping himself up against the sideways seat. "He's been shot through with an arrow."

An arrow?

Eve unsheathed her dagger and moved to push the door open again.

"What are you doing?" Liam demanded, grasping the hem of her skirt to stop her. Eve shoved him off with the nudge of her boot.

"We can't stay here," she said, carefully peering out of the door. All she could see was the empty forest.

"Isn't that more reason to stay inside the carriage?" Liam argued. "Or are you hoping to get shot?"

"I'm not going to be a sitting duck," she said, climbing out of the door.

Liam grumbled something under his breath, but he followed after her, rolling off the carriage's surface with another grunt. Eve used the side of the carriage as a shield, ducking behind it until she maneuvered her way around to the dead driver.

Beneath the cloak, the driver was more skeleton than man, with his skin pulled tight and an unnervingly impassive face for someone shot through the neck. Blood soaked his cloak, but based on the artery hit, it must have been a mercifully quick death. Eve was glad for that, at lea—

Liam yanked her back against his chest. An arrow whizzed by where she'd stood, narrowly missing her head.

The duo snapped their attention in the direction it had come from. A figure stood in a narrow gap in the trees, the white fur of his cloak disguising him against the snow. Her heart dropped. Recognition flashed across his face.

Eve. Colton mouthed the word, too far for her to hear. Eve dared not move. Dared not *breathe.* The needle pulsed in her pocket, small and useless.

There was a fondness in the softening of Colton's expression as he lowered his bow that nearly made her puke.

The bastard had the nerve to *smile.*

A blind, wild rage overtook her. Eve raced forward, nearly tripping through the snow as she ran as a bull rushes to red.

The dagger was an extension to her arm, and Eve imagined all the terrible ways she could stab him with its blade. A horrible, thrilling glee sent shivers down her spine at the mental image of his blood staining her feet as she carried her prize to the High King.

This was what she had been missing from Logan's botched assassination. A primal, visceral hatred shuddered through her. It serenaded her bloody hunger like a lost lover returned home. She would kill him, just as he had done to her.

Eve focused on the soft flesh of his neck and pulled her dagger back—

"I thought you were dead," Colton said, and pulled her into his arms.

The world grew cold. Eve stumbled, nearly choking from the shock. Colton held her close and sighed in relief, his grimy fingers running through her hair.

Don't touch me! Don't touch me, don't touch me, don't touch me! her mind screamed. Blood and iron wafted from him, but it was the touch of his hands her that made her skin crawl. Even the press of his body against her through his thick cloak made her nauseous, but the shock of his hug left her speechless and immobile.

"When I saw your necklace by Nick's clothes, I thought you'd died too," Colton explained obliviously. Bile rose in her throat. "Logan and I searched everywhere for you. I knew you were here, and I'd hoped you were alive, but—Well, I should have known the demons kidnapped you."

His words were muffled static in her ears. As the shock wore off, panic settled in. He was too close. His hold was too tight. Eve's breaths came short and sharp, her lungs unable to pull in enough air.

"Let go," she gasped. Her head was dizzy, her heart beating too fast. A scream caught in her throat. Eve was malfunctioning as the pieces she'd spent ages putting back together broke apart at an alarming speed.

Colton did not hear her. Or he chose not to. He was talking, but the words did not pass through her ears. All she could hear were the alarms blaring in her skull.

Let go.

Let go!

"LET GO!"

Eve did not remember doing it, but her blade pressed beneath his cloak, digging into soft flesh. Colton gasped and shoved her away, one hand pressed against the wound she'd inflicted on his side.

A wicked sense of satisfaction fell over her. The voice in her head was buzzing with delight, craving more. She moved to stab him again, but Colton was prepared this time. He threw her back into the snow, her head barely missing one of the trees' trunks.

"Oh, Eve," Colton sighed with pity. He pulled a bloody hand away from his side and held his bow tight. His white tunic and green trousers were ill-fitting, clearly scavenged from one of the Fae. "They've gotten to you. Did you forget to beware of false prophets?"

"Eve!" Liam's voice bellowed from behind. She glanced back in time to see Liam duck to the side, missing one of Colton's arrows from a few yards away. Colton was a good shot. A horrifyingly good shot.

He must have mistaken the fear on her face for admiration. Colton regarded her with a bashful smile. "My father used to take me hunting every year. It was a relief to find that these demons use the same tools. I'm not sure how I would have survived this winter otherwise." His laugh grated on her ears. "I'll admit, I'm rusty, but the hunt isn't all that different—it's only the prey that's changed."

Colton readied his bow again, but Eve dove in front of him—and promptly threw up on his cloak. Colton grimaced in disgust. It wasn't the sort of disarming she'd planned on, but it got the job done.

"Don't," she gasped, then retched again before steadying herself. "Don't shoot him."

"Demons don't deserve to live, Eve," Colton said gently. "You don't know the sins these creatures commit. The lengths they'll go to for corruption."

"Humans are no better," she spat. "You've done worse."

Colton appeared solemn. "I have repented for my sins, Eve. God has forgiven me for all that I've done. If not for these demons and their endless temptations, none of it would have happened. It is not me you're angry at—it's them."

"No," Eve growled. "It *is* you I'm fucking angry at. You—You—" Her eyes stung with fresh tears. Her entire body shook, angrier than she had ever been. It was as if a black hole had opened in her heart, threatening to swallow everyone with it. "You fucking *raped* me. All *three* of you."

"Under *their* influence," Colton argued, his voice pleading. "Can't you see it? It's all real. Everything the Bible has warned us about. *They* are the ones doing this. It's *their* fault."

That destroyed her. Eve could accept the disgusting enjoyment from Nick, the remorse from Logan, but to refuse any accountability, to find a scapegoat for his actions? To not even apologize?

Eve would not merely be content to kill Colton. She would revel in it.

She swung her dagger again, moving as Liam had taught her. Colton stumbled back, the wound in his side bleeding into the once again pristine fur of his cloak. It faded away with what Eve could only assume was some kind of magic. Which Faerie had he killed to steal this from?

Colton readied his bow again. Eve knew without thinking that it couldn't kill her—she was too close. Whatever strength he put behind the pull would be useless from where she—

He released the arrow. It flew past Eve, missing at a wide berth.

Liam cried out in pain.

Thirty

Eve saw red. Liam collapsed onto one knee, gripping the arrow that struck his good arm. She turned on Colton and swung her dagger recklessly, screaming with every bit of rage that festered inside of her. Those fantasies of his death were nothing compared to what she dreamed of now.

She would paint Killian's entire dining room with Colton's blood. She would wear his intestines as jewelry. His family jewels would be fed to Liam's horses, and she'd mount his head on the wall as her finest trophy. She would make even Evren blush with her brutality.

Perhaps she belonged in the Unseelie Court after all.

Colton used his bow as a shield, the well-crafted item clearly another one of his spoils from the hunt. It irked her even more that he should condemn the Fair Folk yet use their things as if they were his own.

"You're making a mistake, Eve," Colton chided, dodging a blade to the face. Eve wished it had taken his eye out. "Don't get hysterical. He's manipulating you."

"You don't get to *say* that!" Eve screamed with her full chest. Her throat burned raw, and yet he hadn't heard a word she'd said.

"We need to go." Liam's distant rasp barely registered in her ears. The fire in her gut propelled her forward, one strike at a time. *"Eve."*

"I know Liam," Colton said. "He led me astray, too." Eve winced as Colton's bow smacked hard against her hand, but she did not relinquish her dagger. "Let me save you. God can—"

"There is no God," she spat. "And He sure as hell won't save you from me."

Eve took another swipe. Colton gritted his teeth as the blade nicked his cheek. He slapped her with the back of his hand and Eve reeled, catching herself on one of the trees. Her cheek stung red.

"Eve!" Liam shouted. He tried to move, but a smear of stone crawled up his neck to his chin.

"I don't enjoy hitting women," Colton said gravely. "But I won't take your assault." He took a deep breath and stepped forward. His face was drawn in pity. "You'll forgive me when this is over."

Eve would never forgive him for anything for as long as she lived.

Colton swung his bow hard against her temple. Sharp pain rattled through her skull. Eve crashed into the too-bright snow, stunned. Ringing pierced her ears as she tried to orient herself.

There wasn't time to think. Colton aimed his bow at Liam, the shot clear.

Eve fumbled with the dagger in her palm and stabbed Colton in the leg.

The priest howled in pain. Eve snatched the blade from his leg, tugging the wound, and scrambled to her feet. Colton swung at her with his bow and missed. Blood dripped in red splotches down his leg as he shuffled forward and drew another arrow.

Eve raced to Liam's side, her boots crunching against the ground as she helped him to his feet. With a glance over her shoulder, she saw that Colton had fallen on his injured leg and struggled to find his footing. A spike of pleasure ran through her at the sight of his agony.

"We need to go." Liam tugged on her arm, his wince of pain bringing her back to reality. She nodded, and they slipped through the trees.

When Eve glanced back, Colton was gone, leaving a path of red splotches in his absence. She must have cut him deeper than she realized.

Liam winced when his wounded arm swung too far.

"Are you okay?" she asked.

"Are you referring to the arrow stuck in my arm or the disease steadily rendering my body uninhabitable?"

"I meant to walk home." Eve grimaced, glancing at the wreckage of the carriage. "But all of it applies."

"I can walk," Liam said, although they both knew that there wasn't much of a choice. The road home loomed ahead in bitter frost and a darkening sky. "If we move quickly, we'll be back before nightfall."

Eve matched Liam's staggered pace on their trek back. She watched him in her peripheral vision, worrying at the corner of her lip until it bled. His limp worsened in the cold, and Eve's fingers twitched to catch him should he fall.

It was his face that stopped her from assisting. Anger clouded his expression, worsening with each silent moment that ticked by. Eve couldn't help thinking that it was directed at her. She was the one that made them leave the carriage. The one that picked a fight with Colton. Who failed to deliver the items of his quest on time.

Guilt ripped through her sharper than a blade. Not the kind built from Catholic shame, but a true failure that was all her own.

"I'm sorry," she said, her voice too loud in the quiet forest.

Liam's step faltered. "You aren't to blame."

"I am. I shouldn't have made us leave the carriage. Hell, I should have never asked you to kill them for me in the first place."

"You had a good reason," Liam said firmly. Regret flashed across his face. "I should have killed them when you asked me to. I didn't... I never thought they'd..."

Her cheeks burned as his implication settled in. Eve had forgotten Liam was there, listening to her rant at Colton. To what had happened.

Eve ducked her head and shoved her shaking hands into the thick pockets of her cloak. She couldn't bear to see the judgment on his face.

Her fingers brushed against the silver needle. The pulsing had stopped when Colton left.

Should I have tried to use this against him? Would it have even made a difference? What could this measly thing do? What could *she* do?

God, she was going to be sick again. The tops of her boots blurred in her line of vision, and Eve had to blink away the stinging tears in her eyes before they could pool over.

The lack of Liam's footsteps registered too late. Eve nearly stumbled into his chest, surprised to find that he'd blocked her path and forced her to face him. She tried to avert her gaze, but the stuttering of her heart made it impossible. Eve half-gasped a sob. Liam reached for her, but she glared up at the trees instead, willing her burning eyes to dry.

"Don't," she said fiercely. "I don't need pity."

"I don't pity you." Liam sounded truly baffled, but Eve didn't trust herself to look for confirmation. "I could never pity you." He swallowed hard, struggling to meet her gaze in turn. "I've failed you in one of the highest regards I can. I don't know how I will make it up to you yet, but I will do everything in my power to make this right."

Eve sniffed. There was no pushing the tears back now. She quickly scrubbed her eyes with the edge of her cloak. "I want to kill them myself."

"Then I will make it happen." His gloved hands slipped into hers, gentle but firm. Eve finally met his eyes, his face blurring in and out of focus with her tears. "Make use of me as you wish. Use me, command me, break me; I am your willing pawn. I ask only one thing in return."

Magic always came at a cost. "What's that?"

Liam gently brushed a tear from her cheek. "Make them suffer thrice the torture they put you through."

Thirty-One

Liam, despite all his bravado, was an utter wimp when it came to first aid.

"Would you hold still?" Eve snapped, dipping a clean rag into her bowl of antiseptic. She'd managed to pull the arrow out of his arm, leaving it in two broken, bloody pieces on the floor, but he'd been relentless in avoiding her medicinal care. "I need to make sure it doesn't get infected."

Liam shifted uncomfortably on the bathroom stool, jerking his exposed forearm out of reach. "Can't you bandage it up instead?"

"And let it fester? No." Eve yanked him forward by the wrist and pressed the cloth to his wound. "How were you fine taking an arrow but not this?"

"I had other things on my mind," he grumbled. "That doesn't mean it didn't hurt."

"Less than this?" Eve held up the rag dubiously.

"The arrow doesn't *sting*."

"That's the dumbest thing I've ever heard." He tried to pull his shirt sleeve down, but Eve smacked his hand away. She opened the jar of healing salve—the jar was already half-empty from her own use. "Don't be such a baby. I'm not *torturing* you."

"Aren't you?" he grumbled.

"Poor Liam," Sage said from the doorway, startling them both. "Did someone drop a thistlebee's nest on you again? Nasty little creatures."

Liam glowered at her. "That hasn't occurred since *you* dropped one on me."

"It was an accident." Sage smiled. "I never intended for them all to attack you."

"I have my doubts about that," Liam muttered. He hissed between his teeth as Eve seized the opportunity to apply the healing salve to his wound.

Sage took in Liam's battered state and the broken arrow with curiosity. "What *did* happen?"

For a moment, Eve worried that Liam's disease had been exposed. She searched his upper body, relieved to find that he was still covered aside from his wounded arm. A creep of gray peeked out at his elbow. Eve prayed Sage wouldn't notice.

"None of your concern," Liam said, shifting to move his injury from Sage's view.

"Did you anger the wrong Faerie again, Liam?" Sage cocked her head with a vicious grin. Her lilac hair swayed with delight, buoyant with her amusement. "Don't tell me you fought with Killian again."

"Killian?" Eve raised her brows at Liam, but he refused to meet her gaze. "The *Blood Court* Killian?"

"Who else?" Sage tapped her long nails against the door's frame. "Liam's brother is quite a handful, isn't he?"

"*Half* brother," Liam snapped. He softened at Eve's stunned stare. "Through my mother's side; he has no claim to the Bone Court. This has nothing to do with him."

"What trouble did you get into, then?" Sage asked before Eve could question Liam further.

"Why do you care?"

"Because someone has to be responsible for maintaining relationships with our clientele," Sage scoffed. "What remains of it, anyway."

"What is that supposed to mean?" Already Liam appeared as though he regretted asking.

"Father tells me the Faerie murderer has become a real thorn in the side of the nobles. Fair Folk are turning up dead. Mutilated." Sage's gaze flickered to the broken arrow on the floor, then back to her brother. "You've already heard that the High King wants his head."

"He's offering a boon for it," Eve said quietly. Sage snapped her attention to Eve, as if she'd forgotten she was there.

"It would be foolish to pass up the opportunity." Primal hunger shined in Sage's gold eyes. "The only thing Evren loves more than his wine is a sport of bloodshed. If I bring him the head of the man murdering half of his clientele, then he has to make me his heir."

"You'd give Father the High King's boon?" Liam asked warily.

"I've considered it," Sage said. "Or, perhaps, I will take it myself. Evren will be satisfied either way."

Liam swallowed carefully. Eve couldn't be certain which was worse—Evren with any boon of his choosing, or Sage with her vendetta.

Sage noticed their uneasy glances and scowled. "You want out of this annoying competition as much as the rest of us. The sooner I finish, the sooner you can go home."

"You actually plan on letting me go home? After everything?" Eve challenged. Sage did not respond right away, but Eve saw her reluctance. That was good. Maybe. "What would you ask for as a boon?"

"A way for Hailey to love her, I'd guess," Liam cut in. "Or to make her happy in some way or another while my sister rules the world. You're doing this because she still won't speak to you. Is that correct?"

He directed the second part toward his sister, whose face twisted with rage. Eve thought her braids might extend out to slap Liam across the face.

"I want to inherit the Bone Court. You've always known this."

"You want to be respected by our father, and you believe the court will give you that," Liam countered. "Tell me, Sage, will Hailey still respect you once you've tricked her into loving you?"

"I would never do that to her. She already loves me." But Sage's shoulders hunched as the fight left her in a puff of smoke. Uncertainty crept into her voice, whispering across the worried pinch between her brows.

"Even so," Liam said gently. "Do you think that will continue if you inherit the court and everything that comes with it? Duties and all? Consider it, Sage. What is more important to you?"

Sage's nails dug into the wooden door frame, anchoring her there. She stared at her brother with a mixture of anger and betrayal—but most of all, fear. Eve could see the knowledge settling in—the realization that Liam was right.

What did Sage love more? Power or Hailey?

The pixie collected herself and presented a smile befitting of an ice queen. "The heir chooses what happens to the losers in this game, Liam. Remember that."

Sage left the room with the sharp flap of her wings to carry her out. Eve watched her go, fighting against the uneasy twist in her stomach.

"Are we finished, then?" Liam stood to leave. Eve lightly shoved him back onto the stool. She was still nursing a slight headache, and Sage's visit had done nothing to help.

"Let me put the bandages on first," she murmured. For once, Liam didn't put up a fight as she wrapped his arm.

A familiar numbness blanketed her emotions as she worked. The events of the past few days weighed on her. All Eve wanted to do was curl up in a duvet and hibernate until spring. What was the point of fighting to escape if every decision she made led her down the wrong path? Eve was drowning, and it was getting harder to beg for air.

Liam nudged her lightly with his shoe. She hadn't realized that she'd finished bandaging his arm. Eve picked up the medical supplies and returned them to the closet with effort.

"You're quiet," he said.

"I'm tired."

"If this is about Killian—"

Eve snapped the lid to the healing salve's jar shut. "Why didn't you tell me he was your brother?"

Liam reached for her as he stood but dropped his arm as he thought better of it. Good. This was how things ought to be. She should have never let him in in the first place. "I didn't think it mattered."

"After warning me about him, after everything I went through in the Blood Court, you didn't think it *mattered?*"

Liam glanced down in shame.

It shouldn't bother her. Liam was allowed to have secrets—God knew she had plenty herself. It wasn't as if they were dating, either. They had only shared a kiss—those things meant nothing to people her age.

Yet, it stung. Betrayal burrowed deep within her, wrapping its thorns around her heart. There was a reason Eve did not grow attached to others; the walls she'd built had made a fortress to protect her. But Liam had chipped at the stone until the cracks were too large to ignore. He left a gaping hole in his wake that left her vulnerable and weak.

He must have seen the ice that frosted her heart, because Liam stepped forward and grasped her hands in his. Eve flinched away, but he held firm, the stone on his hand beneath his glove solid and unyielding.

"You're angry," he said softly. His voice took on an edge of pleading. "I should have told you, but he is not someone I want in my life. Preece is the only brother I care to acknowledge."

Eve could sympathize with that. There were plenty of people she wished to remove from her life entirely. "Still, you could have asked him for his hair."

"You've seen how he despises the Bone Court, Evie," Liam argued. "He would have never given it to me."

"Then *I* could have handled it differently." Frustration pulled against her heartstrings. "I would have known what I was walking into. I could have bargained better, or figured out another way, or *something* that didn't leave me in a cell for three days."

Liam brushed a few stray blond curls from her face with the back of their joined hands, his touch impossibly gentle.

"I want to murder him for what he did to you," he confessed with a glint of ire in his molten eyes. "I fantasize about the ways I would tear the bones from his flesh and use them for jewelry. I imagine flaying him alive and serving his blood to his own court."

Eve's cheeks warmed with unexpected affection. She stared at their hands, afraid to hold on. Afraid to let go. "That's... unusually violent coming from you."

"You make me want to commit atrocities." Liam grinned, lopsided and charming in all the ways she feared. "I dare say you're corrupting me, Evie."

"You were already corrupted." Eve snorted, letting their hands drop. She returned to putting away the first aid supplies, the grip of his palms still tingling on her skin. It was not... unpleasant.

Her instincts told her to repress such traitorous emotions. Touch was dangerous. Affection, even more so.

"You know, I killed the last man that kissed me," Eve said. The nightmare of Nick's body drowning in the bloody water stuck in her mind. "I'll kill the man who broke my heart, too. Does that make you afraid of me?"

She wasn't sure if she presented a threat or a plea. *See me. Hate me. Fear me.*

Forgive me.

"I am terrified of you," Liam said, and Eve believed him. "But I am more afraid of what I feel for you."

That makes two of us, Eve thought.

THIRTY-TWO

Unbeknownst to Eve, Hailey waited for her directly outside of the bathroom. When she had finished bathing for the evening and swung the heavy oak door open, her friend's face was inches from hers.

Eve screamed, almost slamming the door back in her face.

"Are you busy?" Hailey asked, brown eyes wide as Eve clutched her chest.

"Jesus Christ, at least *knock* or something," Eve hissed, trying to still her racing heart.

"Sorry." Hailey's lips curved into an apologetic smile. The dark circles under her eyes were plum as bruises. Was *anyone* in this cursed mansion getting enough sleep?

"What's up?" Eve made a conscious effort to soften her tone as she led Hailey to her bedroom. Her wet hair was short but tangled, and Eve picked up a wide-toothed comb made of bone from the desk to remedy the situation.

Hailey plopped onto Eve's bed without question, kicking her legs freely off the edge. She was in her pajamas, too—a cream night shift that puffed out in a cloud formation. "I was wondering if you were busy."

Eve jerked the comb through her hair. "Is everything okay?"

Hailey nodded. "I've been looking around the mansion for something to help us leave..." She must have noticed the hope in Eve's eyes because she quickly waved her hands in front of her as if she could dispel the emotion.

"I haven't found anything, but I haven't checked the distillery yet. I was hoping you'd come with me?"

"Sure." Eve set down the comb and shrugged on a plush robe from the closet. Hailey sighed in relief and hopped up from the bed.

"Thank you!" She clasped Eve's hands in hers, almost in prayer. "Oh my God, it's *so* creepy down there, Eve. You have, like, no idea. Every time I tried to go down by myself, I freaked out and couldn't do it."

Eve chuckled, giving Hailey's hands a gentle squeeze. "Don't worry, I'll protect you."

"You'd better," Hailey whined. Eve moved past her to pick up the dagger from under her pillow—then the needle from a locked drawer in her nightstand. Just in case.

Hailey eyed the sewing needle with confusion. "What's that for?"

"Don't worry about it," Eve said, tucking it in her dress's pocket. Hailey frowned. Could she sense the magic radiating from it, too? Was she aware of its dark vibrations that pulsed in time with Eve's heart? "The distillery?"

"Right!" Needle forgotten, Hailey led Eve downstairs, her slippered feet almost dancing across the moss carpet. Hailey bent her head and greeted the cloaked servants with a smile as they passed, unbothered when they did not respond in kind.

"You know some of them are dead, right?" Eve whispered.

"Of course," Hailey said. "I think the dead deserve our respect even more than the living."

Eve didn't know what to say to that, but she found herself murmuring small greetings to the staff as well.

Hailey hesitated once they entered the kitchen and reached the staircase that led to the basement. Small sconces were half-lit down the stone steps, the arch wide and rounded similarly to a gaping mouth.

"You haven't explored the basement at all, have you?" Eve guessed.

"I checked some of it when the brownies were working," she admitted. "But there's a lot I didn't cover."

Eve sighed and took the first step down. Hailey followed close behind, her nervous breath brushing the top of Eve's head. The sight would be comical to anyone that found them: Hailey and her tall, spindly limbs trying to hide behind Eve and her lackluster height. She barely reached above Hailey's shoulders.

The mental image kept Eve's nerves at bay as they sunk lower underground. Carved wood turned to solid bone the deeper they went. Dark shadows danced across the ground, flickering with the dim sconces.

Eve understood why Hailey was hesitant to go down by herself. There was a creepy stillness as they landed off the last step, the hallway's length barely visible from the stairs. Eve lit cobwebbed candles on the walls as they went, passing by closed doors marked by bronze plaques: the larder and various storage rooms. Curiosity pulled her toward a door marked "Remains", but she hesitated to peek inside.

"We should search in each of them," Eve said, catching the dread on Hailey's face.

"I was hoping you wouldn't say that," Hailey muttered, glancing around the hall. It wasn't only creepy—it was cold. Hailey's breath came out in a thin white puff, and Eve passed over her robe. "Thanks."

"Let's split up." Hailey paled. "It'll be faster that way."

Hailey obviously wanted to do anything *but* that. With a small whine, Hailey left to explore one of the storage rooms closer to the staircase. Maybe she thought she'd have a better chance of escaping that way.

Suppressing a shiver, Eve rubbed her arms and slipped into the nearest room. It was a storage room with various mushrooms. Probably not what she needed, but Eve explored the space anyway, drawing on knowledge she'd picked up from the Bone Court's library to identify them. Unfortunately, none of their properties offered a way home.

Eve parsed through a few more rooms, picking through raw food and forgotten relics that had been left to rot underground with everything else Evren and his children bored of. She admired a wall of half-empty snow globes, wondering which family member they belonged to.

A dusty vanity sat in the far back, its wooden drawers sticky and its mirror cracked. Eve fiddled with the drawers until they yanked open. Tarnished jewelry and small trinkets clattered inside, spilling over onto the ground.

An opal brooch caught her eye. Two brass dragonflies held the opal between them. Eve picked up the brooch from the drawer, turning it over between her thumb and forefinger.

The needle in her pocket pulsed violently against her thigh. It reacted the closer she brought the brooch to it and damn her if she didn't see the thing *glow* in response.

Eve dropped the brooch back into the drawer. Whatever was happening, Eve didn't want to be a part of it. The last thing she needed was for her needle to break because she was messing with magical items in the basement.

She dug through a few more rooms before meeting Hailey back in the hallway, her search not yielding anything useful.

"Any luck?" Hailey asked, and Eve shook her head.

"There's still the distillery," Hailey pointed to the open archway at the end of the hall. Eve recognized the rows upon rows of enormous barrels and copper stills that took up most of the space.

Her nose wrinkled at the sickly sweet scent of magically aged alcohol. There was a mix of flavored scents, but one stuck out to her, worse than the phantom of her memories. Eve pictured its dark blue hue playing on Colton's lips and tinting his vicious smile. She remembered it staining her favorite sweater, drowning her in its cloying scent.

"Eve?" Hailey glanced over her shoulder when Eve did not follow. She had paused at the threshold, queasy as she gripped the archway.

"I'm coming," she promised. Each step forward screamed against her instincts to run. She kept going, and Eve found it easier with Hailey at her side.

The two girls lingered over inked labels and specialty crafted brews that had fermented in the heart of the Bone Court. Crates of finished bottles sat by the nearest wall. Eve examined them first, turning the beautifully crafted glass over in her hands. They were all written in a language she couldn't read.

"Citronale," Hailey said, picking up an amber bottle. "Enhance your creative vision."

Eve nearly dropped the bottle in her hands. "You can *read* them?"

"Yeah." Hailey's brow furrowed. "I guess I can."

Hailey shrugged, pushing the thought aside as she moved onto the next crate. Eve lingered behind, suspicion gnawing at her gut.

"Did Sage teach you?" Eve tried to sound casual as she passed a familiar bottle with a shimmering, dark blue shade of wine. It took everything in her not to smash the entire stash against the wall.

Hailey cocked her head to the side, but as she thought, Eve could see a glaze sweeping over her eyes. Her answer was slow, uncertain. "Maybe? I'm not sure."

She was not as adept at hiding her concern as she was before Eve had told her about the missing memories. Hailey continued to read off the list of wines, her voice forcefully upbeat, but there was tension in her body as their search narrowed. Hailey may not know why she could translate Faerie script, but Eve knew she suspected. That was enough to put her on edge.

Did she talk to Liam yet? Eve hadn't dared ask. Hailey had already been overwhelmed when Eve told her the truth. She didn't want to push her friend further.

Eve focused back on the task, thumbing through crates as Hailey read out what each labeled bottle said. Eve was on the last crate, her hope diminishing, until she came across the familiar pale liquid from her birthday.

"Captimist: Use for realm confinement," Hailey read for her. Her eyes brightened, and she nearly dropped a bottle in her excitement, clumsily catching it between her elbows. "That's it!"

"Any hints on how to undo it?" Eve squinted at the script as if it would translate itself for her.

"It doesn't say anything else," Hailey confessed. "Nothing about an antidote, or a reversal, or... anything."

"What about the crate then?"

Hailey was already digging inside, clinking bottles together as she searched.

"Nope. Nothing in here."

"Shit." Disappointment left an acrid taste on Eve's tongue. "What now?"

"Maybe there's one that Evren is working on. We should keep looking."

Eve wanted to argue in favor of sleep instead. Everything was aching and she shivered in the cold basement—but the thought of missing a vital clue nagged at the back of her mind.

She dragged herself through the distillery at Hailey's side, certain that they would find nothing. Everything was properly labeled—at least Evren believed in some form of organization—so it was easy to dismiss the wines they'd already investigated.

It was soon clear that Evren did not keep his notes for experimentation in the distillery. A few pieces of parchment had been tacked on here and there, but otherwise the room operated as a well-oiled machine. If he had been working on some reversal to the Captimist, that information was not kept down here.

"Eve?"

Eve turned, surprised to find that she'd been lagging behind. Hailey stood up ahead, her body half-obscured by a stack of enormous barrels.

Eve rubbed her eyes as she approached. The hair on her arms stood up with the chill, and Eve wanted nothing more than to crawl under her covers and go to sleep.

"What do you think this is for?" Hailey asked. Eve tiredly followed Hailey's gaze. A rounded door was inlaid into the packed dirt wall. A heavy brass lock hung from the handle.

Eve glanced at the barrels, then at the hole. "I'm guessing this is how Evren transports the wine out of here."

"It's easier than the stairs," Hailey agreed. "But I don't feel a breeze or anything on the other side. Do you?"

Eve leaned against the door. It was the same temperature as the rest of the room—freezing, but no more than the basement already was. She couldn't hear anything on the other side of the door either—no wind, no animals. Complete stillness.

"Maybe it has great insulation?" Hailey guessed. "We're underground. You think there might be a ramp that goes up?"

"Maybe." Eve still expected to hear *something* from the other side. The deafening silence was eerie. "Do you see a key anywhere?"

"I'll check."

Eve kept her gaze trained on the door, even as Hailey's footsteps rescinded. A heavy bronze padlock hung through a metal loop attached to the wall and door. She tried the knob anyway, and the door wiggled before catching on the padlock.

Hailey returned empty-handed. She pouted stubbornly at the door, as if she could pry it open with sheer willpower alone.

Wait. Maybe they could.

"Forget the key," Eve said, grasping the slight edge of the door. "Help me pull this open."

Hailey obeyed, crouching down and shoving one foot against the wall for better leverage. Digging their nails into the wood, the girls pulled, grunting and groaning as they tried to force it open.

The meal loop in the dirt wall shifted, but didn't give way. Eve wasn't ready to be dissuaded. She considered the lock for a moment, weighing the heavy metal in her hand.

She pulled out the needle from her pocket and wiggled it into the keyhole.

"You know how to pick a lock?" Hailey asked, surprised.

"No," Eve admitted. "But it's worth a try."

She knew the basic mechanics of a padlock and assumed the ones in Faerie worked the same. There were a series of pins inside that, once set evenly with the key's jagged edges, would pop open the lock. Since the needle didn't share the same characteristics, she would need to test each pin individually.

Eve had watched short how-to videos throughout middle school that offered little tricks to pass the time—such as how to pick locks or fold an origami swan. She hoped that she remembered enough to do it correctly.

It was a far more challenging task than Eve had expected. She poked and prodded at the lock's pins, occasionally trading off with Hailey, who wanted to give it a try, before ultimately resetting the lock and starting over again.

There was a collective sigh of relief when the lock finally snapped open. Eve tossed the dreaded padlock aside and shoved open the rounded door.

Not a ramp, nor a way out—the girls stepped into a small, dark room inlaid with shelves upon shelves of sealed bottles. There was no light inside. Instead, they used what little leaked in from the distillery to examine the small space.

Most of the bottles were dusty and individualistic in nature—whether from their unique shapes or labels, no two bottles were the same. Eve picked up one with deep green tinted glass in the shape of a serpent.

"This must be the expensive stuff," Hailey guessed, squinting at the labels. "There aren't any huge batches of anything."

"Sounds right." Eve found herself drawn to the bottles, as if their magical potency was pulling her in. She scanned the labels in search of anything useful. "Do you think any of it's poison?"

"Probably." Hailey picked up a small violet bottle. "*Concentrated Nightshade*. Definitely."

Eve regarded the bottles with heightened caution. Even if there was something useful here, she wasn't about to accidentally poison herself. *Again.*

A small bottle tinted in teal caught her eye. Eve picked up the glass, turning it over in her hands. She handed it over to Hailey.

"*Voyager: A temporary transport through...*" Hailey frowned. Part of the front label had worn with age, rendering the rest of the translation indecipherable. "Transport..." Hailey's eyes widened. She held the bottle up to the light. "Wait, do you think this could get us home?"

"I'm not sure," Eve hedged. "It says temporary. If we can get back, I don't think we'll be there for long."

"That's fine," Hailey said with determination. "I just want to make sure everyone is okay."

Eve's heart twinged as Nan came to mind. She wanted the same.

"It's worth a shot," Eve conceded, gingerly taking the bottle. There was a list of instructions scrawled on the back, barely legible enough to read. Hailey translated for them, speaking with slow deliberation.

"*Step One: Swallow one teaspoon of the tincture and no more.*"

"*Step Two: Close your eyes and visualize the location to which you aim to travel.*"

"Step Three: You will have one hour to complete your duties and no more. You will return to your body where you left it. Bring what you wish, but you may take nothing back."

The instructions were simple, if not vague. Questions buzzed in Eve's mind, but she had no one to ask for clarification—not without admitting she'd broken into Evren's private stash.

Hailey searched the room for measuring implements. Luckily, a small work desk was cluttered with various tools and jars of herbs for creating tinctures. She grabbed a teaspoon and poured the unusual clear liquid into it.

"Good luck," she said with a smile. Hailey swallowed the spoonful, making a curious face after. She settled onto the floor and closed her eyes.

Eve measured out her own amount and brought the liquid to her lips. She wasn't sure what to expect, but she settled on the ground and squeezed her eyes shut tight. For all she knew, this wine didn't work on humans.

She pictured her nan's home anyway; the small, two-story brick house with the gable roof and creaky wooden porch. Eve imagined herself in the living room amid the yellow floral wallpaper, surrounded by Nan's favorite fake plants and the old-fashioned box TV in the corner. She could almost smell the vanilla scented plug-in by the front door.

Slowly, Eve grew lightheaded. A deep drowsiness took over, pulling her under. Eve was glad she'd settled beside Hailey first, because as the darkness swirled in her vision, she heard her body thump to the floor.

THIRTY-THREE

Eve opened her eyes to her nan's living room. It was mostly the same as she'd left it, with the exception of a few pine needles on the floor where the Christmas tree had been placed and removed in her absence. Eve brushed her fingers over the loose strands of tinsel on the floor, surprised to find that she could not feel them at all.

Nan sat in her usual seat by the TV, engrossed in an old western movie as her fingers nimbly toyed with a ball of yarn in her hands. An unfinished knitting project sat over the arm of her chair, forgotten against the captivating moving pictures of Clint Eastwood. Eve secretly wondered if he was another one of her grandmother's childhood crushes.

A nurse in her late twenties sat beside her on the couch, only halfway interested in the film. Eve didn't recognize the woman, but her light purple scrubs and pulled-back hair were recognizable enough. She glanced toward Nan occasionally, checking in on the woman's health before relaxing again.

Eve waited for them to notice her. To say something. Anything. They watched the television instead, oblivious to her presence.

"Nan," Eve finally said. Nan's head did not turn. "Nan. *Nan.*"

Nothing.

She can't hear me, Eve realized with a wave of despair. So much for providing reassurance. Without a way to communicate with her, Eve would instead be forced to witness Nan's struggle in her absence.

Except Nan wasn't struggling—not as Eve had feared. The elderly woman was thin, but no more than when Eve had left her. Her silver hair was tidy and pulled into a loose bun, and a knitted afghan hung over her lap in squares of brown and orange. She took a sip of the tea on the end table beside her before resuming watching the film.

The front door creaked open. Eve stepped aside on instinct to make room for the newcomer, but it was deemed unnecessary. Their guest, a tall woman with blond hair and a camel-brown trench coat, stepped *through* her, sending a shiver down Eve's spine at the eerie sensation.

"Hey, Mom," the woman said, bending down to kiss Nan's check. Eve's eyes widened. Nan only had one daughter—Aunt Sam.

Eve could see the resemblance between them—their pale hair and freckled skin. Her great-grandmother's Irish roots were stronger in the trickles of red that caught in the light in Aunt Sam's hair.

She hadn't seen her aunt in years. Not since she'd been exiled from the family. Eve was barely seven at the time, and her concerns had aligned more with the fruit snacks hidden in the pantry than with the family drama occurring in the next room over.

No wonder Nan confused them. Eve was staring into a distorted mirror, seeing a version of herself that might have existed in another life.

Nan smiled at Aunt Sam, squeezing her hand once before returning to the television set. Aunt Sam and the nurse shared a glance before they retreated to the dining room.

Eve followed them with the presence of a ghost drifting through the house. She hung back in the doorway, keeping one eye on Nan while the women talked.

"How was she today?" Aunt Sam asked, removing her coat and gloves. The nurse picked up a medical bag from one of the chairs.

"She's alright. Got her to eat half a bowl of soup and some tea, but she's still low on her daily calorie intake," the nurse admitted, pulling a sheet from her bag. She scribbled down a few things in a chart. "Keep having her take the supplements with her meals and make sure to stick to her routine. She's stubborn today; you might have trouble getting her to take her nighttime medicine."

"I'll do my best," Aunt Sam promised with a smile. "She's always been stubborn, so I'm not surprised."

"If you can, try to have her get up and do something physical with you," the nurse continued. "It doesn't need to be exercise necessarily—baking, cooking, what have you—just something that gets her muscles moving. I want to see her a bit more active than she's been."

"I've been trying." Aunt Sam glanced into the living room through Eve. "She's been reluctant to leave the house except for church. I got her to go to the post office with me the other day, though. That was something."

"Something is better than nothing."

Eve watched the nurse pack up and leave. Aunt Sam sighed, hanging up the rest of her winter wear before joining Nan in the living room. Eve lingered in the doorway, feeling like an intruder.

Her aunt was different than Eve had imagined. More... mundane. Ben had always spoken of his sister as if she were the devil, and everything he said had only created a more glamorous image of her in Eve's mind. Aunt Sam was... disappointingly normal. She watched some of Nan's movie before checking the temperature of her mother's teacup.

"I'm going to warm this up for you, okay, Mom?" she said. Aunt Sam had to repeat it a couple of times before Nan understood, then retreated to the kitchen. She did it all with a gentleness Eve hadn't expected from her.

What brought Aunt Sam back here to care for Nan? As far as Eve knew, their relationship had been strained since Nan blacklisted her from the family. If Eve had been treated that way by her own parents, she would've cut everyone off. A part of her still wanted to. Why did her aunt come back?

Eve stalked Aunt Sam to the kitchen, using her invisibility to peer over her arm and read the texts that popped up on the phone in her hand. A couple were clearly from coworkers regarding work, but Eve's curiosity rose when she saw her father's name on the screen.

She tried to poke at the cell phone, but her hand fell through it. Thankfully, Aunt Sam opened the messages to respond, giving Eve enough time to briefly glance at the previous texts.

There were a few links to nursing homes from Aunt Sam. She sent another one, and Ben called immediately after.

"Stop sending the damn links," Ben snapped before Aunt Sam could greet him. "There's a nurse there now. It's fine."

"*It's fine?* Someone has to pay for said nurse, and I don't see you contributing." Eve followed Aunt Sam through the kitchen as she prepared dinner.

"We did—"

"You sent a *teenager* to watch our mom." Aunt Sam was rearing to fight but decided against it. With a heavy breath, she asked, "Speaking of, have you heard anything?"

Heard anything? How long had she been gone?

"I told you, she's doing it for attention. She'll come home eventually." Ben's voice cut like a spear through Eve's heart.

"I can't believe I have to have this conversation with you," Aunt Sam scoffed. "Teenagers don't just run away for attention."

"Some do."

"Jesus, Ben, you can't be serious—"

Eve stopped listening then, her heart tight with emotion. Attention. Her own father thought she was doing it for *attention*.

Was that what he thought about her incident at her old school, too? And what happened with Colton, Logan, and Nick? Did he believe she'd done everything for... attention?

Disgust sailed a ship on stormy waters in the depths of her stomach. Aunt Sam fought back, but Eve wasn't ready to hear anything else they had to say.

There was some irony in being right. Eve knew her parents didn't care—not in the ways that a parent should. Knowing Sharon, Eve imagined her mother was worried, but she couldn't know for certain. And Ben... Her father didn't bat an eye.

Eve stumbled back into the living room. She could not feel the tears streaming down her face, but she knew they were there, making stark lines across her cheeks. She collapsed beside Nan's chair and rested her head against her grandmother's knee.

"I hate this," she sobbed to no one. "This isn't fair."

"Sammy," Nan breathed. Eve glanced at the doorway, expecting her aunt to walk through—but then a gentle hand rested on her head, bony fingers gently brushing her hair.

Eve snapped her attention to her grandmother, who smiled down at her fondly.

"Don't cry," Nan said, brushing a finger against one of Eve's tears. "Everything will be alright."

"Nan." Eve couldn't *stop* crying. How had her grandmother seen her? How did she know she was there? It shouldn't be possible. Eve had tested it.

Yet Nan brushed her hair, providing a comfort Eve desperately needed. She cried against her grandmother's knee, hugging her spindly legs as she sobbed.

"I love you, dear," Nan whispered. She did not stop stroking Eve's hair. "Even when we're apart, I love you always."

A gentle kiss pressed at the top of Eve's head—and then her vision faded.

Time was up. The world fuzzed at the edges, then blurred entirely. Nan disappeared, along with the world around her.

Eve gasped as she was sucked back into her body. Her limbs ached from the awkward position on the distillery floor, and a sharp chill ran under her veins. Her teeth chattered as she sat up and reached for her robe, only to realize it was still wrapped around Hailey's body.

"Here," Hailey said, returning the robe to her shivering friend. "Thanks for letting me borrow it."

"N-No problem," Eve chattered, clutching onto the fabric's warmth. Relief washed over her as she realized she was back in Faerie. Coming to her senses, Eve recognized the sting of her eyes and the path her tears had taken down her cheeks. Hailey helped her to her feet, rubbing Eve's arms for additional heat.

"You okay?" she asked softly.

"I'm fine," Eve said too quickly. She scrubbed her face with the back of her hand. She didn't want to get into the conversation she'd overheard. Not now. "What about you?"

Hailey sighed, her bottom lip slipping into a pout. "Okay, I guess. I tried to go home, but no one was there. I was in an empty house for an hour."

"Oh." Eve wasn't sure what to say to that. A part of her wished that had been what happened when she returned to Nan's—but she could see that Hailey was disappointed by the whole thing. "I'm sorry."

"It's fine," she said, placing the bottle back on the shelf. "I saw some missing posters, which was freaky. They didn't even choose a good picture of me! Like, if you're going to search for me, at least make it cute, right?"

Hailey's voice pitched too high, disclosing her anxiety. Eve had no clue what kind of photo her own parents would use for missing photos—she wasn't even sure any recent ones existed.

Did Dad even put any up? she thought miserably, then dispelled the thought. Eve was glad she didn't see them, if they even existed.

"We'll keep searching for a way home," Eve said quietly, more for Hailey's reassurance than her own. Eve wasn't entirely sure she wanted to go home—and not only because of the conversation she'd overheard. Returning to the house had been an odd experience. Unwelcoming. As if she were a stranger in her own home.

Waking up in Faerie had been a relief. It was alarming, the security she found here. The more Eve interacted with this world, the more it became a part of her, planting seeds of comfort in her bones until she did not know which realm to call home.

What would become of her when vengeance was accomplished and a path to her realm opened up to her? Would she take it? Or would she stay?

Eve had never imagined a future past her junior year of high school, but here she was. Older. Wiser.

And Eve had no idea what to do.

Thirty-Four

Sage was gone the next morning, off to fulfill her quest to bring Colton's head to the High King of the Unseelie Court. Eve almost wished she'd gone with her—Sage undoubtedly knew the region better than Eve did—but pushed the thought aside. She needed to be better prepared before she faced Colton again. If she was going to glean any satisfaction from his death, Eve had to be sure she could do it.

She doubted Sage would've let her accompany her anyway. If she did, the chances that Eve wouldn't find herself at the end of Sage's blade were slim.

Some things were better off handled on her own.

Eve caught Hailey glimpsing out the frosted windows as she tried her hand at crotchet. Preece had lent them both supplies, but Hailey was the only one to take him up on the offer. She chewed her lip in between stitches, scanning the white expanse for what Eve could only guess were a pair of shimmering wings.

"Did she tell you where she was going?" Eve asked. She had found a deck of cards stashed away and entertained herself with a game of solitaire at the table.

"Yeah." Hailey pulled her lip under her teeth, glancing down at her hands in shame. "I told her that she's going to get herself killed. Do you think I should've stopped her?"

"Would she have listened?" Eve countered. Hailey ducked her head, silently confirming what they both knew. "She'll be fine. It's only one guy. She might not even find him."

"How do you know it's just one?"

Eve's cheeks pinked as she realized her slipup. She hadn't told Hailey anything about Colton—not of her past *or* the fact that he was slaughtering the Fair Folk. Something *she* was responsible for, Eve realized with a wave of shame.

It won't last much longer, she told herself. The needle pulsed in her pocket as if in agreement. Eve remembered Liam throwing her mortal-made handsaw into the fire when she'd fought off the asrai. The magical strength of the flames had turned her weapon into molten silver on the logs.

The sewing needle in her pocket was made by the Fair Folk—or maybe even the gods. The metal was stronger, the edges pointed and wicked in a way no human could achieve. Magic flowed through it, tingling against the thick fibers of her woolen skirt. Colton may have stolen Faerie armor from his victims, but Eve was certain she could pierce through it—with as much damage as a needle could do, anyway.

All of that would have to wait, though. There were more pressing matters at hand.

"Do you know where Preece is?" Eve asked.

Hailey pointed to the back of the manor. "I think I saw him in the backyard with Logan."

The mention of his name left a vile taste in the back of Eve's throat. She nodded her thanks, leaving Hailey to her distractions while she sought out Liam's brother.

If there was anyone that would have information on Liam's disease, it was Preece. As a member of the Court of Knowledge, Eve suspected he would have access to more history on the disease than the common Fair

Folk. Maybe there would be a way to cure him, too—or at least something to help with that awful riddle.

Blood from stone, bind with thine own. Ash to root, a seed awaiting her fruit—lay to rest, the newt.

Eve had been mulling over the riddle for over a day now. The words turned over in her head often enough that she'd begun to wonder if they were her own.

"Why does everything have to be in riddles?" she grumbled.

Eve found Preece in the courtyard playing a sport resembling croquette. Instead of metal arches, a dozen snow sprites held up giant snowflakes in the sky, moving the goals around the air at an incredible speed. How Preece had managed to recruit snow sprites for a game, she had no idea. Maybe this was an elaborate prank, and Preece was going to squash them with his mallet.

I wouldn't mind seeing that, she thought. The marks from the snow sprite's slashing of her leg still lingered, although the pain had vanished.

In addition to his game, Preece was trapped in a one-sided conversation with the enemy. Logan eagerly prattled away while Preece nodded along, more habitual than interested. Eve wasn't sure she'd ever seen Preece this *bored* before.

Eve's footfalls crunched as she approached them, and Preece gave an audible sigh of relief, frantically waving her over.

Logan stiffened. He took a step back behind the Fair Folk—as if expecting Preece to protect him. Eve wasn't sure what Preece would do, but she suspected that saving Logan from her blade wasn't high on his list of priorities.

"Eve!" Preece greeted her with a wide grin, extending his slippery hands in a welcoming gesture. "What a lovely surprise. Have you come to finish the boy off?"

Logan shot him a horrified look, but Preece did not spare him an ounce of attention. Apparently, the frog-man would not be his savior after all.

Eve considered it. The fact that he was terrified of her was good enough—for now. Logan was a coward. When she was ready to kill him, Eve wouldn't need to wait for an opportunity to present itself. She could pick and choose exactly when and how it would be done.

That delighted her more than it should've.

"Not yet," Eve said with a pointed glare at Logan. The man shuffled in place, his face turning red. His discomfort brought her a sense of satisfaction. "Actually, I wanted to talk to you about something."

"But of course!"

Preece swung his mallet, blasting one of the snowflakes into a flurry of smaller ones. The snow sprites scattered off before creating another.

Logan took this opportunity to escape before he found himself face down in the snow again. Eve let him go, watching his slight figure race back to the servants' quarters tucked far across the yard until he disappeared entirely.

A part of her wished he'd tripped on his run back. He did not.

"What curiosities shall I lay to rest?" Preece asked.

"What do you know about people turning into stone?"

Preece pressed his pale green lips together and cocked his head in thought. "It is not within my primary field of study, but I know of many myths that carry that sentiment across various realms—including your own. Are you seeking a story in particular?"

"Do you know anything about it happening through a disease?" Eve asked.

"I... do not," Preece said after a contemplative moment. "Again, it is not within my field of study—that does not mean such information does not exist. Why do you ask?"

Eve almost told him the truth but held her tongue. This wasn't her secret to tell.

"Just wondering," she said with a stilted shrug. The curiosity in Preece's eyes told her that he didn't believe her lie for a minute. "There should be something about it in the Court of Knowledge, right?"

"Only if it has been documented," Preece hedged. "That would be a few days' trip, at least in this weather." Preece grimaced distastefully at the snow on the ground, as if it had fallen purely to spite him. "Even then, it is not guaranteed I would have access to those records—if they should even exist."

Eve deflated. The stone crawled in her mind as it did up Liam's neck, a stark reminder of how little time was left.

"No need to be dour," Preece said. "It is not an impossible task—merely one with involvement. You're lucky, though; I was planning to join my father on his trip to the Spring Court for his meeting with Lady Acacia. There is some business I have to attend to as well, but I should have time to spare for a short trip to the Court of Knowledge."

"For a price," Eve said flatly. She could hear the insinuation in his tone. Preece shrugged with a helpless smile.

"It is the way of doing business," he confessed.

"I'm getting real tired of making deals with Fae," Eve grumbled. Preece grinned with unrestrained amusement. "Can't you do anything because you *want* to? Without strings attached?"

"Of course we can—but then you'd miss out on all the wonderful stories people have to share. All the new information in the realms from here and beyond. I understand that is not the desire of every Fair Folk, but I have yet to meet a single creature that hasn't taught me something interesting, whether I wanted to learn it or not." He paused, then turned toward the servants' quarters where Logan had disappeared. "Then again, perhaps I spoke too soon."

Eve toyed with the string on her cuff, silent. She had plenty of stories to tell—and no doubt they would captivate Preece's attention—but it was nothing she wanted to share. Those private secrets were kept in the vault of her memory, sealed away where they could do harm to no one but herself.

In her heart, Eve knew they wanted to be told—and a part of her wanted to tell them. That was how her confessions came out, her slipups in front of Liam. There was a painful release in speaking the dark truths that haunted her. There was freedom in sharing her burdens.

Once they were out in the world, she could not take them back. Eve could not stop changing the way people stared at her or how they spoke of her—*to* her—and cast their judgment. In their eyes, she was a vile temptress or a pitiful girl that tarnished everything she touched. She had no control, and that frightened her.

Liam didn't think either of those things, a small voice whispered in her mind. Eve shrugged it off. Liam was a fluke. Maybe he didn't think it now, but there was still time for those thoughts to change.

Eve knew what kind of ugly, twisted creature she was. If Liam did not see it yet, time would teach him soon enough.

"I'll tell you a story," she offered. Her saliva was hard to swallow. "If you go to the Court of Knowledge and see what you can find."

"It would need to be an awfully good story," Preece said, his webbed fingers tapping the elbow of his crossed arms. "A quest this involved will take time."

"It will be," Eve promised. She knew what Preece wanted and, if it was in exchange for Liam's cure, she would give it. That was the least she could do. "I'll tell you everything that happened between me and Logan *after* you find everything you can on this stone disease."

There it was, that gleaming interest in Preece's eye. To her surprise, he sighed and stared out across the yard—back toward the servants' quarters.

"I should confess, Logan told me this story already," he said. Eve's blood went cold. "I imagine he painted himself in a kinder light than your truth would reveal. I am more interested in your side of the story, but I am aware it is a difficult one." He turned to her then, not with pity but with a severity that made her muscles clench. "If you are not ready to speak it, I would accept another story in its place."

Eve nearly forgot how to breathe. Preece *knew*. He knew, he knew, he *knew*. Her gaze shot to the servants' quarters, and she had to hold herself back from barreling through the front door and splattering Logan's guts along the wall.

This was not his secret to reveal. He had no right to tell him her deepest shame. *No. Right.*

"If you already know, then it doesn't matter, does it?" Her voice was even, but the anger thrived underneath, snapping each word into place. What must Preece think of her now? Had he told anyone else? Had *Logan* told anyone else?

She would kill him. Eve *had* to kill him.

"I have heard the cowardice confessions of many guilty men," Preece said slowly. "And I will tell you firsthand that they are not worth much. It is the voices of the survivors that matter a great deal more."

He met her gaze and something shifted between them. An unspoken understanding.

Survivor. He did not speak it with pity, but with strength. Preece saw her for what she was—and he did not pity her. He did not condemn her.

He wanted to know her truth.

The heavy weight that suffocated her lungs eased. She did not want to trust him. She *shouldn't* trust him. Yet, the Fair Folk could not lie, and a tiny part of her that she'd worked hard over the years to squash down lifted her hopes.

"I'll tell you my side when you find the information I need," she said, and did not deny herself the fear that came with speaking those words aloud. "Not a minute sooner."

"It shall be done," Preece said, bowing with a flourish. It wasn't hard to see that Evren's air for the dramatics lived on through his children.

As she turned to leave, another thought struck her.

"One last thing," Eve said quickly. "Do you know what this riddle might mean?"

She repeated the riddle for Liam's cure. Preece paused and considered. "I am at a loss. Does this relate to your search for stone mythology?"

"Sort of."

"Shall I investigate it on my trip?" Preece offered. Eve *was* tempted, but something told her that this wasn't the kind of puzzle Preece could find the answer to in a book. This task was all her own to solve.

"No," she conceded. It probably wasn't a good idea to make too many deals with the Fair Folk anyway—a lesson she was poor at learning. "I'll figure it out on my own."

"I'd be intrigued to hear the answer when you do."

With that, he shattered another snowflake.

Thirty-Five

No one had seen Sage. Eve tried not to let herself worry as the servants brought out their dishes, but Hailey wouldn't stop fidgeting in her seat and staring at Sage's empty chair.

Eve wasn't sure she'd be hungry enough to eat, even without Hailey fretting across the table. Tonight's dinner was meat pie with a flaky, egg-washed crust. The crow-shaped dough was screeching up at them, its open beak stuffed with shiny red cranberries. Eve wondered if it was trying to warn her.

She tried to tell herself that Sage was fine. Even if she wasn't, why did Eve care? Sage had tried to contract her into killing her own brother. *Then* she'd tried to kill Eve. Twice. Eve should have been glad that Sage was gone.

The worry did not cease. They had been friends once—even if it was one-sided. It was not as easy to forget that as Eve would have wanted.

Evren did not comment on his daughter's disappearance. He tore into his pie with the refinery of a king too high above to hear the screams of his people. Disgust sloshed in Eve's stomach as she watched him dab a smear of red from his thin lips with a black cloth.

Eve had once thought there was no worse man than her father. Then again, she had thought the same of Colton. Now, she watched Evren enjoy his feast, while his daughter fought tooth and nail for his scraps of approval. Eve wondered if it was not the men in her life that grew worse, but her growing awareness of how little her life—and the lives of other women—were valued.

"Okay, I can't do this anymore." Hailey threw her napkin onto the table. Her silverware clattered onto the wood, clinking against her untouched glass of wine. "Isn't anyone else freaked out? Sage has been missing for two days. She told me she'd be home by now, and she's not, and *no one* cares."

"We care plenty," Preece said. "I've already sent some of the servants to investigate."

"Have they found her?"

Preece frowned, poking at his meal with the tip of his fork. "Not yet."

"Then what are we *doing* here?" Hailey waved her arms at the table. "She's going to get herself killed trying to win this stupid game!"

This piqued Evren's interest. The elder Faerie dabbed his lips again, his strange gold eyes flickering over Hailey in her distress. "What danger, precisely, has my daughter found herself in now?"

Hailey glared at him, her hands shaking in tight fists at her sides. "She's trying to take down the weirdo who's been hunting the Fair Folk. She thinks that bringing you his head is going to make her your *heir*."

She spoke the last part with disgust, her lips curling into a sneer.

"Does she, now?" Evren chuckled and spread a dollop of cherry jam over a biscuit. "Foolish child. That wouldn't do anything."

"Why not?" Eve asked. There was a mischievous glint in Evren's eyes that disarmed her.

"Preece, how would you describe the general atmosphere of the Unseelie Court?" Evren asked, as if they were speaking about the weather.

Preece listed them off. "Reckless, capricious, brutal—"

"Brutal!" Evren cut in with a grin. "Yes, I would agree. Unfortunately, the High Unseelie King does not view the Bone Court as the house of massacre we had once been. Does he, Liam?"

Liam scowled but said nothing.

"The Bone Court had once been second hand to the throne," Evren continued. "My father accomplished such a feat when he took the seat from the previous lord."

Power is bestowed upon the strongest contender.

Evren's words from their earlier conversation about the High King lingered in the back of her mind. The Fogtrees had not always overseen the Bone Court, she realized. They had simply managed to hold on to it.

"I hear the whispers. It is clear to me that our court has fallen from the king's favor, and that our family shares a weak reputation because of it. Thus, I have created a game to rectify the situation."

Hailey shook her head. "Isn't what Sage is doing enough? She's going to bring you a freaking *head*—that's pretty brutal."

"Killing mortals is no more impressive than squashing a bug," Evren sighed with the dismissive wave of his hand. "Perhaps there is a bit of a thrill to it—oh, we do love a hunt—but it does not show me that my children are ready for leadership.

"What I require—and what you have all failed to realize—is that leadership comes with sacrifice. Especially that of something you care about."

Evren glanced at Eve, then at Hailey. There was something knowing in the way he watched them. A tingling sensation lingered on Eve's tongue as the pieces clicked into place.

"You poisoned me," Eve whispered. The bottle of concentrated nightshade in the private distillery room flashed in the back of her mind. "*You* poisoned me with the pie."

"Yes and no." Evren's lips quirked into an unnerving smile. "There was a poisoned pie, yes, but it was not of my making. That credit can go to my daughter."

"She did try to poison Liam," Hailey whispered to herself. Even though she had accused Sage, it was as if she didn't believe it. Didn't *want* to believe it. Liam's lips set into a thin, pale line.

"I couldn't risk my potential heir dying, and no one would have been the wiser if the pies were to switch. I never predicted my children would *help* once the symptoms kicked in," Evren drawled. "It is a shame. We could have ended the whole charade quite early."

Eve stood from her chair, head swimming. "You tried to *kill* me."

"What other purpose would your presence serve here?" Evren turned to Preece with a hint of regret. "I tried to acquire one of your mortal friends, but they weren't nearly as willing to make the trek. It is fortunate that I found someone at the last minute."

"Wait a minute." Hailey pressed her hand to her head as if trying to block out this dreaded knowledge. "You kept us here because you want to *kill us*? Like, am I totally insane, or did he just say that?"

"No, you heard quite right," Evren said calmly. "Not all of you have to die, of course. That will be up to the decided heir once their partner is slain, as I promised. It is quite simple."

Eve and Hailey stared at each other from across the table. Eve almost couldn't believe what she was hearing. Kill them. The only reason she and Hailey were there was for Liam and Sage to *kill* them.

"I'm not *murdering* my friends," Liam said sharply.

"And why not? Is it so different from what you did to your mother?"

"His mother?" Eve echoed. Liam avoided her gaze, his gloved hands clasped tightly in his lap.

"Has he not mentioned?" Evren's eyes twinkled with mischief, something Eve had seen on Liam's face too many times to count. It was unnerving on Evren, alarming in his malicious intent. "Liam murdered her."

No one spoke. The reality settled over the table in an unsettling blow.

Eve turned to Liam for an explanation, but he couldn't meet her eye. She knew he'd killed before—he confessed as much all those months ago—but Eve never imagined the victim would be his own kin. His own *mother*.

"It was a delightful spectacle," Evren continued, ignoring his son's blatant discomfort. "I knew any child Liadain bore would be ruthless—but even she couldn't predict that it would turn back on her."

"That does not mean I will harm my friends," Liam said, his words venomous. Eve recognized the flicker of fear in his eyes as his secrets came to light.

It was not disgust or fear that held her tongue. Eve yearned to chip away at the cracks that held his secrets. To learn the language of him until she was fluent. Between Killian and his mother, what else was he hiding?

Eve knew better than anyone the time it took to earn trust. She would not push him if he was not ready.

It was anger that captured her heart instead, its entirety reserved for Evren.

"You have grown soft by your siblings' influence," Evren said, disappointed. "We both know what you are capable of, Liam. You need only prove it once more to secure your rightful place in my court."

"That's why you decided to kill me?" Eve snapped. "So you could cheat at your own game and force Liam to be your heir?"

"I underestimated his attachment to mortals," Evren confessed. His jaw ticked with annoyance. "Leaving you to die would have been the same as poisoning you himself. It would have been sufficient, albeit far less entertaining."

Eve's fingers twitched to grasp his neck. She swallowed her rage, harboring her resentment into the pool of hatred that fueled her very being. Given a spark, she would explode.

"I intend to retire by Ostara," Evren continued, his voice firm. "I will *not* allow the title of lordship to fall into another house's hands because my children are too inept to take it for themselves."

His gaze flickered to Liam. "You are all aware of what this court demands. If you cannot make the necessary sacrifices, this court will fall, and all of us with it. Did you forget what happened to the Dust Court?"

Liam gritted his teeth but said nothing. Preece frowned at his lap, abashed.

"What happened to the Dust Court?" Hailey asked before Eve could.

"They were a well-established court under Unseelie rule some time ago," Evren said with the flippant wave of his hand. "It came down to two heirs: one who shared no interest in ruling, and another who took up the role out of necessity. Alas, he could not stomach the decisions necessary to keep the court in favor. A stronger family of Fair Folk beheaded them—the spare included—and took over the mantle.

"The replacements were not versed in ruling. Eventually, the Blood Court did their people a mercy and took over their land, dissolving the Dust Court entirely."

"That won't happen," Liam said with a scowl. Evren steadied his gaze at Eve.

"I know it won't. I will not allow it."

Thirty-Six

Eve let Hailey share her room that night. It was not wise to sleep alone, not after their conversation at dinner.

They huddled together under the blankets, limbs tangled as Hailey clung close and snored gently in her ear. The physical touch brought an unusual comfort to Eve. There was no threat from Hailey, her body thrown haphazardly across the bed in such a way that Eve had to contort herself into a fetal position lest she fall onto the floor.

No, the greater threat was all around them.

Eve stared up at the heavy canopy. Listening. Waiting.

The manor was silent, save for the soft sounds of sleep, but Eve was restless. She tossed and turned, expecting to find Evren or one of his servants hovering at her side, dagger drawn in the air.

There wasn't time to sit around and wait for Evren to strike again. He'd made it quite clear that Eve's life would be a small price to pay in exchange for a ruthless heir. She needed to bring Colton's head to the High Unseelie King and leave Faerie as fast as she could. For Hailey's sake. For... her own.

I don't want to leave. Her heart ached. What was waiting for her back in the mortal realm? Nan was taken care of. Her father didn't care. The impending doom of graduation and college and her unplanned future nipped at her heels. If given the chance to catch up, it would devour her whole.

In Faerie, Eve could breathe. She could *live.* There were no condemnations to hell or the suffocating expectations of her family. No one shamed her for the violent fantasies that raced through her mind. Some even *admired* her for them.

Yet, this world rejected her humanity. Her mortality. Could she ever truly be happy in a realm that sneered at her existence?

Would she ever know if she didn't try?

Panic set in when Eve found her bed empty. Eve groped the vacant sheets, searching, before she flung herself off the mattress and yanked on her robe.

She should have never gone to sleep. That had been her first mistake. They should have taken shifts watching over each other through the night. Or set up a defense system before they slept—an alarm or trap of some sort.

Anything but leave each other vulnerable and at Evren's mercy.

Horrible scenarios ran through Eve's mind as she crept through the manor. She conjured images of cloaked servants dragging Hailey from her bed for the shadows to consume. Evren, in all his arrogance, twisting the knife in her throat. Her body, once full of life and joy, left abandoned to the vultures.

Eve tripped over herself in the hallway, cursing under her breath as she frantically peeked into open doorways and dimly lit corridors.

She's probably in the bathroom, Eve told herself. When she peeked inside, Hailey was not there.

Cold sweat trickled down the back of her neck. Eve took the stairs two at a time, robe fluttering behind her as she scrambled to the first floor.

What if she was too late? Memories of the Bone Court's servants descending upon the corpses at Yule burned fresh in her mind. She imagined Hailey in place of the dead, her thin lips drawn in horror as they pecked at her bones. Hailey ripped apart by Faerie scavengers, her pieces left to rot back into the earth until the soil bled.

Hailey sitting at the kitchen table, sipping a cup of tea.

Eve nearly collapsed with relief. Alive. Her friend was *alive.*

"What are you doing down here?" she asked, her voice chastising when she had not meant it to be. If it wasn't for the moonlight streaming through the window, Eve wouldn't have even seen her. She hastened to light one of the candles on the wall using a set of matches tucked away in one of the drawers. "Can't sleep?"

Hailey shook her head, staring at the mug in her hands. Eve sat with her at the table and noticed that the untouched tea had gone cold. How long had she been down here?

Eve reached across the table, not quite touching her hand, but close enough to draw her friend's attention. "What's wrong?"

Hailey opened her mouth, but for once, the words were lost on her. She promptly snapped her lips shut, fingers trembling as she gripped the cup in her hands. The moisture in her sad brown eyes made her even more pathetic and helpless. A lost pup that wanted to go home.

"I went back."

Eve's brows furrowed. "Back?"

Hailey fingered the handle of her mug. She sniffed, wiping her tears with the back of her hand. "I drank the wine."

It took a moment for Eve to register what she meant.

"Why did you do that?"

Hailey shrugged helplessly. "I don't know. I wanted... I thought if I pictured Sage hard enough, I'd find out where she went."

"Did you find her?"

"No." Hailey played with her loose hair over her shoulder, twisting and unwinding the dark strands into tight knots. "Nothing happened, so I visited my family instead."

There was a quiet dread in the way she spoke. Hailey stared at her fidgeting fingers, haunted.

Eve swallowed hard. "What did you see?"

"My family," Hailey admitted quietly. "They were in the living room talking. I guess none of them could sleep either. I thought maybe they would be able to see me, but they didn't even know I was there."

Eve frowned. It had been the same for her, too. She wished too late that she would have said something to Hailey earlier. Something to spare the inevitable disappointment.

"I'm sorry—" Eve said, but Hailey carried on without having heard her.

"My mom was furious. Like, I'd never seen her this angry, Eve. They were talking about me, and she just—she lost her freaking mind." Hailey's voice hitched, but she pushed forward. "I thought she would be worried or scared or-or something, but she kept ranting at my dad, screaming at the top of her lungs. She thinks I ran away with Sage—or you. That I did it before Christmas to spite her."

Eve grimaced, unsurprised by Catherine Boyle's outburst. After having met the woman at one of Hailey's sleepovers, Eve got the impression that Hailey's mother did not handle situations beyond her control lightly.

She didn't want to point this out, though, afraid that Hailey was already too shaken from the experience to think rationally. The last thing Eve wanted to do was cause her friend more pain.

Hailey was a kinder soul than Eve ever could be. She didn't deserve a mother who blamed her for her own disappearance. Hell, she didn't even deserve to be trapped in Faerie. The world should have been kinder to girls like Hailey—so why wasn't it?

You know it doesn't work that way. Hadn't she, too, once been kind? Eve picked at her sleeves. It was easier to believe the things her parents said about her—to see herself as flawed, troubled, and prone to sin. That made the misfortunes that befell her easier to stomach after a while.

But bad things happened to all sorts of girls, kind and not. So, what did that make Eve?

"I don't get it." Hailey was still talking, and Eve forced herself to pay attention. "Nothing she said made sense, and sometimes while she was ranting, her words would just—stop. Her mouth was moving, and I knew she was screaming, but there wasn't any sound. I thought I was dreaming."

"Are you sure you weren't?" Eve pressed.

"I'm sure," Hailey insisted. Then quieter, "It happens sometimes. Once in a while, my mom and dad will mention something, and there was silence. There are times I don't even know they're talking to me because it's just... nothing."

"When that happens," Eve said slowly. "What are you usually talking about beforehand?"

Hailey cocked her head and thought seriously. Tense concentration drew firm lines across her forehead. Her eyes clouded for a moment. Then, nothing.

"I can't remember," she said, her voice laced with a trickle of fear. She stared at Eve, wide-eyed and afraid. "It's on the tip of my tongue, but I can't remember. You don't... You don't think this has something to do with Liam, do you? With—with my memories?"

"It might." Eve

gripped her nightdress's sleeves, pinching the lace between her fingers.

"I think... I think you need to ask Liam for your memories back."

There was a long moment of silence. Hailey frowned at her hands, uncertain.

"I think you're right." Her laugh was on the verge of hysterical. She scrubbed her moist eyes with the back of her hand again. "I'm so stupid."

"You're not stupid. You had your reasons."

"Do you know what memories I gave up?" she asked, sniffling. Eve nodded guiltily. "Can't you tell me what it is?"

"You might forget what I tell you," Eve pointed out. "Or won't hear what I say."

"Oh. Right."

A long silence passed between them. Eve could see the candles on the walls inching downward, their wax dripping slowly down their thin pillars. Someone would replace them in the morning. She never saw who.

"I'm scared." Hailey's trembling whisper broke through the quiet.

The confession went against everything Eve had learned. *Don't show fear. Don't show weakness. You must be the scariest thing in the room.* But the way Hailey spoke, as afraid as she was, came with a sense of courage. To speak her fear aloud was what made her brave.

Eve squeezed her hand again, holding it firmly.

"You're not alone."

The tension in Hailey's face softened, and a small smile pulled at the corners of her lips. "Thanks."

"Anytime."

Hailey pulled away then and quickly wiped her tears as she stood. "God, it's probably like, two in the morning. We should go to sleep."

"Time doesn't matter here," Eve said, but rose from the table and put out the lights.

THIRTY-SEVEN

The Lord of the Bone Court and his froggish son left for the Seelie Court in the early hours of dawn. Eve, unable to rest, watched from her bedroom window as they prepared to depart. Servants bustled about in the snow, their cloak hems damp as they piled cases of liquor into a separate wagon attached to the back of the carriage. Others settled trunks of luggage into the carriage, arranging them underneath the seats.

Evren had been furious when he found out about the state of the other carriage. Eve was secretly pleased that Liam had made that confession after dinner, souring his father's mood for the rest of the night. Servants had already been sent to reclaim and repair the broken vehicle, but the damage hadn't been fixed in time for their trip.

Sucks to be you, she thought, glaring down at him.

Evren stood tall, a blot of red and black ink against the white snow. His auburn hair shimmered in the early sun, standing out even brighter against his dark fur cloak. Bones swung like fringe from his shoulders and ankles, dragging against the snow as he lazily paced the front lawn.

Preece defied his father in a contrast of dusty blue no darker than ice upon a lake. The color was woven into every inch of his clothes, blending nicely with his greenish skin and hair. It almost reminded Eve of the rococo paintings she'd seen at the museum.

Was this how he usually dressed in the Seelie Court? Eve had only seen him in the dark colors of the Bone Court, but the pastels suited him better.

Preece caught her eye through the window and waved with a smile. Eve timidly waved back, too tired to return his enthusiasm. She let out a staggering breath when the vehicle finally took off, both men sequestered safely inside.

Eve fidgeted with her robe, hopeful that Preece would find some information on Liam's condition in the Court of Knowledge. Waiting was always the hardest part.

What if he didn't find anything? All that time wasted while Liam slowly turned into a lawn ornament.

There has to be something else I can do.

The little bottles of paint from the marketplace caught her eye, untouched atop the blank canvas.

Perhaps there *was* something she could do.

"This place is *insane!*" Hailey gaped in awe at the busy underground marketplace, her attention flitting from one booth to the next with childlike fascination. She turned on Liam, her lips drawn into a pout. "Why haven't you ever taken me here before?"

"You never asked," Liam said bluntly. Hailey made a face, then tried to wander down one of the aisles. "Don't go too far—it's not safe on your own. Stay close to us."

"Then hurry up!" Hailey bounced on the balls of her feet impatiently. Liam did his best to walk casually, but the limp in his gait was prominent enough that even Hailey noticed.

Before she could ask, he simply said, "Sparring injury. Don't worry yourself."

Hailey nodded, but Eve could tell Liam was grateful she walked slower down the aisle. Eve wandered behind both of them, sticking close.

Liam hadn't mentioned a word about his mother since last night. Eve hesitated to bring it up. Tension corded through his slender form, his gaze sweeping over her before she could read the emotions hidden underneath.

He's allowed to have secrets. Eve had plenty of her own. Yet it bothered her, not knowing this part of him. If he got to know her deepest secrets, why couldn't she know his?

Hailey hadn't said anything about last night, either, but Eve saw an extra push from her friend for normalcy. Extra wide smiles and a bubbly disposition were her armor, and Hailey wore it well.

She's probably more worried about Sage anyway, Eve thought. *We all have our problems, I guess.*

Eve's gaze lingered on Liam's gloves, picturing the stone underneath. She redirected her attention to the stalls lined up on either side, scanning their contents for something useful.

She didn't know what she was searching for exactly. A cure for Liam's disease wasn't likely to be found sitting out with wares and goods.

Although, Eve thought as they passed a booth selling specialized glamours, *it wouldn't be impossible.*

Rust-tinted bottles and liquid tinctures caught her eye. Eve examined the heavy salves in tin containers and foul-smelling remedies that were questionably medicinal in nature. Her finds never did what she wanted them to, though. Some promised enhanced beauty, while others offered various ailments against one's victims.

"This will stop a heartbeat for ten minutes once consumed," one shop owner said, pointing at the purple glass bottle Eve had been staring at.

"Wouldn't they die?"

"They are put into a stasis. Can't do a thing until those ten minutes are up."

Eve considered the bottle—not for Liam, but to use against Colton. She had no idea how she would get him to consume it, though, and reluctantly moved on.

"Find what you wanted?" Liam asked when she rejoined them at the next booth. Hailey was examining a necklace with heavy black stones on display.

"No," Eve sighed.

"What *are* you looking for, exactly?" Hailey asked, still enamored by the jewelry.

"I wish I knew." Eve sighed and readjusted her cloak. "I'll know it when I see it."

Liam shrugged, then hooked Hailey's arm in his and dragged her away from the booth. Under his breath, Eve heard, "That jewelry is cursed, Hailey. You don't want anything from there."

"But it's gorgeous..."

Eve browsed more stalls with growing dissatisfaction. The Unseelie market had everything for sale—poisons, weapons, spells, glamours, bones, cloth, enchantments, memories, regrets, tears, teeth, dreams, nightmares, humans, animals, and creatures Eve had never seen—some she never wanted to see again. Everything but a cure.

They eventually came across an apothecary's stand with shelves and displays littered with black corked bottles labeled in inky script. Eve paused, carefully reading each label with discernment.

"Is there something in particular that you require, child?" The apothecary was a tall, angular man with bluish skin and eyes as black as obsidian. A thick, velvet robe hung down past his feet, the fabric hissing as he moved behind the stand.

"Yes," Eve said, carefully glancing at Liam out of the corner of her vision. He was already following Hailey to the next booth, likely discerning that she had a higher risk of getting tricked by one of the Fair Folk than Eve. Still, Eve kept her voice low as she said, "I'm trying to find a cure for a rare disease. Do you have anything that could help?"

"I have tinctures for all sorts of maladies. You will need to be more specific."

"Do you have one for someone that's turning into stone?"

"I do not dwell in remedies for curses," the apothecary said with a dismissive wave of his hand. "You will need to speak to an enchantress for that."

"It's not a curse," Eve insisted. "It's a disease."

"I know ailments, girl, and the curse of stone is not a disease," the apothecary said. "And it is not nearly as rare as you are led to believe. You will find no treatment for it here."

Eve scowled but left the booth.

Had the hags been wrong? Everyone assumed Liam's disease was actually some curse—one that could be easily broken with the spell of an enchantress, no less. If that were the case, wouldn't Liam have already tried that? And if so, then why was he still turning to stone before her eyes?

The next stall had several thin wooden boxes with different compartments, their contents displayed by panels of glass. Rows and rows of various beetles with jewel tone carapace glittered inside. Eve thought they were dead until the stall's owner—a woman with an eagle's beak and feathers adorning her body—opened one of the displays and the beetles' antennae twitched.

"If it's a missing item that you seek," the eagle-woman said, pointing to a beetle with large pincers at the front. "This one will bring it to you directly."

"What about a person?" Hailey asked.

"Living or dead?"

Hailey faltered. "Living, I hope."

The stall's owner plucked a small beetle with a shimmering ruby carapace. "Speak to it the name of whom you seek, and it will lead you to your missing companion."

"A beetle bloodhound," Eve remarked.

"Far more efficient. I know of no hounds that work without a scent," the eagle-woman said. "Obedient though they may be."

"It's perfect." Hailey reached for the beetle, but the owner snatched it back, holding the insect in a loose fist.

"We haven't discussed the subject of payment. A creature of this sort is rare—you will not find many that can seek what you desire by words alone."

Hailey dug into her pockets. "I don't have money—"

"Coin!" the stall's owner scoffed. "We do not trade in coin here. No, I think I should prefer an innocent memory. Such things are rare to come by here."

Hailey stared at the clutched fist, wavering. Her memories were already so finicky. Eve could see that she was reluctant to lose another.

"I'll—"

"I'll do it," Eve said. The eagle-woman smiled, displaying an unnerving row of human teeth beneath her beak, and gestured her forward.

Liam's fingers brushed her elbow, giving her pause. "You don't have to do this. I have plenty of memories—"

"It's fine." Eve stepped away, closer to the stall's owner. Her talons clicked together as she pressed her free hand against Eve's skull.

"Close your eyes and think of a time of innocence," the eagle-woman instructed. Eve glanced at her talons, shuddering as they tapped her scalp.

She did not ask if it would hurt—Eve was certain she would find out soon enough.

She would pay the price either way.

Closing her eyes, Eve did not need to think hard to pinpoint the memory she wished to give. She remembered herself as she had been nearly three years ago, her long hair braided and her academy uniform chipped with paint she'd yet to scrub out. It was early spring—too cold to forgo stockings, but warm enough that Eve savored the sunlight streaming in through the windows of her art room.

Class had ended, but a few students had stayed behind to finish projects. Eve was among them, her sleeves rolled to her elbows and beige apron doing little to keep the paint from her hair. She couldn't remember what she was working on, but she recalled the blond-haired boy nearby, and his growing frustration as his watercolors dripped in the wrong sections of his paper.

"Your brush might have too much water on it," Eve said after another one of his failed attempts. "Try to swipe some of it off on a paper towel. Otherwise, it'll all kind of wash together."

The boy took her advice, swiping his wet brush before applying the next blot of color. Sure enough, the paint didn't absorb into the rest of the painting. "Thanks."

"No problem."

"Logan! You ready to go?"

Logan glanced up from his watercolors. Colton strode into the room with a smile that could stop time. Eve averted her gaze back to her painting, but her focus was lost.

"Yeah, let me clean up," Logan said. Colton took a seat while his friend tidied, peering curiously over at the watercolor painting. He caught one of Eve's furtive glances with a bemused grin.

They did not speak, but Eve's cheeks heated under his gaze. She had seen Colton around school before—everyone had—but he'd never looked at her. Never *noticed* her. She shakily continued painting, secretly pleased that he did not turn away.

"Ready to go?" Logan nudged him out of the corner of her eye. Colton nodded, his stance almost reluctant as he followed his friend out of the room.

The edges of the art room blurred. Eve blinked as something dug into her mind, replacing the memory with a vague, foggy recollection of her first crush... her first... her...?

When the beaked woman stepped away, Eve couldn't recall the memory she'd focused on. A wall of fog swirled in her mind, filling up the hollow space where the memory had lived.

"The innocence of first admiration," the eagle-woman cooed, sticking her talon into a little glass bottle. The extracted memory poured in a pink, foggy swirl until the stall's owner capped it off with a cork. "The first is always a treasured memory."

"I wouldn't know," Eve said with a hint of irony.

The eagle-woman smiled back at her, amused, then plopped the beetle into Hailey's open palms. The beetle twitched in her hands and settled down as if for a great nap.

"Don't get too cozy," Eve said. "You've got work to do."

One of its antennae twitched in response.

"Thank you," Hailey said as they left the marketplace. She had trouble meeting Eve's gaze, focusing instead on the beetle in her hands. "I... You didn't have to do that for me, you know. I would've given them something."

"I would have as well," Liam said.

"I wanted to do it," Eve said firmly. "I'm glad to get rid of that memory anyway."

"You don't even remember what it was."

Eve shrugged. "I don't regret it—and I knew going in that whatever I gave them, I would be happy to get rid of."

Hailey bit her lip but didn't interject. From what Eve could tell, she still hadn't asked Liam about restoring her memories. Was she afraid? How far would that fear hold her back?

There were plenty of things Eve wanted to forget—and even more, she refused to, lest she make foolish errors of judgment again. The past was what made people into who they were. While she could spare one here or there, Eve was protective of those memories, as horrific as they were. Without them, she would never learn.

"Should we start the search party now?" Hailey asked, hopeful. Eve shook her head.

"We should get back first," she said. "Eat, warm up—we don't know how long we'll be following this thing around."

"She's right," Liam agreed. "It'll get dark before we know it, and we're not prepared in the slightest. Best to take as many precautions as we can."

Hailey stroked the beetle's carapace with a frown. "Tonight, then?"

"Morning would be best—" Liam said, but Eve interjected before Hailey could argue.

"Tonight," she promised. "We'll find Sage tonight."

"Tonight," Hailey agreed, softening. Eve wasn't sure Hailey would be able to last another sleepless night without knowing if Sage was safe. Eve wasn't sure she could, either.

Thirty-Eight

They reconvened in the foyer after dinner. Eve readjusted the satchel underneath her cloak, the bulging leather filled with emergency supplies: food, candles, a fire starter, first aid supplies, four heated gemstones in addition to the ones she'd tucked into her gloves and boots—and her sewing needle. Hailey's bag was bigger, filled with an extra set of clothes for Sage in case she needed them.

"Do you even know how to use that?" Eve asked, pointing to the thin rapier strapped to Hailey's waist. Hailey pulled on her cloak, disguising its gold hilt.

"You didn't think Sage was going to let me stay in Faerie without teaching me how to defend myself, did you?" Hailey said. "You're not the only one with private training sessions."

Hailey winked, and Eve blushed.

"I don't know what you're talking about," Eve said hastily, which was a horrible mistake because Hailey grinned even wider.

"Oh, really?" Hailey nudged her playfully, giggling as Eve's ears burned. "So you're *not* gawking at Liam every time he walks in a room?"

"No."

"Not even a little?"

"*No.*"

"You're so cute."

"Shut up."

Eve, despite the embarrassment crawling over her skin, instinctively glanced up as Liam hobbled down the stairs. From the corner of her vision, Hailey smirked. A childish part of Eve almost won out and shoved her. Eve gripped her satchel instead, silently willing her blush to evaporate.

"I suspect you two are ready to go, then?" Liam asked, his otherwise pleasant voice strained. His body was entirely covered, but even his clothes couldn't hide the solid stone that crawled up the back of his neck and consumed his left ear.

Eve's breath caught. His ear hadn't been that way an hour ago. The disease was spreading much faster than she'd realized.

She fidgeted with the hem of her cloak. What if Preece didn't find the information they needed before Liam turned entirely? What if he didn't find anything *at all?* Time moved slowly as Liam pulled on his boots, his movements stiff and irregular. Even Hailey noticed how he struggled to bend over, his fingers grinding together with effort to pull at the leather.

"You can't come with us," Eve decided. Hailey nodded in agreement. A troubled frown pulled at her lips as Liam struggled with his boots.

"I'm not letting you two go out on your own," Liam scoffed. "You'll get yourselves killed."

"We can handle ourselves." Hailey swung an arm around Eve's shoulder for emphasis. Then she pulled at the brooch of red berries pinned to her cloak. "See? We shouldn't have any problems with the Fair Folk."

"It is not the Fair Folk I'm solely concerned about," Liam said, frowning at Eve.

"We'll be fine," Eve reassured him. "We don't even know if Sage found him."

"But if she did?"

Eve considered. With the brutality Colton had been showing the Fair Folk, Eve wasn't certain Sage would've made it out alive. She wasn't about to say that in front of Hailey, though.

"She's my sister," Liam insisted. "Regardless of her hatred, I do care about her. I want to find her."

"You can't go out in your condition. You can barely stand!"

Liam wanted to argue, but his silence proved that he knew it would be a lie. He finished putting on his boots, but the laces were tricky. His fingers were unable to bend with the flexibility they used to, making the task impossibly difficult.

"Eve's right," Hailey said. "You're hurt, Liam. You need to stay here."

"I'm going."

"Back to bed, maybe," Eve mumbled. Liam opened his mouth to protest, but Eve slapped a hand over it, silencing him. "Stop. If you try to come along, you're going to slow us down—or worse. You know that."

Liam glowered at her. When she pulled her hand away, he sighed, the argument flooding out of him all at once. "What do you suppose we do, then? The Unseelie Court is dangerous, particularly at night, even without the brute making a nuisance of things." He glanced at Hailey, noting her confusion. "If this serial murderer *does* have my sister, I doubt he will simply let her go because you ask nicely."

"I'm not going to ask him nicely," Eve muttered, her fingers brushing against the dagger strapped to her hips. Liam half-smiled, his eyes sad.

"I don't believe he will let her go at all, regardless of how you ask."

"We don't even know if we'll run into him or her or whoever," Hailey said. "But if we *do*, there's two of us. We can distract him."

"He's not going to listen to anything we have to say." Eve recalled how poorly her last confrontation with Colton went. "*If* he shows up, though, a distraction would be nice."

"That's all very well and good," Liam said. "But how do you intend to do that?"

Eve turned her attention out the window, scanning the dark expanse of forest outside.

"I know someone that can do it for us."

The freezing winter was nothing compared to the iciness between Eve and her enemy. She trudged on, eyeing the little beetle in Hailey's hands, its shell reflective against the moonlight. Hailey followed at her side while Logan trudged miserably behind. Eve knew he was still there by the steady crunch of his boots in the snow.

It had been easy to convince him to come along. Showing up in his room with a dagger pointed at his throat made for simple bargaining.

"You want to use me as bait?" he'd whispered. His Adam's apple bobbed against her blade.

"You owe me," Eve reminded him. "This doesn't even begin to cover it."

"What if he's not even there?" Logan argued.

"Then you have nothing to worry about."

Logan trembled, but didn't fight. He'd gathered his things and met them at the edge of the manor, carrying himself like a sacrifice prepped for slaughter.

Hailey held the beetle to her lips and whispered, "Francis, please go find Sage Fogtree."

The little beetle hopped off her hands, leading the way. Eve rose a brow. "Francis?"

"I figured he needs a name."

"It's nice."

Their conversation had lapsed after that. Eve reserved her focus for the beetle, watching the tiny creature brush along the snow without impact. If it wasn't for its shiny carapace, they would've lost it a while ago.

Maybe we should've *waited for daylight.* Too late now. Eve wasn't sure if she wanted Sage to have found Colton or not. On one hand, it would make it easier for her to kill him—supposedly. With Logan providing a distraction, Hailey could grab Sage, and Eve could stab him in the back. That was the ideal scenario.

Considering how things went last time, I doubt it'll be that easy...

If Sage hadn't found him, well, not much would change—except that Eve had to endure a late-night traipse through the woods with one of the men she hated most.

Logan coughed behind her, and Eve turned to glare at him briefly before continuing forward. She preferred to pretend he didn't exist, but Eve knew she had to make sure he was still with them and listened for his footsteps. Each sound from him made her want to rip her ears off.

The silence must have been too much for Hailey because she cleared her throat and asked, "So, uh, how'd you two meet?"

Eve kept her gaze forward. "He was in my art class."

"Oh! Did you guys have any projects together, or...?" Hailey glanced between them cautiously, sensing the frigid waters she was wading into.

Eve wasn't in the mood for niceties. "You want to tell her, or should I?"

Logan started, his eyes wide and uncertain, as if he expected it to be a trick question. "Do you... *want* me to talk about it?"

A part of her did. After Liam and Preece's reactions, Eve found herself... wanting to tell Hailey what happened. To give her best friend a secret as deep as the ones Hailey couldn't even remember.

"I'm not the one who's going to look like shit if you do," Eve said a beat too late. His cheeks flushed in shame. Logan struggled to meet either of their gazes, his attention focused on the toes of his boots.

"I... We... I wasn't a great guy in high school. I mean—"

"Don't try to make yourself look good," Eve snapped. "Just tell her what you did."

Logan shrank into himself. His pathetic passivity infuriated her. *You're not the victim!* She wanted to scream. *You were NEVER the victim!*

But she waited. Logan glanced at her, searching for help—for *her* to do the dirty work—but Eve refused. He didn't deserve to have her soften the blow.

Logan swallowed hard. Each word he spoke barely carried above a whisper. "We did something unforgivable. I... I'll carry that for the rest of my life—"

"*Coward,*" Eve seethed. Sickened rage roiled inside of her, blood pounding in her ears. Her hands itched to strangle him where he stood. She should have never let him live.

Begging for his life when it was the two of them was one thing—but to refuse to admit what he'd done in front of someone else? Eve was reminded of her initial confession to the school all over again. The sobbing, the begging for someone to hear her. To *believe* her. It was her word against theirs, and Logan had been silent then as he was now. Why did she ever, for a moment, trust his word? Why would she ever believe he might have changed?

Eve was used to screaming in an endless void. Deep down, she begged to be heard.

Yet, why was it that her heart thundered when she parted her lips to speak? The confession caught in her throat, anxiety slicking her hands with sweat.

Just do it, she told herself. *You told Liam.* But that had been an accident. The truth had slipped from her tongue before she could reel it back in. The last time she'd told someone with intention had been...

Freshman year. Fear coalesced in her veins, pricking at her confidence with its thorny reminders. Her father yelling. Her mother denying. The church, the boys, the school twisting her pain into a mangled fib that could be brushed under the rug and left to fester in its own rot.

They didn't believe you. They'll never believe you. You can't trust anyone.

That wasn't true. Liam *did* believe her. He'd taken her word when no one else had.

Maybe... Maybe Hailey would, too.

"He raped me." The words were foreign to her ears. They sounded distant, as if another girl had spoken. Someone much braver than Eve.

She glared at Logan's shrinking form, daring him to contradict her. It was real. It happened. She'd... said it.

Hailey stumbled. "He *what?*"

"He raped me," Eve said again, swallowing past the lump in her throat. Speech came easier a second time. "In my freshman year. He and his friends. They got away with it. The guy Sage went after, the one killing all the Fair Folk... he's one of them."

When she met Hailey's eyes, Eve expected pity. Maybe disgust or accusation. She remembered the blame her parents had heaved upon her shoulders. The weight of their disappointment—of their shame—had crushed her. Every kick after from her parish, her school, and her friends had only added more salt to the wound.

Eve was not expecting the unbridled rage that burned in her friend's eyes.

Without a word, Hailey spun toward Logan—she towered over him by nearly two inches—and punched him square in the nose. A loud *crunch* echoed through the forest.

"Fuck!" Logan howled, clutching his face as Hailey held her fist in the air. When he pulled his hands away, blood gushed down his chin. "Jesus—*you broke my nose!*"

"I'll break a lot more if you lay another hand on her," Hailey spat viciously. She wrapped a protective arm around Eve's shoulders, tugging her close. "You want me to kill him for you, Eve? I'll do it. I have a sword."

The threat pulled Eve from her stunned stupor. She nearly choked out a laugh. "What happened to *thou shalt not kill*?"

Hailey leveled a glare at Logan over her shoulder. "Even God breaks his own commandments."

Affection swelled in Eve's heart. She tucked her chin in, hiding a stupid smile behind the hood of her cloak. Eve had never been more grateful for her friend.

The beetle took them further through the woods, and Eve had to squint through the darkness lest she trip. The pine trees condensed the further they moved in, forcing their little group together as Francis led the way.

Hailey stopped abruptly. She reached for Eve's arm, squeezing tight.

"What is it?" Eve dropped her voice to a low whisper. She almost growled when Logan bumped into her from behind. He mouthed a quick *sorry* and stepped back.

Hailey pointed ahead. At first, Eve didn't see what she was gesturing to. Then the clouds shifted, and the glimmer caught her eye.

An arrow stuck out of a nearby tree. Eve shuddered, remembering how easily one had sliced through Liam's shoulder. The arrow's tip was embedded deeply into the rough bark, but caught between it was a thin, sheer piece of fabric. If it weren't for its reflective shimmer, Eve would have never seen it.

She approached the arrow cautiously. *Not fabric,* she realized. Dread pooled in her stomach as she brushed her fingers along the insect-like material.

Wings. Pixie wings.

THIRTY-NINE

"Your beetle's still moving," Logan whispered, pointing to where Francis hopped ahead. In the time Eve avoided him, he'd wrapped his scarf around his broken nose to clot the bleeding.

The beetle did not wait for them to catch up, and Eve took a few instinctive steps forward to follow it before it could disappear between the trees.

Hailey did not move. Her face had grown pallid, her gaze locked on the scrap of wing. Carefully, she pulled it out from under the arrow, wincing as it ripped, paper-thin between her fingers.

"We don't know if that's hers," Eve said, ignoring the hopelessness of her own voice.

"It is," Hailey whispered, cradling the piece of wing close to her heart.

"It doesn't mean anything. We haven't found her yet—Sage could still be alive."

Unshed tears glistened in Hailey's eyes. "Do you believe that?"

No. But Hailey didn't need that right now. What she needed was a friend.

"Sure," Eve lied. "Let's keep going."

Hailey nodded, still clutching the torn wing. Logan was up ahead, shuffling awkwardly after the beetle. He didn't seem to know whether to keep following it or stay, but he kept an eye on the bug before it could get too far.

The girls caught up to him and pushed forward. There was a solemnity to their trek through the woods. Eve almost expected to find Sage's corpse buried among the bramble. Even Logan was eerily quiet.

Eve wasn't sure if it was from the pain of his broken nose or his fear of disturbing what Fair Folk lingered in the forest. Either way, she was glad for his silence.

Francis led them through the trees and to a narrow stream. Dark water lapped over the smooth rocks and bent in a winding arc through the forest. Eve couldn't tell how deep the water was—and she wasn't willing to check. There was no sign of Sage. Or any life, for that matter.

Weird. Now that she thought about it, Eve hadn't seen—or even heard—any of the Fair Folk traipsing through the woods for some time. Usually, she would have been swatting away snow sprites by now or steering clear of the sharp-toothed creatures that eyed wanderers as prey.

Their trip had been easy. Quiet, even.

Far too quiet.

Unease crept up the back of Eve's neck. The light hairs on her body rose in the chill. The Unseelie Court thrived in the darkness. She'd seen firsthand how their power grew, as if the sun itself were a force meant to weaken them. They should have passed some—if not several—hungry eyes by now.

Where are the Fae?

Francis the beetle did not stop at the stream. Eve followed with far more caution as they carried on. She glanced at the trees, the water, the sky—searching for any kind of life. The stillness of the forest only made her jumpier, as though some monstrous force was keeping the Fair Folk at bay.

The beetle led them to the open mouth of a cave, its tiny body disappearing into the dark. Eve and the others hesitated outside, sticking to the shadows of the forest.

Boot prints overlapped on the snow outside of the cave, the shapes crisscrossed and snowed over with time. Even in the dark, Eve saw the glint of iron protruding from the ground as a barrier—and the blood that stained the ground underneath.

"We should go back," Logan whispered. His nails dug into the bark of a nearby tree. Eve could smell the fear on him from a mile away—and she was certain the Fair Folk could, too.

So, why aren't they coming?

They crept around the edge of the trees, Hailey's fist in Logan's cloak to drag him along. The scent of decay wafted toward them as they approached the entrance. Dark patches of blood stained the floor, and iron bars had been shoved jaggedly into the earth like crooked teeth.

A shudder ran through Eve. Now she understood why there were no Fae: this was the work of a human. No Fair Folk would create a barrier of iron in this way—not even to repel their own.

"We need a lookout," she said, locking her gaze onto Logan. The young man blanched.

"Me? You want *me* to stand here and watch?" His voice rose in pitch, nasally from his smashed-in nostrils. His pale eyes darted across the landscape, as if anticipating one of the Fair Folk to attack while his guard was down.

"You *were* going to be the distraction," Eve said. "We better get some use out of bringing you here."

Hailey nudged her in the side. "I don't know, Eve. Are you sure you want to trust him to keep watch? You're not afraid he's going to bolt off into the woods?"

Logan appeared as though he might do just that. Eve shrugged, speaking loud enough for him to hear, "If he wants to run off by himself and get eaten in the woods, be my guest. The Fair Folk are less likely to attack people in groups, anyway. You and I are fine."

She had no idea if that last part was true—and somehow doubted it was—but it was enough to make Logan reconsider his earlier plans for escape.

"I won't run away," he said, more of a tentative choice than a promise. Logan gingerly removed his scarf and applied some snow to it before retying it around his face in an attempt to ice his broken nose. "Just... be quick, alright?"

"No," Eve said. Logan's face hardened, but he took up his half-hidden post beside one of the iron bars.

Eve turned toward the cave, its entrance a gaping maw.

Dread pooled in her stomach as she stepped past the threshold. Eve clutched the matches in her pack, desperate for light, but unwilling to give her location away. *Was* this Colton's doing? Surely other humans had come through Faerie. Eve had seen them with her own eyes.

But the primal survival instinct to it all... It screamed calculation. It screamed *Colton*.

The girls stumbled through the darkness, their fingers brushing along the jagged walls to guide them. The scent of decay lingered, molding and wet, akin to rotten leaves left in the rain. It grew stronger the deeper they traveled, the musty rot cloying in Eve's nose.

She stepped onto something squishy and recoiled. *Please don't be a dead body.*

She did not smell death. Eve kept moving forward.

"You shouldn't... be here..."

They froze. The voice—so startlingly close—left Eve's heart hammering in her ears.

"Sage?" Hailey whispered. Metal clinked in response. Hailey lit one of the matches and held it up toward the voice, her breath shuddering.

Sage had never been worse for wear. She hunched against the cold, wet floor in a shivering heap. Purple bruises circled her golden eyes, but Eve couldn't tell exhaustion from fists. Her normally buoyant lilac hair hung low, disheveled and tangled with debris. The once mystical wings on her back had been shredded, leaving pale green tatters dangling limply from their tattered frame. Her clothes were damp with grime, her cloak and boots missing entirely.

Francis sat atop Sage's shoulder. Eve wasn't sure Sage even noticed him.

What happened? Eve's gaze fell to the chains at Sage's feet—and then the iron clasps around her wrists and ankles.

The skin underneath had been burned as if touched by acid. Bile rose in the back of her throat as she saw the raw, pink muscle poking out from the gaps. Sage remained utterly still, the clasps on the ground positioned in a way that her wrists could hover between them. As if she feared the metal would touch her again.

Eve followed the trail of chains and gasped. Three Fae corpses sat shackled to the wall, their thin wrists clasped in iron. Their jaws hung open in silent agony, their pelts and flesh meticulously stripped the same as the not-deer in the woods. They did not smell as corpses do, but instead of decaying leaves, and Eve realized where the musty scent was coming from.

"Dear God." Hailey fell to her knees and touched Sage's battered face with the gentlest care. "What happened to you?"

"Ambition." Sage forced a weak smile. Trickles of blood colored her pointed teeth. "Stupidity, I fear. Once I saw it was a mortal, I did not take the threat seriously." Her smile faded, a darkness pooling in her eyes. "You have to leave. Both of you. Before he gets back."

"I'm not going to leave you here," Hailey snapped, then reached for the iron chains. To Eve, "Help me find a way to get these things off."

Sage pulled her wrists away, hissing in pain when the metal touched her. "Don't! It's pure iron—even our metals are not strong enough to break it. You need the key."

"Okay, where's the key?"

Before Sage could answer, a set of footsteps echoed distantly from the cave's entrance. Eve tensed as a second pair fell in line. Colton had returned.

"We have to hurry," Eve all but mouthed to the others. "Turn the light off."

Hailey extinguished the match. They fell into pitch-black darkness again with only touch to guide them. Eve felt around on the ground, following the line of chain to Sage's cuffs. Sage tried to pull away, but Eve took her hand and held it tight.

"We're going to get you out of here," she whispered as close to Sage's ear as she could. The Faerie's hands were ice.

"Why?" Sage's words were barely audible over the sound of Colton's and Logan's footsteps down the tunnel."

"Because we're friends."

Sage was silent. It was too dark to read her emotions, but her hand tightened in Eve's palm.

"Where's the key?" Hailey whispered, leaning in. Sage sighed heavily.

"He keeps it on his person."

Great. Eve bit her lip, thinking.

"I'm going to try picking your lock," she said. "Don't move."

Sage was silent as Eve dug into her pouch. She didn't have much for this kind of situation: the needle and her matches were the smallest she could fit into the keyhole. Removing the pulsing needle from her pouch, Eve slipped it into the hole.

The mechanism was different from what she'd attempted on the door in the distillery. Iron clicked against silver. Nervous sweat slicked her hands, and when she tried to wiggle the needle inside, it slipped from her grasp and fell to the floor.

Shit. Eve touched the ground, but it was nowhere in sight. *Shit!*

There wasn't time to look for it—not now.

Eve tried not to think of the dire consequences that awaited her for losing the valuable tool. Instead, she traded it out for one of the matches and got to work.

The match broke at once, snapping in two.

"Shit," she muttered, grabbing for another one.

Quiet, Hailey mouthed, gesturing down the tunnel. The footsteps were closer. Eve could pick out bits of their conversation, no longer merely echoed voices.

She bowed her head and worked, jerking the matches in the hole.

"...came back, you were gone."

Snap! Another match.

"I was, in a sense. I thought they were going to kill me."

Snap! Snap!

"I'm surprised they didn't."

SNAP!

The final match trembled between her fingers, a last beacon of hope. She willed herself to be strong. Precise. Efficient.

She jiggled the match against the lock.

SNAP.

Eve did not dare seek out her friends' disappointed faces. She stared at her traitorous hands, shaking in response to her failure.

The men were close now. Eve saw the edge of a light dance across the slight bend of the cave. Logan's distraction had done nothing. Perhaps he hadn't tried all that hard to begin with.

Hailey rose from her crouch beside Sage and unsheathed her rapier. Sage grew rigid, wide eyes flashing up to her.

"What do you think you're doing?" she demanded. Hailey did not bat an eye.

"I'm going to get you that key."

FORTY

"You barely know how to wield that thing," Sage hissed. Her chains rattled as she moved. Sage recoiled, trying not to whimper at the pain. "He'll kill you."

"We're not leaving here without you." Hailey was unusually calm. There was a focus in her eyes, the same Eve had seen when she'd practiced basketball.

Eve scrambled to her feet and unsheathed her dagger. Maybe if they could take him by surprise—

Colton turned the corner first. A small lantern attached to his hip lit up the cave, casting an eerie green glow from the fireflies stuck inside. Logan was at his side, his blond curls matted to his forehead with nervous sweat.

Now that there was light in the cave, she could see the collection Colton had amassed—clothes, furs, arrows with tips of both bone and iron. Various other materials and trinkets the Fair Folk had made. They sat in organized piles, some layered over stained patches of blood on the floor.

Sage's chain extended across the room. It looped through a small hole in the cave wall, just big enough for the chain to pass through.

"Where's the key?" Hailey demanded, pointing the tip of her rapier at Colton. A flicker of surprise crossed his face but smoothed over instantly.

"You're not one of the demons," Colton mused. He was not intimidated by Hailey's sword by any measure. "You wouldn't have been able to pass the barrier. A human?"

"The only demon here is you," Eve snapped. Colton's gaze fell on her. The pity in his eyes made her nauseous.

"Eve." Her name was a curse on his lips. "We can make this quick. Logan, grab the holy water over there, will you? The bottle."

Logan glanced at the girls uncertainly but obeyed, too cowed by Colton's presence to resist.

Traitor, Eve thought. If he was only closer, she could stab him. *I should've never let him live.*

"We don't want whatever you're doing," Hailey said, her chin held high. "Give us the key so we can take our friend and go."

Colton smiled patronizingly and spoke as if to a child. "I'm afraid I can't do that. I'm sorry, you must understand; I can't risk letting these creatures corrupt anyone else."

"That's what this whole serial killer shtick is about?" Eve asked, waving her dagger toward the trinkets collecting along the wall underneath scratched tallies. Trophies from his kills. "You're trying to play God?"

"Of course not." Colton pressed a hand to his heart, offended. "I am merely doing the task God assigned to me. There is only one reason he would bring me back here—bring *us* back here, Eve. He is giving us another chance to atone for our sins by wiping out the devils that have found their way from hell to our home."

"Oh my God. You're, like, actually insane," Hailey said without thinking. She took a step back, the weapon still gripped tightly in her hand.

"Actually, I wonder if I'm the only sane one here." Colton smiled bitterly, lifting the bow slightly in his hand. "Now, I'd suggest you put that down. Please. Before someone gets hurt."

"Not until you give us the key," Hailey insisted, but there was a quiver in her voice now. She'd never faced someone like Colton before, drunk on his own power and narcissism.

She could taste the lie in his excuse. Eve knew it was not delusions that led Colton here. It was his refusal to see himself and recognize his own actions that led him here. It was easier to blame the ones who passed him the alcohol than to accept the choices he made under its influence.

"You won't make this easy, will you?" Colton stepped forward, the tip of her rapier pressing lightly against his chest. Hailey took another step back. "Please. I'm trying to help."

"You're *hurting* other people!" Hailey threw one arm back to gesture at Sage, tears brimming in her eyes. "How can you call this *help?*"

"God works in mysterious ways. I am only his messenger."

Eve noticed movement behind Colton. Logan caught her eye, shifting uneasily from side to side. The bottle Colton had requested was still in his hands, waiting to be used. Based on its awkward hold, Eve guessed it was heavy and feared what might actually be inside it.

Logan glanced at Colton. Then the jar. Then Colton again.

Do it, Eve mouthed. She saw the way Logan's gaze lingered on the back of Colton's head, the jar slipping in his hands.

Logan lifted up the jar and smashed it as hard as he could against Colton's head.

The jar *thunked* against Colton's skull, then fell to the ground in a shatter of glass. Clear liquid spilled out onto the cave floor. Colton stumbled forward, grabbing onto the wall for support. Unharmed.

Logan inched back, his whole body shaking with fear. The momentum hadn't been strong enough. *He* hadn't been strong enough.

Run, Eve thought, surprising even herself. *Run!*

Logan did not move a muscle. Colton turned with a dark change in his expression. Shivers rolled down Eve's spine.

Without a word, Colton grabbed one of his arrows—and stuck it through Logan's neck.

Eve gasped. Hailey screamed, jumping back. Logan stared at them, pleading with his eyes, but there was nothing to do. He choked, gurgling on his own blood as he collapsed onto his knees and pawed helplessly at the arrow.

Colton watched over him with the same dead-eyed expression. He said nothing.

Logan's body convulsed, then stilled. The scent of iron swirled in Eve's head, momentarily placing her back into the Blood Court. All that blood, drowning, seeping into the cracks...

She shook her head and swallowed hard, forcing the thoughts away.

"I made sure I would hit an artery. He was my friend, after all," Colton said, emotionless. "It wouldn't be fair for him to suffer."

Eve didn't know what to say. She'd fantasized about killing Logan almost every night. Now, staring at his corpse, she wasn't sure what to feel. Relief at his death? Pity for the man he was?

Or fear of the man that now stood before her?

Grasping the dagger in her palm, Eve ran at Colton's back, arm raised to strike. He turned before she could—the blade embedded itself into his side instead. He let out an angry, pained cry and struck her with the back of his hand. Eve fell, but took the dagger with her, refusing to let it slip from her fingers again.

Colton grasped his bloody side, gritting his teeth in pain. He grabbed an arrow from the quiver slung over his shoulder.

Hailey swiped her rapier at him. Colton twisted his body away, the blade missing by inches.

Eve was on her feet again, breathing hard. It was two against one. Eve liked the odds with Hailey on her side, but Colton was still bigger than both of them. Stronger. His head nearly brushed the top of the cave, his body blocking the narrow bend that led to their exit.

She glimpsed Sage out of the corner of her vision. Sage was trying to pull her wrists free, but either the cuffs were too tight or the pain was too much to bear. Tears poured down her cheeks, and Sage watched helplessly as Hailey fought for a way out.

Hailey struck again. And again. Colton blocked her with his bow, knocking the blade hard enough that it dislodged from her hand. The thin weapon clattered to his feet. Colton raised his bow to smack her in the head.

Eve struck his arm, her blade scraping uselessly against the protective leather armor tied to his elbows. Hailey dove for the rapier. Colton kicked it out of her way, behind him, and knocked Eve back with his bow. Eve kept her footing but barely dodged his next attack.

Hailey lifted her legs and kicked his shin. Colton cried out, momentarily shifting away from the tunnel's gap. Eve scrambled for the rapier.

The weapon was unexpectedly light. Eve swung it at Colton, but her lacking experience was obvious. The weapon swung too loosely in her hand, threatening to fly out from her grasp. Unlike her dagger, the sides of the rapier were not sharp. When she landed a blow to his back, the hit relied entirely on her own weight behind the strike—of which there wasn't much to begin with.

"Stab him," Sage ordered. "You have to *stab* him!"

"What does it look like I'm doing?" Eve's patience was running thin. She tried to return the weapon to Hailey—it was difficult holding both the dagger and rapier at once—but Colton blocked her at every chance. She tried thrusting the rapier at him instead, point forward, but Colton easily knocked it out of his way. Hailey, on her feet again, raised her clenched fists in a boxer pose.

"You don't know what you're doing." Colton's voice was pleading, even as he dodged one of Hailey's blows. "Whatever they've promised you, it's not—"

"I *chose* this," Eve snapped. She pointed the end of the rapier at his chest and thrust.

Colton grabbed the blade before it could pierce and yanked it violently over his shoulder. Eve cried out, her own shoulder popping with the sudden force. His knee rose instantly, jabbing her hard in the sternum. Air knocked out of her lungs as she collapsed onto the ground.

Eve struggled to breathe. Logan's blood pooled underneath her, seeping into her clothes, her hair, her skin. Eve coughed, gasping for air, while Hailey continued to fight.

What now? What now? No matter if they fought separately or together, Colton still came out on top. He had muscle and experience on his side. What did Eve have?

Her gaze fell onto the lantern swinging from his hip. Ghastly shadows danced across the cave walls as he fought, his irritation growing as Hailey dodged each of his attacks. Hailey was stronger than Eve realized—but even that strength could only carry her so far.

The rapier glinted under the shifting light. Colton had tossed it down the tunnel, out of reach from either girl. Eve couldn't get to the rapier, but maybe...

Grasping her dagger, Eve dragged herself forward and smashed her dagger against the glass as hard as she could.

Fireflies fled from the lantern. They hovered above them all, as if stunned by their new freedom. Then they soared out of the tunnel in a blast of green light.

Darkness shrouded the cave. For a moment, no one moved. Colton's foot nudged Eve. She rolled out of the way, but did not miss the kick of his toe as it smashed against her back. A painful moan bubbled up as her dagger skidded out of reach. Eve held her whimper back, scrambling to her feet against the cry of her aching muscles.

Eve reached through the air blindly, nearly jumping out of her skin when she touched an arm—only to realize it was far too thin to be Colton's. Hailey grasped her wrist in the dark and silently stepped closer.

They shuffled along the wall at Hailey's guidance. Colton ignored stealth as he prowled the area, grasping blindly for the girls. Eve shuddered when his fingers come near, but they did not reach her. He moved on, slamming his hands against the walls and stomping on the floor as if they were bugs he could squash.

Hailey leaned in, her hair tickling Eve's cheek.

"On three." The words barely left her lips as she whispered in Eve's ear.

On three, what? Eve didn't have a chance to ask. Hailey stuck her leg out, and Colton tripped with a yell. Still gripping her hand, Hailey dove forward and Eve clumsily followed, both girls tackling the man from behind. Colton landed on the ground with a loud thud and a shout of rage.

He tried to flip them over. Together, they pushed him back down. Hailey grasped at his body, her fingers slipping in and out of pouches and pockets as quickly as she could. Eve tried to hold him down on her own; she grasped his hair and smashed his head against the cold floor. Once. Twice.

On her third try, Colton stuck his arms under himself and threw the girls off. They cried out, scrambling back as he righted himself.

"I got the key," Hailey choked out. "Sage?"

"Here!" Sage sounded distant, and Eve wondered how far away they'd traveled when the lights went out.

"Don't," Colton growled. Hailey cried out, and Eve heard her fall hard onto her back. As her eyes adjusted to the darkness, Eve saw Hailey's legs kick wildly in the air, one ankle captured by Colton's fist.

Eve slammed herself into his body with everything she had.

Colton faltered on his knees, but didn't fall. His grip loosened enough for Hailey to scramble away.

"Eve?" Hailey's, voice filled with panic.

"Go!"

A moment of hesitation. Hailey's footsteps thudded in an echoing distance toward Sage.

Eve was on her own.

Colton's fists came down on Eve's arms. She cried out as he threw her onto the ground, pinning her underneath his large body.

Panic clawed its way up her throat. Eve squeezed her eyes shut, but she couldn't quiet the haunting memories that flooded to the surface. This was too familiar. Too *real*. Her breath came quick and shallow, pitching into gasps as she begged her body to remember the danger she was in.

The problem was that it already knew.

"Calm down, please," Colton said. The soft gentility in his voice made her nauseous. "You're confused and making things harder for yourself. I'm on your side."

Adrenaline pumped through her veins, but Eve stopped fighting. She lay there, waiting. Biding her time.

Cautiously, Colton sat up on top of her. Maybe it was the shuddering of her breath or the tension easing from her body, but Colton must have sensed he was safe. She would not hurt him.

That was the mistake you made with predators; if you let your guard down, you were sure to be devoured.

Eve slammed her knee into his crotch. Colton shouted, bending over. He reached for her throat, but Eve raked her nails down his exposed biceps. Colton tried to shake her off, but Eve used her grip on his flesh to haul herself upward—and sunk her teeth into his shoulder.

He screamed, pushing her away, but Eve tore a chunk of flesh with her. Hot, metallic blood stained her lips and teeth. She spat the flesh away, trying not to think too hard about what she'd done. Colton was still screaming, but he was moving, too. Toward her.

It was time to go.

Eve ran as fast as she could in the dark. Tunnel walls appeared where she did not expect them, and Eve pushed off, ignoring the growing pain of bruises that blossomed on her skin with each reckless thunk.

Colton charged behind her. He grunted in pain with each step, the distance between them growing further and further apart. Eve didn't stop to see what gave him pause. She just ran.

When she reached the mouth of the cave, Hailey was already racing back inside. She skidded to a stop as Eve ran past her.

"Eve! Oh my God, you're okay!" she cried out. Eve did not stop running. Hailey struggled to keep up as she grabbed Sage's arm and helped the Faerie go after her. "Wait! Eve, slow down—"

"We have to go."

Hailey glanced back at the cave. A figure appeared at its mouth, pushing past the iron bars.

The three women grasped each other's hands and fled into the night.

FORTY-ONE

Francis was, admittedly, useful. Hailey used the little beetle to find a way back to the Bone Court, where Liam waited for them anxiously in the den.

"Sage—" His expression fell upon seeing his sister's tattered state. His brows drew together, and his voice was sharp when he spoke. "What happened?"

"Talk later," Eve said. She was already locking the windows. "Hailey, can you—"

"On it." Hailey ran off to put more locks in place.

Liam reached for Eve's arm. "Are you okay?"

"Later," she promised. Sage stood awkwardly in the corner, blankly staring at the crackling flames in the fireplace. "Can you get the doors?"

Liam glanced down in shame. "I... can't. I'm..."

He held his hands up helplessly, but even that movement was small and not without effort. Liam could barely lift his arms past his waist.

Eve exhaled shakily. It was getting worse, so much worse. Anxiety spiraled in her head, but she couldn't worry about that now. One thing at a time.

"You should be resting," she said. "Leave Sage to me and Hailey. We can—"

"I want to stay here." Liam spared another worried glance at his sister. Eve didn't understand it. Sage had tried to kill him *twice*, and yet he was afraid to leave *her* alone.

To be fair, I don't think Sage is going to be killing him anytime soon. She understood that faraway stare in the pixie's eyes all too well.

"Keep an eye on her for me, alright? I'm going to take care of some things."

Liam nodded and uncomfortably settled down in a chair by the fire. Sage did not move. Eve wondered if she saw him there at all.

Eve triple checked every lock she could think of and washed out the blood from her mouth. Even after scrubbing her gums raw, she could still taste the metallic tang of Colton's flesh and iron on her tongue. Her aim in the dark had been poor. Eve wished she'd torn out his throat instead.

Logan's blood still clung to her in dried patches. Eve cleaned herself up the best she could, promising herself a proper bath before bed. There were other things to prioritize now.

By the time she rejoined the others in the den, Hailey had wrapped a blanket around Sage's shoulders and given her a cup of tea. They sat close to each other on the settee, Hailey's head resting atop Sage's as she quietly sipped her tea. Her shimmering wings fluttered weakly underneath the blanket, rising no more than an inch or two before falling limply back in place.

Eve took a seat near Liam. He regarded her with a slight nod, but otherwise did not move. Eve wondered if he was even able to. The stone was impossible to hide now—it crept along his hair, freezing the strands in time.

If Sage noticed it, she didn't say so. After tonight, Eve wasn't sure she was paying much attention to anything.

Sage cradled the cup of tea close, glaring into its steam. Her fury was a living thing. It breathed hatred in the way her hair twisted and rose, poised to attack. Sharp claws clicked against the porcelain cup, her earlier numbness making way for the rage pent up in her heart.

"I've never been treated with such insult," Sage muttered, more to herself than anyone around her. "By a *mortal*, no less. I will have him groveling on his hands and knees for mercy for what he put me through."

"How did you find him?" Liam asked.

Sage tapped her nails against her teacup. "I questioned the Fair Folk in the area. They mentioned a cave that no one dared approach; it smelled too much of pure iron. He is craftier than I gave him credit for."

Her wings—what little remained—twitched underneath the blanket.

"Where did he get all the iron?" Eve wondered. Bandages covered Sage's wrists, disguising the exposed muscle underneath. "I thought pure iron was rare in Faerie."

"It is, but pure iron has been passing through Faerie for thousands of years," Liam explained. "You won't see much of it in the Seelie Court, but the Unseelie find that its benefits outweigh the danger. There is no telling how many hoards have been stashed around."

"What does he need all that for?" Hailey asked. "I understand the pure iron and the weapons, but there was a *ton* of stuff in there."

"Pieces for survival," Liam guessed. "He's had to live out there somehow."

Sage shook her head. "Not even the Fae kill that much for survival."

Discontented quiet fell over the room. No one was particularly eager to carry on the grim conversation.

"I need to rest," Sage finally said, rising from the settee. Hailey followed suit.

"That's a great idea," she said quickly. "We'll come together with a plan tomorrow. I think we could all use some sleep."

"You go on," Liam said with a well-practiced smile. Pain flickered across his eyes when he glanced at Sage's wings. "I intend to stay up a while longer."

Hailey nodded, and Sage followed her upstairs, away from the others. Liam stared into the fire, his smile slipping. The pain of their conversation weighed on the crease between his brows, the hunch of his shoulders. Liam slumped into his chair as much as the stone would allow, pulling him down into the pits of remorse.

"You didn't know," Eve whispered.

"I should have done more."

"You couldn't have changed it." The words left her before she could catch them. Eve curled up on her chair, legs tucked against her chest as her own declaration settled in.

I couldn't have changed it. The what ifs had haunted her for too long. Eve knew what happened was not her fault, but that did not stop the questions from creeping in. The accusations that if she had done things differently, dressed differently, was simply a different girl altogether, this would not have happened.

Those thoughts would drive anyone to insanity. They were best left alone altogether.

Liam shifted in his chair. The movement was stiff and halting. Eve could hear the grind of his stone-laden skin as he struggled to find a comfortable position. Liam gave up and fell back against the cushions, breathing hard from the exertion.

"It's almost time, isn't it?" Eve asked. She slipped onto the floor to sit closer to the fire. Closer to Liam.

"I've been playing the old hag's riddle over in my head since it was spoken," Liam said. "I suppose it's too late now to figure it out."

"There's plenty of time. You can still talk, can't you?"

"Not for much longer."

Eve met his gaze and frowned. His hopelessness was contagious, and Eve wasn't sure she could save Liam *and* kill Colton at the same time. Honestly, she wasn't sure she could do either one to begin with. Her doubts increased tenfold as the stone solidified over parts of his face, freezing his scale-freckled skin in that moment in time.

She wanted to reach up and tear the stone away. She wished to claw at the ugly gray granite until it cracked and splintered like chipped paint. Until she could see Liam's face and stop hating herself for her failure.

Desire rivaled with fear to kiss him. Would it be their last? What if she did, and she couldn't let go? The macabre part of her wondered if the stone would spread to her, trapping them together as eternal statues in the den. They would be left as Evren's decorations, his golden boy and the filthy mortal that dared to ensnare his son's heart.

Eve did not think this was love. She wasn't sure she was capable of such a thing. Still, the stirrings of affection mangled her heart in ways she could not explain. One look at his handsome face, and she was made a fool.

"A bard."

"What?"

"A bard," Liam said, staring at the fire. The flames danced in his golden eyes, bringing them to life. "I want to be a bard. Instead of running the Bone Court."

"I don't know what that is."

"They tell stories," he explained. A wistful smile touched his face. "Sing songs, play music, make people laugh. They aren't well off but find fulfillment in other ways."

It was the first Eve had heard of it. Warm affection spread through her at the thought of Liam gallivanting from town to town, leaving taverns of laughter in his wake. "I didn't know you could play music."

"I can't. Not well, anyway," he admitted. "I have a pan flute upstairs. Father complains that it bothers his ears. I've only practiced when he's not around. He says there isn't much use for instruments among his heirs."

"There's always a use for art," Eve argued. Liam smiled wanly.

"If only everyone shared that view."

I want to see him play the pan flute. It was only upstairs, but she did not get it, did not mention it. A new resolve settled inside of her.

She would save him. If she could not stop what was to come, she would find a way to undo it. Eve made this promise to herself, helpless to fight against it and unwilling to let him go.

This was bigger than a crush or a kiss. If there was any hope for her, for her soul—damned to hell or otherwise—it was tied up in his life.

There was a long moment of silence. Eve stared at the drifting embers of the fire, the crackle of flames on wood drifting her into a quiet stupor.

"I did not mean to kill her."

Eve's head bobbed awake. She blinked up at Liam, confused, as his words slowly registered in her brain.

"Your mother?"

"Yes." His expression strained. "I don't want you thinking I did it for pleasure. It was an accident. I didn't mean—I only wanted her to stop."

Eve's brows furrowed. "Stop what?"

"Hurting me."

Her heart sank. Liam kept his attention focused on the fire as if he, too, could burn with it.

Eve knew the pain of a parent's hatred like a self-orchestrated symphony. She still winced at the clink of metal on belts and when a man's voice rose too high. Ben did not try to kill his daughter, but there were times Eve knew he wanted to.

"I do not want to become them," Liam whispered, almost too low for her to hear.

Eve grabbed his gloved hand—all but stone in her palm—and squeezed it, nonetheless. "You are not them. You're not anything like them."

"How can you be certain?"

"Because I know *you*," Eve said with conviction. "That tells me all I need to know."

Liam's breath shuddered. He gave her fingers a gentle squeeze in return.

As the fire dimmed, Eve rested her head against Liam's leg. His gloved hand came to rest on her hair, the fingers too solid to be comfortable but providing comfort, nonetheless.

I'll paint him something beautiful after all this, she thought sleepily, remembering the untouched paints and canvas upstairs. Her eyelids drooped as the night dragged on. *It will be the prettiest thing he's ever seen.*

I won't even have to use blood.

FORTY-TWO

Embers still glowed in the fireplace when Eve awoke from her nap, but the cold was quickly seeping in. She sat upright, stretching her stiff muscles before rubbing her arms for warmth. The moon hovered in the sky outside of the den's window, casting silver light across the room.

"Liam?" Eve turned and reached for his leg. Rough, solid stone scraped underneath her fingers. She shuddered, standing quickly to observe him. God, even his clothes had turned to stone. "Liam?"

Eve shook him—as much as she could do to a statue. Liam grumbled something out of the corner of his mouth, half-asleep.

He's alive. Eve sat back on her calves in relief. In the dim, flickering light, Eve saw that the stone had overtaken most of his face. Patches on the left side remained untouched, allowing the corner of his lips to twitch in discomfort.

There would be no moving him upstairs. Eve reached for a blanket strewn across the back of the settee and hung it over his shoulders, tucking it between him and the chair to stay in place. Eve wasn't sure how he slept at all in that position, but what choice did he have?

Tentatively, she reached for his calf and attempted to straighten his leg. The stone would not budge.

"If you intend on feeling me up, I'm afraid you'll be sorely disappointed by my current state," Liam said drowsily, the words half-muffled under his stone lips. "Unless you are into this sort of thing. Is this what you mortals mean by having rock-hard abs?"

Eve smacked his leg, wincing as her knuckles rapped against stone. "I was trying to help. That can't be comfortable."

"It's not," Liam agreed. His single golden eye solemnly flickered to the dying embers. "I won't make it through the night."

Eve couldn't bring herself to argue. It was a painful revelation, but she could only imagine how much harder it was for him.

"Preece is searching for information," she said quietly. "There's still a chance we can reverse it."

"Do you believe that?"

"Someone has to." Eve grabbed the poker and nudged some of the logs, if only for something to keep her preoccupied.

"You should rest," Liam said. "It's been a long night. One of us ought to get some sleep."

"I'm not that tired." A yawn betrayed her. Eve scowled at Liam's attempt at a smirk.

"Try anyway," Liam said. "I will be here in the morning. There is nothing to be done about it tonight."

She hated that he was right. Eve reluctantly climbed to her feet, adjusting the slipping blanket on Liam's shoulders again before trudging up the stairs.

A film of sweat and dried blood clung to her skin. A large bruise throbbed on her hip where she'd fallen in the cave, and smaller ones decorated her arms and legs in black-blue blossoms. Eve diverted to the bathroom, where she settled in the large porcelain tub and scrubbed away the grime and filth until the touch of Colton's hands was only a lingering nightmare on her senses.

Bathed and refreshed, Eve changed into her nightdress and collapsed on her bed, willing sleep to take over. Her body ached with exhaustion. Yet the bed was only a small comfort to her racing mind. Thoughts spiraled one after another, trying to solve mysteries she was too tired to contemplate.

Blood from stone, bind with thine own. Ash to root, a seed awaiting her fruit—lay to rest, the newt.

Blood from stone... Liam's blood, maybe? Was she supposed to draw blood from him? What did the ash and root have to do with it? Seeds and fruits and newts... What the hell did any of that *mean?*

Her attempts at sleep defeated, Eve threw herself out of bed. Darkness loomed outside, still too late for the sun to rise. She tied on her robe and crept into the hall, the moss carpet squishing under her feet. If rest wasn't an option, maybe some caffeine would get her brain to function.

Eve glanced into the den, relieved to see Liam's eye shift under the lid, before she moved to the kitchen. She put on the kettle and slumped against the counter, thinking.

Bind the threads with no eye, unravel the ones seen.

Free those which have been cast in stone, behold an empire grown.

A new age is upon us.

Why couldn't you say what you meant? Eve thought in frustration. Tea ready, she took up residence at the nearby table and glared out the window, mentally willing the trees to give her the answers.

A soft noise of surprise caught her attention. Hailey lingered in the doorway, hair loose and messy. "Can't sleep either?"

Eve shook her head. "Water's hot if you want some."

Hailey nodded and prepared her own cup of tea. Eve could smell the thick layers of sugar and honey inside from across the room. She settled in across from her with a sweet-scented teacup in the shape of a tulip.

Eve stirred her spoon idly, glancing toward the ceiling. "Is Sage...?"

"Asleep," Hailey confirmed. "Finally. She wouldn't say it, but I could tell she was in a lot of pain. I'm going to figure out how to get a doctor, or a healer, or whatever they use here over in the morning. Her wrists were awful, and her wings..."

Eve winced, a phantom pain dancing across her spine where Sage's wings would've connected. "Did she say why he kept her locked up?"

Hailey stared into the depths of her teacup, her thumb stroking the rippled edges of the lip. "He had been torturing the Fae to figure out their weaknesses. She lasted the longest."

Eve cringed, recalling the other Fair Folk chained to the cave. Did Colton ever replace them when he was finished? How many Faeries did he hurt?

They drank in quiet, ruminating over the hardship of their night. At one point, Hailey refilled their cups and gathered leftover cranberry scones from the pantry. Eve nibbled one, too tired to resist.

"So, what's the deal with Liam turning into a rock?" Hailey asked. "I didn't want to mention it in front of him, but it's kind of hard not to notice."

"He's sick," Eve explained with a sigh. She caught Hailey up with the information she had, relaying her request to Preece and the riddle they'd been given to solve. Her friend listened with concentration, lips pressing into a thin line as Eve described his current state. "I don't know what else to do."

Hailey sat back in her seat, nails clinking against the side of her teacup. "We'll figure something out. It's not like we'll let him turn into a garden gnome."

"I thought we'd have more time," Eve said. "I thought we'd at least be fine until Preece got back, but..."

"I could've helped sooner if I knew about it." There was an edge of dissatisfaction to Hailey's voice. "I could've helped with *any* of this stuff if you guys had just *told* me what was going on. Why didn't either of you trust me with this?"

"I..." Eve wasn't sure what to say. She took a sip of her tea—cold now—and averted her gaze. "I wasn't ready to talk about some of it."

"No, I get *that*. God, I can't imagine. But still." Hurt flashed across Hailey's face as she gripped her teacup tight. "We're friends, and we're supposed to be there for each other. I can't do that if I don't know what's going on. Maybe I wouldn't have been helpful for any of it, but I won't know unless I try."

Eve sucked in her lip, the guilt crashing down all at once. Hailey was right. If Eve had said something sooner, maybe the extra help would've saved Liam. Maybe Colton would've never captured Sage at all. How much pain could have been avoided if Eve had simply talked to someone and asked for help?

Would she have believed me? Hailey had proven herself without a doubt that she trusted Eve, but a small part of her still wondered if that would have always been the case.

Meeting Hailey's gaze now, Eve wondered how she ever could have doubted her.

"I'm sorry," Eve whispered. The anxious scrutiny made her jittery, and Eve gathered up their scones and dirty utensils, quickly moving to clean up as she talked. "I didn't mean—I don't want you to think that—" *Ugh*. Why was talking so hard? "I didn't think Liam's situation was mine to tell. As for the rest of it, I... I'm not sure what to say. I didn't know—"

A loud clatter, followed by the sound of breaking glass, made her jump. Eve spun, finding the table empty. "Hailey?"

Her friend's responding groan was enough for Eve to scurry around the kitchen island. Hailey lay collapsed on the floor, the tulip teacup shattered in pieces around her. Sugary tea spilled through the cracks in the stone floor, food for the ants and centipedes that lived underneath.

"Hailey." Eve dropped to the floor and helped her stand. Hailey swayed, one hand pressed to her head as she squinted against the dim candlelight as if it beamed from the sun itself. "What's wrong? What happened?"

"My head," Hailey whimpered, leaning on Eve for support. Eve helped her into one of the chairs, propping her up against the wall so she wouldn't fall. She parted through Hailey's dark hair, searching for a wound.

"I don't see anything. Did you hit it?"

"No," Hailey breathed. Sweat pooled at her forehead, slipping down in small trails. "It's—There's so much—"

"We need to get you a doctor." But who could she call at this time of night? Where did she even find doctors in Faerie?

The den, Eve thought. Surely there had to be a piece of paper or a notebook or *something* with information on this kind of thing.

"I'll be right back," Eve promised. Hailey whimpered in response. Eve thought she saw something shift in the darkness outside the window but set it aside as she rushed to the den.

Liam had not moved an inch. Eve only caught a glimpse of the stone side of his face before she rummaged through the bookshelves and drawers.

"Liam, I need your help," she said, tossing envelopes and papers aside. "Hailey and Sage need a doctor. Do you have anything around here that tells me how to contact one?"

Liam did not answer.

He must be asleep, she thought. Eve didn't want to wake him up—it must've been hard enough to fall asleep in that position—but this was an emergency.

"Sorry, Liam," she said, reaching for his shoulder. "I really need your help right now."

She nudged him, but there was no response. The embers in the fire had turned to ash, leaving half of his face in shadow. Eve reached for the fleshy part of his skin, hoping a small pinch would be enough to awaken him.

Her hand met stone.

Eve recoiled with a sharp gasp. She reached again, trembling, searching for the warmth of his skin.

Her fingers brushed the cold, lifeless stone instead.

No. No, not yet. Eve grasped his face between her palms, as if the heat of her skin could transfer onto him instead. Liam remained still beneath her touch, frozen in time by unyielding rock.

"Shit. *Shit!*" She kicked a nearby chair, toppling it over. Panic crawled through her skin. Gone. He was *gone.*

Not gone, she told herself. A statue. He was a goddamn statue.

This wasn't helping her panic.

Eve took a deep, shaky breath and turned back to Liam. He appeared peaceful, almost asleep, as his stone body slumped against the chair. She hoped it hadn't been painful. Why hadn't she stayed with him after she woke up? Why leave him alone to suffer in her absence?

No, she couldn't think about that now. She couldn't change what happened, and Hailey was still waiting on her for help.

I'll fix this, she promised him. Another pledge added to her debt. At least this one she intended to keep.

Eve shuffled through the room, sifting through papers until she was certain there was nothing to be found. She retreated back to the kitchen, wondering how to deliver the news of Liam's current state.

Hailey smiled tiredly from beside the table, a broom in one hand and a dustpan in the other. The color had returned to her cheeks.

"Hey," she said, brushing the broken teacup into the dustpan. "Sorry, watch your step. I'm almost done."

"I could've gotten that," Eve said. She reached for the broom, but Hailey shook her head. "You should be sitting down."

"I'm fine now." Was she? Eve sensed her friend's troubled thoughts, made heavier by the hunch in her posture as she cleaned the mess on the floor. "I just... remembered."

"Remembered...?"

Hailey met her gaze. "I *remembered*."

Eve's eyes widened. Hailey's memories—they'd returned. *But how...?*

Eve glanced back down the hall toward the den. Sage had said weeks ago that if Liam was dead, his deals were moot.

He wasn't—he couldn't be *dead*, right? A shiver ran down her spine. *What am I supposed to do?* Doubt snuck in, twisting her gut with hopeless failure.

What if he can't be saved?

Stop it, she scolded herself. *You can still help him. You* will *help him.*

Eve leaned against the kitchen island, her spirit as beaten as her bruised legs. A dull ache throbbed behind her left eye. Her entire world was collapsing around her one hit at a time, but she had to keep going. What other choice was there?

"You okay?" Hailey placed a tentative hand on Eve's shoulder.

"I should be asking you that," Eve mumbled, burying her face in her folded arms. Hailey laughed humorlessly.

"We're both dealing with hell right now," she said. "But at least we're in it together."

"Yeah." Eve stretched her arms out, joints cracking. "Yeah, we are."

She gathered the remaining teacup to clean while Hailey finished sweeping the floor. They were both walking back down the hall when the first window broke. Then another.

Eve turned in time to see a hairy creature crawl through the broken glass.

FORTY-THREE

Run. Her legs wouldn't move. Eve froze as more creatures crawled through the window after one another.

Squat and humanoid, the creatures were large—nearly the size of a calf—with long, dragging arms and reflective, beady eyes. Mangled hair sprouted from their heads and limbs, poking out between scraps of ragged clothing. Noses twisted and curved like branches, as pointed as the fingers that scraped across the floor. Gray-green skin peeled back to reveal sharp yellow teeth.

Men, or as close to it as they could get. A dozen of them clambered into the kitchen, tossing over chairs and furniture in their wake.

Hailey grasped at the air beside her hip where her rapier would normally be. Eve's own vulnerability shook her. The mental image of her dagger lost to the cave taunted her in its absence. A weapon. She needed a *weapon*.

Eve sucked in a sharp breath, grabbed Hailey's arm, and ran. If the men hadn't noticed them earlier, they certainly did now. Claws raked against wood and dirt behind them in a stampede down the hall. The pungent odor of rot and mildew wafted forward as one snuck up behind her. His hot breath brushed the back of Eve's neck.

The girls rushed into the den. Eve snatched the fire poker from beside the mantle and thrust it toward the beasts. Hailey followed suit, using the brass tongs intended for logs.

Only three of the creatures had followed, but they stopped as the weapons swung in their direction. They inched forward, trapping Eve and Hailey in a semi-circle against the mantle.

Destruction echoed from the kitchen; the clanging of pots and pans hitting the floor, of plates and glasses shattering against the walls. The chaos carried into the hall, where portraits smashed and wooden paneling splintered. Cheers rose amid the raze—strange, wild hollers that could only be interpreted as joy.

More were coming. How much longer—?

Claws swiped at Eve's face. She knocked the man's arm away with her poker, but not before it grazed her cheek. The fresh wound stung and reeked of earthen rot. Eve gritted her teeth, swinging the poker again.

The creature hopped back, then swiped again, nearly missing her shoulder. The other two joined in, crowding around Eve and Hailey as they swung their brass weapons in a clanging arc.

"Don't be difficult, lass. 'Tis only business," one said from the middle. The familiar voice startled Eve, and she forgot to block an attack from her right. Claws dragged down her arm in jagged lines, tearing through the fabric of her nightgown. Red bled into white. Eve hissed, knocking the beast back with a swift hit to its head.

"*Gotwin?*" she gasped. Hailey's jaw dropped as she stared at the creature.

"Thought ye'd seen the last of me, eh?" Eve recognized the brownie's patchy trousers and wiry hair, but he'd changed vastly in their time apart. This was not the same hardworking chef Sage had exiled from her home. He had changed into something darker. Something vengeful.

"Okay, I get you're mad. *Totally* understandable. Why don't we talk this out?" There was a tinge of desperation in Hailey's voice as she blocked another attack from her left. The girls tried to step back, but their backs pressed firmly against the fireplace: there was nowhere to go. "I'll make some tea, and we can sit down, maybe work this out without all the hitting and stuff."

A man on the right grabbed Hailey's ankles and yanked. Hailey screamed, falling onto her back with a hard thump.

Eve moved to help, but the other two focused on her, their claws spread wide as they snagged on her dress and flesh. She smacked their heads with her poker as hard as she could, ignoring the sharp hisses they gave in return.

Hailey struggled on the ground, holding the tongs out wide at the creature's neck to push him back. The beast hissed in her face, his gray skin wrinkled in the pale light. She held him off with her slippered feet, sweat brimming at her brow.

With a hard swing, Eve knocked one of the not-brownies onto his back, banging his head for good measure. She drove her fire poker into Gotwin's eye. He wailed, clawing frantically at his face as Eve yanked the poker back.

Hailey's grip was slipping. The creature inched toward her face, the tongs doing little to hold him back.

Eve drove the fire poker through his back. The man let out a wild roar, twisting and shouting against the brass pole lodged in his organs.

"Don't take it personally," Eve grunted. She pushed the fire poker deeper through his torso until it slipped through his chest. "It's only business."

The man stilled. Hailey used her tongs to throw him off her while Eve struggled to retrieve her bloody poker.

Gotwin and his friend were back on their feet. Hailey held them off long enough for Eve to yank her improvised weapon from the creature's back.

By then, the other not-brownies filtered into the room. Eve weaved and dodged through the reckless chaos, slipping out of Gotwin's grip as he trampled after her. The others did not pay her or Hailey much mind—they were lost in their own destruction, tearing apart every inch of the room they could touch.

She was nearly at the doorway when Liam's statue tipped over. Eve spun, her heart hammering wildly in her chest as three creatures picked him up from the chair.

"*No!*" she screamed too late. One hand reached out to stop them as they lifted him above their heads.

Liam's body crashed into the fireplace and shattered.

A strangled cry choked Eve's throat. Pieces of the young man scattered across the room in a burst of dusty gray confetti. A pointed ear there. A long-jointed finger there. Scraps of his annoyingly beautiful face cracked and split, discarded into rubble on the floor.

He was more fragile than she'd anticipated. Her hope shattered on the floor with him, easier to break than he had been.

"Eve," Hailey urged, her voice distant to Eve's numb ears. She stared at the pieces on the floor, wondering how to put them back together. If it would even matter if she did.

Her attention drifted to a piece underneath the settee. Eve wasn't sure what drew her to it. With all the chaos in the room, it was hard to keep track of any single thing, but a steady pulse inside her chest urged her toward the broken shard.

Eve crawled onto the floor and snatched the piece of stone.

A sharp pain shot up her leg. Eve cried out as she was violently pulled out from under the chaise. A single reflective eye glared down at her, the other dark and mottled with blood. Gotwin snarled at her from above.

Thunk!

Gotwin fell to the side. Hailey stood where he'd been, the tongs gripped tightly in her hands.

"Come *on*," she said, forcibly pulling Eve to her feet. Eve stumbled after her out of the room, the poker tight in one hand and the stone balled in her fist in the other. Some creatures grabbed for them with little effort, and they instead reveled in the damage they wrought.

Smoke trickled into the hall from the kitchen. Eve's lungs stung with each breath. She caught a glance of movement from the kitchen—something tall and armored—but the shadow vanished as the smoke thickened.

Eve reached for the front door, but Hailey spun toward the stairs. Right. Sage.

She chased after her, ignoring the shuffling and clawing from downstairs as the creatures moved to their next location. The not-brownie's excitement turned into panic beneath her. Warmth spread through the floor under her feet, drying up the moss between her toes. Smoke followed them, rising higher still as they threw themselves into Sage's room.

It was gloomier than Eve remembered. Darkness shrouded the black room, from the heavy drawn curtains to the charcoal-painted walls that stretched high above their heads. Sage's handcrafted figurines sat in a neat little line on her desk, while several half-finished ones were dispersed throughout the room in no particular order. Eve imagined Sage trailing through the room, whittling away on one, only to set it down as another distracted her.

She lit some candles to help her see while Hailey tried to rouse Sage from the bed. The pixie grumbled irritably, her words muffled under the thick velvet blanket tucked up to her shoulder. Francis twitched tiredly from the nightstand, and Hailey tucked him into her pocket.

Scattered about the room were pieces of parchment with frantic scribbling, some crumbled in frustration while others had been smoothed over on the desk. It only took a cursory glance to realize they were plans for inheriting the court. Eve noted that the ones involving murdering her brother had the most creases. Had that decision eaten at her more than Sage let on? How many times did she deliberate how to curry her father's favor before accepting the truth that stared her in the face?

"What's that smell?" Sage asked groggily, pulling on the set of clothes Hailey frantically tossed to her. Smoke drifted in through the cracks in the door. Eve could almost hear the crackle of flames reaching the second floor. "That noise—what's going on?"

"Your house is on fire," Hailey said matter-of-factly. "And I think we're being invaded by brownies."

"*What?*"

Sage threw open the door with a gasp. Thick smoke burst into the room, and the girls coughed and covered their faces with their tops the best they could to filter it out. Horrible, agonized screams made their way upstairs. Flames licked the walls, spreading quickly through the hallway—and blocking their exit.

One of the hairy men ran by the door entirely engulfed in flames. He collapsed a few feet down the hall, wheezing against the plume of smoke.

Sage slammed the door shut.

"My house is on fire," she said calmly.

"Yes."

"The Court of Bones is on *fire*, and there are *Boggarts* running in my hall."

"It appears so."

Sage rubbed her face, and Eve swore the pixie aged by a decade in that moment. "Where's Liam?"

Eve and Hailey exchanged a glance—Hailey had seen what happened to Liam's body, too. Eve cleared her throat against the smoke, the air too dry for tears. "I'll tell you about it later."

"Of course he'd run off." Sage's face heated with accusation. "That complete *idiot*." She sucked in a sharp, rattling breath before running her hands down her tired face. "*I'm* the idiot. I should have known this would happen."

"Blame yourself later. We have to leave," Eve urged.

They glanced at the door again. No one attempted to open it; where would they go? The fire was spreading quickly, consuming every inch of the estate. Eve heard the creak of the stairs and knew they were at risk of collapsing. The second-floor balcony didn't offer any cushion, either—the servants had cleared the snow beneath it for the carriage, revealing hard, packed dirt and stone.

"Do you know an easy way out of here?" Eve asked. Sage considered.

"There are a few passageways, but the only one that connects to my room goes to the basement."

"Why does it go to the basement?" Hailey asked. Sage shrugged.

"I didn't build this place. How should I know?"

"The basement works," Eve said, but Hailey shook her head.

"The fire is already in the kitchen, remember? Unless there's another way out of the basement..."

"There's a tunnel that connects down there. We use it to haul things out of the distillery," Sage said. "I think that's the last place we would want to be right now, though."

Eve paled. The *distillery*. The whole mansion was a ticking time bomb.

"Oh God," Hailey whimpered, her bravado cracking. She paced the room, using one of Sage's accessories on the dresser to pull her hair up tight. "Crap. Crap, crap, *crap*—"

"Breathe," Sage instructed firmly. Hailey obeyed, her breath shuddering. "We'll find a way out of here."

Pushing past Eve, Sage stared down at the bare walls under her windows. Eve had already considered escaping through the window and deemed it useless. There was nothing to grab onto.

The nearest tree was too far for any of them to jump—which Sage would have to do with her wings out of commission. There was snow beneath them, yes, but also the patio that overlooked the backyard. Throwing themselves out would be risky. Eve wasn't sure she could convince herself to do it, let alone the other two.

Think. Think! There had to be a way to fix this. Eve just didn't know how.

And the fire was growing closer.

"Sage?" Hailey asked, peering out of the window. She grimaced at the height, swallowing hard. *What a time to be afraid of heights.* "Any other ideas?"

"No," Sage said, defeated. She tried to hold it together, cool and collected as always, but Eve saw the cracks in her façade.

Eve tightened her fist—the one she still held the remains of Liam in. She would not die today.

A pitcher of water remained untouched on Sage's nightstand. Eve ripped long pieces from her dress—it was ruined anyway—and dunked them in the water, passing them around.

"For the smoke," she explained.

Hailey frowned at the door. "You want us to go back out there?"

"Do we have a choice?" Eve said. Hailey blanched, but didn't object. They each wrapped the wet scraps around their faces.

That should help, Eve thought. She tucked the piece of stone into her dress pocket as Hailey murmured a prayer. Who knew how far the fire had spread by now? How long did they have before the distillery blew them into bits?

Or before one of the Boggarts got to them first?

The ground rumbled beneath them. Eve imagined the foundation failing, the mansion collapsing. Maybe it wouldn't be the fire that killed them—it would be the house itself, burying them under its bones until their bodies were no more than fertilizer for the next one.

The ground rumbled again before she could open the door.

Pause.

Again.

Pause.

A flutter of hope lifted in Eve's chest. She ran to the window and stuck her head out. Between the smoke billowing from the mansion's foundation, it was hard to see but—no, those trees were moving, and it was not from the wind.

"Cinder!" Eve cried out. Her voice was dry and cracked from the fire, but she tried again with all her might. Never had she been so happy to feed an oversized cat. *"CINDER! OVER HERE!"*

Eve knew her friends thought she'd lost her mind. She could sense their stares on her back, the caution with which Hailey approached her side. Eve kept shouting, searching through the smoke even as her eyes dried from the blaze below.

Sage yelped as the fire blasted through the door. She hurried to join them, glancing dubiously at the ground below. Fire burst from the windows underneath, blowing out into the cold.

Come on, Eve thought, squinting out at the forest. *Please!*

There was a crash outside the room. They were running out of time—and options. Eve shakily climbed onto the windowsill. If she had no other choice...

Tufts of gray fur emerged from the trees, almost blending in with the smoke. Cinder meowed, its large eyes glaring at the flaming estate with suspicion. Eve coughed and stood on the windowsill, gripping it tightly as she waved for the Yule Cat's attention.

"Cinder! *Cinder!*"

Sage grabbed the back of Eve's gown, nearly pulling her from the ledge—or pushing her off it. "What are you *doing?* Are you trying to get us *killed?*"

Eve ignored her, still waving for the enormous cat. Cinder hesitated. Even the magnificent beast saw the danger they were in and had no desire to involve itself.

Yet, Cinder crept forward, moving its face close enough to the window for Eve to touch. Hailey and Sage stumbled back, shaking—but Eve threw her arms around the cat's nose, nuzzling it in relief.

"Thank you," she whispered. "*Thank you.*"

Cinder purred in response and bowed its head. Eve climbed up onto the bridge of its nose, gripping its large tufts of fur for support as she climbed to the top of its head.

"Come on!" she called. Hailey and Sage hadn't moved an inch. Hailey glanced at Sage, who was horrified by the prospect, and gently extracted her hand. She stood in front of the Yule Cat who, after a few sniffs, allowed her safe passage onto its head.

"Sage!" Hailey waved their friend onward, but the pixie didn't move.

"I'll be fine!" she yelled back, staring at Cinder with wide, frightened eyes. "I can fly!"

"No, you can't." Sage winced. Hailey crawled down Cinder's face—much to the cat's annoyance—and offered her hand. "Please."

Sage glanced back at her room. At her home. At everything she had worked hard for, the very thing she lived for, burning up in flames before her eyes.

She took Hailey's hand.

FORTY-FOUR

Early cracks of dawn encroached on the horizon, subtly shifting the light over the clouds. Day inched over the sky in paling shades of blue and pink.

It would have been a gorgeous sunrise if not for the plumes of smoke that bled through the trees.

Cinder carried Eve, Hailey, and Sage away from the estate, pushing through pines as if wading through water. They could still see the Bone Court's skeleton aflame in the distance.

"Gotwin," Sage muttered, shaking her head. "I didn't think he'd turn into a *Boggart*. Vengeful little bastard."

"I didn't know he could do that," Hailey murmured. Eve saw Gotwin's snarling face in her mind's eye, the twisted creature a far cry from the chef she knew.

Cinder moved over an awkward patch of rocks, jostling its company. Sage gripped onto the fur at her sides, inhaling sharply. "When you offend a brownie, you risk the alterations that come with it."

"Well, you *did* frame him for trying to kill me," Eve said sardonically. "And Liam, I guess. Is it *that* surprising?"

Sage's shoulders slumped. "I suppose not."

"Can they change back?" Hailey asked. She relaxed into Cinder's fur, occasionally reaching out to pet the skin underneath. Cinder's purr rumbled through the forest.

"No," Sage said.

Cinder crested over a large hill. The Bone Court faded over the trees, and only the wisp of smoke remained.

The girls were silent for a long time. Morning arrived in full, shedding light on the extent of their disastrous appearances. Eve curled into Cinder's fur, grateful for the warmth against the chilly winter air.

Without death lurking at her feet, the adrenaline in her body faded into new pains and aches her body didn't know what to do with. Eve yawned. The fact she hadn't slept all night was finally hitting her. While there was nothing she longed for more than a soft bed, Cinder's fur was a fine replacement.

She was drifting off when Hailey asked, "Where do we go from here?"

"The Seelie Court," Eve said, surprising them both. "Evren will need to know about the estate." *And I need to see if Preece found anything on Liam's condition.*

"To the Seelie Court, then," Sage said. Hailey nodded her agreement. They sat close together, almost snuggling but not quite. A new dynamic had shifted between them—one Sage had not yet come to know about. Hailey did not look at her directly, as if Sage would see the resurfaced memories playing in her eyes.

Eve reached into her pocket and retrieved the stone piece—Liam's piece— and turned it over in her palm.

A salamander. The stone had been perfectly carved into the shape of a salamander lying flat on its belly, asleep. Eve brushed her thumb across its tiny head. She could have sworn the figure was *warm.*

No— it's a newt, Eve realized, her eyes widening.

Lay to rest, the newt.

Hysterical laughter burst from her lips. She clutched the newt to her chest, tears springing to her eyes in relief. One piece of the puzzle found. One part of the riddle solved.

One step closer to bringing Liam back.

Epilogue

An explosion rattled the forest. The screams within silenced as rubble and ash spewed across the estate grounds, singeing the earth they'd once stood on.

Colton watched it all with an impassive stare. It was the same expression he'd worn when he'd met the hairy beasts in the forest and bargained for directions to the Fogtree manor. And again when he'd lit the estate aflame, trapping the little devils inside.

Little idiots, the lot of them. Perhaps it was their own rage that had blinded them. The Boggarts had their own vendettas against the Fogtree siblings. Who was Colton to deny their revenge while enacting his own?

Not revenge, he told himself. *Justice.*

Most of the explosion had occurred underground, leveling the estate to ash but keeping the fire contained. It had not reached the servant's quarters in the back of the estate grounds—that dusty wooden structure Colton had spent over a month lingering inside, serving these wretched beasts' every command with a beleaguered smile and addled mind.

Colton hadn't known that was what he was doing. He'd been tricked, as all the other poor souls enslaved to these monsters. Illusions of priesthood had played before him, each command a whispered wish from God himself to serve the saints he'd prayed to for guidance.

Then that illusion shattered. Colton found himself thrown into a pile of bodies: some half-dead, cold and stiff with rigor mortis. Others struggled to remain conscious, their flesh deathly pale from blood loss and starvation. The not-so-distant noise of revelry and music spun in his ears in a disjointed cacophony as he staggered out of the corpses' cold embraces.

The spell had worn off, and Colton found a new purpose.

He lingered in the servants' quarters now, pitying the poor souls that were still trapped in their own delusions. Perhaps they could be saved, but at what cost? He'd seen what destruction had been done to his own soul, and these people suffered far longer.

Colton cradled an old man's head in his arms, gentler than a babe. He was thinner than any human had a right to be, with gray eyes as hazy as the clouds above. The old man stared, unknowing, unflinching, as Colton's hands drifted to his throat.

"May God have mercy on your soul," Colton whispered.

Snap.

The body fell limp against its meager cot. Colton moved onto the next.

Smoke and ash clung to the furs of his cloak as Colton embarked on the return to his cave. His lower neck throbbed where Eve had torn his flesh. Thankfully, she'd missed the vital arteries that would've killed him. Once she vanished, Colton had quickly washed the wound in the creek and stitched the flesh back together with a needle and thread he must have procured from one of his raids.

He'd been right not to toss anything he gathered. The needle might have been missing its eye but did the job all the same.

Colton resisted rubbing at the bandaged spot now, glancing at the silver compass in his hand to guide him back to camp. Logan's body would still need to be dealt with. The ground was too frozen to break, but he could find a cold spot to store his body until spring. Did the bastard even deserve a burial? Logan had betrayed him. Abandoned him to the woods on his own. Tried to *kill* him.

No, there would be no burial. Let his body rot in the woods for the demons to make do with.

Colton shook his head, the horror of those demons' unnatural faces sending a chill to his core. It terrified him to think of what they had almost gotten away with. Those he once considered strange friends had quickly revealed themselves to be the same demons his pastor condemned.

It had to be a test of his faith. Did God not order Abraham to murder his own son as proof of his loyalty? Was this not the same thing? This strange land was the source of his corruption—the inspiration for his pursuit in theological studies and seminary training after. Why else would God ordain his return?

His footsteps slowed as the iron bars came into view, guarding his camp from monstrous intruders. It had taken weeks to forage these spare pieces.

The iron bars were not as he remembered them upon his arrival. They leaned too far to either side, their gaps more than enough for his body to slip through.

Colton paused outside the cave in alarm. Had he forgotten to push them back into place before he left? Did Eve or her spindly companion do this? Colton ran a hand across the sharp metal, scanning the snow for footprints.

None. Not even his own.

Colton did not have time to react. Four sharp, pointed claws pierced into his back from behind, lifting him up into the air. Colton gasped from the pain as his body flew to the side. His head slammed into a nearby tree, and he crumpled to the ground.

Demons. He tasted the blood on his lips. *Demons.*

He tried to sit up, but the pounding in his skull disoriented him. Colton blinked against the spots in his vision, his body limp and vulnerable in the snow.

Figures appeared around him in varying shapes and sizes, their features sharp and alien in nature. A tall man with antlers and a vicious smile stepped forward, his long hair cascading in a black curtain to obscure Colton's view.

"The little murderer is a mortal," he mused, tapping his chin with long, claw-like nails. "Whoever would have thought?"

Two large ogres grabbed Colton from either side and flopped him onto his stomach. He tried to wriggle free, but they were too strong—and he was too dizzy. The world spun around him in a flurry of black and white. Bile rose in his throat, stinging his insides with its acidic taste.

"Tell me, why did you do it?" the antler-headed man continued, crouching down until his face hovered above Colton's. The thick stench of blood and roses wafted off him, turning Colton's stomach. "I'm curious whose head I will be bringing to the High Unseelie King."

His head? Colton writhed under the ogres' grips, snapping his teeth at anyone that ventured too close. More figures adjusted to hold his kicking legs down, pinning him to the ground with violating ease.

Colton was used to fighting from afar, knocking his victims down one-by-one before he finished them off. He'd never had to face a group this up close before. He'd never been stupid enough to try.

Somehow, they'd found him.

When Colton did not answer, the antler-headed man frowned and backed away. Another demon took his place—this one with a sharp ax that glinted under the breaking dawn.

Colton swallowed hard. Was it another test? Would God spare him now, knowing he had proven his loyalty, or condemn him for his failure?

The creature lifted his ax, and another held Colton's head down, stretching his neck long. A perfect opening.

"Wait!" Colton shouted. He heard the whoosh of the blade. "*Wait!*"

The ax paused above his neck.

The antler-headed man lowered his palm, having stopped the executioner. "You wish to speak your final words?"

"No," Colton said. "I want to make a deal."

The antler-headed man raised a brow, but did not call off the executioner. The weight of the blade still hovered over Colton's neck: a promise waiting for fulfillment.

"I'm listening."

He had to think fast. Colton had learned much about these creatures during his time here, and he knew their desire for bargains was outmatched. If there was a deal to be made, they would listen.

What sort of deal would be worth his life?

"You said that you're bringing my head to the king," Colton said slowly. Stalling. "Why?"

The antler-headed man cocked his head. "Why are you concerned?"

Because it's life or death for me, you idiot. Colton breathed deeply, doing his best to ignore the weapon dangling over his throat.

"Can I assume your king has a bounty out for me because I've killed his people?" The demonic creature said nothing, but his silence was truth enough. "Strange that a king would make others hunt for me and not do the work himself."

A few figures shifted around him. Apparently, this was a spot of contention for some of them—and that was something Colton could latch onto.

"It's not a true show of leadership, is it?" Colton pressed. "If your king was strong, he would have handled the threat on his own by now."

A few murmurs of agreement whispered in his direction. Colton watched for a reaction from the antler-headed man—their leader, he understood, based on the respectful way the others moved around him—but his face remained taut.

"What is your point?"

"Spare my life, and I assure you, I will send your king back to the hell in which he belongs," Colton said, meeting the demon's eye.

The leader laughed. "What makes you think that I wish the king dead?"

"Don't you?" Colton glanced at the man's companions, at their disgruntled expressions at the mention of their king. "I sense some ambivalence against him among your friends here. Am I mistaken?"

They did not reject his claim. Instead, they watched the antler-headed man for his response—but the anger was there. The displeasure was written across their faces.

The antler-headed man tapped his claws over his crossed arms. "It is a bold assumption you make to assume I could not handle the king myself, should I wish it."

"Of course you could. You're obviously capable." Colton nodded to the ogres on his back. "But the risks are high, aren't they? If you're caught, things get complicated. Messy. If I'm caught, though, well, I'm just one mortal. What is there to lose?"

There was a ripe tension in the air. As the demons stared at him, Colton thought for a fleeting moment that this was it. He'd failed God and forfeited his life with it.

"Your name," said the antler-headed man. "Give it to me."

"Colton Anthony Davis."

"I see." A smile flickered across the demon's face. The executioner stepped back with the wave of his hand. "Come, Colton Anthony Davis. We have much to discuss."

CONTENT WARNINGS

Below is a list of some of the sensitive topics that can be found in this book.

- Rape

  - In Past, Not on Page, Not Described

- Sexual Trauma

- Mentions of abuse from a parental figure

- Religious Trauma

- Self-Harm

  - On page, not graphically described

- Panic Attacks

- Mentions of Suicidal Ideation

- Violence, Death, Gore

- Terminal Illness

- Family member with Dementia

ACKNOWLEDGEMENTS

Screaming, crying, throwing up, *book two is done!* There isn't a hope in the world that I would have accomplished this without the endless support of my friends, family, and team, so let's jump into it.

To my in-laws and their endless outpour of interest, love, and support, I cannot thank you enough. The release party you put together for my first book will live in my heart and memories forever.

To my family, thank you for your enthusiasm and thoughtfulness in every way. You have all made my dream come true, and Uncle Mike, I'll cherish that *Sin and Bones* slab to my grave. An extra thanks to my Grandma Carol and Vicky, who hosted a signing event for my family and surprised me with the most delicious, beautiful cake of my first book, and my Grandma Linda who brags of my creative endeavors to anyone with a listening ear. You have all warmed my heart beyond comprehension, and I hope to continue to make you proud.

Abbey. JC. Micah. Elliot. Emmy. My people, my loves, the found family that carry the torch of remembering my ridiculous thoughts, laughing through my bad puns, and reading my stories whether you want to or not. Thank you for putting up with me and for supporting my dream (even when I don't shut up about it). I love you guys.

My VMKM family, you guys have been so relentlessly supportive that it makes me cry. I'm so honored to be your friend and to share my life's work with you all. Parker, thank you for letting me use your kitty's name in the book. May he be remembered always. I love you guys, and I hope life brings you nothing but joy and fulfillment on the same level you have brought me.

To my ABC family, how do I even put into words how grateful I am for you all? Pete, thank you for letting me advertise and sell my books at the coffee shop; without you, I wouldn't be nearly as successful as I am today. Manny, Megan, Liz, Sam, Mark, Shiloh, Dutch, Buffy, and all of the amazing regulars and customers that step into the coffee shop, thank you, thank you, thank you for all of your kind words, encouragement, and support. I'm so grateful to know each and every one of you; may life bring you every success!

Maddi Leatherman, my editor and the queen of unhinged commentary. Thank you for all the laughs, critique, and notes that brought this book to life and made it is what it is today. I'm so grateful to you and your hard work. I can't wait to finish this trilogy with you!

Jessica Sherburn, the artist who brought my book cover to life AGAIN! Your creative vision, artistic skill, and eye for detail never cease to amaze me. Your art is breathtaking and I'm so grateful to have you as my cover illustrator. Looking forward to book 3's cover; in the meantime, I can't wait to see all of the brilliant pieces you put out!

To Maple and Caramel, who trampled over my keyboard numerous times during my writing and editing process so that their voices would be heard too. Thank you for your help and I'm sorry I had to delete your contributions. I'll give you both extra churu treats when this releases to make up for it.

Of course, to Connor, my husband, who has shown his endless support in all of my writing, past and present. Thank you for endlessly listening to my rambles, plot holes, character arcs, and for pointing out when I (or my story) has gone a little off the rails. You are my greatest supporter, my greatest love, and I look forward to giving you a lifetime of stories to laugh, bond, and cry over. I truly couldn't do this without you by my side. Thank you, darling.

And to every reader that picked up my book and gave it a chance, thank you from the bottom of my heart. There is no possibility in this world that I could do this without you. May your pillows always be cold and your blankets warm. Most important of all, *thank you, thank you, thank you!*

About the Author

Paige N. Regan is a dark fantasy author with a BA in Screenwriting and a penchant for laughter amongst the macabre. She is the author of the *Sin and Bones* trilogy and *We Are Buried in the Garden*. Outside of writing, she can be found gaming with her husband and spoiling her cats. You can follow her writing journey on social media @pnrwrites or learn more at her website: pnregan.com.